Phoenix Republic

The Lone Star Gambit

By
Danielle Wedgeworth

Copyright © 2013 Danielle Wedgeworth
All rights reserved.

ISBN: 0615847269
ISBN-13: 9780615847269
Library of Congress Control Number: 2013912955
Once Upon A Time Press, Cedar Hill, Texas

Dedication

I would like to offer special thanks to my partner, Gail Wedgeworth and stepmother, Bobbie Wedgeworth, for their endless hours reading and correcting mistakes and for their invaluable advice. Tom Terrell, thank you for sharing a guy's point of view and sanity checking the fight scenes. Gail, thanks again for the trailer art and putting up with me for the last year and a half. Finally, Lucas Wedgeworth, your cover art is amazing. You really do great work.

Regarding research, I would like to thank Associate Professor Brent Sasley, of the University of Texas at Arlington, who offered advice related to the Middle East. Mucho thanks to Rodney Walker, for kindly sharing his experience as a chief of police. Finally, I would like to say thank you to Glenn Repp for his perspective on Texas politics, based on his time as a state senator, and mayor of a large metropolitan city. Any mistakes that go to believability are mine alone, and in no way reflect the information so kindly provided by these very nice people.

Table of Contents

Chapter I
Hunted

Irritated, Sadie Cline stormed out of the Carrollton police station totally frustrated, followed by Detective Fernando Reyes. It had now been two months since he had first notified her that her mother had been murdered in her home. "Ms. Cline, please don't be upset. I know that this has got to be very hard on you, but I can assure you that we are all doing everything that we can to find out who did this to your mother. I look at it every day. We just do not have any leads."

Sadie stepped off the curb in front of the suburban police station. As pleasant as the quiet, tree lined medians in front of the station were, they still only represented one thing to her. It was the place where she first learned that her life had been completely turned upside down, and there was nothing anyone could do about it. Although frustrated and furious, she had to admit that the detective had been kind, and probably was trying his best. As she neared the end of the line of cars where she had parked, she paused. She turned to face him, knowing that she should at least give him the opportunity to explain.

"Ms. Cline, Sadie, please give us some time here. There were no fingerprints, and nothing was stolen; thus, there is nothing to track in pawnshops. All we know for sure is that ballistics said that a nine millimeter pistol was used in the crime. They could not match the rifling on the recovered bullet fragments to any weapon in our files."

In spite of herself, frustration had pushed her beyond her limit to accept.

"Detective Reyes, I know that you are trying, but it has been two months and all you can tell me is that my mom was shot with a nine millimeter pistol. I am a nurse, Detective. I work at a hospital, and I could have told you she was shot with a nine millimeter by looking at what the bastard did to her. Let's be honest, what with all the Solidarity Movement protests you guys are dealing with, you are not spending time on Mom's case. You don't have the time to really dig for an undiscovered clue. Am I right?"

"Ms. Cline, we are looking, and we won't quit either. The budget is tight, but we will do the best we can. We will find out what happened, and who did this thing. Please give us some time."

Angry, but now feeling a little guilty about unloading on the man, she responded in a more reasonable tone. "I will check back next week. Please try to uncover something, anything to move us forward." She forced a smile, nodded and turned to go. Unlocking her car, she decided that the detectives were just out of their depth and had no clue how to find her mom's killer, or for that matter, why she had even been killed. Slapping her hands in frustration on the steering wheel she forced herself to calm down. It was almost not worth taking the half day off from work. Her boss had been really supportive, but she also knew that the chief of medicine at Texas Health Presbyterian Hospital was not known for empathy.

Soon she was turning onto North Josey, and accelerating hard. Heading for the Turnpike, she thought about what to do next. The cops just were not going to resolve this. "Like I care about their stupid damn budget cuts!" They went through the same details from the case file they told her about a month ago.

The only new development was that ballistics indicated there was something odd about the bullets they recovered. They could not match the markings on the bullets to any known rifling pattern. The other thing not making today's visit a complete waste, was that Detective Reyes believed that the death was professionally executed due to the lack of evidence, and due to the oddity of the weapon used. He had said that their department was fortunate to have a true expert in firearms. If their guy thought the weapon was foreign, then Reyes was probably right in thinking it may have had something to do with her mom's past. She wondered for a fleeting moment if it was possible that she and her mom being of Persian heritage could be a part of this, but if so - why? We don't have any connection to the Middle East any more. Her mother told her that she was barely pregnant when she left Iran. Sadie turned it over in her mind. Mom had moved here before I was even born in 1983. She changed her name when she arrived in the United States specifically to make a clean break with anything from her life before coming here.

Why now, after almost thirty years, would anyone from her mom's previous life, have a reason to kill her now? Stopped at the traffic light, Sadie picked up her phone to call Reyes with another thought. Exasperated at getting his voicemail, she sighed before leaving a message. "I will get you mom's old letters and stuff from the shoe box that she, has on a shelf, in the top of her closet. It is all old stuff from when she lived in Iran. I don't know if that can help, but you said the gun was weird. Please let me know what you find out." She closed her phone as the light turned green. Stepping down hard on the accelerator, the Hemi under the hood of her Challenger propelled her forward sharply. She made the right turn and entered the on-ramp to the freeway.

Killing her blinker after a lane change, she caught a really odd look from the guy to her right, as she passed him. Momentarily distracted from her thoughts by the dark haired guy, she decided some music might clear her head of the omnipresent thoughts about her mom's killers until she got back to her apartment. Sadie drove on, trying to relax with mixed results, as she listened to the Rolling Stones and fumed about how angry she was at life just now. Turning her mom's past over and over in her mind, it just did not make any sense. Mom came here about the time I was born, so she obviously had something or someone she needed to get away from, but what or who? All I know is that she wanted to be an American. She never talked about her life before. If it was because her mother converted to Bahá'í, that might make someone angry, but why thirty years later? We don't make a big deal out of it, and anyway all our beliefs are about peace and the acceptance of God. Sadi shook her head, for she was not an overtly religious person herself, and to think someone might want to kill her over such things was strange.

Soon enough she exited the freeway, turning onto Parkwood and into her parking garage. Pulling up to her reserved spot, she rolled her eyes, noticing that the light over her space was out again for the third time this month. Losing her thought, for the moment, she heard Jagger belt out her favorite signature line from his song *Beast of Burden*. It did little to abate her foul mood as she pulled into her parking spot.

Putting the car in park, she angrily yanked her purse from the passenger seat and in the process spilled some of the contents, including her cell phone onto the floorboard opposite the gearshift of her beloved black Challenger. "I am a freaking beast of burden!" Exasperated, she reached over – stretching to retrieve the fallen items as the sound of gunfire erupted, and glass exploded, sending fragments raining down all around her.

Frozen in place, time slowed to a crawl. She could almost feel her heart stop. Her eyes fixed with terror. Her blood now running cold, she knew she had to react. She reached back with her left hand to jerk the gearshift into reverse and stepped hard on the gas. The Challenger's Hemi roared to life, slamming the car back and to the right – in the direction from which it had just come. Bullets continued in thunderstorm torrents of sound, as they punched holes all around her. Showers of the sparks from the tearing metal danced along the side of the car as lightening to the storm. The Challenger scraped a concrete pillar and smashed into the SUV parked behind her. Still leaning over, but now rising up enough to see, Sadie slammed the gearshift into drive. Again she floored the accelerator, inadvertently clipping her assailant, knocking him into the concrete wall where he had been standing as he loaded another magazine in to his pistol. As she passed the man, she sat up and headed for the garage's exit.

On the street now, she knew that she was driving erratically. Blind with terror, Sadie thought of nothing but evasion as she drove away in a near panic. Wind blowing relentlessly through shot out windows created a slipstream, as a tornado vortex of her own long black hair whipped about her head, stinging her face. Thankful that her windshield at least was still mostly intact and that the car seemed to be performing for the moment, she accelerated away.

Driving madly and with no thought about where she was now going, Sadie realized that she should look down to see if she was hit. She knew that shock and adrenalin could mask pain from any wounds that may have already been inflicted on her. Finding no blood or perforations, she drove on, accelerating hard at every turn, of which she was taking several, in a blind rush to get away from her attackers. Looking nervously out through the opening where her back window used to reside, she didn't see anyone following. Thinking hard, she realized that she had no idea where a nearby police station was located. The only one she knew about for sure was in Carrollton. If the guy that attacked her was the man that killed her mom, he might figure that she would go there and cut her off.

It then occurred to her that she could call the police. She reached down to recover her cell phone from the passenger side seat where she dropped it when the bullets tore through her car. Retrieving it, she just stared at the device, realizing that it had one corner missing, having been shot to pieces moments before. Starting to shake now, she looked back again to see if she was being pursued. Seeing nothing that she could identify as a pursuer, she slammed a hand down on the dash of the Challenger. "I don't know what to do! I don't know what to do! Oh God, where do I go now? Why is this happening to me?" Once more, finding herself back near the expressway, she finally made a decision. She would just have to go back to Carrollton.

Pulling on to the on-ramp she felt no hesitation at driving there at the speed of her choosing. The trip back to Carrollton seemed to only take moments before she was once again back on North Josey, this time headed south. Stopping at a red light in front of a high school, just south of the expressway, she was on alert for the late model sedan that was screaming up from behind her. She watched, her pulse racing, as it pulled even with her in the left turn lane. The car slammed to a halt beside her, only a couple of feet away. The man that she thought had looked at her so oddly before, raised a pistol in what felt like slow motion.

Time almost seemed to stand still. Her eyes going wide with terror, she saw the black hole at the end of the barrel on the intended instrument of her death. It was rapidly moving into position to carry out its appointed mission.

Terrified she floored the accelerator, summoning the valiant Hemi forth once more to be her defender. The Challenger instantly sprang to life as Sadie pulled hard on her emergency brake and cranked the steering wheel hard to the left. As had happened when her friend Doug taught her the maneuver when she first bought the car, the back of the Challenger spun around, pointing the nose of her car north once again.

Still in slow motion, she could see others around her screaming in their cars as well as see that her assailant was robotically adjusting his aim to accommodate for his highly mobile target, struggling to get a bead on her. He did not get the opportunity, as she rocketed forward leaving only the smell of burning rubber behind her. Looking anxiously in the mirror, she saw her opponent attempt the same thing, only to be T-Boned by a Fed-Ex Truck that had just entered the intersection.

Terrified and frantically looking all around her, Sadie drove off yet again towards the freeway.

Chapter 2
The Daily Grind

"Crap! No way, it was morning already. Where the hell do my weekends go?" The soothing harp music on her iPhone alarm was pleasant but persistent. "Damn it, I just want to sleep." Catherine thought that it was probably a good thing that she didn't stay in the army. She was just not a quick riser. She admitted to herself that in spite of being only thirty one years old, alarms, regardless of how gentle, made her furious. This was especially true at five-thirty in the morning. Lying there flat on her back, she blinked away the sleep. She recalled that it was Janice who suggested using soothing harp music to prod her awake without jarring her to consciousness – thus pissing her off before the day even began.

As she lay there, trying to get the nerve to face another day, she began accessing her agenda. It was a Monday, so she had to get the trash out to the street and get to her new temp assignment. Sighing, she realized that this gig was the one that was located all the way across town in Plano, so she would have to fight morning traffic for the next four months until the assignment ended. Perhaps she should have considered getting a place somewhere north of I-30, to be in a more central location, closer to where potential jobs were. Still, she loved the dilapidated old frame bungalow, purchased after her divorce, irrespective that it was located on the southern edge of the Dallas – Fort Worth metro area. The neighbors were reasonable enough, and it had a nice yard for her best friend, a boxer named Maggie. As her mind began to awaken, she realized that she felt more at home here than she did in the Mc-Mansion that she had shared with her ex-husband Dan. Catherine rolled over snuggling deeper into the soft blankets. "Really sorry, Dan, but I just couldn't pretend any longer. You are a decent guy even if you are a prick half the time. Still, I know that it was my fault really, and you were damn sure sick of me griping about politics and about how things were headed into the toilet all the time. Trust me, you are better off." Closing her eyes, she blinked away the single tear that was threatening, as she thought of what a wreck her life had become. "Dammit, I didn't ask to be born gay. Aw, hell, Daddy! I tried to be what everyone wanted, I just couldn't do it."

She reflected that although she did graduate from college, she hadn't exactly done a stellar job with her life since leaving high school. In only a decade, she was encouraged not to reenlist after her four years were up, because the colonel said she was not a good fit for his army, and she had managed to gain, and then subsequently lose, both a good paying job, and a husband. To top it off, she disappointed her father by announcing that she just wasn't into guys, and was tired of trying to fake it to fit in. Now, she thought with a snort, she could not even keep her current love interest, Janice happy because of their disagreements on, well, just about everything. To be fair to herself, she decided, journalist or not, Janice was completely intolerant of anything she disagreed with, and she had absolutely no regard for facts.

Rolling over in bed, Catherine was immediately irritated as she rolled over potato chip crumbs left from the Thursday before, thus eliciting a diatribe aimed at her offending but absent culprit. "Damn-it, Janice! I hate that you eat in bed. Reporters are such pigs. I swear that I've just about had it!" Rolling away from that side of the bed, she recalled the previous weekend.

It was Friday night, and they were supposed to be going out to dinner and then to the Cinemark to watch a bunch of explosions and car chases. Instead, Janice started a fight about Catherine's food storage taking up most of the space in the laundry room. She hardly even used the washer and dryer, and yet she was mad because Catherine thought things were going to get ugly and wanted to have some food around.

She could hear Janice's words now. "It is ridiculous to have all this food; it isn't normal. A disaster isn't going to happen, Kate. You will never need a year's worth of food. It is just a stupid waste of money."

Reliving the fight, she should have known right then that the evening was hosed. The debate soon morphed into how terrible it was that banks ripped off college students and how education was really a right that should be financed by the government anyway.

Snorting in derision, Catherine recalled her benign comment that nobody forced anyone to borrow six figure loans every year so they could go to their snotty Ivy League schools and party.

That was enough; however, the comment sent Janice into hysterics about how evil rich people were always getting what they wanted.

Groaning, Catherine knew she just needed to get up. Reliving her argument with Janice was going to do her no good, but it was all just so frustrating that she continued to replay it in her mind, searching for something she could have done to achieve a different result.

When Janice got wound up she decided any logical argument was pointless. Pointing out that many of the kids protesting were going to the best schools in the country and had rich parents was pointless. Janice would simply not acknowledge the stupidity of spending that kind of money for something like Women's Studies, and then being surprised, when they couldn't get real jobs to pay back their student loans.

Regardless, Janice left abruptly, saying she would come over after work on Monday to talk things over.

"Fat chance that will end well, it's hard to argue with you when your feelings trump facts; and I'm not just going to drink the damn Kool-Aid to have a love life." Catherine closed her eyes in frustration knowing that their problem was that they were both opinionated, with radically different world views. Anyone not mainlining fairy dust, she thought, could see that her view was, of course, the right one.

Looking down at the time displayed on her phone, she realized that her morning was going to be gone if she didn't get a move on. Swinging her feet out from under her comforter and onto the cold wooden floor, she stood, stretched and pulled on her old threadbare robe. She then stumbled towards her bathroom and then on to the kitchen for some coffee. She hoped that she could find something tolerable in the way of food to eat for breakfast. With her head in the fridge, she felt Maggie's cold nose nudging her, lest she forget that she too enjoyed eating things which originated from the refrigerator. Reaching back to scratch the light tan boxer on her head, she pulled out the last of her lunch meat and what was left of a package of sausage. She handed the lunch meat to Maggie. "You know that you are the only creature on God's earth that really gets me. Why can't people be more like dogs?"

Thinking about what she had that was reasonably clean to wear to work, Catherine trudged over and placed some buttered toast into the little toaster oven and began frying the last two links of sausage. Rubbing her face, she decided that grey suit with the black velour collar would be a sufficient compromise between looking professional and being comfortable on another first day. Thankfully, it was not too badly overdue for the cleaners.

As the smell of freshly brewed coffee filled the tiny kitchen, she poured herself a cup and nodded at the back door to let Maggie know her wait was over. She let the boxer out, almost tripping as the animal charged out the door after an insolent squirrel, taunting her from the back yard.

An hour later, her makeup applied and dressed for work, Catherine left a note for Janice on the dry erase board mounted to the wall next to the fridge. She wanted to let her know that she had no idea what to expect about when she would be home since her job was across town and there was no telling what sort of idiot she would be working for this time. She read the message one more time and shrugged.

If you want to hang out until I get here, perhaps we could grab some pizza and watch a movie. Hesitating a moment, she picked up the marker and added one last thought. *I will try to call this afternoon if I can.* With the note complete, she went to the back door, whistling for Maggie, keys and coffee in hand. Watching her running through the yard, Catherine realized yet again that she really loved this little house. She decided that although it might not be fancy, it was home. She could afford it, and to be really honest, the most important thing for her was that it reminded her of a simpler and more honorable time. With news stories every day about Europe going into the toilet and Israel preparing for war, at least her little corner of the world felt comforting. She had at least some protection from what she knew was coming.

❧

Catherine's black four-door Jeep Wrangler threaded its way past another fair sized group of loser protestor types that kept clogging up major intersections. Stopping at the traffic light, a pretty young blonde woman with manicured nails and wearing an SMU sweatshirt began chanting and pounding on her driver's side window. "Capitalism is murder; we are the 99%! Stand in solidarity with those taking back what the bankers have stolen!"

Rolling her eyes in exasperation, Catherine decided that she was in no mood this morning. When the light was about to turn green, she toggled the window switch on the center console of the jeep to lower her driver's side window. As the window disappeared into the door, she flipped off the girl. "Grow up, Loser Bitch! Why don't you try being responsible for yourself for a change." Somewhat cheered by the look of shock on the girl's face, she turned on the radio to find the news emanating from the vehicle's speakers.

"...Iran's Chief of Naval Operations warned this morning that his country can easily close the strategic Strait of Hormuz at any time. While this is not a new threat, the administration reiterated once again, that the United States and our allies, cannot, and will not accept any threat from Iran, that seeks to disrupt the freedom of nations to trade such a vital resource. As the Strait of Hormuz is located at the mouth of the Persian Gulf, the passageway through which a sixth of the world's oil flows, the industrialized nations simply cannot tolerate any such provocation. The United States continues to work with Israel and other parties in the region to lessen the tension caused by that country's declaration that it will never accept any peace proposal based on a border being set along the 1967 lines..."

Fed up, Catherine pounded the dash to exorcise her fury. "How can so many people be so damn stupid?" Like you political assholes don't realize that you are leaving the Israelis with no viable options! She thought. "That's right, dip-shits, keep supporting the Islamo-fascists and then act all surprised when they start another freaking war." Once again, she was completely pissed off before nine in the morning. She didn't care what the idiots in D.C. said; she would stand with Israel because they are God's people, not to mention that they actually have freedom and respect women. They didn't just give the idea lip service.

Shaking her head at the colossal stupidity of politicians everywhere, she switched the dial to her favorite CD. Forty five minutes later, Catherine pulled into the visitor parking lot in front of Texas Health Presbyterian Hospital to start yet another first day. Taking the keys from the ignition, she heard her phone beep to let her know that she had email. As she was a little early, and did not really want to go into the building anyway, she pulled the phone from her purse and flipped open the cover. Tapping the email icon revealed that Dan wanted to once again talk to her about some urgent matter of the highest importance. She decided that as a responsible and a career oriented young woman, she could not deal with him now after all. Smirking, she put the phone back into her purse. Dan would just have to wait. Her parents always said that it was important to be early on a first day anyway.

"Well, Daddy, here I go again." She wondered if he, or anyone for that matter, realized how hard she was trying. She thought that someone should give her some credit for that much at least. I keep getting up, after being knocked on my ass over and over again. The severance isn't going to stretch much further, and the contract gigs are getting pretty sketchy, too. "They may say that unemployment isn't over ten percent, but they don't count me, do they?" She fumed that if you gave up job hunting, worked part time, or worked in a lesser job than you used to have, then you didn't count. "If the bastards were honest, unemployment would be closer to thirty percent." With that thought, she checked her look in the rearview mirror. Her warm reddish brown hair was reasonably together so she grabbed her nerve, her wit, and her purse and headed for the main lobby entrance to the hospital.

❧

As she sat alone in a pleasant corner of the onsite cafeteria, Catherine opened her phone to her email. Five messages were now present, as indicated by the numeral 5, highlighted with a small red circle, indicated in the corner of the email icon on her screen. Opening her email she was presented with five nice little blue dots corresponding to the five messages. Listed atop her older messages were the unread emails arranged from newest message to oldest. Leading off was a note from Dan, then Janice, her sister Meg, the earlier email from Dan and an email from Dennis, the local Tea Party leader. Deciding that the curiosity would get to her if she didn't look, she tapped on the last note from her ex-husband.

Hi Kate, I just got my appraisal back on the house. I told you that I was trying to do the refi thing. Anyway, the appraisal value sucks bad! We need to talk about the arrangement that we came to. If you recall, it was based on an assumption that the market would recover in time. I know you won't want to hear this, but things are not recovering. Call me.

"Like that is gonna happen dumbass." Deleting the message brought up Janice's email.

Sorry I got mad at you on Friday. I know that you are just having a lot of stress and that you didn't mean that stuff about college kids being coddled and stuff. Don't worry, I have forgotten all about it. I'm not mad, I promise. Looking forward to seeing you tonight! Hugs, J.

Delete.

Just checking in with you, Sis. Don't have much time, but wanted to see how you were. I realized that you called me a week ago, and I never got back to you. I am totally loving life here in New York. You really should visit now that you have the time. I have been invited to a Giant's game next weekend. We will be in a sky box complete with a full bar and catering. Have I mentioned that I love this job? Anyway, let me know if you need to talk. I am always there for my big sister. Love you, Meg.

"Yeah Sis, that's right. I am not really employed, so I have nothing at all to do but come listen to you talk about yourself and your self-important corporate bigwig friends. Must be nice."

Delete.

Hey Kate, I have some news to talk to you about. Can we meet for drinks?

Love ya, Dan.

Acknowledging her ex-husband's attempt, she smiled weakly. "Well, at least you lead with a pleasant opening."

Delete.

Hey Kate, we are going to do another talk on preparation for a Tea Party group in a couple of weeks. Can you do your readiness training class? Call me, Dennis.

Reply.

Not sure, Dennis. You guys have not been all that accepting of me in the past. Besides, I just started another temp gig. I will let you know. Depends on how late this thing goes every day.

Send.

Shaking her head she got up, looking around for some clue as to where one might dispose of a lunch tray. Seeing Jack Reynolds, her good looking, twenty something cube partner and supervisor from the hospital's little project office, she forced a grin, acknowledging his help as he pointed to indicate where the trays went. Moving the direction indicated, she dropped off her tray to find Jack waiting for her by the entrance to the cafeteria.

"So, how did you like our elegant and ever-so-well equipped dining opportunity?"

"It's not too bad. Do you guys always eat here or do you ever go out for lunch?"

"We used to do that more, but lately there is usually just too much work to afford the time required to eat out." That his mind had just drifted back a year or two was visible on his face. "We used to do that a couple of times a week but layoffs and extra work put the kibosh to the practice."

Nodding in complete understanding, Catherine walked back to their cubes with him. Once there, she nodded politely and headed for her cube. Reaching her desk, she sat down and clicked on Fox's website for the latest headlines.

Radioactive Material Stolen in Egypt was the lead story. Catherine really didn't want to read the story, but knew that she would wonder what happened until she did. She clicked on the link.

Breaking news... Sources associated with the Egyptian government's Dabaa power plant project admitted today that nuclear material is missing from the plant following continued tension between secular Egyptians and the Muslim Brotherhood. When asked about the theft, leaders with close ties to the Muslim Brotherhood denied that there was any terrorist connection to this crime. IAEA, (International Atomic Energy Agency) officials confirmed that this incident is the second time in the last two years that radioactive material was stolen from the facility. More than twenty people were wounded last week when military police confronted hundreds of angry Egyptian protesters, demanding that constitutional guarantees be reinstated.

Catherine sighed, having seen far too many stories like this, over the past few years. No one seemed to really care. Shaking her head, she wondered how long it would be until some terrorist did something that people did care about.

Chapter 3
Into the Dark

Upon arriving home after her exciting day at First Texas Health Presbyterian, Catherine noticed Janice's yellow hybrid Lexus parked in her gravel driveway. "Why you think that thing is attractive I will never know." Getting out of her jeep, she grabbed her purse and reached back in for her coffee mug from where it rested from the morning drive. Fumbling with her key ring, she singled out the key for her house, and walked towards the door on her small screened-in front porch. Hearing Maggie's urgent barking from the back yard, she smiled. As she reached the screen door on the porch, the front door to the house opened to reveal Janice, smiling, her silky blond hair hanging down, partially obscuring bright green eyes.

"Hi Kate, I am really sorry about the weekend." Catherine could see that Janice had a look on her face that announced that she was back to thinking of her as the woman with which she wanted to make a life. "Kate you are hardnosed and stubborn, and you get ticked off at someone about something way too often, but no one would deny that you are sincere. Anyway, I am glad you are home."

Relieved not to have to put up with the argument that she was expecting, Catherine let her partner help her by taking her purse, keys, and coffee mug as they made their way into the house.

Catherine smiled. "Thanks, Sweetie." She realized as she took the screen-door from Janice, that she was really relieved to see her smiling warmly back at her. "I am really glad that you are here and not angry."

Janice waved away Catherine's comments. "You know, I love your smile. You are beautiful Kate, how can I stay mad? Besides, we are just too great together, if you know what I mean? Still I am insanely jealous that you get the soft curls around your shoulders without even trying and my hair requires actual work to look good."

"Give me a break Janice, you always look great, and you know it."

"Well, I guess, but I just love it when you tell me." Janice winked. "Did your day go ok by the way? You didn't blast anyone this time for not caring sufficiently about your conspiracy theories, I hope."

"No, as a matter of fact, I did not, as you say, blast anyone. Besides, that was last year."

"Ok, you're right. It was mean to bring that up. Oh, by the way, we have company."

Catherine grabbed the worn handle on her front door, waving off Janice's apology with a tired but heartfelt smile as she crossed the threshold into the little house for Maggie's enthusiastic welcome home. Once in the house she noticed her human best friend Drake Sabol sitting on the couch with his feet propped on her coffee table watching the news. He turned it down as she came through the door.

Thinking that Drake really was nice to look at without being over muscled, she sighed and began the relaxation process after work. She had always admired his piercing blue eyes, athletic build, and his easygoing manner. She smiled recalling how they met. He pulled her over the day she moved to Cedar Hill. Having just left the court house following her divorce in 2008, she was a complete mess and blew past a stop sign. He followed her for two blocks to her coworker's house where she had been staying since she had moved out of the house with Dan. Recalling that day always made her feel better about people. Seeing that she was distraught, he was decent enough to take the time to make sure that she was ok.

"So Kate, now that you are home, where is my beer?"

"You are a funny boy, aren't you? Are you always this cute, or did they teach you that in cop school?"

Drake snorted and shrugged, deflecting Catherine's look of protest. "Besides, I gave up bringing beers to men a while back, if you will recall. I tried driving stick because I loved my family and wanted to be Daddy's Little Girl, but let's face it, men are fun to hang with, but you just can't live with them and stay sane."

Laughing, Drake shook his head in mock despair. "If someone would have bet me in college that my number one wing-man would be a hot woman with no appreciation for a man's unique and adorable qualities, I would have lost for sure."

"Yeah Drake, that's me, a freak of nature. I'm an enigma for sure. Not a lot of unemployed, lesbian, Tea Party types, running around bitching about the need for small government, for sure."

"True enough, but you left out impatient, short tempered, and overly critical of others."

"Thanks, just what I wanted to hear after a long day's work. What is on the news by the way?"

"The usual depressing stuff, of course. Some radicals stole radioactive material in Egypt and another ass-wipe killed his entire family in some sort of honor Jihad thing. They were just talking about how the daughter would come to school crying, saying that her father was nuts. He spied on them, followed them, etcetera. It was the usual story; Western culture is corrupt and must be snuffed out."

Catherine sighed, rolled her eyes and turned the sound back up on the television.

"... Iran's chief religious figure, Ayatollah Ali Khamenei said earlier today that Iran will support any faction, or any nation that confronts the cancer that is Israel! Further, he admonished worshippers at prayer in Tehran to remain vigilant and warned that any military strike by the U.S. or Israel would only make Iran stronger. 'We have no fear expressing this. The age of Western dominance is now at an end.'"

Catherine snorted her disgust. "Augh, I get sick of hearing these dirt-bags."

"Yep, and yet most of the country could care less."

Sighing, she changed the subject. "You staying for dinner aren't you, Drake?"

He smiled innocently and gave a knowing look of amusement at Janice. "I am not staying long. Ginny had a late interview for the Assistant City Manager's job around the corner at City Hall. She is nervous and wanted the support, just not too much support, if you know what I mean. She didn't want me watching over her shoulder, so she dropped me off here until she finished up."

Catherine nodded. "I knew that she was concerned about things over at Arlington. Is she worried about getting laid off before she can find a new gig? It would be really great if she didn't have to make the drive to Arlington every morning."

Janice headed back to the kitchen to look after dinner. "I saw your note about pizza, but I finished early today and went to the store so I could make a nice dinner. How does lasagna sound to you? I made it with hamburger instead of sausage just like you like it."

Kate glanced towards the kitchen. "I noticed the aroma when I came through the front door. You really didn't have to do that, but it would be illegal to argue with lasagna. I wouldn't want Drake to have to arrest me or anything."

Smiling from the little galley kitchen, Janice continued. "I made a nice salad, and I know that you can smell the garlic bread, too. I tried to convince Drake to stay, but he has yet to agree."

With a small shake of her head, Catherine smiled at her friends. "Let me go change. I will be right back." She headed for her bedroom followed by Maggie, who always demanded to be the center of attention, if possible. She closed the bedroom door and again, thinking of how she met Drake; she chuckled. They bumped into each other again at church a few days after her stop sign encounter, and again the following week, when he witnessed her breaking a teenager's nose as she came out of Penny's. The nimrod tried to take her purse in the parking lot. Drake had just finished his shift, so he took her to dinner to help settle her nerves.

"It really was nice of you to take an interest, Drake" she mumbled to herself, as she recalled the day. It was cool, too, that we both grew up so close together, she thought. You from Weatherford, and me from Mineral Wells, how could we fail? I knew that you got me when you were cool even after you realized that I just was not interested in putting up with a man in bed again. What we have now is a much more relaxed and comfortable friendship than I have ever had.

Returning to the front room, Catherine plopped down beside her friend.

He smiled at her. "So! Do you think that you will be able to afford Ranger's tickets again this year?"

"I would sure like to but honestly, I am not sure. You know I wouldn't go with anyone but you. Besides, Blondie in the kitchen there is pathetic about sports."

⁂

As the two couples ate lasagna with hamburger instead of sausage, Janice suppressed a grimace, realizing that she was about to have to endure another Ginny story when Catherine asked her about her interview.

"Actually, I think that it really went well. I was able to relate well to the structure here in Cedar Hill since Arlington also has a city manager as well as a mayor. It didn't hurt that I have lived here since 2009." She looked fondly at her soon-to-be-husband. "It always helps to have a local cop in your corner, right? The biggest issues here, like everywhere, are about the drastic budget shortfalls that everyone is facing."

Everyone but Janice nodded assent with Ginny's comments. Janice smiled inwardly as she noticed that Catherine held her tongue, no doubt because of how well things were going tonight. Drake, on the other hand, was not so restrained.

"Despite the grand pronouncements made by pundits on television and by the nauseating platitudes made by government leaders at all levels, no one who's honest in America today is unaffected by the disastrous economy. Everyone with a job is holding on to it for dear life. I don't know anybody who is about to take any risks, or invest in anything until something changes in the debt picture, both in and out of government."

Janice just sighed and listened. Thinking that it was better to let her mind drift than to point out where they fundamentally didn't understand the drivers behind what was happening every day. She decided that with Catherine in a good mood, maybe she could be enticed to give her a nice massage after Ginny and Drake left. Thinking about her strategy for the evening she effectively avoided much of the tale of civil tedium that was Ginny's interview. Looking on blankly, Janice noticed that Catherine gave her a subtle but sultry look, and blew her a kiss. She then mimicked a smile as a reminder to remember to be polite. Janice shook her head to acknowledge her lover's request, but she decided that way too many of Catherine's friends viewpoints were just simplistic. It always had to do with an antiquated view of the Constitution or about God's law. Texas had been a reasonably decent place to get sent by the network, at least compared to some third-world location, but the self-righteous stuff here was getting really old. Making up her mind she decided to send another email to Rodger about getting a temporary assignment some place less provincial.

"Are you ok, Janice? You seem a little out of it." Coming out of her reverie, Janice saw that Catherine was eyeing her closely.

She smiled sheepishly in response. "I'm fine. I guess I just went down a rabbit hole about something at work. The network has me on the road a lot in the next few weeks. Anyway, I'm sorry. What were you saying Ginny?"

Ginny looked at her fiancée. "Um, I was asked about police budgets. Drake just asked me how I thought that we should deal with the cost overruns the police were faced with as a result of the constant protests that seem to be a fixture of modern life these days. He said the police budgets were really being strained."

Drake looked fondly at his wife-to-be. "What did you suggest?"

Ginny shook her head sadly. "What is there to say or do, really? I shrugged and said that if a group of people wanted to force a city to spend money for police and the cleanup resulting from a protest, there was not much a city could do. A governmental body cannot really prohibit people from congregating without getting sued for civil rights violations. Anyway, I thought about it for a bit, and said that any answer would have to be based on transferring the costs of the protest onto the protestors. I said that there might be a way to recover the costs in permit fees, etcetera."

Regretting that she was back in the present, Janice rolled her eyes. "Humph! You have got to be kidding me Ginny, really? The Solidarity and Occupy protestors are really struggling, and there really is no way out for them. They don't have Halliburton or the Koch brothers paying their way."

Drake cut her off in mid thought. "You're right; they have Soros, Bloomberg and Buffett."

Janice's voice rising, she replied to his challenge. "Do you think it's fair for the Wall Street ass-holes to make all that money when most Americans are being forced into poverty, or have to live on the street? These people may not be polite and civil but who can blame them? They are being ripped off daily! Come on guys, I am really concerned here. If this country doesn't find a way to have more fairness, there are real problems coming!" Janice looked from face to face, trying to make some sort of connection. "Who can blame the protestors? Back in 1980, less than 30 percent of all jobs in the United States were low income jobs. Today, that number is almost 50 percent! I get that you guys don't see this all the time, but I report on the crap that some greedy bastard does almost every day."

Catherine snorted. "I am sure that government over-regulation has absolutely nothing to do with any of that."

Ginny glanced at Catherine before responding in her usual controlled manner. "I can't say about Cedar Hill, but it occurs to me that most of these jerks, in Arlington at least, are often bussed in and paid to protest. I am not saying all of the Occupy stuff is fake, but at least some of the outrage, maybe a lot of it, is made up! The truth is that too many people expect others to take care of them."

Janice saw that Drake patted his fiancée's hand in an effort to keep a lid on things. He then nodded at her encouragingly. "So what did you tell them, Ginny?"

"I said that maybe we could find a way to charge anyone coming here from outside the city by implementing a fee based on the transportation angle perhaps."

Truly angry now, Janice replied, her tone ice cold. "You should have asked what the city was doing to help those who are forced to rely on low wage jobs. I am not saying that there are not professional protestors, but I think that we can all agree that people are really hurting. The answer to all of this is to level out the disparity in wealth that exists before things get worse. I was covering a story two weeks ago where a company put a bunch of people out of work just because the greedy owners simply refused to pay them a living wage!"

She didn't miss that Catherine rolled her eyes again, but she thought that at least she didn't say anything. Likewise, Drake passed a subtle look to Ginny who finally seemed to realize where she just went and where things were headed.

Ginny's tone becoming more conciliatory, as she looked down at the table. "Look, nobody wants people that are honestly trying in life, to suffer. Everyone at this table agrees that there are some really greedy people out there in corporations and in government. Actually, there are greedy people all around the world. I was just making a point that there are folks here in the U.S. and internationally too, that are trying to ruin things for everyone." Surprised by Ginny's intensity, Janice found herself looking into her eyes as she, too, was trying to make a connection. "I have no problem with government, Janice; I work in government for heaven's sake. We all just need to find a way past all the hype that we know that the politicians trade in. Anyway, let's change the subject." Janice was about to reply when she was interrupted by the obligatory emergency tone, broadcast from the television in the front room. As the tone died away it was replaced by an official announcement.

"An explosion took place moments ago in..." In mid-sentence the lights went out in a wink following a loud pop coming from down the street.

Chapter 4

The Players Take the Field

The waitress brought drinks and more hot wings for the little knot of well-dressed patrons enjoying the game far below. The New York Giants were in the playoff hunt and were hosting Philadelphia for the second time this season. The Giants were favored to win but only slightly favored. Megan Danvers knew football and could talk about it seriously enough, but honestly she couldn't have cared less. Smiling, she watched the game with feigned interest. She thought how easy getting invited to this suite, and earning this lifestyle had been. I am living life at the top she thought. At twenty-seven, I am extraordinarily young to be a top executive. I am only five years out of college, and I am here because I listened when Daddy told me to follow my instincts – to trust myself and play like I mean it.

"Are you having a nice time Meg?" Turning she noticed Richard Blake, her boss and her date tonight, walk through the door to the posh skybox.

She smiled even more brightly. "I was beginning to worry that you were not going to make it. I was fully prepared to be quite disappointed with you. After all, tonight is my reward for placing our opponents on the Sykes deal in shall we say, a no-win scenario, giving us a way to showcase our superior capabilities for the client." Blake mirrored her expression as he reached to take a large shrimp from the crystal serving dish set out on a nearby table and dipped it into the cocktail sauce.

"Sorry about that. I intended to be here ahead of you, but the old man had to tell me about a last minute assignment for the two of us, just as I was leaving. You might say that we have a target of opportunity tonight." Smirking, he popped the shrimp into his mouth, and taking Meg by the elbow, he maneuvered her to the corner of the room. Smiling like a wolf, he sampled more of the gourmet food offered in the executive suite, while briefing his beautiful *La Femme Nikita* about their assignment this evening.

"It appears that things in Europe are finally coming to a head, and it seems that there is very little that can be done to avoid some pretty ugly outcomes there. John asked me to see what we can learn from any conversation that Nathan Sykes and Congressman Tibman may have. Everyone knows that Sykes is greasing Tibman." Richard nodded slightly, indicating the congressman, seated near the floor to ceiling windows. "The congressman was apparently briefed on what the central banks are saying will happen in the next month or so. Between the two of us, we need to find out what is coming so that we can get our positions secured out in front of any watershed movements overseas."

Looking intently into Richard's rich brown eyes, and nodding, she pondered how vulnerable both she and her boss would be should they become a liability. Due to the fact that just about everyone considered her and Richard to be too young for their titles, they would be easy to blame. They had made their rise in the corporate world at an amazing rate.

Meg knew her looks were part of that rise as well as her single-minded attention to winning. She took a moment to appraise her boss. He had dark brown hair, piercing eyes and a bit of a Mediterranean look. Obviously his good looks made him the male embodiment of the firm's desire to portray Sterns and Becker Investments as being managed by attractive executives, as well as traders who were ruthless in their willingness to win for their clients. Meg pondered whether she should express the misgivings she had about the old man's request. As Richard relayed what was needed, her eyes darted to the middle aged man drinking and laughing with their host tonight, hedge fund manager Nathan Sykes. Megan covered the debriefing with a playful giggle as she memorized the face of the middle age guy, Anthony Tibman, the Honorable Congressman representing the 16th district on Manhattan Island.

Megan's mind drifted to the risks and consequences of the intrigue with which she was being requested to assist. To herself, she went through the angles. She could likely do this with no problem, nine times out of ten. It was the one in ten that was the sticky part. Should the dice not come up in her favor, she realized that she could easily be replaced. She arched an eyebrow and regarded her boss carefully. "Richard," she said in a cool tone, "you do realize that they are getting us to do this sort of thing, because we are expendable should things go awry?" Returning her seriousness in full measure, he only gestured with an almost imperceptible shrug – expressing without words that this was why they made the big money.

An amused expression returned to her face regardless of her reservations and the guilt plaguing her heart. She gracefully turned toward the seating area of the skybox. Raising her right arm up towards her boss's face, she extended her exquisitely manicured right index fingernail to casually caress up along her boss's throat above his shirt collar. Forming her finger into a slight hook, she lightly tickled her way up to his chin, leading him as if pulling her prey behind her.

The game was a close one. As it progressed, the camaraderie amongst the fans in the posh skybox was to be marveled. Megan felt she was every bit the head cheerleader, her youthful exuberance and her self-confidence infusing all of the guests present with a light hearted mood. Artfully she smiled at Sykes's security man, playfully teasing him off and on throughout the night. She wanted him focusing on her as much as possible. She knew she had to be adept at getting everyone in the suite to relax, have fun, and most importantly, to drink with relish.

Megan saw that for his part, Richard chatted amiably with Sykes about their recent deal and with Tibman about football and current events. He, of course, was careful not to get in too deep on anything, focusing instead on playing the role of the guy that just landed a big contract. She watched him laugh and joke with their hosts. After almost an hour, she adroitly distracted their target and the watchful eyes of Sykes's security for a moment of cheering, allowing Richard the opportunity to place a small transmitter under the table where the two men sat.

As the game ended in disappointment for the Giants fans, the guests said their goodbyes, took a couple of pictures together and consoled each other about the loss. Tibman shook Sykes's hand and left them to make his way to his awaiting limo. Sykes and Richard chatted as they left the suite, followed by Megan who abruptly stopped when the little group made their way out the suite's door to the walkway beyond. Rolling her eyes, she looked embarrassed.

"I left my purse on the couch by the window. I will catch up to you boys momentarily." Grinning, she bounced back into the suite to retrieve the forgotten item. Upon reentering the suite, she made a beeline towards her purse, deftly recovering the small transmitter on her way past Sykes's and Tibman's table. She grabbed her purse, turned and made for the door, but hesitated a moment. Acting on a whim, she did a cursory search of the waste basket located on the wall adjacent to the table that had been her focus tonight. Sure enough, right on top was a crumpled napkin with writing on it. Feeling smug, she snatched the napkin, pushing it into her purse. With any luck, there would be something useful on that small piece of paper. In a matter of seconds, Meg rejoined the group of men who were still waiting for an elevator to whisk them to the stadium's ground floor.

~

As Richard's limo pulled up to her apartment between Lexington and 3rd Avenue, Meg knew that her boss would soon be hinting that she should invite him up to her place for a night cap to celebrate their successful activities this evening. She liked Richard, and he was cute, but she also knew from the jump, how that kind of thing ended up. She was young, but she was not stupid. As the car slowed and pulled into the drop off lane, Richard made his play.

"We did a good job tonight. You were amazing. I was concerned about Sykes' body guy, but you had him laughing and watching you more than he looked after his principle or the game for that matter. They never really had a chance did they? Anyway, I do have a bottle of champagne in the car that we could share if you want to celebrate." His eyes were smoky and his grin enticing, but Meg just demurred, hinting with non-verbal cues that the timing was not good from a biological perspective.

Regardless of his defeat with Meg, he nodded. "Another time perhaps."

The driver got out to open her car door. Watching him, she decided that she in fact was in a mood to celebrate by burning off the adrenalin and stress of her little victory, just not with her boss. The thought was sublime.

She smiled, grabbed her purse, and exited the back of the limo when the driver opened her door. Walking to her building's front door, without turning, she gave him a friendly wave, satisfied that Richard was almost sure to be watching her leave. As she approached her building, she smiled warmly, and greeted her doorman before entering her building.

❧

Megan entered her small but very well appointed apartment and hung her purse on the elegant standing mirror and combination caddy which stood just past her entry way. Her warm brown eyes briefly took in the image staring back at her in the mirror. She reflected that her grin really was infectious. It was right at home on perfectly shaped lips, which in turn were just right for the artistically pleasing shape of her face, delicately framed by dark brunette spirals which had partially escaped the elegant up-do for tonight's event. She was the kind of woman who was beautiful, but beautiful without appearing unapproachable. She decided that if she were to fit into a category, at five feet eight inches in height, she would have said she was the girl next door. Annoyingly, others had said she was more like a glamorous model from the cover of a magazine. She felt certain the comment was meant to somehow trivialize her as just a face. Blowing out some of the stress from the evening, she kicked off her pumps on her way to the sofa. As she walked, she straightened out the napkin she had just retrieved from her purse. Sitting down, she read the one line cryptic message.

Demise of Dexia & La Banque imminent. Structured Collapse of the EU unavoidable!

She read the note and pondered its implications. Hearing movement behind her, she turned to see her bedroom door opening. A smiling, Matt Regan emerged from her bedroom. Although they didn't exactly date, they had been very close, almost from the time she came to New York. He was in his early thirties, athletic, with closely cropped light brown hair. Although not exactly handsome, he had a barely tamed rugged appeal that Megan decided was intoxicating. He was wearing only the bottoms to a pair of scrubs. As he walked confidently over to her carrying two wine glasses, he smirked.

"So, how did it go? I saw that the Giants lost. Was the food good?"

"Of course the food was good. It would have been better with you to enjoy it with though. Have you eaten? I can order something for us if you're hungry." Matt stepped over the low back of her modern contemporary sofa and plopped down beside her. Looking at the napkin that she had just straightened, he cocked his head to one side and passed her an inquisitive look. She shook her head, and turned the small square of paper over and over between her fingers. "I guess you could say that it's intel. John sent Richard to the game tonight with an assignment for the two of us. He wanted to know details about the mess going on in Europe from the Congressman, who was in our skybox to meet with Sykes. As usual the old man tries very hard to leave nothing to chance."

Taking the napkin and examining it a little closer, a cautious look settled on his face. "What is this then? You know that the guys you were with tonight are serious players. You could end up way over your head and not even know it."

She nodded. "Tell me about it. Richard got what he needed. I just found this in the trash next to where Sykes and Tibman were sitting. I was the only one in the room when I found it, and we all left together; so there is no way he would have even gone back for it. Something big is coming and everyone is freaked out about it at work." She looked into his seasoned eyes. "I am a little scared about, well I don't know why exactly, but I am."

He raised a questioning eyebrow at her remark.

"Why do you think I fell for a certain rugged, good looking, ex-Army Ranger? What could go wrong?"

"You fell for me because your college roommate dumped me the last time I went over to Afghanistan, and you just couldn't resist my rugged good looks and rapier wit, even if Dianne could. Still, if your gut is telling you to feel queasy about this stuff, I would trust that feeling. Your subconscious is what keeps you healthy when things get rough."

She noticed that he looked directly into her eyes with an expression that left no room for misinterpretation. "These guys won't fool around if they think that you are a problem for them; you may not know you are a problem for them until it is too late. The most effective way for you to protect yourself from trouble is to not be around should it come calling."

She nodded seriously. "Anyway, I'm sick of thinking about this stuff. Why don't you find some clever way to distract me from work? I will decide what, if anything, to do with this in the morning."

Matt feigned being oppressed. "Some people are so demanding." Delighted, she watched him set down his wine glass and lean in on her. She felt a little jolt from his nipping her ear-lobe with his teeth, whispering; "I think I may have something that may help." She sighed, relaxing and turned to kiss her rugged soldier passionately on the mouth, her tongue darting to meet his.

She loved looking into his sharp hazel eyes. He was the one man that had always made her feel safe in the big city. He was quiet and often reserved, but no one who knew him ever confused this with his not being completely aware of his surroundings at all times. She adored that although he was a hard practical man, he had never been threatened by her in any way. She earned many times what he did, and he knew it, but did not resent her for it, nor did he look down at how she accomplished that particular trick. She loved his quiet confidence. She from Texas, he from New York, they came from completely different worlds, but they just clicked regardless. It was as simple as that. Her favorite thing on earth was being with Matt Regan and running her fingers through his closely cropped brown hair. She decided that she might even care for him as much as she cared for her fancy title: Senior Information Officer at Sterns and Becker Investments.

In only moments his kisses completely supplanted any thought other than of the sensations she was experiencing as her man kissed her repeatedly.

As they paused to take a breath, she took a sip of wine. She marveled at the electricity that shot through her when Matt lightly caressed her face. He massaged her temples, while taking her hair down from where it was pinned. Giggling, she returned his affection after a time by lightly raking her nails along his naked biceps, to his shoulders, and down his muscled back on either side of his spine. She saw the sly look he gave her as he shivered slightly at her touch. Taking her glass, Matt returned it to the sofa table. She felt herself being pushed back on the luxurious sofa. Still giggling, she saw him move his right knee sensually between her legs, forcing the short red dress to move up a bit as he cradled her head with his right hand. He supported her head, fiercely kissing her receptive lips. Sighing with pleasure, she squirmed as he tickled the tip of her tongue with his.

Megan smiled up at him. "You know I want this, Matt." She awkwardly reached for the remote on the sofa table and fumbled with it briefly before finally finding the button to remotely lower the lights in her living room.

Now bathed in near darkness, she ran her fingers through Matt's closely cropped hair and sighed yet again with pleasure. She tasted him as he repeatedly kissed her. He began to explore her body through the soft slinky fabric of her dress. Her nerves tingled from his nipping at her earlobe and the soft kisses along her jawline. She could feel his interest growing quickly as he moved over her. Draping her arms around him again, she traced the muscles of his back with her nails, leaning her head all the way back to let him have easy access to her neck. Laughing together, the real world quickly receded to irrelevance. Her dark hair splashed all around her on the crème colored sofa as they sought each other's souls, her willing that he never stop kissing her. Becoming even more heated, Megan hooked her right leg along the back of Matt's left, pulling him even closer to her. As she brought her leg up, her desire was simply to devour him completely.

"Meg, you are a temptress. You make me helpless before you and you know it."

She laughed. "Who are you kidding? I am the addict in this relationship, but if you are powerless, then I command you to take me to the bedroom."

"As you wish." He stood, and she smirked with raised eyebrows, his scrubs inadequate for the task of hiding the center of her focus. He reached down and scooped her into his arms and strode purposefully to the bedroom. Dropping her lightly onto her feet, she felt him gently clasp her face with both hands and kiss her as she wrapped her arms around his waist. They just stood there tasting each other for a moment, and soon she detected him unbuttoning the front of her dress while simultaneously offering her his thigh to ride, as they consumed each other in the half light. In a moment, the dress was a puddle of soft liquid fabric surrounding Meg's feet. She pulled the drawstring to his scrubs revealing what she needed so urgently, allowing his clothing to join hers on the floor. Dying to lie with her man, she climbed on board, wrapping her feet around his waist. He cradled her, laying her back gently onto the soft comforter atop the bed. Watching him, he kneeled before her, and she felt him move her legs apart and onto his shoulders. She gasped as he lightly kissed her inner thighs, reveling and shuddering with pleasure as he worked his way home.

Sighing with pleasure at Matt's efforts, she reached between her breasts and undid the clasp to her bra, gasping as she then teased her nipples. His efforts were soon rewarded with an orgasm that washed through her body. She simply found herself without any composure whatsoever. "Please, Matt I need you. Please – up here on the bed." He looked up at her, his admiration clear on his face. She scooted back on the bed to make room for him and he did as she wished. She felt him impale her just as her head reached the pillows. Breathless, they rocked together in harmony. Again, she flooded, losing all thought as the waves of pleasure rocked over her in limitless succession.

Lost in the luxurious feel of his attention, she gasped as he leaned down to deeply kiss her again. Happily sighing, she felt tears trace down her face as she wept with joy. She felt him touching her, pleasing her, for what felt like an eternity, until she could sense that his need had become intolerable. Pulling him into her with all she had, they achieved ecstasy together.

~

When she awoke Meg was still tingling. She sighed happily, content with the world. She turned her head to see Matt's rugged face lying next to her. She acknowledged that her life was truly blessed. As she lay there she wondered if it was possible for her joy to continue over a lifetime. In the darkness she reflected on her life. The truth was hard to avoid in the silent stillness of the night. She loved her job, but knew full well that she had to compromise her values to have this life. She knew that her father would never approve if he knew some of the less than savory details of the many deals of which she had been involved. Deep in self-reflection, Matt's whispered voice intruded on her reverie.

"You know your breasts are exquisite in this light."

She smiled at him as she felt his fingertips trace her nipples, again kindling fire within her. She moved to kiss him, immersing herself in the feel of his body next to her. Moments later his fire reignited, she used her fingers to stroke him back to life. Moving on top of him, she felt him tease her as well. Sitting astride him she moved carefully into position, arching her back, knowing how he loved to look up at her breasts when she rode him. Smiling softly, she grasped his hands as they reached up to caress her breasts. She covered his hands with hers as together they teased her nipples. Moving together steadily she soon felt herself begin to vibrate with a sensory rush that was indescribable. Unbelievably happy, she closed her eyes, wanting to relish the feedback of every nerve ending. Contentedly, she rocked atop his warm welcoming body. Quietly they traded kisses. She relished the texture of his mouth. Again, reaching the pinnacle of pleasure, she collapsed exhausted on top of her man. Soon, she knew no more as almost immediately she gave in to asleep.

The radio beside the bed startled them to life after only a few hours of sleep. Glancing at the clock on the bedside table, Megan saw that it was 6:00 AM and understood that a new week had begun. Matt rolled over with a huge bemused look on his face. Sheepishly, she made a face at him and headed to the bathroom and a shower. When she came out Matt looked concerned.

"The phone rang while you were showering. It was your dad. His message said that you needed to call your sister in Oklahoma. He sounded pretty serious. Do you want me to play it back for you?" She did, and he reached over to the replay switch.

Chapter 5
Trials and Tribulations

Russell stormed out of the little house, slamming the front door so hard the pictures on the wall rattled and looked as if they might fall. Annie sat stunned at their little dining room table with huge tears falling freely from her eyes.

"Why do you have to be so unreasonable?" She whispered to no one in particular. "I didn't say that our money problems were your fault, but we still have to do something. These bill collectors are making our lives miserable." Amazed, she realized it had only been three months since Russell was laid off at Garriott's, and now they were on the brink of disaster.

She pondered the high points of their dilemma. They could not quite make their truck payment, the air conditioner in her Taurus was broken, and it had a flat tire. The house payment was getting later each month. Annie closed her eyes as she tried to calm down. Again, she faced the fact that her husband, who said that he loved only her from the day they first met, went out and slept with Renee Darnell the day they were all laid-off. The thought tore at her heart and again she focused on her breathing.

To complicate things further, she had to admit what she had proven repeatedly. "Three little plastic sticks aren't all wrong; I'm pregnant. Oh God what will Russ think? How could things go so wrong, so quickly?" Looking through her ceiling and into the beyond, she sighed. "God, how can you allow this? I did what I was supposed to do, what my father taught me was right. I didn't get messed up with drugs, I got married, I have a job, and so did Russ until... What do you want from me? We are trying! In Jesus's name help us, we are in trouble here." Shaking herself out of what was going to be a dark downward spiral, Annie rose from her chair.

She looked around at her cute little frame house, where she lived on a quiet street, in the nice little town of Enid, Oklahoma. "Well, I don't go to work until four, so I can at least get the house cleaned up before Russ comes back." As she began to move about the tiny bungalow, she leaned over to pick up Russ's soiled socks from the previous day. Not even bothering to straighten up, she took a step to retrieve their tiny Pomeranian puppy, Bridgett's stuffed chew toy from where it lay near the coffee table, and tossed it over to the dog's bed. In cleaning mode, her mind went to work on something positive she could do today to improve their situation. As she had done countless times, her thoughts traveled over the same worn out path in her mind. She had been down this path a thousand times since Russell was laid off from Garriott's Fence and Metal Works last fall. The situation just didn't work. With them both working they were able to save a little, but that savings was gone now, along with most of the trust she had in her husband.

Picking up the stack of bills from the table, she lingered on the payment booklet for the pickup. In a moment of complete honesty, she knew that it was a mistake when they bought a new truck when they should have gotten a used one. She remembered telling Russell not to use the couple's credit card to buy the barbeque grill, but she did agree to the new flat screen television.

Now it was all on her, and her job just didn't cover all of their bills. "I know that you don't want any handouts Russ, but if we got food stamps, we would at least be covering food and shelter. I am sick to death of hearing about your pride." Her father always taught his girls to mind the basics first, and then worry about things that you might want. Smiling weakly, she repeated his eternal mantra. "Pretty clothes and fancy gadgets were fine, but they are luxuries. As long as you have shelter from the elements and food to eat you are better off than most." She even raised her hand, shaking her finger to emphasize the point. "Oh, Daddy, was it this hard when you and Momma started out? Sometimes I wish I was back there. Nothing bad could ever get past you to worry us any." The tears threatened anew. "I love you, Daddy." Feeling a little better, she turned the one hundred year old crystal door knob on the closet door, and took out the vacuum cleaner. Soon she was softly singing a song from the radio while pushing her vacuum around the tiny house. It took her a moment to realize that someone was knocking on the front door. She turned off the ancient Kirby and answered the door. "Hi Jana, come in the house this minute. Your timing is perfect I could use a break."

Chuckling, Jana came in, giving Annie a hug. "I guess your door bell is broken again. I thought Russ fixed that a couple of weeks ago."

"He did, but the wire still shakes loose when the door slams over and over again. It isn't quite long enough, so we continually have to reattach it and tighten the little screw. Come sit with me, I could use a friend about now."

"Sure, Honey, what's up with you? I was going to run over to the mall, and I thought that you might want to come with me."

Shaking her head wistfully she responded. "I would love to, but it would only bum me out to see something and not be able to buy it."

Smiling like the woman who sold them their pickup, Jana pressed further. "Come on, if you do see something, I will just get it for you. Things will get better for you guys real soon, I bet. You can pay me back then."

Motioning Jana to the dining room table, Annie headed into the kitchen for coffee. Returning with two steaming mugs, she looked seriously at her best friend. "Russ wouldn't stand for it. We just had another fight about food stamps." Embarrassed, she took a sip and looked down.

Jana patted Annie's hand. "For heaven's sake girl, you are only twenty three, you guys are supposed to be broke at your age. Also, that man of yours doesn't have much room to complain about anything after what he did. You listen to me cause I am older and oh so wise." Smirking, she continued. "I know that it's been tough lately, and Russ will just need to learn some humility. It is people like you guys that food stamps were intended for, not the lazy creeps that just want to lie around."

Taking a sip, Annie's hand trembled just a bit. "There is something that I want to tell you. I need you to promise not to say anything though, at least for a bit. I need time to think. Ok? Do you promise?"

Jana nodded and tilted her head just slightly to indicate her suspicion, but she agreed. "Sure, Honey, as long as it isn't something I have to do something about."

"It isn't like that." Annie took a deep breath. "I don't know how, but I am pregnant."

Sitting up straight in her chair, Jana's eyes glistened with surprise. "Do we need to have that little talk again, Girl? Oh my God Annie, congratulations! I mean it! You will be a wonderful mom. I guess that the timing sucks, but it will work out."

Almost panicking again, Annie looked pleadingly at her friend. "I haven't told Russell yet. I don't know what to do about all of this. What if he is furious? He is under so much pressure already, and who knows what he will think after the thing with that bitch Renee. My pay check is all that is keeping this roof over us."

Jana squeezed Annie's hand even harder. "There is nothing you can do Annie. You have to focus on the things you can control. A child is a gift from God, growing inside you. Russ will just have to deal with it. You aren't thinking about...?" Her voice trailed off and her eyes were wide with concern. As she leaned in, Annie realized that her friend was looking directly into her eyes for the answer to her unspoken question.

"Jana! Of course not! How could you even ask if I could kill my baby?"

Embarrassed, but sighing with relief, she just patted Annie's hand and reached over to take away her coffee. "Sorry, Honey. No more of this for you for a few months. It isn't good for the baby. Anyway, you guys have family and friends who love you. Of course you both should be in church more. You used to go all the time. Now, I don't think that I have seen you there in over a month. You know inside that you already have what you need. You just need to have your faith and keep doing what you know is right. It really is that simple. God will take care of the rest. It may not be what you want exactly, but Russ will be fine. You will be fine, and you will have a wonderful baby in a few months. You just cling to your faith and what you know to be right. God will look after you just wait. You'll see."

As they talked, Annie realized that she was feeling quite a lot better. Between Jana's words and her father's, she was ready to be about doing what needed to be done. "Thanks Jana, I appreciate you more than you know."

"No problem, Girl; that's what friends are for. I will pray for you guys, and it will be just fine. Now I have to run because I absolutely have to see what is on sale at Dillard's."

Annie nodded and hugged her friend as she walked her to the door.

❧

Annie was just finishing getting ready for work. She had just pinned her name tag on her uniform when she heard Russell pull up in the drive way of their little house, reminding her that she was tired of asking him for things. If you don't fix the flat tire on my car, I will just do it myself tomorrow, she thought. Calming herself to face her husband, she closed her eyes, said a quick prayer for strength, and walked out into the living room. Looking out the window, Russ was just sitting there in their little truck. Sighing, she picked up her purse off of the side table and reached down to scratch Bridgett behind her ears and walked out to face her shift.

She walked across the yard to the truck, opened the door and got into the cab. She noticed that he didn't even want to look at her. "The doorbell came loose again, Russ."

Finally, he turned to look at her and nodded. He put the truck into gear, he glanced back over his shoulder and pulled back out of their driveway.

Annie adjusted her seat belt, and tilted her head forward just a bit to see her husband's face a little better. "Where did you go when you left? Are you ok?"

His head gave no indication that he had heard her question, his eyes steady on the street ahead. After a moment or two however, he responded. “I went over to the University, to their maintenance building. I talked to the guy about maybe working there.” He looked down slightly. “They only have a part time opening doing grounds work, but he said that I might could work my way into full time once I was in their system.”

Brightening a little, she smiled at what she hoped was an opening. “That was a good idea, sweetheart. That would be something at least.”

Turning, He looked at her finally. “I have told you Annie, I have to have full time work to even hope to cover my education loans for welding school. If the suits weren’t so damn greedy the country wouldn’t be screwed up like this. It is all them Mexicans that came here to get our jobs!” Slamming his hand on the steering wheel Annie could see that Russ was almost shaking with fury.

Ignoring his childish outburst, she changed the subject. “Jana stopped by for a few minutes today.”

Russell rolled his eyes and scowled even harder. Making the turn onto Owen K Garriott, he was gripping the steering wheel so tightly that Annie would not have been surprised if he broke it off.

“She is our friend, Russ! She has been there for us since we got married, and she is someone I trust. If you would consider listening to advice from people who know stuff once in a while we would be better off.”

“Is that right, Annie? What did she have to say today?” His voice rose again. “What pearl of wisdom did the Little-Miss-Know-It-All have for me today?”

Annie closed her eyes – visibly struggling to keep her temper in check. A moment later she turned to face her husband. “She said that we needed to have faith in God and get to church once in a while. She said that if we had faith and did our best to do what is right, God would bless us and take care of the rest.”

He rolled his eyes. “God expects a man to take care of his family, Annie. Nowhere does it say to sit around and wait for God to pay the bills." Russ pulled the pickup into the Applebee's parking lot and began scanning for a parking space.

"Grow up, Russ! You are twisting what she meant and you know it! No one is saying that you just lie around and wait for God to fix your problems or your screw ups. What it means is that you do your best, and try to be at peace, trusting in God to provide."

Russ again slammed his hand on the dash! "You expect me to believe that was all she was saying? I know how she looks at me. I know what women talk about; she wants to get you to trust her so that you will believe her when she tells you that I can't be trusted ever again. She is probably telling you that you can do better than some washed up, out of work jerk who got drunk and cheated on his wife."

Annie just stared at him with disbelief. "You are completely out of your mind, Russ. Believe it or not, we barely even talked about you at all. I know you think that the world revolves around Russell Davis, but I have news for you; it doesn't! No one has said any such thing to me, much less Jana." She pointed at him for emphasis. "Your problem is not Jana, but you! You are embarrassed that you got fired, and you are humiliated that the great and noble Russell Davis fell off his precious little pedestal by sleeping with that stupid little slut Renee. That's right, I said it. Yes, I am beside myself with fury at your stupidity, but I happen to love you even if you are a colossal idiot! I have done nothing but tip toe around this for three months, and I am sick of it, Russ! You need to think about things really hard. This isn't some television show where it all works out by the top of the hour. This is our life, Russ. You find Pastor Defenbaugh or someone to talk to and get over yourself."

Russ opened his mouth to retort, but Annie held up a hand to stop him from speaking.

"I don't want to hear it anymore. You are doing all you can to find work. That is all we can do about that, so I have had enough of your ranting about how everyone is screwing you over! I am going to go to work now. You go home and think about things, because I have news for you; we are going to have to find some help to make it through, and pretending we don't is just stupid."

Annie got out of the truck, reached back in for her purse and looked directly into her husband's eyes. "And one more thing, I have something important to tell you, so you better put on your big-boy pants and get down on your knees to pray, because when I get home we are going to make some decisions. We are going to find a way through all of this."

As she slammed the truck door shut she paused. "And don't be late tonight! Be here by 10:00. That means here in the parking lot, not leaving the house." With that she turned and stalked off towards an evening of smiling at customers and trying not to be nauseated as she heard the sound of squealing tires. The scent of burned rubber floated past her as she stormed into the restaurant.

Chapter 6
Innocence Destroyed

Both couples sat stunned for a moment in complete darkness, staring wide eyed as their eyes worked to acclimate to the darkness. Catherine wasn't surprised to see that Drake reacted even quicker than she did, feeling his way to the little living room to grab his jacket off the couch. She moved towards the kitchen to grab some candles. Watching him through the cut-out between the kitchen and the dining room, she saw Drake's face lit by the glow from his phone as he dialed the police station.

"Hi Sam, its Drake. Is everything ok? We had the TV on in the other room while we were eating. All we got was the emergency tone and something about an explosion; then our power died. I thought that I should check in."

Consumed in darkness, Catherine rummaged through her emergency drawer to get a couple of candles. In less than two minutes, she came back into the dining room, setting the candles lit from the stove, on the table between the lasagna and the salad. The firelight flickered whimsically. It suddenly transfigured their dinner into an intimate affair as Drake finished his call. Catherine sat back down in her chair and looked expectantly at Drake as did the other two women.

"There aren't many details yet. Apparently there is a problem at the Comanche Peak power plant. Oncor is only going to be able to provide power to critical need infrastructure until they can access how serious the issue they are having is. According to Sam, they are saying that there was an explosion outside the plant, and the safety shut offs engaged, taking the reactor off line. We get a lot of juice from Comanche Peak so all of the non-critical stuff is just going to have to deal with the darkness until they know what they're looking at."

Catherine began to press him further, but Ginny spoke first, looking concerned but calm. "You guys don't think that it could be terrorism do you?"

"I just don't know, Honey. Sam said that we were not being brought in yet, so that is at least a hopeful sign."

Ginny nodded with concern obvious on her face. "Oncor has shut down several coal plants in the last few years or so because of federal mandates. Maybe they can be leveraged back into service to make up the difference if the problem is one that will take time to fix."

Catherine added another bite of salad to her plate, and added her own take to Ginny's statement. "If only the feds were not so stupid and overbearing. By forcing Oncor to shut down perfectly good coal plants before they had new capacity to take their place we are now sitting in the dark."

As she expected, Janice sighed and added her perspective. "It is hardly the fault of the federal government that power plants here refused to keep up with pollution and efficiency standards. They have been given ample warnings that they would have to become compliant."

Catherine rolled her eyes and replied. "Give me a break Janice, The EPA is overly oppressive and everyone knows it. The Feds may have some concern about environmental issues, but what they really care about is gaining power over us. They are doing their best to train everyone to be obedient."

"Kate, that is ridiculous on its face. I promise that the boogie man is not out to get you, Sweetheart."

"I know Janice, I know, the Feds are all about goodness and light. We will just have to agree to disagree. At least we have our own power grid here in Texas. All a terrorist would need to do to really hurt the United States would be to set off an EMP. That would really screw over a lot of people. Having our own power is nothing but a good thing."

"Ok Kate, we have all been down that road. Let's not do that tonight."

Catherine nodded; smiling at Janice's look of encouragement. 'Alright Sweetie, but you have to admit that having a few supplies around is only responsible. What if this power outage goes on for months like what happened in Japan after the Tsunami?"

Catherine could see that Janice wasn't going to accept her point and merely rolled her eyes in exasperation, but she smiled so it looked as if maybe there wasn't going to be an argument. She returned her lover's smile with one of her own, thinking that with any luck, maybe she could actually get though the evening with a real opportunity at some intimacy later.

Looking at Drake, Catherine noticed that he worked quickly to finish his dinner. Looking up, he gave Ginny a significant look. "Baby, Sam didn't say so, but I should probably go to the station when we finish dinner. I am sure that everything will be fine, but they might need me if there is a problem. Besides maybe we can find out what is going on." Ginny grabbed her fiancée's hand, giving him a supportive look to let him know that she understood.

Catherine nodded and thought that she was really glad that Drake was so intuitive, but offered a proforma protest in the name of good manners. "You guys don't have to run off."

"The dinner was great but we should get going. I will let you guys know when I hear something, but I suspect it is likely not that big of a deal," Drake said.

Taking another drink of tea, Catherine saw that Janice dropped her fork, her eyes fixed on Drake as alarm became evident in her voice. "Wait a minute; Comanche Peak is just west of here on Highway Sixty-Seven. It isn't that far away really." Janice grabbed Catherine's hand. "Maybe we need to get Maggie and leave until we know what's going to happen. I knew that something like this would happen one day."

Catherine patted Janice's hand reassuringly. "Come on Janice, we are going to be just fine. The power has to come from somewhere. If the left doesn't like nuke plants and you don't want them to hand out new permits for coal plants, or even natural gas plants which really are clean, what exactly are we supposed to do?"

She stared at Janice a moment knowing that she would have no response.

Drake interceded. "The fact that we are sitting here in the dark is a good thing. It means that the safeties worked. Whatever happened, they took the plant off line before there was a problem. I am sure the worst of this will be the inconvenience."

Catherine passed a knowing look at Ginny, hoping she would take the hint. She in turn, smiled at Janice and added her own perspective. "I am sure that it will be alright Janice, I saw on the news like two weeks ago that TXU was saying that they were really worried the transmission infrastructure is getting to the point that it needs to be replaced. Transmission infrastructure has nothing to do with plant safety. I am sure that the power plant is inspected all the time. I bet that it is just the transmission station or something."

Catherine finished off the last of her salad and was considering another roll, but sat back in her chair as the others finished their meals. She saw that Drake too had placed his napkin on the table. She noticed that Ginny, however, was slow on the uptake and continued to discuss the power outage.

"I recall a briefing that Oncor did for the city of Arlington. They said that the power plant is certified until 2030, so I doubt that there is anything too wrong. There is no way that any of the local city officials would allow something like what happened in Japan to happen here. We will probably know more in the morning. It may even be fixed by then." Smiling reassuringly at Janice, she finally placed her napkin on the table. "Don't you worry, Janice it will be ok, I promise."

Catherine noted that Drake winked at her and then flashed his best cocky look of assurance at the women. "Absolutely. You guys will see, by tomorrow everything will be just fine." Getting up, he offered a hand to help Ginny to her feet. "Well ladies, I hate to eat and run as they say, but we really need to get going."

Ginny smiled, patted her stomach and sighed with pleasure from eating a wonderful meal. Ginny handed Drake her plate as she reached for the salad bowl. Catherine smiled at the look of surprise on his face. "I think that you can wait until we clear off the table, Honey. Janice and Kate are not our personal servants." Catherine decided that although her world was pretty messed up; actually, messed up beyond recognition, she at least had some good friends as both couples finished clearing the table.

As Ginny's car pulled out of the drive onto the dark street amid Maggie's barking her good byes, Catherine gave Janice a reassuring hug and followed her back into the house. "Well, so much for the movie idea. It looks like we will have to do the dishes by hand. It was nice of Drake and Ginny to help get them to the sink and put away the food, so all that we have to do is the actual washing."

"Aw crap, you are right, what about the hot water? We should probably save that for showers, shouldn't we? Maybe we just rinse the dishes and do them in the morning. With any luck, they will have things fixed by then.

"OK, so it is now official. You clearly never listen to anything that I tell you. I am starting to think that you are just with me for my pretty face." Janice returned her gaze with a look of complete confusion.

Catherine gave her partner an impatient look. "I have gas, Janice."

Processing her partner's statement, Janice blinked and then began laughing uncontrollably.

Realizing that the look of confusion that was on Janice's face was likely now mirrored on her own, she gave her a 'what the hell look,' before realizing what she had just said.

"Oh for God's sake Janice, really? What are we, twelve?" Rolling her eyes, she rephrased.

"I have natural gas, so we have as much hot water as we want. Even if I didn't have natural gas, I have two camps stoves and a field-shower if we were really desperate."

Jumping as Catherine swatted her playfully on the butt, the two women headed for the tiny kitchen to begin the cleanup.

Janice sighed resignedly as her mirth subsided. "Or we could just drive to my house and have hot water."

"Aren't you assuming too much. You may not have power at your place either."

"Oh crap. I just bought steaks. They better get this fixed or I am going to be pissed."

Catherine moved back towards the sink. "It isn't so bad, doing these by hand, but it is nice to have the dishwasher when you have company though." As the soapy water filled the sink Catherine began washing the plates and handing them over to Janice for rinsing. The intimacy of the moment was a welcome relief to the tension that had permeated things between them the past few days. As she watched her partner's hands rinsing the dishes, a smile began to blossom on her face. She watched Janice's nimble fingers deftly manipulating the glasses and plates, rinsing the suds away, then prop the items on a dish towel on the far side of the sink. After a moment, Janice noticed that she was being watched. Catherine gave her an appraising look, then nodded in the direction of the clean dishes that were stacked neatly to one side. "And I thought that you only knew how to smile into a camera lens."

Janice responded by splashing water from her side of the sink. "That's how it is, is it? Just a pretty face reading a script for a camera you say? Maybe I need to work harder at keeping you in line."

"Maybe you do at that Blondie, otherwise how will I ever learn to take you seriously?" Not caring to be the only one wearing a wet t-shirt she retaliated in full measure. The water fight didn't last long as the couple was soon kissing in a full embrace as the candle danced impulsively, providing them with mood lighting in front of the little sink.

❧

The alarm on the iPhone was as persistent on Tuesday as it had been the day before. Catherine reached over to silence it, feeling Janice stir as well. Blinking, to focus on the time, Catherine confirmed what she already knew. It was five-thirty in the morning. Lying on her back, staring blankly at the ceiling, she noticed that Janice had rolled over and was leaning her head on her hand. Regarding her closely, she smiled sympathetically. "What are you thinking, Sweetheart?"

She snorted. "I am thinking the same thing that I always think this time of day Janice, that I hate my job, and I don't want to go there anymore. Is it too soon to say that after only one day?"

"It is perfectly alright as far as I'm concerned."

Swinging her legs out on her side Janice got out of bed. As usual, she was wearing her favorite fleece Kitty Cat pajama bottoms and her favorite little white tank top. "I will go fix the coffee."

Catherine was still staring at the same place in the ceiling. "How exactly are you going to do that without power?"

"Magic of course! Either that or just use electricity. If you were even a little inclined to occasionally look on the bright side, you might see that the lights are on in the bathroom. If you were really optimistic, and observant, you might possibly notice that there is light under the bedroom door. We obviously left them on in the dining room too."

"Oh right, I guess that Drake was right, the crisis is in hand after all. Told you so by the way." Catherine followed Janice's example. She struggled to her feet and headed for the bathroom.

Entering the kitchen, the smell of ham cooking and brewing coffee made Catherine's stomach rumble. She walked up behind Janice, and gave her a hug to thank her for breakfast. Inhaling the fragrance of Janice's hair, she realized that Maggie was already out in the back yard.

"Thanks for letting Maggie out. What did you find to cook with the eggs? It smells wonderful.

"I picked up a couple of things yesterday when I shopped for dinner."

"Thanks, I appreciate it. I really need to go to the grocery store in the worst way. I figured it would be cold cereal this morning."

"Amazing! The woman, who has a year of food storage, has no breakfast meats in the fridge. How does that work, Miss Prepper?"

"Cute Janice, with fresh perishables, I am just as subject to having time to go to the grocery store as everyone else. Still, we won't starve when the economy finally tanks."

Janice sighed but Catherine saw her swallow a snarky retort. "How does scrambled eggs smothered in cheddar cheese with chopped onions and shredded lunch meat sound to you?"

"It sounds like a perfect breakfast. Actually, it's just the way I like it."

"Good, go relax then. I will bring it to you. You also had better turn on the TV to check on the traffic. You need to see how ugly your morning commute is going to be."

Catherine stumbled into the front room and fingered the remote, bringing her flat screen to life. As expected, she was greeted with the inane chatter of the morning crews on various stations, as she flipped through looking for what freeways to avoid. "For God's sake, show me the freaking traffic!"

"Are they saying anything about the power from last night?"

"Not yet, besides, wouldn't a story like that be at the top of the hour anyway, Reporter Girl?" Flipping back to channel four, she saw that there was a wreck on I-35 at the merge, and she learned about overnight road work on the toll-way not yet picked up.

As she watched the screen, Janice sat a plate on the coffee table and took a spot on the couch next to her. A reporter standing in front of the freeway with the tardy road crew in the background explained the construction delay. Catherine realized that she really could care less about most of what the various newscasters believed to be important. She looked over at Janice to see that she too was busy eating her eggs and toast and trying to wake up. Content, she decided that she enjoyed their early morning wake up routine.

Glancing at the time displayed on the corner of the TV screen, she realized that it was six o'clock as a noise at the back of the house indicated that Maggie requested and required the immediate assistance of someone with thumbs to let her back inside. Catherine rose and headed to the back porch.

"Who's a good Girl? Did you catch that mean old squirrel this morning, Maggie Girl?" Catherine patted her head and was thinking about getting her a treat when she heard Janice gasp.

"Kate! Come here! Quickly, Honey, you need to see this." Kate rushed back to the front of the house to see Janice leaning forward on the couch with the remote, already backing up the news story that she was watching to its beginning.

"...Three people killed yesterday afternoon including a seven year old child. Two other men were also injured in what was apparently a preplanned attack in Carrollton yesterday afternoon. The attack took place on North Josey Road, at approximately 2:00 PM, not more than a few hundred yards from the Carrollton Police Department. Killed in the incident were Darla Reins, age 31 and her son, Danny Reins, age 7, and another man who has yet to be identified. Witnesses at the scene said the man appeared to be of Middle Eastern descent and was screaming at bystanders in what sounded like Arabic as they tried to assist him." As Catherine watched in horror, the reporter began to interview a witness. "My name is Jamal Norton; I was in the car just behind the family. I was looking down to see what time it was when I heard screeching tires. When I looked up, the Middle Eastern guy just pulled up and started shooting at some woman in a black sports car. He tried to go after the other lady but he got creamed by that FedEx truck."

Catherine looked on in disbelief. "There is no way that Darla and Danny could be involved, right?" She looked pleadingly at Janice. "It can't really be them can it?"

Catherine felt herself being pulled into Janice's embrace as they both watched the rest of the story.

"Also injured in the attack was Martin Johnson, age 62 who was shot in the hand and a Mr. Bang Winn, age 22 who was driving the FedEx vehicle. Both injured men were transported to Baylor Medical Center. Witnesses described a fierce gun battle that began when the Middle Eastern man pulled alongside a black late model Dodge Challenger and opened fire. Carrollton police have declined to comment on the case citing an ongoing investigation, but did emphasize that at this time there was no credible evidence to indicate that this incident had any terrorist connections. Carrollton police detective, Fernando Reyes said that they have been working on a related case for some time, and were actively pursuing leads in the matter. He stated that it was a matter of time before all those involved with this incident were apprehended."

Staring in shock at the television for several seconds, Catherine just blinked at the news that her ex-husband's sister was just brutally murdered in some sort of shootout. "Oh my God! Oh my God! Poor Darla! I wonder if Dan knows yet." Catherine immediately dug in the pocket of her robe for her phone.

"Of course he does Sweetheart. I am sure that the cops have contacted him Katie – right? If he doesn't know, are you sure that you want to be the one to tell him?"

Catherine ignored her partner as Dan's phone began to ring.

"Hello."

"Oh my God Dan, I just heard. Please tell me that this isn't right. This just cannot have happened, right?"

"I wish that I could say it was a mistake but it isn't. I found out late yesterday afternoon. I had jury duty, so I didn't have my cell phone turned on. I guess that I should have called you, but it was just too much, you know? Mom is just destroyed, not to mention Bob, losing his wife and son. He lost his whole family, they were just snuffed out that fast."

Catherine knew that she was losing it, but tried valiantly to keep herself under control for Dan's sake.

"I am just in shock Dan, this is insane. My God why would someone want to shoot Darla and Danny? It is getting as bad here as it is in Europe, or the Middle East. I said that this would happen." Swallowing her tears and the blind emotion threatening to overwhelm her, she continued. "It will only keep getting worse until Americans wake the hell up, and..."

"Stop it Kate. I have heard it all before. I just can't listen to one of your diatribes right now."

"I am so very sorry Dan."

"The cops said it had nothing to do with us. Darla was just in the wrong place at the wrong time. The son-of-a-bitch was trying to get the woman that drove away. Yes, I guess it was another one of those Sharia things, but I just don't want to think about the global implications if you don't mind. I wish to hell that somebody would send all of them back where they came from." As she listened to Dan's words, she also heard something that he hadn't heard since they divorced. He was crying. It was all she could do not to join him as her emotions too, were overwhelming her ability to cope with them. The moment with Dan turned into two; Catherine realized that she was shaking, as grief and sorrow overwhelmed her. Suddenly unsteady, she sank onto the sofa in a heap, as weakness overtook her. Swallowing her pain for the moment she stammered on, wanting to comfort the man on the other end of the phone.

"Is there anything that I can do? Oh my God Dan, I cannot even talk, I am in shock. The world has gone to hell and everybody just continues on like it is no big deal. I am so very sorry. You know how much I love Darla. I know that you guys are... were close."

As she spoke the full impact of what had happened seeped through the shield of her shock, making her light headed and a little nauseous. "My God, I am so very sorry. I just can't believe this. Poor Danny, please tell me that they didn't suffer."

Dan's voice cracked but nothing intelligible came out for several seconds, again creating dead air on the phone. "I don't know Kate, I am still in shock. I hope not. I just don't understand it. Nothing seems real any more. Ever since I found out yesterday, I just keep staring at the wall. I keep expecting Darla to call and ask why I haven't been by. She was the last person to have to worry about something like this."

Catherine took in a deep breath and exhaled slowly. Grabbing the cuff of her tattered robe, she dabbed her eyes. Her breath was still ragged, but she willed her emotions into submission just a little longer.

"Do they know anything about the guy that did this?"

"They said that they think that it may have something to do with some sort of international thing, but I don't really think that they have any clue. The Carrollton police said that they are going to bring in the Feds now."

"That's just crazy. Darla and international murder plots? It is just crazy. I am so sorry Dan. I really am. I wish I knew something to say to comfort you. She really is, was about the nicest woman that I know. The world just keeps getting more and more evil I think. It stopped making any sense to me a long time ago." Leaning back on the couch, she looked up at the slowly spinning ceiling fan. Again, she used her sleeve to dry the tears in her eyes.

"I told my dad last week that I give up because everything is just too screwed up to ever hope to fix." Shutting her eyes, she just wanted to somehow make the world reset.

"Thanks for calling Kate. I appreciate it, and I know that you care. I have to go now. I just can't talk about this anymore right now."

"Sure Hun, you call me though, if you need to talk. I mean it Dan; I really do want to be there for you if you need me."

"Thanks Kate, I appreciate it. Anyway, I have got to go. You keep a sharp eye out for what is going on around you. I couldn't take it if something were to happen to you, too."

"Sure Dan, I will be careful. You too, ok?"

"Sure Kate. Give my best to Janice." With that, the line went dead. Catherine set her phone on the sofa table and sighed, a hapless look on her face. Her tears, finally unrestrained, came on strong, her body shuttering with the pain of her loss and hopelessness.

Janice patted Catherine's arm. "I am sorry Kate," Janice whispered. "Dan is tough and he will get through this. If I could make guns just vanish you know I would." Janice stood up, and took the dirty plates to the kitchen. Catherine just rolled her red and now swollen eyes. She sighed tiredly at her partner's retreating back as she made her way into the kitchen. She couldn't bear the thought of yet another defeat in her life but knew it was inevitable. Taking a breath, she resigned herself to the idea that some things in life were just not repairable, for her, for Dan, or for the world as a whole.

⁂

Catherine drove north, on Beltline so that she could jump over to 161 and avoid some of the traffic mentioned on the morning news. She thought about her conversation with Dan. Tears came unwelcomed to her eyes as she remembered what a sweet little man Danny was, and she thought of how happy he was just a year ago, telling her about his new puppy. Coming to a stop at the light, just south of I-30, she realized that she was actually screaming her rage at the world. "Ass-Holes! Everyone is so dammed concerned over offending someone that we don't stand up for what's right any more. We let the Rat-bastards run over the innocent because we are too busy, and too greedy to be bothered!"

The light turned green, and she accelerated through the intersection, almost clipping two of the protestors that were standing partway in the street, shoving their signs at passing cars. Shaking herself mentally, she realized that she needed to get her emotions under control before she had even more problems.

She made her way onto the on-ramp and accelerated to reach the seventy mile an hour speed limit. As she pondered the world, she again reached the conclusion she always reached. The world was a cesspool, and it was only getting worse, not better. "Oh God, how can you allow this to happen to people like Darla and little Danny?" Darla was one of the kindest women that she had ever known. "Why do good people constantly have to pay for all the stupid fucking evil in the world?" As she approached the mix-master at I-35, she clamped down hard on her emotions. She knew that she could not allow herself to be too worked up on her way to what would be her second day at the Presbyterian gig. She let out a long steady breath.

"And people wonder why I am such a pessimist and have zero trust in anything or anyone." She thought that most of the idiots in the world were either too selfish to care about what goes on around them, or too damn stupid to know the difference between good and evil." As she drove she decided that her father just didn't understand. It just wasn't the world that he grew up in any more. Everything had changed. It is utterly hopeless, she thought. You can't have an honest debate on anything when those debating are no longer honest, or even interested in finding a solution. She sighed, thinking that the leaders in the media, only knew how to profit from issues, not how to solve them. That is it in a nutshell, she thought. There is no honor in people any more, so they do whatever they like, including killing innocent women and little boys without regard. Catherine exhaled another long cleansing breath and reached over to turn on the radio, now willing to endure the news, rather than think about her outlook on life.

"...Israeli Defense Minister Ehud Barak warned in his Monday press update from the Herzliya Conference that time was growing short. He said that the international community would have to take positive steps beyond sanctions soon. The community of nations has now tried sanctions for almost half a decade, and yet today the world still faces the grave reality of a nuclear armed Iran. If sanctions fail to achieve their desired aim fairly soon, the world community must consider more direct steps. The Defense Minister further stated that Iran, not the community of peaceful nations, was alone responsible to demonstrate its good intentions by turning away from its nuclear ambitions. We are quickly moving into a phase where things become immensely more complicated and dangerous. Very soon it may come to pass that a physical strike would become impractical..."

Catherine made a right turn into the employee parking area at Presbyterian. She pulled into a space, shut off the engine to her Jeep. She reached for her purse and paused a moment for one final prayer. "Dear God, take care of Darla and Danny. Maybe they are the lucky ones after all. Please be with Dan and the family, I cannot even imagine what they are going through. Amen!" Stealing herself to face the day she got out and strode with purpose towards her appointed task.

Chapter 7
Realizations

Lying in the unfamiliar surroundings of her new bedroom in the temporary lodgings that Sadie called home since the horrific attack earlier in the week, she realized that she would have to go back to work. She couldn't just stop living her life, could she? She couldn't live forever on her savings. She decided that the Courtyard Residence Inn just north of George Bush at Preston was close enough to work without being too close, but there was absolutely no way to afford two places.

She still shook when she thought about driving into the police department from the back side of the parking lot three days before. The police cars were already screaming out of the opposite end of the parking area onto Jackson Road, on their way to where she had almost just been shot to death. Getting out of her car, she ran in near panic towards the lobby.

Detective Reyes was standing there, leaning in to the front desk as he strained to listen to dispatch describing the shootout. He turned as she entered the building, screaming at them for help. "They are trying to kill me now! Just now! Just now, they tried to shoot me! You have to do something! It isn't just my mom; they want me dead, too!" Reyes rushed over to her as she collapsed in his arms. "They were at my apart...."

"Shush Sadie, try to calm down. We got you. You're safe now. Nobody can hurt you here. Come on; let's go someplace where you can lay down. I don't want you going into shock. Then I want you to tell me what happened. Did what just happen to you, take place on Josey a few minutes ago?"

Too terrified to speak and shaking terribly, Sadie bobbed her head up and down furiously, as she allowed Reyes to lead her to his captain's office so she could lie down on his couch. Feeling her knees beginning to give way, she felt him take her weight as he looked back over his shoulder towards the desk sergeant. "Mike, get me a cup of coffee for Ms. Cline and get Doctor Riker to come in here please."

Sadie's eyes were full of tears and shock, pleading with Reyes to make it all stop. "I don't understand; I don't. Why is this happening to me? I have never done anything to anyone. My mom never did anything to anyone, and people are trying to kill me. My God, why is this happening?"

Officer Nate Phillips handed Reyes the cup of coffee and left as the police psychologist rounded the corner of the adjoining hall. He stopped abruptly at the office door to lean in, to see what was going on.

Fernando Reyes handed her the cup of coffee. "Just take a minute or two Sadie. Drink some coffee and give your body some time to realize that you are ok now. The adrenalin will have you crashing now that you are safe. When you're ready, tell me what happened."

Trying to get her breathing under control, she sipped at the cup in her hands. Seeing that the men before her stood patiently waiting. She took a couple more cleansing breaths and relayed the events of the last hour or so, beginning when she left the station earlier.

Now, three days later, she was lying in a hotel room, too afraid to go back to her apartment. She recalled how Reyes said that the man she had run down was nowhere to be found, although there was blood on the pillar. Swallowing her anxiety, she decided that he really was a good guy. He arranged for an officer to stay with her the first night. He advised her to avoid going anywhere she was known to frequent, including work, until they could figure out who was behind the shootings. Still racked with guilt and grief that an innocent woman and her son had been killed in her place, she shivered with the emotion from what had become of her life.

Closing her eyes to squeeze out the horror of her chase, she whispered her damnation of the men who wanted her dead. "I am so glad that at least one of you died, you sick bastards! Why couldn't I have killed that guy in the garage?" She could not put out of her mind that the man who tried to kill her, and who likely killed her mother, was still out there.

Tired of lying there feeling sorry for herself, she sat up and again took the new revolver out of the drawer of the nightstand beside the bed. Being careful as the salesman instructed her, she popped the cylinder out to check that it was not loaded; regardless of the fact the she had never loaded it with any of the bullets from the weighty little box still in the drawer beside the bed. She was still a little surprised at how heavy the thing was. Replaying the instructions in her mind, she decided that she would call the number for the instructor after all. She knew that if she was going to carry this thing, then she would have to learn to be comfortable with it, but she had another call to make first.

Sighing, she placed the pistol back into the drawer, got out of the bed, and walked through the door into the suite's tiny living area. Sitting at the little desk, she dialed the hospital. "Hi CC, it's me. Is Becky around?" Her colleague confirmed that she was, and a few moments later, the head nurse for Sadie's section came onto the line.

"How are you holding up Sadie?"

"Ok I guess; I am pretty bored. I have decided that premium channels are designed to never have anything good to watch, unless you are unable to do so. Anyway, I can't stay here forever. Can I come back to work? I am probably safer there than anywhere else anyway."

"You have been through a lot, Girl, I went to the chief, and he said that you were good, salary wise. He said that the hospital would comp you for a couple of weeks, so you don't have to worry about paying bills because of missing work."

"I am going nuts here Becky, I need to work. Every day, all I do is think about what happened. I would rather be helping others."

"I can't even imagine what you must be feeling."

"Thanks for that, Becky. I really appreciate your support. I guess that I am just doing the best I can. The worst is not having my mom to talk to about it."

"Have the police made any progress?"

"They don't know very much, really. The guy in the car didn't have any ID on him, and they said that they can't find his fingerprints on file anywhere. The FBI is involved because they think that the guy is Iranian. It may have something to do with my mom before I was born."

"Oh my God Sadie, that is crazy! Why now?"

"That is what a lot of people are asking. Anyway, can I come back to work?"

"I don't see why not, but I had better run it past Dr. Lohan."

"Thanks Becky, I really appreciate it."

"Well, I have to go, Girl. You don't worry about us and just be careful, ok? You are one of my best nurses."

"You guys are the best, Becky. Thank you so much. If it's alright, just put me back on the schedule for next week, ok? I will be better by then."

"You got it, Sadie. Stay safe and you call if we can do anything. Anything at all, ok?"

"Thanks, Becky. Tell everyone hello for me."

Sadie pushed the button on the phone base to hang up and dialed the number on the card for the man that the salesman recommended. "Hello, Mr. Peek? My name is Sadie Cline. I just bought a pistol, and I need to learn how to be responsible and defend myself with this thing."

Catherine pulled her jeep onto the gravel drive, climbed out and sighed with relief at being home after a long day. She took in a deep breath and smiled. "Thank God it is Friday at last." Digging for her keys, which seemed to have a unique talent for hiding in some dark fold of her purse, she walked to the house. She opened her front door and Maggie pounced on her with an abundance of joy. Feeling grateful for the weekend after what she decided was probably one of the crappiest weeks in her life, Catherine dropped what she was carrying on the dining room table, stopped at the fridge for a cold diet RC, and headed for the back yard. Reaching the back porch, she bent down to pick up Maggie's knotted rope toy. Maggie was wagging her stubby tail so hard that she risked breaking herself in half. Catherine opened the worn back door and stepped onto the back porch, as Maggie charged forward, criss-crossing the yard to find just the right spot to take care of her concerns. Catherine sat down on the steps and reflected on her week. She was getting settled in at work, but she realized that she could take or leave her coworker. Jack was good to work with, but he was preachy and completely full of it with regards to what was going on in the world. Watching Maggie chase a squirrel, she thought that at least Jack was sort of cute as long as he didn't open his mouth.

"Who am I kidding? I keep thinking about anything to get my mind off Darla and Danny." Even arguing with clueless people, who think everything will turn out just fine, is not working to make me feel anything. She knew that she had been spiraling down into a very dark place for over a year. Sitting here watching her dog, it dawned on her why she was despondent. "Son-of-a-bitch! I have no purpose in life." She turned it over in her mind. Everything I have worried about for two years is happening and nobody gives a damn. How can I or anyone else have a future with the world cratering like it is?

"What kind of world has this much evil happening on a daily basis?" She looked up into the darkening sky. "I have never questioned why crap happens to good people. Everyone has to make his or her own choices, so evil is going to happen, but there is just too much of it lately. If you are up there, God, You had better do something or the result will not be what You want."

She had already decided that people living through World War II must have thought similarly dark thoughts. The good guys won that war, but what good came from it? Millions of people are still killed by evil and sadistic bastards every day that would trade a life for twenty bucks, or even just for fun. “Come on, God, we need some help here. Between Islamo-Nazis working with the Drug Cartels, or the political weenies stealing everybody blind, how are we supposed to have any chance? I give up. Fighting back is pointless.”

Catherine decided that the best she could do was to shut out the world and seek joy where she could find it. Feeling Maggie’s cold nose nudging her for attention, she threw the tattered rope toy deep into the yard. Maggie rocketed forward to thunder after the rope. “Go get it girl, bring it back to Mommy!” Nodding to herself, she realized that this was as good as it would ever get. She would just have to learn to focus on the world that she could control, and that wasn’t going to be much. Maggie was soon back to fight her for the rope and for the privilege of another throw. The game went on for several minutes as Catherine’s troubles and stress began to slowly leach onto the concrete under her, dripping insolently down the steps, to soak into the ground. She was just going to have to learn to cope with things as they were. She thought that if she couldn’t change anything, why even try?

Breathing in the beginning of a new weekend, Catherine smiled slightly, thinking how much she enjoyed simple pleasures like playing fetch in the back yard at the end of a bright blue day. She threw the rope deep into the yard again, only this time she noticed that Maggie was losing interest. Standing up to go back into the house, she realized that her phone was ringing. Hurrying inside she reached into her purse for her phone.

“Hello?”

“Hi, Honey, it’s Janice. Are you off work yet?”

“It’s after six so yes. I just got home. I take it you are back from doing the Austin story?”

“Sure am. I filed it just after lunch and hit the road for Dallas. I suspect that the network will decide not to air the piece, but what the hell. There is not much I can do about that, I guess. I would like to see you, Sweetheart. Jason, Rick and Terri from work asked if we would join them for Mexican, then maybe one of the clubs to see if there are any decent new bands playing. I know you are probably not really feeling up to it after what happened on Monday, but I really think you should at least go through the motions of having a good time. My treat, if you are interested."

Catherine knew she really did not feel like going out, but decided maybe Janice was right, that she should make an effort. "I could eat some Mexican, I guess. Ok, where do you want to meet, or should I pick you up at your place?"

"Just pick me up here in like an hour. Does that sound ok?"

"Sure, Janice, but I may not be the best of company."

"It's ok Kate, I will cheer you up."

"OK, let me change real quick, and I will head out."

"Ok, so see you in an hour. Hugs Kate, love you!"

❧

As Catherine pulled up to Janice's condo it gratified her that Janice must have been looking for her as she emerged immediately from her front door. Catherine pulled the jeep to the curb, tapped the horn lightly and waved. Janice waved back and jogged over to the Wrangler. She opened the back door for her purse and then jumped into the front with Kate for a welcome back kiss. "I missed you, Katie. How are things? Is Dan hanging in there ok?" Janice settled into her seat and fastened her seat belt.

"I don't know; about as well as you might expect, I guess. I just keep thinking about it. One minute they were sitting in their car, minding their own business with no worries; the next, their bodies' are shattered by some primitive asshole with a hatred for women. You probably know more about it than I do, but it looks like the FBI is thinking it is a simple hate crime. The guy was probably just another loser asshole trying to enforce Sharia law or whatever - all pissed off when his daughter or sister decided he was a primitive moron and wanted out. Then the incompetent bastard ended up killing Darla and Danny because he just fucked up. Anyway, you don't want me going down that road"

"I know, Honey," Janice sympathized.

Catherine smiled weakly and pulled away from the curb.

Janice sighed. "I heard they said, it was probably related to an honor killing. The government really must do something. They are going to have to find a way to relate to these people. It has been like years and the so-called War on Terror has not accomplished anything."

Catherine exhaled without taking her eyes from the road. "If I recall, they tried dropping the War on Terror language years ago. It seems to me the Islamo-Nazis just keep pushing us, don't they? I keep trying to tell you that Nine-Eleven was not about what we did, but about their nut job views they want to push on everyone else."

Raising an eyebrow in anticipation of Janice's retort, she was surprised to see her swallow her reply.

"Look Janice, I have had a really hard week. Let's just drop it. If we are going to have any shot at a pleasant evening, I just can't think about it anymore."

"Oh, right. Sorry, Katie, I guess I wasn't being sensitive to your needs, was I?" Janice squeezed Catherine's hand nodding her agreement, that dropping the subject was a good idea, and gave her a winning smile. "You really look great by the way. I absolutely love that dress. Very slutty! You will absolutely drive the men nuts."

"You do, too, but then you always do, don't you?"

"I try, Sweetheart."

Focusing for a moment on the busy traffic as she pulled into the flow, Catherine was grateful that Janice took her hint about not discussing what happened to her in-laws. She smiled as she felt Janice's hand reach out to caress her cheek.

"I really missed you this week," said Janice. "I had wanted to get to Austin, but as usual, with my luck being what it is, the big story was here. Ripley, of course, got assigned to chase it, and you know that he is not about to share anything."

Catherine nodded, her eyes not deviating from the road. "Drake said it was a suicide car bomb. They just drove through the fence and detonated near a transmission station. He said the FBI was looking at Al Qaeda or Iranian terrorists. Evidently, it took down several of the towers feeding the metro area."

"Yes, that much is true, but what Drake is leaving out is that the terrorists could have taken out our power for months. They were spotted on camera after trying to crash another fence that protects the transmissions towers. Ripley has a source that said that they apparently panicked and took off towards the highway. Anyway, I guess they decided that their chances to get away were not all that good, so they broke through a fence further down and drove their truck right next to one of the main transmission towers."

Catherine sighed. "At least the bastards were killed I guess. It would be nice if the Feds would get serious about the border. This sort of crap is only going to get worse."

Catherine was surprised to see that Janice nodded in agreement.

"If the terrorists had hit the tower they were initially trying for it would have been much worse." Janice shuddered. "The one they got was downstream from the primary distribution hub. Had they taken out the one they were trying for originally, there would be no way to get power out of the plant until the towers were replaced. It could have taken months."

Shocked, Catherine stole a glance at her partner as she stopped at a red light. "Oh my God, Janice, we are in such trouble. You have to admit that things are going to hell quickly now. It is really obvious, right?"

Janice smiled patiently. "Honey, I have never said that things were good, but just that the government is taking care of it."

Blinking, Catherine simply shook her head in disbelief. "We are doomed. All the Feds want, is power. They say they are fighting terrorism, but their PC approach will not work, and it violates the US Constitution four ways to Sunday."

Janice gave her a patronizing smile. "Anyway, we are almost there, so let's see what we can do about having a good time and getting some good food to eat."

As Catherine pulled up to the restaurant, she and Janice were both quiet, but smiling. Parking the jeep, they walked in to Chuy's, hungry and looking forward to a fun evening. As soon as they went inside they saw that Rick, and his wife, Terri, were already there.

Catherine smiled at the couple who seemed to her to always be attached at the hip. She liked that they really and truly were each other's best friends. Both Terri and Rick had jet black hair and blue eyes. Terri was thin and classically beautiful and Rick, though not exactly a male model, was athletic and had a perpetual look of mischief on his face. Catherine decided that he resembled the prototypical World War II British fighter pilot in a movie. Genuinely smiling now, she stepped forward to greet them, thinking that they looked as if they belonged together.

Terri hugged her laughing as they met. "I am so glad you guys came. You both look wonderful."

Catherine exhaled, releasing some of her tension, as Janice hugged her friends. Looking around at the restaurant's eclectic decorations, breathing in the aroma of the grilling meat of the fajitas, she could feel her stomach rumble its demands.

Terri turned to her again, smiling warmly. "You know Kate, if I was ever inclined to walk on yours and Janice's side of the street, I would just have to dump Prince Charming over there, and chase you both without any shame." She patted her husband affectionately on the arm and smiled brightly at the little group. "By the way, Jason just called a bit ago. He said that he was like five minutes away and we should go ahead and get a table."

Looking mortally wounded by his wife's comment, Rick displayed his best pouty face. "Getting rid of me already? They do look great, but they can't provide you the one thing that I can." Smirking, he seemed more than confident, knowing that he had nothing to worry about. He stepped forward to hug Janice and Catherine in turn, as the waiter asked the group to please follow him to their table. They took their seats. "So Kate, what have you been up to? Have you landed a new job yet?"

"Not exactly, Rick. I am still doing whatever contract work I can find, but that is about it. I still send out resumes, etcetera, and I go to the networking group thing every couple of weeks, but the story is the same old same old. The problem could just be my winning personality and positive outlook on life, but I have come to think that actually it may have more to do with the fact that nobody is really hiring. Too much regulation and too much cost associated with hiring people."

Janice's smile dimmed for a moment, but Jason walked up before she could respond.

"Hi guys!" He looked at Rick, and wiggled his eyebrows knowingly. "Dude, we have it made tonight bro, two mutts like us, and yet we are surrounded by the most beautiful women in the joint." Pulling out a chair he sat to Janice's right. The waiter came up, with a menu in hand, but he waved him off with a smile and put in his order. "I will just take the house beer if you would, and I will just have another of whatever Rick ordered."

Rick smiled at his friend. "We haven't ordered yet, but if we all know what we want, we can do that now."

As everyone made their selections, Catherine watched the little group out for some weekend fun, and realized that as bad and as crazy as things were, the craziness didn't extend to everyone. As long as you managed to avoid being laid off, she realized that life was much like it had been. Give or take having to deal with the constant harassment by the Solidarity protestors blockading something, or the fact that everything was costing more and more every day, life was going on for many Americans. She decided that the media and popular culture didn't care, so it was easy to dismiss the problem.

Watching the little group, she wondered if it had always been that way. It was human nature to only be concerned when, as Daddy would say, it was your ox being gored. After all, like the Great Depression, most people were working.

After giving her order, Janice changed the subject to another of her favorite topics. "I have been in Austin most of the week chasing a story on a study that is about to come out. It pretty much supports that idea that the rich are getting richer while most of us are really hurting." She smiled at Catherine for emphasis. "For example, if you can believe it, thirty-seven percent of all households in the United States that are led by someone under the age of 35 have a net worth of zero or less than zero. A higher percentage of Americans are living in extreme poverty now than have ever been measured before. In fact, homelessness in children is a third higher than it was back before the crash in 2008."

Terri's mouth dropped at the statistics. "That's terrible; I am shocked it is that bad." Nodding towards Catherine, she extended her a sympathetic look. "I mean, I know that there were a lot of good people out of work, or really hurting, but a third?"

"Sucks, doesn't it?" Janice continued. "Sadly, child poverty is out of control all over the country. According to the National Center for Children in Poverty, over a third of all children who live in Philadelphia are living in poverty. The number is over forty percent in Atlanta and over fifty percent in Cleveland and Detroit."

Rick thought over the statistics that Janice rattled off. "Did you talk to any of the political types in Austin? My question is, what do they plan to do to fix this mess?"

Janice gave him an imperious look, followed by attempting a caring expression for Catherine. "Every time they try to pass more relief, the Tea Party types throw a fit. They are out of step with modern life, but they have enough support to stop everything the more sensible legislators have tried."

Catherine rolled her eyes. "You can probably make stats look like they support whatever you like, but that isn't going to change the reality of what is happening. I may not be a reporter Sweetheart, but I can read, and I look at the stats too. Today, one out of every seven Americans, and one out of four kids are on food stamps. Almost half of all Americans live in a household that receives some form of government benefits. The federal government has had a budget deficit of over a trillion dollars every year since Dan and I divorced in 2008. Come on, guys. You could take every penny that guys like Bill Gates have, and it wouldn't even last the year. Then what would we do about next year? I do not know anyone that wants poor people, or kids, or anyone else, for that matter to suffer, but the government can't help anyone if they don't have the resources to help them. Your buddies in DC and Austin talk about social justice and sharing, but the math just doesn't work, and they know it. They are lying and half the country just believes the lie. It is that simple. We are now at what is called a stalemate. There is no more money available to give to people. They have been lied to for so long though, that they are pissed and in the streets because they expect the impossible. I don't know when, but this will not end well."

Catherine could see that Janice was torn. She obviously didn't want to have another fight, but she could not help herself. "Honey, I don't understand how you could be so uncaring when people are hurting. It's not just adults, but kids that are going hungry."

"Who said that I don't care? In case you haven't noticed, I am out of work myself. My point is that government types couldn't fix this train wreck if they wanted to. It is too big. They have taxed and regulated and spent money we don't have and now the economy is a mess, and we are all going to have to accept that fact. That is why we had all better get ready to get by on our own. I am here to tell you all that the government is not going to be able to take care of it if things really go badly."

The table was quite for a moment when Terri spoke up. "Well, we all can agree that it is a terrible problem, but we are not going to be able to solve the problems tonight. I vote that we just focus on having a nice time."

Catherine gave the group a shrug and a contrite smile. "Good idea, Terri. Janice, I apologize for being a downer. We are going to have to learn to not touch on certain subjects when we are trying to have fun. I am really sorry if I dampened the party. I have just had a really tough week, and I get really angry at the drop of a hat."

Janice reached over to pat Catherine's hand. "It's ok, Kate. We all know that you mean well. You have enough to worry about lately. No one expects you to have the time to follow the details on this stuff. I only know it because I follow it for a living. I still believe it will all work out." Janice looked at her partner hopefully. "Smart people are working on this stuff every day. You can bet that they will find the right mix of laws to fix things."

Catherine just sat there looking stunned at how arrogant Janice could be, but decided there was absolutely no point to any further response. Pushing down her emotions, she smiled weakly as the appetizers arrived. Looking across the table, she studied

Janice from an analytical perspective for once, disregarding how sweet and caring she could be, or how beautiful she was, or even how much she liked their intimate moments. Smiling and trying to relax, she decided that maybe a love life was worth drinking a little Kool-Aid. Unfortunately, she knew that the truth was that a real relationship would be all but impossible over the long run. It was only a matter of time.

Chapter 8
Deterioration

Megan sat behind her desk in a comfortable oversized leather chair with her back to the door. She just sat there staring out the window at her million dollar view with her shoes off, her feet propped up on the credenza behind her desk. She decided that she had not experienced quite such an eventful few days at work in some time. She took in a deep breath and exhaled as she considered her week and the events driving her life. Ticking off the key points in her mind, she considered the current state of play.

She and Richard had both been in and out of meetings all week regarding what moves their teams should make. European leaders were just not going to deal with the emergency. Germany's Chancellor, Anna Hoffman, was diligently attempting to force strict adherence to the austerity plans all the European nations agreed to when they accepted their bailouts over the last two years.

Megan smirked, and tossed the ink pen she was nibbling onto the credenza, turning the situation over and over in her mind.

France, of course, was much less keen to impose its will on sovereign nations. She chuckled darkly. "I bet you don't want to intrude on others sovereignty," she whispered. "You would not want to set a precedent of strict adherence to the bailout agreements, now would you? You know that you are also in line to face the very same consequences."

She realized that Europe's regional recession was becoming critical, making budgets impossible to meet, and they were only expected to get worse.

Megan shivered at the thought of what Sykes, Tibman, and the Board believed would happen. It was clear by the middle of the week, that what was coming would not be anything like previous downturns anyone had ever seen. Rubbing her temples, she stared out at New York City as it moved below her. Watching the denizens, she tried to work though the angles from their perspective. She thought of how the people below her would react, and what responses those reactions would provoke. Public reaction would be of crucial importance. She realized that she was actually a little scared of what seemed to be unfolding. Feeling chill bumps raise on her arms, she spun around and blinked, to clear her mind.

She decided that she just needed a few minutes to unwind after the heated discussion with her second largest client about the losses the company was taking as a result of the unfolding mess, but staring out the window was clearly not reducing her stress.

The quiet ended a moment later when her phone buzzed sharply, bringing her out of her thoughts. She tapped the device in her ear to answer. She knew it was Richard calling without looking at the caller ID or hearing a word.

"Megan Danvers."

"It's me. The EU Ministers just came out of their conference, and they announced just what we expected from them. The austerity matter will be deferred to the larger group of Eurozone members."

"Well, Richard that is it then, isn't it?" Megan sighed audibly. "They are stalling. This means any decision that could allow them to avoid disaster will now drag on for months, into the spring at the very least."

"Yep, that is pretty much what it means. Following Germany's reluctance to back the plan to intermingle all European debt by issuing Eurobonds, the IMF began work to set up its own mechanism to create a new bailout fund to provide capital to weak nations. That capital, in turn, will be loaned to the IMF by the Eurozone's central banks."

Megan rolled her eyes. "What a joke. I swear I cannot understand what they hope to accomplish. Every bailout they try is less effective than the one before it. Actually, forget that. We both know what the current strategy is about. The elites started with the bailouts to prop up their friends. Now that their populations are beginning to realize that only the big lenders are getting anything out of the bailout efforts, things are coming apart. Simply put Richard, they are just buying time to keep their populations mollified until they can position themselves to survive."

"That is my take on it, too, Meg. Where John is on the matter, is that we have acquired a good share of that money, but it is now time to short the market and secure our positions. The information we obtained last week validates that Europe is toast. The riots in Athens, Rome, Paris, and even London are getting bigger every day."

As Richard spoke, Megan retrieved another pen and tapped the end of it against her lips as she considered the week's events. Pondering deeply, she realized that her instincts were saying that shorting the market might not do them a lot of good if the markets themselves completely collapsed. She gasped in horror as her mind went again to the denizens below. What the market players did or did not do would pale in comparison to the reactions of average people. She realized that she really needed to take a fresh look at the angles behind the current crisis from the populist perspective, and she needed to do it quickly. An icy foreboding enveloped her, and she knew she needed to focus on the average person, and the motivations that drove them. Looking down on the street, she realized that her free hand was shaking. "Um, Richard, I have another call. Why don't we meet for lunch?"

His voice was a little off, but he responded quickly enough. "Sure Meg, Lunch. That sounds good. We can talk more then."

She tapped on the device in her ear and reached for her iPad, and tapped the icon for her assistant. "Liz, something has come up today, I need you to reschedule my next meeting." Hanging up, she again stared out at midday New York City. Returning to the key points of her dilemma, she began the systematic process to work out the motivations of the various actors in the unfolding drama. We have verified that the European Union is doomed to fail because the monetary divide between the northern and southern countries is just too large and the debt amounts are, at this point, just too extreme. Europe and the United States too for that matter, are far too leveraged. If the U.S. dollar was the safe haven leaders were trying to sell it as, it would be rising against all currencies.

Instead, like Europe, the U.S. dollar is setting new record lows in trading. Europe is failing, but so also is the United States. It was just behind the curve, a year or two. She felt her mouth go dry as she realized that she suddenly felt a bit ill. If she were completely honest, that year or two was likely too generous of an assessment.

Spinning in her chair, to face her desk, she took out a legal pad to outline the relevant points of her assessment. Copying the items she had come up with so far, she tapped her pen on the pad as she continued her mental dissection of events. When she got to the bottom of the sheet of paper, she realized she had goose bumps.

While most of the key players were focusing on the Eurozone debt crisis, and had been for the last year or so, concerns about the United States, too, were continuing to mount. In spite of two credit downgrades in the U.S., Congress still failed to agree on a long-term plan to deal with the nation's staggering debt. Americans were largely apathetic, but that would not continue. Overall, the public was not yet panicking, but anyone with any brains was now beginning to wake up.

As she outlined the problem, she noticed that one word was common to multiple groups of people. Stabbing her legal pad with her pen, she underlined the word in each column. "BLAME."

The accreditation agencies were promising another credit downgrade by the end of the year if spending was not addressed, but she realized that would not even come into play as things would develop into a crisis long before the end of the year arrived. Shaking her head as things came together in her mind, she realized that Europe going down would be the catalyst. The average citizen in such a scenario would certainly be outraged, and governments throughout Europe would fall. She smirked, vocalizing the salient point under her breath. "That is what has all the power players alarmed. Elites everywhere don't have a clue how to stop this and are rightfully concerned about peasants with pitchforks and torches."

Megan laid her head on her hands, trying unsuccessfully to will away how this drama would play out, but time after time she came back to the same conclusion. Europe would likely collapse and probably fairly soon. She confirmed the note on the napkin that she obtained, and from the actions taken with such urgency by her own firm.

"My own firm," she said out loud. Peasants with pitchforks would be coming for people just like me. As she processed the thought, a new set of angles began bouncing around in her head. Thinking it through, she again tapped an icon on her tablet to dial another number as she listened to the tones through the device in her ear.

Within two rings her broker answered his private line for key clients. "Dan Marley, How can I help you?"

"Dan, I have had a change of heart on the order I placed earlier this week. Can you get me back in?"

As he spoke, she could almost see the baffled look on his face, superimposed across New York City, reflected in the glass of the window in front of her. "Of course I can buy back your positions, but it has only been a few days. You will be taking a considerable loss." In addition to her almost being able to see his face, she could all but hear him question if there was something that Meg knew that he should act on.

"Do the best you can, Dan, but do it today, alright?"

"Sure Megan, no problem. Consider it done. Um, do you want me to go back into exactly the percentages you had with your funds before?"

"That would be fine, just distribute it in the same percentages. I am calling you with this because I want it done quietly and done today. Just do it like we talked about in our conversation on Monday." Cringing at her loss, she hung up the phone before Marley could say anything else.

Well, she realized that it was done now. She was probably being stupid, but maybe it would make a difference should peasants with pitch forks decide to storm the Bastille. Now, somewhat depressed, she reluctantly dialed another number. She was almost relieved to get Annie's voice message instead of her sister.

"Hello, Baby Sister, how is my favorite Okie? Dad said things were tough for you and Russ. Finance is my thing, so he asked me to call. I will try you back another time."

Riding the elevator down to the main floor with Richard, Megan fidgeted with her phone, checking through messages while absently listening to him deliberate lunch options. "How much time do you have Meg?"

Tilting her head just slightly she looked at him askance. "My next meeting is at two, why? What do you have in mind?" Studying him carefully, she hoped he wasn't going to suggest anything extracurricular.

"We have been putting in some wicked hours this week; I was thinking we take in a nice lunch. I know of a quaint little place in SoHo that has the best food in Manhattan. Besides it will give us the chance to talk. What do you say?"

As the elevator doors opened, she saw two executives stride across the opulent lobby to greet their guests by the fountain in the center of the space. She smiled thinking that she always loved this lobby. Highly polished marble on the floors, expensive art on the walls, and the clean lines of glass and steel rounded out the architecture. The lobby had two seating areas, furnished with plush leather seating, tastefully arranged on either side of the fountain. To her surprise, a car not owned by Sterns and Becker was waiting for them in front of the building.

"Sure sounds nice. I assume that you want to continue the conversation from earlier."

Smiling at her, his dark eyes let just a little of the emotion he was feeling make their way to the surface. "You blew me off earlier today. Seriously, saying you had another call is a bit weak as an excuse to use on your boss, don't you think? I assume you didn't want to discuss what you were thinking at the office."

Reaching the limo, Richard opened the door and ushered her in with an understated flourish. Megan climbed in and moved over to allow him to follow. Once they were both comfortable, she looked at him soberly, acknowledging his assessment.

"True enough, I didn't mean to blow you off, but I needed time to work the angles a bit before saying anything more." The silence stretched out for several minutes as she contemplated what she should say. "We have done some pretty intense deals the last couple of years wouldn't you say?" Looking at him, she saw that he nodded in the affirmative. "Let me ask you," she paused, "from the deals that we have done, have you formed an opinion of my ability to predict how various parties will react to the stimulus presented them?"

Looking at him intently, she could see that he considered her carefully, wondering where she would go with this. Megan could tell by the expression on his face that his mind had traveled what was likely a similar path to her own.

"I have, in fact, formed such an opinion, Ms. Danvers. I don't know that I am aware that you have ever made a bad call. What I am interested in at the moment, however, is what you are thinking now." His face grew deadly serious as he awaited her answer.

Looking him directly in the eye, she did not even flinch. "I think that it is very likely that everything is about to come unglued. We have spent the last week moving our assets around and preparing key clients to short the market, yes?"

He nodded.

"What happens if there is no functioning market to short? Look around us. The numbers of protestors we are seeing today in most of the parks that we pass and on the streets are double what we saw even a few months ago. Now everyone is collectively holding their breath, hoping that things will improve. So far, the media has been able to convince most of us that things will turn around. Most Americans are working and regardless of not being able to get ahead, they still have a lot to lose, so they are afraid of making it worse. Still, the disruptions that we are experiencing now are bad. What if the contagion from Europe causes the disruption and chaos to increase even if only by say ten or fifteen percent?" She could see that he was staring into her eyes to gauge the sincerity of her assessment. "Think about it, Richard, if you use the formulas that were used in the seventies, the unemployment rate would be over twenty-five percent or so right now. That figure would be much higher for minorities and young people. When Europe reaches its breaking point soon, that will affect us drastically. Our unemployment will skyrocket as trade dries up."

Richard just stared at her as the car pulled up to their restaurant. She noted that his trying to find a counter argument was as obvious as was his frustration at not being able to do so. Finally, she saw him nod, if only slightly. She laid a hand on his arm to prevent him from exiting the vehicle and paused until she had his full attention. "In that scenario, Richard, a point will come where the social contract fails and the center will cease to hold. Panic will set in."

Megan smiled bleakly. "From a sociological perspective, it only takes about ten percent of a population to create a movement. The Solidarity and Occupy Movements are approaching ten percent of the population now. If you add to their number, people who are unemployed or are in the process of losing everything, it will exceed that threshold easily. There is not nearly enough wealth to spread around, even if they were to liquidate everything that all Americans owned. People will realize that they have been ripped off. Would you care to guess who all of these people will blame?"

She was sure that Richard believed what she was saying because the color drained from his face. After a moment, he blinked and visibly collected his wits, nodding at the driver that they were ready to exit the vehicle.

Megan stepped out of the vehicle into a completely different reality as her world had just shifted in the short drive from the office to the restaurant. Looking down the trendy streets in SoHo, she now noticed small groups of homeless people and protesters mingling in amongst the artists and shoppers that inhabited the area. Looking into the faces of a small knot of people standing in front of their destination, she could see their anger. Looking at Richard, she knew that he, too, saw what she was seeing. Only a few feet from the door to their destination, two twenty something year old guys stood leering at them. Megan made eye contact with the man nearest her. Her eyes went wide as she realized that the guy with dirty blonde hair standing next to him was pointing at her as he whispered something to his friend. She felt a cold chill down her spine as she felt Richard take her elbow to rush her past two dirty men and into the restaurant.

❧

After ordering, Megan sat in silence, reigning in her fear reaction. The couple of moments of silence told her that Richard was likely doing the same thing. Each of them absorbed in their own thoughts and what the end of their way of life meant to them personally. As she watched him begin to eat, Meg realized that he really was attractive, and one of the smartest men she had ever known. She could see him considering their conversation as he ate. Swallowing a final bite, he looked up. "So?"

His sudden statement caught her off guard. "So?" She repeated.

His gaze pierced her like a knife. "So, Megan Danvers, what is our play? You know as well as I do that this is not something that we go to the old man with. Still, not telling John and the Board what we are thinking does not mean that the necessity to make a move outside our roles at the firm isn't warranted."

Again, silence descended on the table. Megan felt almost detached from her body. She could almost see Richard and herself as would an observer. She could smell the spicy meats cooking on the open grill twenty feet away. She watched the other patrons as they moved about, deep in their own conversations. Looking about the restaurant she realized that it was less populated than it should be. She could feel the energy of the city building towards something. Through the windows, she observed wandering bodies pass them by, peering in with fierce eyes.

She again considered the angles of this current scenario as she finished eating her meal and coughed softly to regain his attention. "I see three key aspects to this." She emphasized her point with an immaculately manicured index finger on her right hand. "First, we must deal with our personal positions in the markets. A vast amount of money will be made and lost in the coming months. The key factor in this will be having useful assets that will retain some value on the other side of whatever the contagion does to us." Her second finger joined the first. "Second, we must mitigate our vulnerability with regard to the masses. This will be the most dangerous and the most unpredictable piece of any plan. There is no way to guess how things will unfold. All I can say now is that it will likely not pay to be a Wall Street big shot or a politician." A third finger joined its sisters. "Finally, there is the firm. What do we do with regard to our jobs? Are we really thinking that we should walk away from serious six figure incomes to join the unemployed? The answer to that question may soon be, yes."

Megan noticed that her boss barely looked at her as he considered her words. As their check came, he handed the waiter his American Express card and sat there staring blankly at her. Finally, looking directly into her eyes, he bit his lip and slowly shook his head in despair.

"Just think about it, I guess, Richard. I don't know what kind of time we have. The lid could blow off today or a few months from now. There is no way to tell how desperately people will cling to their normalcy biases. I don't mind telling you that I am scared about all of this."

Feeling him take her hand, he squeezed it and gave her a sincere expression of solidarity. "Look, Meg. We work well together. We will be alright. We just have to trust each other and keep our mouths shut."

Nodding at him, she realized that they would indeed have to be very careful. "Do you think we should move to metal or perhaps diamonds?"

"Of course, but we need to find a way to do it the right way. The firm watches our personal transactions very closely. If we abruptly moved our personal positions into metal they would know immediately. That might not be the best move, if you know what I mean."

She nodded that she did, but suddenly, her eyes went wide with the realization that the old man would already know that she had shorted the market after the previous weekend in the skybox.

Megan could see a question form on her boss's face about her reaction, as the waiter brought back his credit card, and he signed the credit slip. She was not supposed to be privy to any of the data they recovered, yet it was now obvious she was. Worse yet, she realized what her actions today would look like from their perspective. On a whim, she abandoned her play to short the market in an attempt to mollify any future investigation that the peasants, or anyone else for that matter, might undertake when the time came to access blame for the disaster.

Chapter 9
A Sister's Trust

Annie stood in front of the mirror in the ladies' restroom at the Applebee's where she worked. She considered her reflection. Light brown eyes, perfect clear skin, rich brown hair and a nice smile added up to her being attractive enough. At twenty three, she had her whole life in front of her. She had a husband who loved her, regardless of his actions lately, and she would have a baby later this year. Yes, she had to admit that Russ was an idiot, unrealistic, and he was far too proud for his own good. Still, she had to give him credit for knowing when to give in after their last fight two weeks ago. Her mind replayed how Russell had spent his evening after their fight by finally fixing her car. He even broke down and sobbed after Ginger, from work, dropped her off at home. It was slow that night, and they had both been sent home early from work. She surprised him when she walked in the door of their little house. Instead of getting mad, she recalled how he was more worried that he screwed up by not picking her up. She sighed, thinking that she should have told him that she was pregnant right then, but she just could not bear to screw up the tenderness that he showed her when she walked in the door. That was the trouble with him lately, he was unpredictable. One day he was sweet and thoughtful; the next he was angry again.

Coming back to the present, she fixed her hair, washed her hands and after a few moments under the dryer, turned and headed back to work. Walking through the door and back into the dining room, she caught Ginger's look warning her that their boss, Dewayne, had just entered the restaurant.

Smiling her thanks, she walked back towards her station near the kitchen. "Jaden, how much longer do you need on my order for table seven?" She smiled to herself, thinking of the cook. According to Russ, Jaden Schwartz had been a big guy on campus when he attended Hennessy High School with her husband. He was nice enough, but a little too cheesy for her taste. She knew he was once probably a pretty big deal, but he was hardly all that any more.

She watched as he checked the fire under the two grilling steaks, and then looked over at the pasta he was working on for Annie. "Give me like three minutes, Tinker Bell! You won't get much of a tip if the noodles suck."

Rolling her eyes, she went back to rolling silverware in freshly laundered napkins. After going through approximately half of the forks, knives and spoons, she heard police sirens. She looked up, stretching a little to stare out the windows to see if she could see what it was all about as police cars raced past on the street outside the restaurant.

Ginger joined her at their station and began cutting up more lemons. "What do you suppose that is? That is the fifth car to go past in the last ten minutes." Ginger stepped over to the little take out window, craning her neck to see if she could see anything from down the street.

Annie noticed that her table's meal was finally ready and began placing the plates on a tray. "Well, what's happening? Can you see anything?"

"I'm not sure. There are a bunch of cops and like four ambulances at that apartment complex just down from us. It looks like something though, because they're taping off one of the apartments."

Annie moved past her friend and out into the dining room, carrying her stand and the tray of food. Approaching the table, she could see that the two women and a man sitting there were also moving so that they too might be able to see what they could of the events going on down the street. She set the tray down on her stand, and began to recite the order; "Steak, medium with mashed potatoes and fresh vegetables," Three-Cheese Chicken Penne, and of course, the Cajun Shrimp Pasta."

Her guests turned their attention to her, smiling and nodding at the savory smells coming from their meals. Annie was glad to see the women nod in approval. "Thank you, Dear. Could you bring us some extra bread and refills for our drinks?"

Annie smiled brightly. "Of course, I would be happy to." Pointing at each patron, she listed off their beverages in order; Doctor Pepper, tea extra lemon, and a Coke, right?"

All three patrons smiled and nodded. "Perfect!"

Taking her tray and folding up her stand she hurried to fulfill their request. "I will be back in just a moment."

As she filled the glasses, she noticed that Jaden was watching her closely. She looked up, her head tilting just slightly as she regarded his gaze. She filled the glasses and placed them on her tray, wondering what that was about. She looked over at Ginger to see if she could ask her if she thought Jaden was acting weird, but she was busy. She wondered what his deal was as she placed the bread beside the drinks on her tray and delivered them to her guests. "Does everything taste delicious, and may I get you folks anything else?" The answer was apparently a positive one. All three guests replied with thumbs up gestures, or a head nod, but were too busy eating to reply.

Once again back at her station, Annie could still see through the serving window that Jaden was watching her intently. Her curiosity getting the best of her, she stuck her head into the kitchen and motioned at him to come over to her. "Jaden, do you have a moment?"

After flipping a hamburger patty he walked over, giving her a smirk that Annie was pretty sure was his standard expression from the time he had been in high school. "What's up Annie? Why you calling me over, Princess? I'm thinking that you don't want to whine about my cooking."

"Is there a reason that you are staring at me, Jaden? You have been watching me all shift."

"No, I haven't. I got better things to do than..."

"Whatever. You could just say what you have on your mind, you know."

Pondering her statement, his face took on a more serious expression. "OK, I was just trying to be helpful. You are a nice looking girl, and I was just thinking that if you needed someone to talk to I could give you some perspective on things. Maybe we could get a drink and you could talk to me about your, you know, problems. Maybe I can help you with a man's perspective."

Looking completely taken aback, she stuttered. "What are you talking about? I don't need any man's perspective, and for sure, I don't need yours. Maybe you can help me out by not staring at me all the time." Embarrassed now, she could feel that she was blushing. She realized that, somehow, he must know about Russ and that slut, Renee. Of course, Renee must have told him. She probably sleeps with everyone. I should make Russ get tested. God only knows what he may have caught. Exasperated, she turned and rushed headlong out onto the floor, wanting to put as much distance between her and Jaden as possible.

Seething, she bolted right into one of two police officers who had just entered the restaurant. Looking back over her shoulder at the kitchen as she made her escape from Jaden, she had no chance of avoiding a collision. The result was a dented sense of pride as she fell in a heap at the men's feet.

The young black officer reached down to help her to her feet. "Are you ok, Miss? That was quite a spill."

"I'm fine." She instinctively looked up to see who the owner of that voice might be. It sounded familiar in a way, but somehow out of place. Embarrassed and disoriented, she felt a sense of familiarity as she looked up at the officer. His generous smile and warm brown skin overwhelmed her; how could it be?

Getting up, she looked at the attractive young police officer, blinking at him as she did so. "Thank you, Officer... Nathan? Nathan Jacobs, what are you doing here?" Seeing him was disorienting like a scene from the Twilight Zone. Her heart skipped as she blinked in happy surprise.

A smile warmed his face, momentarily erasing the serious expression he wore into the restaurant. "Annie Danvers! I can't believe I'm running into you here. I take it you live here in Enid now? Imagine that, a couple of people from Mineral Wells, literally running into each other in another state."

Annie noticed the older police officer realized that Nathan needed a moment, and proceeded on towards the kitchen.

"Yes, I live here now, Nate. I got married a few years back and moved here with my husband, Russ. His family is from here. It's Annie Davis, now by the way." Looking embarrassed it dawned on her that he had more important things to do just now. Looking over Nathan's shoulder to see his partner talking to Dewayne, she then shifted her eyes in the direction of the apartment complex down the street. "You are here on business aren't you?"

He nodded that he was. "It is a pretty ugly thing, Annie. We were sent to canvas the area to see what people might have seen or heard. When did you come in to work today? Also, did you work last night at all? "

Almost hypnotized by the sparkle in his eyes and how incredibly handsome he was, she had to focus to make her brain function. She could not seem to stop herself from wondering what a different life would be like right now. "I opened this morning, so I guess I was here around nine o'clock." Looking across the floor at Ginger, she continued. "She and I both came in about the same time. She has the key and neither of us worked last night since we opened today."

Nathan copied down her comments on his pad. "Did you hear anything unusual coming from the direction of the apartments this morning?"

Annie looked up and to the left as she ruminated on this morning's set up routine. "Not really, Nate. I wish I could say I did, but I just don't recall anything weird. What happened over there, anyway? Is it terrible?"

Looking grim, she saw his eyes turn hard and cold as they dropped to her feet. "It is really terrible and I'm sorry, Annie, but I really can't discuss it." Looking apologetic, he shrugged. "Ongoing investigation and all, you know what I mean?"

She nodded that she understood. "I am so sorry Nate. It was a stupid question."

When he looked up, she could once again see a little warmth return to his eyes. He was now staring at her as if into her soul. She was suddenly overwhelmed with the charm she remembered from high school as it once again reasserted itself. She realized that she wanted to know more about what he had been up to since high school. She felt a little guilty, but she didn't want the encounter to end.

They just stood there for a moment when he finally spoke up. "Um, anyway, I have to go. We should meet for coffee sometime and catch up on old times." He smiled at her, handed her his business card, squeezed her lightly on the shoulder and then turned to join the other officer. She watched as they spoke briefly before they nodded at her and left the building. Her emotions churning, her heart beat hard in her chest. As quickly as he had come, he was gone.

❧

Annie walked in the front door, followed by Russ who was still complaining about old man Dickerson with whom he had spent his day doing cleanup work in the old dude's barn outside of town. It wasn't that she didn't care, exactly, but rather that she was too tired, from being on her feet all day. She knew she really needed to tell him she was pregnant, but every time she started to get up the courage to do it, something would happen. He would get mad over some bill coming in, or someone would stop by the house, making it impossible for them to talk.

The door closed behind her husband as he finally came in from the truck. "That old coot only wanted to pay like eight dollars an hour! That pisses me off. Who does he think he is, anyway? He tries to pay that kind of money, and then has the nerve to complain that someone might not be overly enthused about crawling through all the junk he has, that he thinks of as priceless heirlooms."

Annie smiled patiently as she listened to him continue to vent. "Look, Russ, he is probably just old. He doesn't realize how much things have changed lately. My dad is always telling how he started off making like two bucks an hour."

Winding up for another rant he said, "A damn insult is what it is. The old bastard knows what things cost; he is just cheap and wants his barn cleaned out for nothing. I told him straight off that I wasn't going out there for eight dollars. I think the other two guys got the hint real quick, too, because they said the same thing. It didn't take him long to fold then, I can tell you.

"What did you end up getting, Sweetheart?"

"Humph! We got ten. Even that is an insult. It was hard work and a man can get hurt in a dump like that, and then what would we do? You know as well as I do, we got no coverage for anything like that happening."

"Any work is honorable Russ. You know that. You made the best deal that you could and did what you had to do for your family. I am proud of you."

He just looked at her, angry at the world because things were just not working the way they should. "Whatever, Annie, whatever, I am going to go take a shower. I hope that we have something decent to eat, I am starving."

Annie sat there, closed her eyes, thinking what a jerk Russ could be. All he ever thought about was how he felt or what he needed. He never once considered that she might be tired, too. She steeled herself to go see what she could figure out about dinner when the phone rang. Rolling her eyes in exasperation, she picked up.

"Hello!"

"Hi there Sis, how is my absolute favorite baby sister? I called you earlier today just before lunch, but I got your machine. Anyway, I figured you might be at work, so I am trying back."

"Oh hi, Meg, it's good to hear your voice. How is life in the big city?"

"My God, Annie, that line is getting so old, but to answer your question, I honestly don't know anymore. The protesters are getting pretty bad lately, but my job is going along pretty well. The firm took me and my boss to a professional football game last weekend."

"That sounds like a lot of fun Sis, but aren't you afraid to go out? I saw on the news that the 'Occupy people' there in New York, tried to stop an ambulance from getting in to help someone. Is that really true? Would someone really do that there?"

"They pretty much would, Sis. What happened is that hundreds of them surrounded an ambulance, as it tried to leave with a wounded cop. He was stabbed trying to protect some Bank of America employees, who were trying to get to work during one of their protests."

"Wow Megan, that sounds awful. You couldn't pay me to live there. I am officially going to worry myself sick about you now."

"I'm fine, Annie. We have really good security at the office and you met the guy I am with last year at Christmas, remember? He can handle himself ok. He is ex-army, so I don't really think that anyone will bother him. Anyway, you just hinted at why I am calling. Dad said that you guys are having a tough time. I wanted to see what I could do to help the two of you."

Embarrassment creeping into her voice, Annie was suddenly tongue tied and awkward. "It has been tough since we, well, since Russ got laid off, but we're doing ok, I guess. I was just freaked out a few days ago when I last talked to Daddy. We were stupid buying a new pickup last year. We spent money that we shouldn't have spent. Now we are having trouble making the payments. He had called to see how I was, and I sort of unloaded on him."

"You know that he always wants to be there for us. He doesn't mind; I promise. Still, I can spot you some money until you get back on your feet. How much do you owe on your truck? Maybe we just pay that off. That would help, wouldn't it?"

"Oh Megan, you are my favorite person in the whole world, but I can't let you do that. For one thing, Russ would flip. You know how proud he is."

"I know, Sweetie. As far as I'm concerned, that is all the more reason to do it. I am absolutely furious with him. The big jerk doesn't know how lucky he is that you are still there with him."

"Megan Danvers! You sound like Katie now. Ok, Russ screwed up, but he took responsibility for it immediately. He didn't even try to hide it. He is a big dufus, but he is my dufus and regardless, I still love him. More than that, he loves me. Half of the problems we are having now are because he is eaten up with his guilt. He knows if he ever did something like that again, we would be done. You don't understand because you are living the high life, but a marriage has to mean something, and we are going to make it work. If Daddy can live with that, then I think that you can, too."

"Ok, Ok, Little Sister. I get the message. I just love you and nobody hurts my family." Now how much do you owe on the pickup?"

"Meg, let me think about it. You are a wonderful sister, but our credit issues are our responsibility. It is bad enough that I applied for food stamps this week. Russ hated it, but swallowed his pride on that. He was even going to go down with me, but I told him it was an on line thing now. He wants so badly to do right, but I don't think that he could bear taking charity from a family member."

"Annie, that is crazy. One's family is supposed to take care of their own, not the government. I want you to talk to Russ about it. You can pay it back when things get better. Anyway, what did they say about food stamps?"

"When I called to see about it, the lady at the welfare office had said that we would probably begin receiving food stamps in one to two months. There are so many people applying now that they are backlogged.

"I am really sorry, Honey. I don't think that I could ever do it. Well, at least some of the truckloads of tax money they get from me is going for something worthwhile."

Annie dabbed a tear from her eyes and realized how much she missed her sister. Her voice shook a little, but she decided that she needed to tell someone in the family. "There is something that I need to tell you, Meg, but you cannot tell anyone. You have to promise me, ok? I haven't even told Russ. God only knows what he will think. He is already under so much pressure that I am worried how he will react."

"Sure, Honey, as long as that promise doesn't count if you could get hurt in some way."

"It's nothing like that, Sis. It is only that, um, well, I found out a couple of weeks ago that I am pregnant. I just confirmed it yesterday. I am about six weeks along."

"Oh my God, my little sister is going to be a mommy! Annie, that is absolutely wonderful news, I am so excited. I can't wait to buy baby clothes!"

"Thanks, Megan. I am really scared about it because we are so broke. Still, I guess there is nothing to do about it now. Anyway, I have to go make dinner. Remember, you promised not to tell anyone yet, not Mom and Dad, not Katie, no one, right?

"I promise Love, I won't say anything, but I am super happy for you. I am even crying a little bit here. Everything will be all right, Annie. I promise you that."

As she hung up the phone, she heard the floor board creek behind her. She turned around slowly, her eyes going wide to see Russell, with a towel wrapped around his waist standing just behind her, dripping water onto the wooden floor in front of her. She could not exactly read the expression on his face, but it was obvious that he was furious.

Chapter 10
Meetings

Sitting in her rent car, Sadie watched in despair to see the first of what must be the funeral party for the Reins woman and her child. The hearse turned onto the little drive towards the tent and the neatly covered pile of dirt beside the family's final resting place. Seeing the scene unfold before her, she decided that she really didn't belong here after all. She accepted that what had happened to this family was not her fault. She did not cause the tragedy, but she felt guilty anyway. A tear threaded its way towards her chin as alone in her car, she whispered a prayer for her assassin's victims. "Dear God, please be with these people. Care for their needs and comfort them through this horrible time."

She paused as she saw the cars park behind the hearse as men and women dressed in dark clothing exited the numerous vehicles that assembled. "Had I not been at that intersection that day a young mother and her child would not be in this place, and the woman's husband would not be watching his entire family lowered into the ground this morning." Numb and in shock, she gazed on the results of blind hatred. Her tears now flowed freely, and her breath came in shuttered gasps. She felt nauseated as she gripped the steering wheel of her car.

She watched as the woman's family and friends gathered to pay their respects to her and her little boy. As it had since that day, her mind screamed that it just did not make sense. Why did this happen? Detective Reyes said that the FBI was now assisting on the case. With FBI help, they had proved that the murder weapon in her mom's case did, in fact, match the weapon that was used to kill the people before her now. Detective Reyes confirmed that it was a nine millimeter Zoaf pistol. He said that it was Iranian made, and they were now convinced of an international connection between her mother and someone that she knew in Iran. If that were true, then all of this must be the result of something that happened before she was even born.

Looking back up, she realized the minister that was presiding over the sad ritual was well into his sermon. Sadie steeled herself to do what she must do, to at least offer a prayer, to express to the woman and child how terribly sorry she was for what happened to them. Clamping down on her emotions, she dabbed at her eyes with a tissue and reached for the handle to the car door. Taking a cleansing breath, she exhaled sharply; picked up the roses she brought, and got out of the car.

She approached the group from behind and to one side, only getting close enough to just make out what was being said. She wanted to be very considerate of these people, thinking that she in no way wanted to encounter them individually. Drawing close to the mourners, she found a place to stand. Looking towards where the caskets were positioned, ready to be lowered out of sight, she felt a jolt of electricity upon seeing the larger than life portraits of a mother and her little boy, smiling out at the distraught family. They were joyous and happy and so full of life she thought. They had no way to know that when they had smiled those smiles their time here was already growing very short.

She really wished that her nightmare had died with the man who tried to kill her, and did kill the family being laid to rest a few yards in front of her, but she knew better. The man in the garage was still out there. She knew that the police had found almost no evidence leading to the identity of the man who attacked her. Except for the broken glass, the paint she left on the pillars of her garage, and the pock marks from the bullets near her parking space, visually it never happened. As she watched some of the woman's family talk about her life, Sadie's thoughts went through what she knew about her situation for what may well have been the thousandth time.

The guys chasing her and her mom were from Iran, probably someone that her mother had known when she was young.

Detective Reyes said that the FBI was working with other agencies to learn what they could. They were trying to match fingerprints and other intelligence they had, to see why this was happening now, after so many years. He said that the Feds believed it was a personal act, but Reyes said that he disagreed, and was looking at other more straight forward motivations.

As she pondered the cause of her pain over the last couple of months, she heard a woman crying out with the heart rending anguish, of which, only a mother losing her child was capable. She looked up to see a silver haired woman being assisted back to her seat in the front row of mourners.

Struggling desperately to fight back her own tears, she whispered another prayer for the woman. "Dear Lord, please comfort this family and all of your children throughout the world. As this family suffers, so also do families everywhere at the loss of a loved one. Please, God, help us all find a way to stop the madness."

She noticed that others were doing what they could for the woman who was likely the victim's mother. "I am so sorry," she whispered. The elderly man who was speaking concluded his eulogy and returned to join the other mourners. An attractive woman with shoulder length, light brown hair, then stood up next and made her way forward. She stopped, and hugged a man standing next to the murdered woman's husband, and went forward to speak. There was something about this woman that was somehow familiar. She had seen her somewhere, but unable to recall where, she dismissed the thought, her mind returning to thoughts of her own anguish and the loss of her own mother.

The detectives had translated what she found in her mom's shoebox. She had been over and over what she had read, but nothing stood out. Whoever was behind all of this must have a motive that had something to do with the early eighties, but all she had were a few letters written in Farsi by her mother, some old photos, and a worn and stained pamphlet with a note scrawled in Farsi on the back dated May 20th 1983.

"It is time, Marta. You are with child. May God bless, and keep you both safe."

Recalling the note, she pondered who would have written it and what it meant. It seemed possible, if not obvious, that it was a warning, but a warning about what, and from whom? It was all so frustrating. It probably had absolutely nothing to do with today, but there was just no way to know for sure. Yet again, the recurring thought of why, plagued her. I am an American and have had no connection to Iran. If it is about something that happened before Mom came here, what do they want with me? Sighing, Sadie knew that there was just no way to know.

She decided that she would do an internet search on Iranian history from the eighties. Maybe she could find something about the pamphlet, at least. Having made the decision to learn what she could about the letters, Sadie sighed, finally escaping the prison of her thoughts, for a while at least.

Looking up again, she focused on what was being said. She saw that the pretty woman had just finished speaking, and was walking back over to stand next to a blonde with an expensive suit, as the minister said his final blessings. Wiping her eyes, Sadie realized that the blond lady with the last speaker was almost holding the woman who had just spoken. As the caskets were lowered to their places, she realized that the last speaker was likely a sister or someone close.

Soon the funeral was over and the grief stricken loved ones began to disperse. She waited a few moments for the husband and the mother to leave. The crowd finally thinned out a little, so she cautiously approached the grave to lay her roses down for the woman and her child. Sadie bowed her head to honor this family that she had led to such grief. "Dear Lord, receive the souls of these innocent people into your arms, amen." Standing there in her misery, she heard a voice from behind gasp.

"Oh my God, Kate, look! That woman by the grave is the lady the asshole was chasing last week!

"What are you saying, Janice?"

"I have been over the video like a hundred times, Honey. This story is the biggest headline I have worked on in a couple of months, and I am telling you that she is involved in this. The cops won't release her name. I need to talk to her. An interview with her would be a major score."

Sadie could feel the eyes on the back of her head as she rose and turned in horror at being noticed. Taking a deep breath, she turned to face the women talking behind her.

"I am very sorry for your loss. Really, I am so..."

Sadie only got a few words out before one of the men who had spoken came at her like a charging lion having obviously heard the blonde point her out to her friend. "What in the hell are you doing here? What the fuck is wrong with you, you Arab bitch!" Sadie blanched, stunned by the ferocity of the man's anger.

She thought he was going to strike her and knowing all too well what he was feeling, she wasn't even sure that she cared if he did. "That woman and little boy over there are dead because of your kind. All of this is your fault. They were the nicest people I have ever known and you and your backwards Arab nut cases took them away." In a full rage, he towered over her and looked like he was about to strike out when both of the women who had first noticed her recovered from their shock to intercede.

"Dan!" The blonde yelled. "Don't! It's not her fault. Please, calm down." The other woman was more aggressive, and stepped between them, actually grabbing his arm.

"No, Dan, No! Janice is right; this isn't her fault. The assholes were trying to kill her too, remember?" Raising her voice as she spoke, the woman with the light brown hair looked directly into his eyes, her voice as hard as steal. Pointing at Sadie she continued. "Apologize to her Dan. Now!"

"OK." He looked furiously into the woman's eyes and then stared coldly at Sadie. "I forgive you, Lady! I am sorry about the primitive, hate filled terrorist crap your kind push on people everywhere. I apologize because your father, or brothers, or whatever, have some twisted sick notion of family honor!" Looking back to the two women he snarled. "How's that?" Turning again to face Sadie he shook a finger in her face. "You got no place here!"

Angry now the darker haired woman took a step towards the grieving man. "Dan! Stop this, and I mean now! This isn't who your sister would want you to be, is it?"

Still shaking with fury, but unwilling to take it out on the woman in front of him, he relented, but only to a point. Pointing at Sadie, his voice cracked. "Get Out! You take your backwards ass, twisted, primitive religion, and get away from my family!"

Sadie closed her eyes for a moment, and lowered her head, grimacing at hearing the man's words. "No apology needed, Sir; there is nothing to forgive. I was just as furious two months ago when these men killed my mother." Working hard to avoid crying again, Sadie lowered her head. "I will leave of course; I just wanted to pay my respects. May God bless and keep your family. I am very sorry for your loss." Numb, Sadie nodded her thanks to the two women, and then simply looked at the man for a moment. She wanted him to know that she cared before she turned to leave.

Dan froze for several seconds, just standing there. Finally his shoulders dropped and he seemed to deflate. He looked exhausted, a feeling she knew all too well. Looking at her with eyes reflecting the emptiness in his soul, he just turned and walked away towards the cars.

"Thank you both, really. I probably shouldn't have come I guess. I am so very sorry. I did not mean to cause your family any further grief. I just wanted to express my sorrow to your..." Sadie looked over at the grave site. "...to your loved ones."

The woman who stood between her and the grieving man smiled tiredly and took her hand. "My name is Catherine Danvers." Looking at the blonde standing next to her, she inclined her head in her direction. "This is Janice Tate. I am very sorry for the loss of your mom, too. I cannot even begin to imagine how to cope with something like this first hand."

Again, she smiled her sympathy. "Really, thank you for coming. Darla was my sister-in-law, and I know that she would appreciate your kindness. I apologize for Dan. He is not like this normally. He is just lost right now. He and his sister were really close."

Sadie nodded her understanding and returned a weak smile of her own. "Well, I should go. You both have been very nice." Nodding slightly to the grave site, she turned and started for her car.

"Wait!"

Sadie paused and turned back to face the two women, to see the blonde woman in the suit urgently digging in her purse. "Um, Can you tell us your name?" The blonde took a step forward, her hand extended towards her with a business card between her thumb and forefinger. "I am a reporter. I work for CNN, and I would really like to talk to you sometime. Would that be ok?"

Catherine's eyes shot daggers at the blonde woman. "Janice – stop!"

Ignoring her, Janice took another step forward, looking sincere and hopeful.

"I am sorry, Ms. Tate, I am not sure that would be smart. Another one of the men who did this is still out there. The police don't have any idea who he is so I really need to not talk to any reporters. It just isn't a good idea."

"Look, I can keep your identity to myself. I swear that I won't tell anyone who you are. I am a professional. Maybe I can even help you figure out what this is all about. If you will let me, that is. I know that reporters get a bad rap and honestly, I do need a good story to make my boss happy and all, but I would never compromise a source."

Sadie considered her for several moments, looking from the woman imploring her with her eyes to accept and then to the other woman who just looked embarrassed. She considered how helpful a reporter could be. Finally, she decided that someone with resources like CNN really could possibly help her.

"When you say that you can help me figure this stuff out, what does that mean exactly? Can you get me some research help with what I know about all of this?"

"Absolutely I can! I will look into anything you like and I won't breathe a word. I swear."

Sadie closed her eyes for a moment then took a step forward and extended her hand. "My name is Sadie. Sadie Cline. I will reach out for you soon, and we can talk about this."

Janice smiled warmly at her. "Thank you. My partner and I are really trustworthy. I look forward to helping you."

Catherine, although still embarrassed, extended her hand. "It really is nice to meet you Sadie."

Catherine held her hand a moment longer and smiled at Sadie, before looking with exasperation at Janice. "I apologize for this, this intrusion into your life, but of all her faults, I do think that she really would not betray a source."

Sadie nodded. "Ok. If you can help me find out what is happening with all of this it will be worth the risk, but you should both realize that whoever these people are, they are very determined. You may think better of all of this at some point." Sadie took a breath and smiled weakly. "Well, Now I really should go. Thank you both for your kindness, and again, please tell your brother that I am very sorry for intruding."

"Sure, we will do that."

Janice nodded, too. "I look forward to hearing from you. You can reach me anytime. Just hit me on my cell."

Feeling a wave of exhaustion pass over her, Sadie nodded and walked away. Arriving back at her rent car, she put the keys in the ignition and looked over her right shoulder to make sure that no one was coming before pulling out. She noticed then she was not the only one in attendance at the funeral who did not seem to know the family personally. A man was staring intently at her. She decided he could easily be Middle Eastern, but she just wasn't sure.

"Am I being paranoid, or is it him?"

Chapter 11
The Firm

John David Sterns entered the dark room. He was glad that the briefing was already under way. He had already skimmed the highpoints of today's report over breakfast. Still, he was a firm believer in seeing the visuals along with a written report. Moving to the head of the table, he sat down in the dark blue leather wing-back chair, leaned back, and folded his hands neatly in his lap as the executive steward placed an ice cold glass of lemon water on the coaster on the table, beside him.

Sterns savored the smell of the leather and the highly polished wooden surfaces of his poshly furnished briefing room. He also appreciated that the room suddenly grew tenser upon his arrival. The group assembled there sat quietly watching the report displayed on the large screen before them.

"...We, of course, expected the British Foreign Office to be prepared for a variety of possibilities. We have now confirmed from multiple sources within the ministry, that British embassies have received instructions on how to aid British citizens should there be a collapse on the continent. They are now taking active steps to prepare for a likely collapse of the Euro. The planning behind this process has been in play for some time since Cyprus began the trend of appropriating its citizens' bank deposits. As things have become more precarious in the Mediterranean countries, the decision was taken three days ago that the inconceivable is no longer as implausible as it was even a few months ago."

Sterns delighted in the prospect that a vast opportunity was opening up. He relished the thrill of what was coming. Slightly raising an eyebrow, he smiled coldly. He realized that he felt more alive now than he had in years. Unlike many of his contemporaries at his club, he was of the opinion they were rapidly approaching a nexus point in history. One after another, virtually every major developed economy in Western Europe had become, or was in the process of becoming, embroiled in the Keynesian Endgame scenario.

"...Our analysts believe that the status quo is changing dramatically. Several major banks attempted to move supplies of cash as close as possible to the national borders of failing European countries, but the cash was depleted in a matter of hours. Obviously, trust is shattered, with bank runs becoming more and more common place over the past few weeks.

The implicit solution from Germany and her acolytes is based on draconian austerity. Clearly, these measures are not sitting well with the populations of many EU nations. Violence is expected to escalate as conditions deteriorate here over coming weeks. As I indicated earlier this morning, the *Telegraph* reported that Britain's Foreign Office is mandating that its overseas embassies begin executing plans to help their expats, should the collapse of the Euro turn explosive in the coming weeks.

Senior ministers are now confirming that Britain has already begun taking emergency action on the basis that a Euro collapse is now a matter of time."

Sterns's eyes focused on his London intelligence analyst's face on the flat screen across the room. As he calculated his plan, he knew timing would be the key. He was actually looking forward to the challenges that lay ahead, and was growing anxious, waiting for things to really get serious. The political puppets here and in Europe believe that they are in control, but soon, he thought, their illusion would be forever shattered. With any luck, he would soon wield an unprecedented amount of power as the so-called New World Order asserted itself over the lives of men.

"...In all of the major cities throughout Europe, students are marching with home-made placards during daily demonstrations. They are protesting cuts and demanding education as a right at no cost. After enduring years of recession prompted by the collapse of a real estate bubble, the tax base has, of course, collapsed, so their demands are impossible. Moreover, Spain's economy is now exceeding thirty percent unemployment. Accommodating them is impossible, but with the exception of a few individuals in the elected classes. The majority of political leaders in Britain, and across Europe simply refuse to address any of the root cause issues. Greece, Spain, Italy, and even France are posting zero growth, with no expectation to improve in the near term. It is the consensus here that Spain will fold within days, following Greece, Italy, Ireland, and Portugal."

Sterns raised an index finger, his head inclining slightly to indicate that he wished to interrupt.

"Yes Sir, Mr. Sterns, do you have a question?"

"I do, Mr. Blackman. I understand that the Italians and the Spanish are now seeking additional international bail-outs by supporting consolidation of European national bonds into a single Euro-bond. What would be your estimation as to timing?"

Yes Sir, timing is key. Well Sir, considering the failures of bail-out measures over the past two years, and considering the failure of any of the countries surrounding the Mediterranean to implement anything even close to an austerity plan that could make a difference, British ministers are warning that the break-up of the Euro, is now likely to occur in a matter of weeks.

As I said, Mr. Sterns, the diplomatic instructions going out from London are to prepare to help tens of thousands of British citizens in Eurozone countries with the consequences of a financial collapse that would leave them unable to access bank accounts or withdraw cash."

"Very well, Mr. Blackman, do focus on timing in coming weeks, if you please."

"Of course Sir."

"Pardon my interruption, Mr. Blackman, please continue." Sterns leaned back once again as the analyst prepared to do just that.

"Yes Sir, of course. Our assessment is that the financial crisis here has entered a far more dangerous phase resulting from the political failures since the warning tremors of 2008. In my estimation, gentlemen, ladies, a catastrophic collapse is inevitable and likely imminent. Dr. Jacobs is predicting that in a matter of weeks, millions will lose virtually everything. To emphasize this point, it is my duty to inform the Board that Dr. Jacobs resigned from Sterns and Becker Investments this morning. He is returning to the United States immediately, along with his family. I understand he has a vacation home in Colorado. In any case, gentlemen, this concludes this week's report unless there are questions."

Sterns appraised the room and inclined his head to dismiss his employee.

The screen went blank and the lights in the room began to slowly return to full brightness. The heads of the assembled leaders turned to face the old man. John David Sterns, Chairman of the Board at Sterns and Becker Investments, let them await his pleasure as he leaned back in the massive leather chair, his fingers steepled at his chest. He recalled fondly his time as an infantry officer in Vietnam, and the sense of power he wielded then. What he had now was definitely preferable he thought, as rules for him were now manageable. The room was silent for almost two minutes as the members who held controlling interests for the firms fund pondered this week's situation report from their European office.

"Well, ladies and gentlemen, have we any discussion on today's topic? It seems events are unfolding apace, does it not?" As his taciturn gaze traversed the room, he studied the gathered expressions presented to him by his staff. The faces watching him were grave but reluctant to kick off the discussion. Most grave of all, was the woman he had charged with the duty to move the firm's assets to safety.

"Ms. Tanner, have you anything to add to your report regarding the readiness of our contingency plans?"

"Yes Sir, Mr. Sterns. Since last week, we have moved most of our technology holdings into conformance, but legal continues to delay our activities. I would mention that we are within the predicted parameters that we set in place three weeks ago when we received the Tibman data. Furthermore, since last week, the net change in the value of our holdings is marginal, but is trending significantly into negative territory. I have confirmed that our key positions have all been moved into our market shorting portfolios except for those that we have purposely left in place to provide plausible deniability that may be required after the event."

The old man nodded to her in appreciation. "I see. Thank you, Ms. Tanner." His calculating stare swiveled to a chair opposite Ms. Tanner's. A sardonic smirk emerged on his face and tilting his head just slightly, his left eyebrow rose as he considered the man sitting there. "Mr. Carnahan, have you anything you would like to add to Ms. Tanners report? It seems your people are hindering the progress of our activities. What explanation would you care to provide for this lack of support?"

Carnahan took in a breath but appeared to be predominately unruffled by the old man's challenging gaze. "As Ms. Tanner just stated, we only received this intelligence three weeks previous to today. Everyone here is well aware of the scrutiny that firms like ours are receiving from the regulating authority here in New York. As you would expect, we are seeing the same level of attention nationally, and even internationally." He casually glanced from face to face, regarding each Board member with a cool expression. "As I recall, we all agreed that it would do little good to beat the market in this emergency, only to have our gains reduced or eliminated through government interference."

The old man regarded with amusement, the agitation his leaders displayed, as they fought for supremacy. Noticing Ms. Tanner's primary ally, motioning for acknowledgement he called on her.

"Have you something to add, Ms. Devaroe?"

"Yes Sir. Thank you, Sir. Mr. Carnahan's argument is a silly one, isn't it? We were all just witness to this week's situation report. It is nothing, if not clear that the collapse is not as structured as the planning committees at the central banks would have preferred. I would submit that, at best, we are at least a month, perhaps two, ahead of what we believed the trajectory of the collapse would be. To be concise, it does us little good to avoid all scrutiny if there is nothing to scrutinize, should the event occur before we are able to make the moves we must make, to take full advantage of what we know to be true. I would suggest that we make our moves expeditiously. That was the entire point of allowing some of our positions to fall victim to the apocalypse, wasn't it? We can be quick about protecting our key positions, and still show that we have some losses, as well, as victories."

John Sterns sat forward in his chair, picked up the ivory pen lying on the notepad in front of him. He twirled it between gnarled fingers as he considered the statements presented along with the reports he had reviewed in his office earlier that morning.

Sterns smiled pleasantly. "It seems that the thing to do now is decide what opportunities might best serve our interests in a somewhat abbreviated time. It seems clear to me that our horizon is much shorter than we anticipated, so we must mitigate accordingly." Looking at the woman at the end of the table, he nodded slightly. "Ms. Devaroe, if you would be so kind, please reconsider your analysis of our action plan. I want to reassess our strategy. Adjust your recommendation to account for a plan that appropriately balances our two stated goals of shorting the markets while leaving enough behind that we are perceived as being relatively blameless. I would like you to focus your efforts on a prioritization matrix that allows us to pursue a flexible approach in executing our plans. Your matrix should begin with what we can move over by next week and what must be sacrificed. You will similarly assess what can be saved with a two week horizon, a three week horizon and so forth. Focus on expected key events that we may use to justify our actions."

Leaning back once more, John David Sterns addressed his entire Board. "It is clear that this exercise will be quite fluid. I would have us meet regarding Ms. Devaroe's plan twice a week."

Turning to Bob Carnahan, he smiled mincingly at his senior counsel. "Mr. Carnahan, you will continue to protect our legal interests as you have, but do consider Ms. Devaroe's point that it does us little good to be free of legal complications if we lose too much. I would ask you to work closely with Ms. Tanner to expedite the movement of some key positions in the next few weeks.

The two of you can decide which of our core businesses we can sacrifice should that become necessary in the short term."

The grim faces in the room all nodded in assent with their leader as he reached down to flip to the next page of his notes.

"Next, what have we to say about the matter of our lovely prodigy, Ms. Danvers, and the personal trades she has made of late? More to the point, what of those trades she placed the week previous?"

The old man's gaze rested on a serious looking black man with close cropped grey hair and piercing eyes. Luther Sterling was his head of corporate security, and was the best in the business if it weren't for his rather narrow sense of propriety. He nodded at the man to speak.

"Yes Sir." Sterling took a moment to select the notes he wanted to present on the matter from his iPad. "It seems Sir, that Ms. Danvers was emulating our public strategy to the letter with regards to all of her trades until the Monday after we were able to obtain our intelligence from Sykes and the Honorable Mr. Tibman. She shorted her key accounts the very next day."

"I see. That is a bit of curious timing, is it not? So, Mr. Sterling what can you share of your investigation into this matter?"

"It is a curious thing, Sir." Sterling touched the screen of his iPod and a timeline appeared on the large flat screen behind him. "As you can see, I have indicated the night we gathered the intelligence and marked it as day zero. Ms. Danvers made the trade in question the following day on Monday as I mentioned. We, of course, had possession of the transceiver from Mr. Blake the evening after the event concluded. He handed the transceiver to me personally upon returning from the football game. I locked it in my safe until Monday at approximately 11:00 AM." Sterling then touched his iPad to change screens. It now displayed a technical depiction of the transceiver with details about how it functioned.

"As you can see, this device is a simple recording device only. It does not transmit its take. As you are all aware, interrupting or detecting a transmission is much too easy to be reliable for our purposes. Furthermore, this device encodes everything it picks up so that the risk of inadvertent dissemination is minimal. We downloaded the take from the transceiver at approximately 11:30 AM. I took it out of my safe and had the device in my possession the entire time. Sterling paused to give anyone with a question, the time to ask it.

"Also, it is specifically designed to only interface with its parent device for playback. It is, therefore, not possible for Ms. Danvers or anyone else for that matter, to have copied or to have listened in on the take from this device prior to handing it off to me Sunday evening." Sterling scanned the room to ensure that the other members registered what he was saying and again touched his tablet to advance to the next screen. "After downloading the take to the hard drive for decoding, we had an issue. The hard drive in the parent device failed and was corrupted. I, personally, took possession of the damaged hard drive and watched as it was destroyed. A new parent device to download and decode the take was now required. I ordered a replacement immediately and again locked the transceiver in my safe. The replacement hard drive arrived the following day, Tuesday, or day two on the timeline. Upon receiving the new device we were able to successfully download and decode the intelligence. As you can see on the timeline, Ms. Danvers placed her sell trade at 9:30 AM on day one, Monday, an hour and a half before I retrieved the device from the safe."

The room stirred on hearing his words but Ms. Tanner was the first to speak. "Ok, Mr. Sterling, you are saying that she could not have intercepted the take and used the information before handing it off to us?"

"Yes, Ms. Tanner, that is correct."

"How, then, do you explain the fact that Ms. Danvers began shorting her positions the day after she and Mr. Blake obtained the information that led us to do the very same thing?"

"There is not a factual explanation for this, only supposition I am afraid. I can tell you that she did not get any actionable intelligence from our device. That much is not possible."

"Alright, Mr. Sterling, I can accept that, but she clearly did obtain the information, so I want to know how she did that? She was obviously present during the information being communicated by Mr. Tibman to Mr. Sykes. She must have overheard the conversation."

A look of impatience showed on the security specialist's face, and he sighed with impatience. "I am afraid that, too, is unlikely, Ms. Tanner. The device is designed to record everything that takes place within its range once it is deployed. Mr. Blake deployed the device once he arrived in the suite that night. We have the entire event on disk. We heard everything that happened in that suite that evening and there was never a time when any of the principles being recorded left the suite. Other than Ms. Danvers efforts to distract the targets, she did not communicate with either Mr. Tibman or Mr. Sykes, not one time. If you have an explanation on how this could have happened, I would very much like to hear it."

Agitated now, Ms. Tanner chewed on her lower lip, but said nothing.

Sterling leaned forward and placed his palms flat on the conference room table, and focused his attention on the entire Board. "It is my opinion based on the facts at hand that Ms. Danvers is a very capable and clever young woman. She may well have found a way to obtain the intelligence and act on it without anyone knowing that she did so. To believe that explanation however, you have to believe that she had actionable intelligence two days before we were able to do so. It is possible that she simply based her actions on the information available to anyone smart enough to be aware of where things are going. This would, however, require a great deal of confidence on her part to bet the amount of money she bet on a mere hunch, but it is possible." Pacing over to the flat screen he moved his finger to the date three days later on the display. "This is the curious date in my view. This is the date that Ms. Danvers thought better of her decision made the previous Monday. She reversed herself completely. She paid a considerable amount in fees to rescind her position. I am quite intrigued as to why she did this. If Ms. Tanner is correct that Ms. Danvers somehow compromised our best security, then after going to such lengths to do so, why would she then turn around and back out of her position? For this I have no answer."

Again the room grew contemplative. The two women present traded furtive glances, but other than fuming, they remained silent.

His fingers steepled on his chest, John David Sterns leaned back in his great chair and regarded his board dispassionately. "Well, ladies and gentlemen, it seems we have a mystery doesn't it? Ladies, I fear that if your suspicions are correct our feisty little Ms. Danvers is even clever than we anticipated. As I cannot determine how this would have been accomplished, I am indisposed to take action on the matter at this time. On the other hand, my great appreciation for her skills and, um, other attributes aside, I am not inclined to tolerate a mystery positioned so close to the heart of our primary strategy to survive and prosper in the coming months. Mr. Sterling, I would have you look into this matter with a little more care. I understand that she lives alone, so I believe that you might be able to look around a bit in our Ms. Danver's personal life with little interference. If she is anything other than a firebrand and a risk taker, I would like to know it, as well as understand the technique employed in such an endeavor. If she represents a risk to our activities, have no fear, such a risk will be removed."

Making his pronouncement, the old man stood, taking his note pad and glass of water and walked out of the room.

Chapter 12
Betrayed

Megan tapped on her earpiece to end her last call with a smile. She decided that she was in the best mood she'd been in for at least a couple of weeks. Done with all her meetings, she had nothing to do for work over the weekend. A thrill ran through her as she contemplated her plans with Matt. Maybe a dinner and dancing would be nice.

Sighing happily, she spun around to face the window and credenza behind her. She opened the lower left hand drawer and took her portfolio from the desk. Closing the drawer only part way she placed the portfolio on top of the files to create a makeshift padded foot rest, so she could put her feet up for a few moments of relaxation.

Luxuriating in her plush office chair, she savored the feel of the exquisite leather as she leaned back and drank in the posh surroundings of dark woods and fine art, elegantly displayed on her walls. The quiet stillness of her office was, in this time and place, a sanctuary.

She sat there watching life on the other side of the glass pulse with energy on the taxi-choked street below. Watching for several minutes, she witnessed what was likely an argument about the price of a couple of hot dogs between a street vendor and a protestor. She noticed that a bicycle courier almost got clipped by a car as he zipped past a maintenance crew valiantly working to remove graffiti off the building across from her.

Megan shook her head in dismay. "What will all of you think a few weeks or months from now?" Not surprisingly, it was only a few minutes before she decided that her sanctuary, far above the street denizens, was perhaps too quiet for her taste. To alleviate this situation, she opened her center drawer and withdrew a remote and clicked on the television mounted to a wall across the room. She had seen enough market news today, so she instead clicked over to a news channel to see what disaster had befallen the world since her morning update.

Instead of the news, Megan saw that there was a group of three pundits arranged around a circular conference table, sharing their so-called 'expert' opinions about the current economic dilemma.

"...As reported earlier today, the financial crisis in Greece, Italy, and Spain has taken on epic and, in many cases, violent proportions. In fact, Wendy, last week the Eurozone's most economically stable partner, Germany, openly demanded that the governments in all three nations be subjugated to governance by the Emergency Planning Authority as authorized by the August 29 bailout plan, agreed to by all of the Eurozone nations."

"Exactly John. That is just the point that I was trying to make. The situation is now so dire, that following the Italian model from earlier this year, the managing Austerity Committee, appointed in Brussels, is now preparing to sell bonds secured with state property from the defaulting nations as collateral to buy back sovereign debt."

"Wendy, where you and Eric are wrong is in misinterpreting the facts here. I agree with you both that the Eurozone State Asset Development Fund was set up last year to manage sovereign asset sales, and that they are working now to create a privatization bond to buy back some of the enormous debts on the secondary market. What you are missing is the implication of this fact. I have said before, and I reiterate now, that there is just no way that government officials in Europe or the US will allow sovereign nation states to simply fail. For every €1 billion earned by the planned bond sale, the government will be able to buy back older debt worth €3 billion at today's depressed values. It is painful, but it will resolve the issues facing these beleaguered nations."

"Come on, John, Not even you can honestly believe that it will work out that way. Eric pointed out earlier that due to the unsustainable culture of entitlements, many public sector employees from France to Italy are right this minute, talking about taking to the streets and rioting over the austerity measures, Not only that...."

Wendy cut him off with a hand motion to add her own comment. "The protestors have a point Eric, and they know it. They were promised lifetime jobs that were guaranteed along with mandated full pensions upon retirement. The current issue underpinning the crisis is that the Eurozone no longer has any money, a rock-bottom fertility rate, and generations of retired public sector employees expecting to collect pension checks from a dramatically reduced workforce that is no longer able to sustain the system."

Following a light knock on her office door, Meg tapped her remote to pause the discussion right where it was. Richard stuck his head in the door.

"Hey there. I am not sure I recall what one does with a weekend away from work. Do you have any plans?"

Motioning for him to come in, she smiled. "Some plans, yes. How about you? Are you going out to the country?"

Richard entered the office, shut the door, and sat across from Megan at her desk. "You know, I think that you have a better view than I do. How did I manage to let that happen?"

"It's simple, you can't walk in heels." Giggling, she reached into her right file drawer and brought out a small bottle of Vodka. "You look like you had a rough afternoon and could use a drink; may I pour you one?"

"Pass." He propped his feet up on the leather chair positioned next to the one he was sitting in and employed his most persuasive smile as he made his pitch. "Actually, I am thinking about a relaxing weekend out of town. I thought I would see if you wanted to join me? There's a small group of us from the club springing for a nice beach house on Nantucket. It'll be full service, and I'll cover the weekend if you're interested. I thought we might be able to have a chance to talk."

"That is a quite tempting offer, Richard, but my date will be here in a few minutes."

"OK, Meg, but you know my idea will have the better upside potential by far." Handing her a note, he winked. "Here is how to reach me if you change your mind. I figured you would be busy, but one never knows. I'm only going because Saloman asked me yesterday when we were playing racquet ball. I know you haven't had any more time than I have lately, so I thought I'd give it a try."

Meg looked down at the note to see that it was a message of a different kind entirely.

"We are being watched. Be careful what you say and who you say it to."

"I guess I should make time to do something like that very soon. I wish I had known sooner."

"Sure, well, I have to go and pack, so I'm out of here. Hope you have a nice time this weekend. See you on Monday." With that, Richard got up, gave her a knowing look and departed her office.

Megan un-paused the TV, but stared after her boss for almost two minutes, completely oblivious to the talking faces proclaiming ultimate wisdom from her flat screen. Her heart all but seized at having confirmation of what she already knew would likely happen. The firm noticed her trades and now they were suspicious of her. Not only her, but apparently Richard, too, so her being able to count on him for support would be of limited use. No doubt the stupid cow, Barbara Tanner, would be behind her opposition. Still, if they had a smoking gun, she would have already been escorted from the building at the very least.

Overcome with nerves, she got up to pace, but realized once she was on her feet, she would already be under surveillance. To cover her movements, and what might appear as guilt to anyone watching, she decided to straighten up her spacious office a bit, and get her things ready to leave for the weekend. Placing a dirty tumbler on her wet bar, her mind returned once again to her primary focus.

Alright, I burned the napkin and washed the ashes down the sink, so there is absolutely no way that anyone, including Queen-Tight-Ass, can have anything more than her suspicion to make a case with the old man. Obviously, Randi Devaroe will be in on it, and she has some good contacts in Luther's department.

Megan checked her watch and moved her key files into her briefcase. Taking a moment to stare out at the always burning lights of New York City, it occurred to her that, regardless of what the two women may want, or who they have in security, Luther was a straight up player. She smiled inwardly, deciding that she really wasn't too bad at this stuff. He would call it as he saw it, and it was obvious that she only had possession of the recording device for a matter of like ten seconds. There was no way to trace anything back to her, so the key would be to support a story around why she did what she did with her trades. She was hypothesizing that the situation might be salvageable after all when her phone rang.

Megan tapped the blue tooth in her ear. "Meg Danvers."

"Hi, you ready to get out of there yet?"

"Hi, Matt, you know I am. I am really looking forward to having a day or two off. It has been absolutely nuts here the last couple of weeks. Where are you?"

"Your lobby. I am sitting by the fountain making your security guys nervous. It seems that they aren't as dumb as they look. I came right over from the office, so I'm still in a monkey suit, yet these numb-nuts haven't taken their eyes off me."

"Humph! You love that, and you know it. You would be insulted if they didn't think you were a bad ass."

"Fair point, still I think that I may have to get one of your snobby-boy haircuts. It is a valuable thing to be underestimated. Anyway, I am starving so you need to get your shapely behind down here."

"On my way, Babe, and just so you know, I am really dying for a nice steak."

❧

Megan smiled at Matt's rugged features, as he held the car door for her, thinking that suit, or no suit, there was no way he would ever look like one of the Harvard boys that he seemed to want to blend in with so badly. "I am really glad to see you Matt. How was your day?"

"Tense as always. More and more firms are moving their assets around, so I get to spend endless hours planning routes to move our client's key assets through the endless protest groups." Her gaze followed the economy of his movements as he climbed into the car after her, once she had scooted over to make room for him in the back of his company limo. She felt herself relax for the first time that day when he reached over to her. His touch and the taste of his lips on hers were just what she needed. The electricity of his kiss filled her with passion and joy as the car pulled away from the sidewalk. As he leaned back, she could see the concern in his eyes. "You really look tense, Meg. Do you want to talk about it?"

She reached into her purse and handed him the note that Richard had given her just twenty minutes before.

His gaze hardened and his countenance took on a professional cast. Matt reached over and toggled the privacy shield, looked right into her soul with an expression that would condone nothing short of a complete explanation. "OK, so is this about the note on the napkin a week or so back?"

"Yes. I shorted several of my positions on Monday morning."

"So your guys are apparently watching your accounts and realized that you picked up on their intel and are less than excited by that fact. Is that pretty much the story?"

"That's my take on it. I'm all but certain that it is Tanner. She has been after anything to keep me out of the boardroom since I came to Sterns and Becker. I think that I would have been ok with shorting the market, but I got cold feet a few days later and reversed myself. That one would be impossible for them to miss if they are watching my account. I suspected this would happen, but when Richard handed me this note, I had confirmation."

She wished that he would say something, but Matt just sat beside her, his face tense, as he considered the facts. After two or three minutes, he spoke again. "You and Blake picked up intel that the firm intends to act on. You had minimal contact with the device that recorded that intel. You acted on it the following day, likely before anyone in your leadership could view what was..."

She cut him off with a hand gesture. "No way that they think that I could have intercepted the data. Luther is thorough, and it really was just luck that I picked up that napkin. You already know that I burned it that night, not to mention that I would have been walked out or worse if they suspected that I had breached their tech."

Looking into his eyes, she shivered slightly at the icy expression reflecting back to her. "OK, so does it matter why they are watching you, if they are?"

"Of course, the fact that I haven't been fired tells me that the matter is still up for debate. On the one hand, as you said at the time, they would not hesitate to protect their interests, but, John is not about to act rashly. Richard and I are assets, and I do have plausible deniability regarding the stupidity of my trades." She pointed to the protesters as they passed through Times Square with its cacophony of garish sights and sounds. "Look at them. Look at their expressions. They're not just pissed, they're resentful, and their numbers are growing. Is it any wonder that I could come up with the notion to short the market on my own?"

He followed her gaze at the so called ninety-nine percent. "Then how do you explain reversing yourself?"

"That is the weakest point, but then again, look at them. When this thing goes south, those people are going to come for people like me in a big way. I just got scared." She looked into his eyes; for once she felt very much like the twenty something college girl he first knew when she arrived in the city. "I'm really freaking out about where all this is going. It was sort of an exercise, or a case study before, but I'm realizing that I made a mistake. Watching the blank faces of men, and women, and even kids, who had long since gone dead inside, she sighed. "These people frighten me Matt."

She felt his arm reach around her to bring her protectively to his side. "We will figure this thing out. I agree with you, though, that things are getting too tense for my comfort. It doesn't take a genius to form that opinion. The only question that anyone on the street or anywhere else, for that matter, should really have is the timing. That, Meg, is what you picked up from your efforts.

What you are going to have to sell now, is that you acted based on a hunch, and subsequently thought better of it. That you are, where you are, supports that you are a risk taker so that's what you go with."

"Why do you put up with me? I know that you've never really loved what I do for a living. I can see it in your eyes sometimes."

She felt his kiss on her temple, as he held her. "I love you because you are fearless, smart, and regardless of your being a Wall Street suit, you are a good person in there somewhere. You wouldn't have even blinked at shorting the market if you weren't. I think that you are still trying to decide where the lines are, but I believe in you."

As the car pulled up to the main entrance of Delmonico's, she realized that her relaxation had dissipated as a result of their conversation. She looked at her man as they prepared to get out. "Don't let this freak you out too much, but I love you Matt."

The door opened, and he stepped out, offering her his hand in assistance. "I know."

Megan joined him on the sidewalk, smiling in an obvious attempt to suppress her anxiety. "Well, I don't want to worry about any of this stuff this weekend. I have been looking forward to it all week. Besides, I am absolutely starving. I just hope that you can make me forget about office politics for a while."

She felt herself being moved forward as Matt, with his hand in the small of her back propelled her past the greeter and into the restaurant. She noticed that his eyes were constantly scanning their surroundings as they made the short journey from the car door through the entrance to the restaurant.

"Is something wrong?"

"Not specifically, just in the habit." Matt Smiled grimly. "Well, that, and I agree with you, there is an increase in tempo with the dissatisfaction amongst the disenfranchised. I want you to do the same thing Meg. You need to be really aware of your surroundings."

"I'm not worried as long as I am with you, but maybe I will start thinking about an exit strategy. I just hate the idea, because

I love this city. Maybe I could have done a few things better, but I will never get a job like this again if I walk away. It just makes me furious that I am here and things are going better than I even imagined, and it may all come to an end, regardless of anything that I can do."

Arriving at the reception stand, Megan saw that Matt handed the trendy young woman a twenty dollar bill which got them escorted immediately to a table.

"Welcome to life, Babe. It may not be what you want, but that is just how life is. I didn't want to go to war, or lose some of the best friends that I have ever had, but it happened anyway. The best you can do is play smart and try to be faster on the uptake than your opponents. What Americans never seem to count on, is that life is like going down a river. The overall current may be mild and lazy, but that has nothing to do with how things might be a mile down river where there may be rapids. Too many people just simply refuse to accommodate for challenges and then expect someone else to make their losses good."

"Is that where we are now, rushing through the rapids?"

Shaking his head, he lifted an eyebrow and nodded in agreement. "Yes, I'd say so, only we have others on the river with us, who will sink our raft if they can. Also, I guess that you could say that we have a tour guide on our raft that is all but positive that there are falls ahead."

Megan shrugged. "And I thought that I was Mary Sunshine. I guess being a tour guide is a better gig."

A tall, very handsome waiter, with jet black hair, olive skin, and an angelic face, walked up to their table almost as soon as they were seated, and handed them menus. "Good evening, my name is Stephan. It will be my pleasure to provide you superior service this evening. May I begin by bringing you something to drink?"

"Iced tea for the lady, and I will have water with extra lemon. We will take the avocado spinach dip and chips, and I will let you know about the meal in a few minutes."

Stephan smiled graciously and nodded. "The gentleman is decisive, I see, an attractive quality indeed."

Megan giggled demurely noticing that Stephan was looking Matt over thoroughly as he left to carry out Matt's instructions. She could see that Matt did not think it nearly as funny as she did.

"You know me, Meg, I am just a realist. I suppose that I got my attitude in Fallujah, in 04."

Megan nodded. "I knew you were there, but don't recall you saying anything about Fallujah before."

She could see in his eyes that she had just sent him back there in his mind. He was reliving it. "It was just before Christmas, when my unit had just come off of a hot patrol rotation. I was in the CP when the warning order came in. The 7th Calvary was ordered in to help out the Marines to retake the city."

Megan noticed a couple at the next table react to his statement with derisive eye rolls, but she took his hands into her own. "What happened?"

"Not the place, Meg. Let's just say, that my point is that we had just taken the city a few months before, after the bad guys did some really ugly stuff. I lost my best friend, Lamont, on that mission because the American public was just too naive to understand just how evil the people we were fighting were. Public opinion drives military decisions. It's stupid, but that is just the way it is. We had tried to take the city earlier that year, but the operation was rash, and our leadership wasn't committed to it. Anyway, my point is, the flow of events is what it is. All you can do is to react to your surroundings, and hope to influence the course you take down that river."

Stephan returned with their appetizer and the drinks, effectively ending the moment. "Have the two of you decided what you would like for dinner this evening?"

Matt snapped his menu closed. "I will have the ribeye, medium, with the mixed vegetables."

Megan smiled at the attractive waiter. "That sounds good to me too, Stephan. Thank you."

Tilting his head just slightly, Stephan added an abbreviated bow for good measure. "I will get your meal right out for you."

Megan's eyes followed the retreating waiter, and again noticed the demeanor of the couple next to them. Apparently, the pair did not approve of their meal choice either. She responded with a raised eyebrow, and her own aloof stare, before returning her attention to Matt.

"I love you, Matt, I really do. The world is coming apart and you are my foundation."

Taking her hand, he squeezed it gently, giving her a satisfied smile, as he nodded his acceptance of her declaration. "We are going to be fine, Meg. We just need to keep our eyes open and be smart..." As she watched Matt, she noticed that he was about to say something else, when he grew suddenly more alert, his eyes darting to the far side of the room, where two men were enjoying a beer and an appetizer at the bar. "Well, your employer didn't waste any time putting someone on you. I just spotted a couple of the guys from your building over at the bar. They're using the mirror to watch you."

"Maybe it's a chance meeting. It is a Friday night after all."

Matt nodded. "It could be coincidence, but, remember, that I don't believe in coincidences. Anyway, that tears it. I am going to pick up a couple of burn phones for us to communicate. From this point on, you must assume you have eyes on you at all times. You know they love their little toys, so you had best assume that they will pull out all the stops to vet you."

"Matt, I can't live like that. I would be nuts inside a week."

"Oh, yes, you can. You have a terrific operations head on your shoulders. It's one reason you are where you are at your firm. Just be cautious for a few weeks. This kind of thing is not cheap, so they will be very much interested in proving their suspicions out one way or another. I think we are going to have to endure my place tonight. They will have my bio and my address, etcetera, by tomorrow morning, but we should be ok to talk there tonight. The most important thing for now is to keep them under the impression that you are a good little girl with no idea they are out there. Can you pull it off?"

Megan nodded, but her thoughts were not as sanguine.

"Good. Well then, nothing to do but enjoy our meal. I will go out tonight and see about lining up a few things. I will buy you some clothes to change into, should we need to quickly disappear.

Frowning, Megan responded. "The thought of you buying clothes for me does not sound all that promising. I can put together a bag if you think I should."

Matt smirked. "I want to be sure that there is no way you can be tracked, should your friends be clever enough to plant a device on your clothing. You will just have to trust me. Also, we are going to start using a code to text that you are safe, like three times a day."

Megan just sat there, not saying anything, realizing that she would soon have to come up with a plan. She almost didn't even look up when their meal arrived. "Thank you Stephan. I appreciate your attentiveness this evening."

The waiter smiled his thanks and disappeared.

As the meal progressed, she turned the matter over in her mind. She analyzed all of the angles. She noticed how Matt reached for her a couple of times, comforting her, but otherwise he was content to ponder his thoughts, and she was grateful for his quiet strength. The key point now was that Sterns was unsure of her. He was probably unsure of Richard now, too. She realized that Matt was right. She would just have to be careful.

A few moments later, she saw Matt text his driver, for pick-up, and their check arrived. She was very much looking forward to being out of view for a while. As they were leaving, Matt as always, held her door for her, and she stepped into the limo. "Thanks Matt."

He smiled. "You're welcome, Babe. As the car pulled away from the curb amongst the jeers of a homeless woman, Meg noted that the two from the bar climbed into their own car. Megan noticed a non-descript sedan with yet two additional men, who appeared to be following the men tailing her. She thought to say something, but decided she was likely seeing things that were not there.

Chapter 13
Arrogance of Power

"Oh my God, Russ! I swear I didn't want you to find out like this." Annie's head moved, but no further sound emitted from her mouth. No rationale came into her mind. She felt as if they were strangers as they stood there staring at each other. Finally, he turned his head, his lips pursed with disgust. Her eyes dropped to his fists balled up at his sides. She could see the goose bumps among the glistening droplets of water that chased each other over his wet skin. Finally, he looked down at the floor. Annie closed her eyes, his pain coursing through her. She could see that he was stunned and hurt far more than he was angry. She looked at him, her heart breaking at how lousy things had been for them the last few months. "I was going to tell you, I was just trying to find the right moment. We have been fighting so much I just hadn't had the chance."

She knew that this was going to be an ugly battle. His head shook slowly from side to side as his mind obviously considered and then rejected her explanation. Staring into his tired red eyes, she saw something that she had never seen before. She saw defeat and weariness as he stood before her, his body shaking with humiliation.

When he spoke, his voice came in a low measured tone. "Damn it, Annie, I am your husband. You don't get to hide stuff like that from me. It's not like I am some jerk like that idiot friend of yours is dating."

She knew well what it cost his pride having to work as a day laborer. If she could only get him to remember how he was a year ago before things went so terribly wrong.

"Annie, I am your husband," he whispered it this time. A pregnant moment of silence passed as she could feel his indignation rising. She could see he was so furious that the water dripping off of his body was almost turning to steam as he stood there goading himself into a rage. "We are family. That means I am supposed to be the first one to know stupid stuff, much less that I am going to be a father."

Watching his anger rise as magma spilling from a volcano, Annie could feel her own temper rising with a heat all its own, to meet his challenge. "Ok, fine. Exactly when was I supposed to find that special little moment to let you know that we are having a baby? You are pissed off every day when you come in."

"So what is that supposed to mean? So what if I am tired when I get home from busting my ass for crap wages? How exactly does that give you the right to hold back information about my family from me? I thought you said I was our family's leader."

Dropping her eyes, she tried to think. If only she could somehow find a way to reach him.

"It is pretty fucking hard to lead, when your fucking wife is keeping secrets from you. Who all knows about our happy news, anyway? Which sister was on the phone, the dike or little miss-fancy pants in New York?"

"Shut up, Russ. Is that the way your grandfather would have you talk to me? Why do you always have to make everything harder? You are so stupid sometimes. This isn't about my sisters. If you were a better husband, I would have told you already. Who could blame me when you act like... like this all the time?"

"I have my reasons, Annie. I got fired and made a stupid mistake. Now you rub my face in my fuck-up every single day! Any man would be pissed off. Now we're pregnant and apparently you go around telling every stupid cow you know, but do you tell me? Fuck, no, you don't."

"I am not doing this anymore, Russ. I am leaving until you get your act together. I don't need the grief. It isn't good for the baby, and it isn't good for our marriage."

"To hell you are, Annie. Don't you move! You are my wife, and you will do what the fuck I tell you to do."

She could feel her world disintegrating around her. She decided right then that she just couldn't take this anymore. "I am sick of the constant fighting, Russ. I have had it!" She could feel the tears coming hot and fast, and she collapsed into the dining room chair next to her. She could tell that Russ was at a loss. He just stood there, with a towel wrapped around his waist for almost a minute. As the moment turned into two, he turned and walked into their bedroom. Hearing the dresser drawer open, she stood.

Numb with fear and disgust, she quietly moved towards the front door. Reaching it, she grabbed her purse, and bolted into the front yard, searching in her purse for the keys to her old Taurus as she ran. She was terrified that he would chase after her, as clumsy fingers scrambled to grasp the key chain. Finding them, she yanked them out of her purse as her eyes darted toward the front door of her house. Her hands shaking badly, she was not sure she would be able to get the key into the lock. In spite of time seeming to slow to a standstill, she achieved success. She pulled open the door, threw her purse onto the seat and climbed behind the wheel. Still shaking, she inserted the key into the ignition and prayed the car would start quickly. Annie turned the key and the engine came to life. A moment later she put the Taurus in gear, spinning tires throwing gravel toward the house as she quickly backed out into the street.

Driving away, she could see in the mirror that Russ had managed to get into his pants and make it out the door, but not quite fast enough to stop her. She turned left and drove blindly away from her home. "Dear God, what am I going to do? I love him, but he is too stupid to live. How can I ever trust him to be a father to my child when he acts like a child himself? Give me some help here; I really need someone to help me fix this."

Without thought, she drove aimlessly around Enid for the best part of an hour as she worked to gain control over her emotions. As her mind began to process once again, she realized she was driving towards the university. Tears washing down her face, she spied Nathan's card in the cup holder. She pulled into the university's administration building parking lot. She sat there for several minutes watching her fingers play with the card. She knew that calling him now was not the thing to do, but she was so tired, and she just couldn't tell Jana about this. Finally calming down enough to speak, she pulled her cell phone from her purse and dialed the number.

"Hello Nathan? It's Annie, are you busy?"

"Annie? Wow, I was hoping to catch up, but I didn't expect that it would be today. Is everything ok?"

She snorted derisively before she could stop herself. "Well, I have had better days. I guess I just needed someone to talk to, and I remembered that I had your card."

"OK, I guess. It really was great to see you today, although I hated the circumstances. Besides I would love to meet your husband."

"Um, I don't have Russ along at the moment, but I know he will want to meet you too."

She heard the hesitance in his voice, but pressed on as if she hadn't. "We will have to do that really soon, but for now, how about getting a cup of coffee?"

He paused, took a breath and then continued. "OK, Annie, how about that Starbuck's over by where you work?"

"I will meet you there in like fifteen minutes then. How does that sound?"

"See you there."

Annie hung up and returned her phone to her purse. She knew that meeting with Nathan was inappropriate, but, for the moment, she just didn't care. She decided she just wanted to feel normal for at least a few minutes. Putting the car in gear, she pulled out of the parking lot and headed back across town, towards Starbuck's.

Driving west again past the little frame houses on Randolph Street, she wondered what it would be like to be with Nathan. She smiled, remembering how they flirted outrageously during high school. Even when they dated other people, it was just sort of understood that they were the best of friends. She thought that her life would be very different right now if she had only been a year older. She sighed. If only she could have been in his class. Instead, he graduated and disappeared from her life.

She knew that Daddy liked Nathan. "I wonder, though, if he would be cool with an interracial couple in the family."

Finally smiling, she imagined how completely hot he was. She remembered how he looked playing basketball on one end of the gymnasium while she and the other cheerleaders practiced on the other end. She giggled as her mind traveled back to that day, of how he looked goofing around with the guys before his practice started. He was shirtless and his abs were to die for. "I wonder what you have been up to, Nathan."

She guessed that it would be tough being a cop's wife, but he had such a good sense of humor.

The light at Second Street turned red in front of her and she brought the Taurus to a stop. "If Russ would just try to lighten up, it would help." She thought if only Russell were more like Nathan, we would never be in this mess.

The stoplight in front of her turned green and she accelerated through the intersection. Her mind reliving the last months since things had gone so terribly wrong, she made her way to Van Buren, and turned left. Sighing at all of the senseless arguments, she decided that she wasn't blameless, but her husband had cheated after all. Who could blame her? Turning right on Owen K. Garriott, her mind finally settled onto the topic of whether she still loved Russell. Her mind replayed the good and the bad. As she drove, she thought that she wanted to love Russell, but she also realized that although she loved him, and always would, she was done with the fighting. She wanted the man she made vows to, back. She needed that man to be the father of her child. She wanted her husband back or things were not going to work out.

She could see her Applebee's on the left up ahead, and just down from that was Starbucks. As she turned in to the parking lot, she realized that she was actually anxious. Looking at herself in the mirror, she did a quick fix of her makeup.

"Why am I anxious? We have known each other for years?" In a moment, she was out of her car and walking towards the entrance. Clearing the doorway, she paused and looked around for a moment, before locating Nathan by a window nearest the street. She realized he had already picked up the coffee. As she approached, a smile lit her face, thinking how much he looked like he did in high school now that he wasn't wearing a uniform.

"Hi, Nathan. It is really a small world, isn't it?"

"It really is, Annie. You look really great."

She saw something in his eyes as she slid into the booth opposite him, but decided it could be anything, and gave him a demure smile.

"I am surprised you called so soon, but I do want to know what is up with you these days."

Looking at him now, she was sure of what she saw. A cautious look crossed his face as she reached for her cup of coffee.

"You sounded a little upset when you called."

Annie looked down. "I was, I guess. It has been really tough lately. Russ got laid off a couple months back. Anyway, we have had a little trouble connecting since then. We had a fight a little while ago."

The concern on Nathan's face was obvious. "It is really tough on a lot of folks lately, Annie. Are your folks doing ok? How about your big sisters? My dad said that Meg was some sort of big executive back East." His smile was warm and genuine. She could tell that he cared, but he seemed different somehow. It occurred to her that this was really a stupid move. Dear God, he probably thought she was pathetic. Regretting that she had called him, she took a sip of coffee to gain a moment to compose herself.

"Mom and Dad are fine. They are doing the same thing that they always do. Dad takes care of the cattle and mom paints. She is actually selling some of her work now. She is even making some good money. Katie is out of work in Dallas, and yes, as you would expect, Meg is living the high life in New York."

Nathan took a drink and smiled at her. "And Annie is married and living in Enid." Annie stared out onto the street for a minute. Looking back at Nathan, he tilted his head slightly to look deeply into her eyes, his body language displaying the question that she could feel he wanted to ask her from the moment she called him. "Can I ask you why you aren't having coffee with one of your girlfriends, or someone that knows you and Russ? I don't think it is really the best idea for a married girl to have coffee with a guy your husband doesn't know, when you need someone to talk to."

His words seared her heart. She shook her head, knowing that the guilt she felt was obvious to anyone that was paying attention. Taking a deep breath, she collected her thoughts, and exhaled. "I, um, I sort of need to talk to someone that I can trust, that doesn't know Russ and everyone else we know, for that matter."

A long moment passed between them, and she continued, now looking up through her lashes into his eyes. "It has been, rough. We just cannot connect lately. Since the layoffs, Russ just isn't the same person he..."

"Is he hitting you Annie? Is that why we're here?"

Her head jerked up, her eyes wide at being startled by his words. "No, Nathan, no; it isn't like that at all. He yells and throws stuff, but he would never do that."

"Then I have to tell you that I don't think I am the one you should be talking to." She noticed that his eyebrows went up and his face transformed into one of skepticism.

"I have to say, Annie; it feels like there is something more here."

Annie looked down. "It's hard to talk about with ..."

She sighed and shrugged. "Nathan, Russ's pride is a problem. He is so damned proud that he won't talk to anyone. He knows that my family and my girlfriends know about what happened, so he is embarrassed. If I talk to someone he knows, he gets embarrassed and it makes him crazy, but I am sick of being yelled at." She looked into her coffee. "I have had it with walking on egg shells, and ...

"Wait, embarrassed that people know he was let go? I don't understand that. A lot of people are out of work. It is hard, yes, but nothing to be ashamed of."

It hit her that she just screwed up. She looked down at the table again. "He got drunk that night after it happened. He and his buddies went out to a bar and had a few too many." She looked up again with tears overwhelming her. "He got drunk and cheated on me with a woman from work. He told me the next day, and our lives have been a wreck since then."

"Oh God, Annie, I am really sorry. You guys really need to get into some couples counseling, though. It sounds like he wants to make things work, or he would have hidden it. I see that sort of crap every day in my job."

"I know Nathan, I know. I have tried to let him know that I still love him. I really do, but I can't take his blowing up all the time. He wasn't like this before. We met the summer after I graduated. I was working at the Dairy Queen in Mineral Wells. Russ was down working at old man Davis's ranch. Anyway, he was always coming in, and we started going out." Her face brightened as she relived the earlier time. "He used to be funny and caring. He was the kind of guy that could do anything."

She could feel Nathan take her hand as he looked into her soul. "Annie, as long as he isn't hurting you, you need to keep trying to reach him. If he got past your dad he must be a reasonably decent guy. You are a Danvers girl, and I want you to go make this thing work, Ok?"

"I wasn't the one that cheated, Nathan. Why isn't Russ the one to make it work?"

"Because, Annie girl, he isn't the one sitting here; you are. If he were sitting here, I would tell him to find a pair, and be a man. He got stupid, and he broke his vow to you. You have every right to call it a day, if you wanted to do that, but you didn't. I am thinking that you must love him, and you must want to be his wife, or you would be in divorce court right now."

Nathan reached for his cup, his eyes never leaving her face as he finished his coffee. "It is a hard thing, Annie, and I honestly don't know what I would do, but you are one of the finest people I have ever known. The bottom line is that a marriage is a sacred thing. If he is a dirt bag then cut your losses. If he isn't, if he is a man who made a mistake in a moment of weakness, you go make it work. Christ expects forgiveness of us all, if we want any in return."

Patting her hands as he rose, Nathan flashed Annie a blinding smile. "You know I have to be the forgiving sort, because you know all too well, some of the stunts I have pulled. Anyway, I have got to go now. I look forward to meeting Russ when it's right. Until then, get some counseling and don't be going for coffee with questionable men." He winked, turned and headed for the door.

Annie took another sip of her coffee and thought through what Nathan had said. She realized that she did love Russ; she just wanted the husband that she married back. She also realized that she messed up today. She may not have really done anything, but she knew that her heart was not in the right place.

Gathering her strength, she started to rise. As she looked out the window, she saw Russ's dad headed her way, and he didn't look happy. He was parked right next to her in the parking lot, so he obviously knew that she was here.

Chapter 14

Pride Goeth Before a Fall

Storming into the front yard, Russell was furious and he just felt like breaking something. He watched Annie's car race off down their street, his embarrassment and rage, his only companions. He seethed, thinking about his wife's obvious lack of confidence. It was clear that she considered him to be no better than his father. Kicking the newspaper from the yard onto the porch, he turned to go back into the house. As he reached for the screen door, he realized he'd had enough of people looking down on him. After all, that is what his dad would do. That is exactly what his dad did do when he was growing up. Standing there with the screen door in his hand, all he could think about was escaping. Setting his jaw, he nodded to himself and slammed it shut so hard the whole front of the screened porch shook with the impact as he went in and quickly finished dressing. He was quickly back out the front door.

Turning towards the driveway, he pulled his keys out of his pocket and climbed into his truck. Inserting his keys into the ignition, he paused a moment, pulled out his cell phone and dialed. His father picked up on the first ring.

"Hello."

"It's me. I don't have a lot of time, but I need to know something. You took off when I was a kid. I want to know why."

Turning the keys in the ignition, he looked up and down the street, put the truck in gear and backed out of the driveway. His father went silent but did not hang up. His anger surging again, Russell slammed his hand down on the dash. "I don't have time for this, Dad. I want to know why you left Mom, and why you came back."

Russell listened, as his stunned father worked to regain his composure. Jack Davis sighed. "That was a long time ago, Boy, and it ain't none of your business. Do you want to tell me why in the hell you are calling me with a question like that? Pissing mad or no, you got no right talking to your pop like that."

"Like I would tell you! You wouldn't understand, anyway."

Hearing the door to his dad's trailer slam, he realized his Pop was moving outside. "Did you and Annie fight, Boy? She walked out on you, didn't she?"

"What the hell do you know about it?

"I know a lot of things Russ. I know that you got a good girl there, and you better find a way to fix what is wrong. If you don't, I promise that you will regret your actions for the rest of your life."

"Like you, Pop? Will I end up like you, with no job, no money, and living in a dump?" As the light turned red, Russell stopped the pickup, but only barely.

"Well, Dad, maybe I've had enough of people looking down their noses at me. Maybe I want something better for my life. You did, right?"

"I made mistakes, Boy, and I was lucky that I married your mom. She is a saintly woman and I know I don't deserve her. I expect you don't deserve your Annie either, but you better try anyway if you know what's good for you."

"You know what, Dad? Forget it. She did take off. I will be dammed if I will go hunt for her, though. I am the man in this family. She can come back to me or not. I don't give a damn!" Completely disgusted, he hung up and threw his phone onto the floorboard on the passenger side. "Fuck it, I'm done!"

Everything within him screamed that he just had to get away from the disaster that his life had turned into, to escape the pain and the humiliation. He just wanted to drive, to leave his trouble behind him. He could see his wife's face in his mind, but he didn't have the first clue what to do to fix their marriage.

"You're never going to let me get past this, are you Annie?" Shaking his head, he pulled to a stop behind a lime green Volkswagen waiting for another light to turn green. "Damn you, Renee. You stupid bitch, why couldn't you leave it alone? I told you before that I wasn't interested, but you had to keep pushing me, didn't you? I hate you." He shook his head in shame and disgust at his weakness. Turning onto Owen K Garriott, the thought crossed his mind that he should look for his wife, but it was true what he told his pop, he just didn't want to. Even if he found her, what good would it do? He didn't want to be here at all anymore, he thought. The little house that he and Annie were so excited to get, their lives together were now nothing but painful reminders of his complete failure as a man and as a husband.

"Screw it, I don't need this grief." Angry and fed up with his life, Russell slammed his fist down again on the dash as he turned south at the next light. Turning onto Van Buren, he just drove, not needing a destination. He decided that he just needed to think, to find a way out of this mess. His thoughts went over and over the sequence of events that led him to where he was. The greedy bastards firing everyone they could find to fire, the stupid illegals who had no right to be here, and yes, his dad too. He recalled his grandfather always saying all that crap about following the rules and working hard. "Screw that, Gramps, I love you, but you just got no idea about things today."

He could hear his dad saying the same sort of thing in his head, even now. "You play by the rules, go to work every day, and you'll be alright, Boy."

"Maybe you should have led by example, you son of a bitch. Where are you now? I will tell you where you are. You're in some broken down mobile home in a crappy trailer park. That's where you are. You ain't got shit to show for your life, do you? All your big words and you didn't do any of it yourself, you drunk, self-serving bastard. You ain't half the man that Gramps was. Mom should have dumped your ass years ago."

Looking up after turning his life over and over in his mind, Russell realized that he had already passed the air force base and was almost to Hennessey. He thought he should turn around, but he realized he really didn't want to. He had nowhere to go, and he knew it, but he was not going to go home, of that he was sure.

He looked out into the cold grey clouds spread out across the horizon in front of him and fumed. He looked for God in those clouds. “Maybe I should just keep driving. How would you like that? You know you ain’t done shit for me lately? I thought I was so blessed when Annie said she would marry me, in spite of her up-tight old man, but that was just your little joke on me, wasn’t it? You had to give me a taste of a good life to make me truly miserable later, didn’t you?”

Now, she gives me that hurtful little look, to remind me what a fuck-up I am.” As the miles of farmland passed, his anger continued to eat him up from within. “I guess you think it is real funny that I am a stupid loser, just like my pop.”

As he passed under the last stoplight in Hennessey, he decided he couldn’t even run for it, worth a crap. He didn’t have any clothes, and he damn-sure didn’t have any money. He could load up the credit card, but even his dad, the worst SOB he knew, would never do that. Looking back at the horizon with its grey clouds, wondering if a cold grey future was what he was destined to live through, he screamed with all the power in his lungs.

“I hate you! If you are my God, and you supposedly love me, then why did you let things turn into crap like this? You are sadistic, so maybe I don’t care what you or Annie thinks. Maybe I start living for me. Doing it your way hasn’t done me much good lately, has it?”

As soon as the words left his mouth, Russell felt guilty. Roaring out his rage and frustration at life and at God drained him of a measure of his rage. He realized that he even felt a twinge of fear at his blasphemy. He knew that his statement was taking things too far, and alone in the cab of his pickup, he conceded, at least to himself, that his problems were of his own making.

As reason slowly reasserted itself, he could feel the rage beginning to dissipate and he smirked. “If I keep going, I really would end up in Oklahoma City.”

He knew that he had to go back, but he would be damned if he was going to take any more crap from Annie or anyone else. He looked down at his watch. To his amazement, he realized that he had only been driving for like forty-five minutes. He could see that he was just outside of Dover, so he thought he would turn around there and head back. He chuckled to himself that this had to be the smallest little town in the country when he looked for a spot to stop. As he slowed the pickup, he noticed a tiny little cafe beside the road. It looked like it had been a gas station at one time. The sign read: *The Dover Market and Café*. He used to go through Dover all the time, but didn't remember this place being here before this.

He pulled into the parking lot and realized that his stomach was in fact demanding his attention. "What the hell! This is just as good as any. Besides, I deserve a meal, out. Screw Annie and her budget." With that, he got out of the truck and walked over to the entrance. Pushing the door open, an old fashioned bell announced his presence. Looking around he saw a woman about his mom's age tease a customer. Noticing him, the woman with collar-length, golden-brown hair winked at her customer and walked over to him.

"Hi there! Sit anywhere you can find a spot, and I will be right with you."

Russell smiled for the first time that day, the smell of home cooking invading his nostrils. He nodded to the waitress. "Nice little place. Smells good."

The waitress smiled back and slid a menu in front of him. "The special today is the meatloaf. What do you want to drink, Hot Stuff?"

"A Dr. Pepper would be great. So, have you guys been here long? I don't recall seeing this place before."

"We have been here for a couple of years, I guess. You are too young to lose a couple of years though. My name is Tracie. I manage the café, and we like to make folks feel welcome, so just yell when you know what you want to eat. Anyway, I will be right back with your drink."

Russell smiled. "Thanks, Tracie, I will." She walked back towards the kitchen, stopping briefly to speak to another woman, obviously another waitress, an attractive olive skinned woman.

Looking back at the menu, he debated with himself about the merits of meat loaf over the hamburger he came in thinking about. In the end, he decided against the idea of meat loaf as the darker of the two women approached him. She placed his drink and a straw in front of him.

"Hi, I am Theresa; here is your Dr. Pepper. Do you know what you would like, or do you need a few more minutes?"

Russell smiled at her. "I'll just take a cheeseburger with fries."

"You got it. We'll get that right out to you." As she returned his smile, he decided he liked this place. It had a homey feeling and everyone was really relaxed. His tension eased as he watched an older couple waiting for their meal one table away. He wondered if he could ever have a shot at being as content as they appeared to be. Looking around, he smiled at how homey the eclectic items scattered around the little restaurant were. Even the three folksy prints displayed on the wall nearest the parking lot made him feel at home. Turning back towards the kitchen, he saw that Tracie was now standing just behind him.

"Feeling at home, I hope? Can I get you a refill or anything?"

"I was just looking at your decorations. They do have that effect on me, I guess."

Tracie nodded. "Thank you. They are mostly related to the Dust bowl and the Great Depression. Sort of appropriate these days I guess."

Russell nodded. "Well, with all the people out of work now, I guess they are."

Looking up at the woman, he saw that she regarded him closely. "You look like you had a hard day, Sweetie. If there is anything we can do to make it better, you let us know, OK?" He nodded, and she smiled her encouragement and returned to the kitchen.

Watching her leave again, Russell realized he really did deserve a break. Looking around, the people here all seemed to be doing alright. It was nice to be around people who weren't looking down their noses at him. When his order arrived and the savory smell of the freshly-grilled burger reached him, he realized that he truly was hungry. Smiling, he took a bite, relishing the juicy burger. As he ate, the little bell announced another couple coming into the café. He nodded at them, and they returned the gesture with smiles on their faces. Russell took another bite and listened to their stories. Both couples talked about the trouble they were having. He decided that it was probably a pretty common thing, after all. Maybe his problems weren't entirely his fault. Maybe it was just crappy luck that things had gone so badly for him.

Getting some food to eat was apparently just what he needed. He was almost done when Theresa handed him his check. He thought that being around these people was cheering him up, and he didn't even know them. Just listening to their opinions reminded him that there were a lot of people suffering just now. He guessed that it was true, that misery loved company. As Theresa came by again, he handed her a credit card, and she smiled her thanks.

Hearing the bell on the door again, he turned his head to see who it was. He saw a tall Hispanic man, about fifty or so, with grey hair and a mustache standing in the doorway. Russell noticed that all of the other heads in the café turned to look, just has he had done.

The man nodded to the patrons. "Any of you boys know anything about welding? I have a hundred and fifty dollars for anyone who can get me back on the road again." He motioned with his thumb pointing behind him. "That guy at the station has a welder, but says he doesn't know how to use it. It would save my life if someone could help me out. I have to get to OKC tonight."

Russell sat there wondering what his story was when he realized that he could do it, and he really did need the money. He raised his hand and stood up. "I'm a welder. I'm not promising you anything, but I will take a look. I just need to pay for my meal."

"I am in your debt, son. I will just be outside. I am grateful for your time."

The man turned and walked out the door, as Tracie brought him his credit card.

"That was nice of you to help that guy out. I hope you stop back in again sometime soon." She smiled at him and Russell realized that he felt normal for the first time in a long time. "You have a nice place here, thanks." Russell stood up and turned toward the door but paused, turning back towards the kitchen. "The burger was really good. Thanks for everything." The women waved, and he headed for the door.

Climbing into his truck, Russell waved to the man to get in.

"The name is Miguel. Miguel Rafe." Russell noticed that the man sort of had an air about him. He was obviously in a jam, yet he sort of had a twinkle in his brown eyes. He smiled a warm smile and extended his arm to shake hands.

"I am Russ Davis, Sir."

"It is nice to meet you, Russ. I am sure glad that this little town has a welder. I would have been in real trouble if you hadn't happened to have been eating your dinner just now." He pointed down the street. "I am just over there. The dirty black Dodge Ram."

Russell nodded and drove down the street to find the man's pickup pulling an overburdened trailer with one of the two arms of the hitch broken almost in two. Russell pulled the truck to a stop and both men got out. Russell examined the break and turned back to the older man.

"Your problem is that you got too much weight on this thing. He looked past the station attendant to his welding rig. "You got fuel in the tanks and wire, etcetera?"

The station attendant nodded. "Yes sir, I got everything for it right here. I just don't know much about no welding. That rig belongs to my brother."

Russell bent down to examine the break in more detail, and then moved to the other side to look for cracks on the other arm of the hitch. After a moment, he stood up and faced the man. "You are going to need some steel to stiffen the hitch, Mr. Rafe. It just isn't designed for the kind of weight you're pulling."

"It isn't that much farther to where I am going. If you can just patch it up that will be enough." He pointed to the trailer. "I have a buyer for some classic car parts back there, but the guy will only be in OKC long enough to eat dinner. I really need the money, so I really have got to get there on time."

Russell thought for a minute, and then turned to the station attendant. "Do you have anything we could use to stiffen these arms? It would need to be steel and solid. I might be able to weld it on the side of the arm to get you the strength you need."

The gas station attendant brightened suddenly. "I have some angle iron in the back!"

"Let's see it. If it's heavy enough, that could work." The attendant smiled enthusiastically and headed for the back of his shop.

Russell yelled after him. "Can I use your floor jack to pick up the end of the trailer?"

"Yeah, no problem, Man."

Putting on his gloves, the owner of the rig walked over to help Russell position the floor jack in a good spot to lift the front of the trailer to take pressure off the broken hitch. "Let me know what you need me to do. I am a mechanic, but I never learned to weld, really." Russell acknowledged the comment, but remained primarily focused on placing the jack where it needed to go. "I guess it is your lucky day, Mr. Rafe, I don't live here. I just happened to be passing through."

"Really? God does work in mysterious ways, I reckon. Where are you from, Son?"

"Just up the road, Enid." Russell inclined his head to the north and replied without taking his eyes off his work.

Miguel nodded. "That is where I first thought that I felt something funny from the trailer. I felt a tremor from the trailer as I left town. I live in Dodge City, Kansas. I have been driving since before lunch. I want you to know that you helping me out like this is really a life saver."

"I will fix you up if I can, Mr. Rafe. It really depends on what the steel looks like that he has to patch this with."

Mr. Rafe grimaced momentarily, but a hopeful look overtook his features. "I know that you will do what you can. I am sure you got better things to do and all. I am just saying that if I don't sell these parts, I am going to lose my house. I got laid off a couple months back, and... Well you know how it goes. It is tough all over, for everyone, right?"

Russell looked at the man, realizing that it really was true. A lot of people were hurting.

"Yes, Sir, you are right about that." Satisfied with the Jack's location, Russell started pumping up the front of the trailer. "Laid-off, huh? That is a tough thing these days. I happen to know a little bit about that actually."

Looking surprised, Miguel nodded. Russell had the impression that he suddenly seemed to understand him.

Miguel walked over and picked up two cinder blocks from beside the garage and brought them back to block the trailer. "I guess there is a lot of that going around these days. To be honest though, my problems are my own making. I decided I deserved a big, new house, and, of course, I paid more than I had any business paying." Miguel set the blocks next to Russell's feet. "My wife, she was against the idea, but you can bet that I got my way. Wasn't long, of course, until the market went south on me. Couldn't sell, couldn't refinance, and now that I'm laid off, my wife is pretty sore about it all." Miguel chuckled, making fun of his situation. "Getting laid off was sure not what I was counting on. Now I have to compete with young fellas like you for any work I hope to get. Still, a man does what he has to do, what he must do to keep his family safe."

Russell picked up the two blocks and placed them under the front of the trailer. He then backed the jack off, letting it settle on the blocks. He noticed that the garage attendant had returned with several lengths of angle iron and had moved up the welding rig for them, but was now helping another traveler.

Russell examined the scrap iron and dry fitted it where he needed it. He slipped the welding mask over his head and motioned for Miguel's attention before pushing the mask down. "Mr. Rafe, can you hold this here until I can clamp it into place? Then I can tack it on."

"You bet."

"Do you mind if I ask you a question, Sir?"

"Shoot. I will answer it if I can."

"You seem to be in a real jam. You screwed up, and your wife is mad at you. I am not sure how to say this, but you don't seem to me to be all that upset." He realized that he was really grateful that the mask protected him from showing any of the emotion he felt suddenly surge through him.

"You misunderstand me, Son. I kick myself every day for letting my pride get the better of me. My younger brother, Gabe, is an accountant and has a nice house. I wanted to be able to show him what was what. Now our whole family knows what a prideful idiot I am. I decided that the only thing left for me, if I was to be any sort of a man, was to cowboy up and admit my mistake."

Embarrassed, Russell realized that tears were threatening to overwhelm him. Steadying his voice, he pressed the man a little further.

"Was that the end of it for you then?"

"Hardly, Son. I had three really sweet classic cars that I had restored over the last ten years. I loved those cars." Miguel indicated the trailer with a motion of his thumb over his shoulder. "In there are the parts for two other projects I had spent the last few years collecting. When I get to Oklahoma City and make this deal, they will all be gone. I even sold my tools."

Russell finished welding the patch onto the trailer, and bent low before lifting the mask to inspect his work and ran his sleeve over his eyes to cover the tears welling up there. Satisfied with the welds, he looked up. "I don't get it. I would be really pissed in your place." He stood up, grabbed the welding rig, and moved over to the other side, to reinforce the other rail of the hitch. Getting into position, he looked at Miguel, his bafflement obvious on his face.

Miguel smiled. "I made a mistake. What good would it do to make matters worse now? There is nothing to be gained by being a sore loser. I gambled by overspending, and I lost. I was mad for a while, but I was lucky. I have a great wife who understood me, and my best friend is my minister. He helped me realize that if I am mad about earthly failures; I am too focused on the wrong things.

I hate losing my hobby, but there is nothing more important than my wife."

Russell finished and looked at Miguel, unsure of what to think. "Not sure it's as good as new Mr. Rafe, but I think you can get to OKC now."

Miguel grabbed Russell's hand, shaking it vigorously. "*Gracias*. I am indebted to you. You really saved me. This deal will give me the money to pay out what's upside down, so I can sell the house now. God bless you, Son. God bless you." Miguel took his wallet out, counted out a hundred and fifty dollars. "Here you go, young man. Good luck with the challenges you are facing."

Russell thought for a moment, and then looked at Miguel with the beginnings of a smile. "I can't take that money sir. Just give me fifty, and we can call it good."

Miguel smiled broadly. "You are a good man, Russell. I bet your people know that too. It is like I said earlier, God works in mysterious ways. What are the odds of us meeting like this? I am going to be praying for you, Son. If I can ask one more thing, will you do the same for me?"

"Yes, Sir, I will. I have said some pretty bad things lately. I hope God will listen."

"He will, Russell. You just get on your knees and leave any pride at the door. God loves us even when we don't deserve it." Unsure, Russell shook his head; but deep inside, he knew that he had his answer. He watched for a moment, smiling, as Miguel grabbed the two blocks to put them where he found them. "It was a blessing meeting you, Young Man. *Vaya con Dios*."

"Good luck to you, Mr. Rafe. Thank you for... Well, just thanks. I know what I have to do now."

Chapter 15
Serendipity

Catherine paced in her small living room, in an all too familiar dance, as once again, she rushed to the breech to defend her point of view. The ongoing battle of ideas with Janice was omnipresent and predictable. Rolling her eyes at her partner's last ridiculous assertion, she noted that Maggie, who had been sleeping in the recliner, seemed almost put-out at having to listen to yet another argument. The boxer stared up at her, exasperated.

"Give it a rest, Janice; all I said was that from an economic perspective, you get more of whatever you subsidize. There just isn't enough money in existence to support what the Progressives say they want. They will never be satisfied because, for one thing, a collective approach simply doesn't work; and for another, supporters of that philosophy are only being used by the political elites to maintain their power. It is no more complicated than that. They are stealing the fruits of productive Americans labor to make it seem as if they care about those who aren't productive."

Exasperated, Janice mimicked grabbing her head to keep it from exploding. "You cannot believe that, Kate! It is a ridiculous assertion, at best. People are hurting, and the rich just keep on getting richer, while the poor are getting poorer." Furious, she wagged her finger in Catherine's direction to emphasize her point. "You know as well as I do the statistics prove that. The government is not stealing from the wealthy. It is those with money who want to keep the majority of people, especially minorities, down for their own benefit."

Catherine rolled her eyes and moved closer to her partner. "Whatever, Janice, like everything else, you only tune in to what you want to hear, and will only accept that which supports your agenda.

The very rich, as a group, are getting wealthier because of the policies your Progressive buddies support. What you don't get is who the people you are worried about, are, or why that statistic is getting worse. For one thing, the poorest of Americans today are not the same people who were in that status a few years ago. In spite of Progressive policies, many of those individuals have improved their lives. The poor today are there because of a lack of jobs. Jobs aren't available because of government regulations, and government starving the private sector of capital to fund their excessive borrowing." Looking at Janice, she realized that Janice was angrier than she had ever seen her. Her pupils were pinpoints, and it looked like she was visibly restraining her balled fists from striking out.

Catherine took a breath, and continued in the calmest tone she could muster. "If borrowing and, in fact, creating money we can never repay wasn't enough, Progressives keep whining about the need for higher taxation. It is a mathematical fact that the Feds could steal everything that every American making over two hundred thousand dollars a year made, and it would barely make a dent. They could steal their homes, their possessions, their vehicles, and even take the clothes off their backs, and it would only fund their out of control nightmare for a matter of months. Then what, Janice? Who will Progressives vilify then?"

Janice looked down, her eyes shut. Catherine continued as gently as possible. "The truth is that the political classes in both parties are sell-outs. The whole argument is a scam to keep the population distracted while they steal us blind."

Janice began to reply, but clamped her mouth shut, clearly considering what to say next. Catherine smiled weakly, adding one final point to make her case. "Look, Janice, I understand that the idea of sharing everything sounds good. I wish human beings were better, but we are not. In the real world, collectives, groups and classes of people don't get out of bed in the morning; individuals do. Individuals must be motivated by personal reward to go the extra mile. Without that motivation, it is only human to skate, and let others carry the load. Government must guarantee equal opportunity, but simply cannot guarantee an equal outcome."

When Janice looked up, something within her had changed. She looked suddenly stoic, her eyes sad. "The world cannot, and will not continue like it has. Look around, Kate. People are in the streets. It is immoral for a few to have vast wealth while others starve. That is the whole point behind both the Occupy and Solidarity Movements. The people are saying they were not given what they were promised. If they know what is good for them, your rich friends had better come through, or we are going to see big problems."

Catherine shook her head in despair. "You just made the point I have been making for two years. The political classes, along with the elites running the corporate world, lied to us all. What the losers on the street want is impossible. Too many have no sense of what earning something is like. Beginning in grade school, many of these people were handed trophies and awards, regardless of how they performed."

Pausing, she gave Janice an imploring look. Unfortunately, she realized she would receive no quarter this morning. "Well, there we are. Somehow it became a bad thing to win in this country. I refuse to give up on my values and this," Catherine pointed to the television, "is what you get as a result. Spoiled, self-entitled college kids who think that society owes them their parent's houses."

"Kate, I am not about to stand here and listen to what is basically hate speech. You always try to oversimplify issues. That is your whole problem. You find one anecdotal example of something you don't like, and try to extrapolate that onto the whole movement. I hate to tell you this, but although the Solidarity Movement, and the Occupy Movement, before that, are both about college kids and ordinary workers who have been unfairly burdened with debts by the banks. Most of the protest movements are just ordinary people, who are tired of your greedy capitalist friends taking advantage of them."

Catherine sighed, resigned to the fact that reaching Janice was simply not possible. "You couldn't have it more wrong, Janice, but I have to let Maggie out."

Janice exhaled and disappeared into the bedroom. Catherine turned to the boxer. "Come on, Girl. Do you want to go outside?" Maggie's ears perked up immediately, as she followed Catherine towards the back door.

Opening the door to let Maggie escape, Catherine considered how angry Janice really was. Her causal comment about the unreasonable demands of the Solidarity Movement caused Janice to go ballistic. She immediately began to throw things into her overnight bag, as she packed for her trip. Sadly, she thought, it wasn't the first time a simple off-handed comment led to an all-out battle between them. Taking a deep breath, she folded her arms around herself, and turned to head back into the living room. She knew this fight was inevitable the moment she spoke. Janice's eyes flared and she scowled in defiance. Catherine realized in a moment of crystal clarity that she was simply never going to be able to avoid her partner's wrath unless she succumbed to her point of view in all things great and small. Leaning on the wood trimmed cased opening between the dining and living rooms, Catherine decided that to Janice's credit, she truly wanted the best for people. It all boiled down to who you trusted, and Catherine knew that she didn't trust anyone, especially not the government. She sighed; weary to her core of the pointlessness of these arguments, knowing the outcome of this fight when it began. As Janice returned with her bags, Catherine took a breath to respond but Janice held up her hand to stop her before she could speak.

Janice zipped up her flight bag, and made a point of not looking at Catherine, as she spoke to the suitcase. Her voice was flat and hard, and rose in volume as she spoke. "Kate, those so called self-entitled Americans have zero chance to have any kind of life, or to have anything like what their parents had, because greedy Wall Street bankers and corporate ass-holes are taking more and more money every year. You know that is true. You got laid off because your own company decided to break their agreements with their unions, and bankruptcy was the only way they could do that. I won't let you denigrate them."

Catherine felt a chill run up her spine. She knew that she was rapidly approaching the point of no return in the discussion. She also realized that giving in on something she believed in was not something that she was capable of doing.

Losing her temper, Catherine's voice finally rose to match Janice's, as her partner grabbed her bags. "As you just said, I got laid off. By your logic, I should be out there crying about it with all the little babies protesting everywhere!" Swallowing, an even more biting comment, she continued. "You may have noticed that I am not out there protesting because it isn't society's job to take care of me. It is my job to do that. If I can't take care of myself, then I guess I would have to go home to my folk's house with my tail between my legs and hope that my father would help me out. And another thing, American Airlines, and all of the other airlines, for that matter, went bankrupt because of greedy unions and their completely unrealistic demands."

Setting her bag by the door, Janice moved towards her, frustration obvious on her face. "You are impossible! Look, Kate, I think you mean well, but your attitudes are out of step with modern life. I should have known you were selfish when I found out that you were involved with the ridiculous Tea Party idiots."

Catherine knew that she should be treading lightly, but her temper was now burning at full force. "That is your problem, Janice; you are just incapable of logical thought. It isn't selfish to want individuals to be responsible for their lives, instead of your idiotic concept of collective salvation. As I said, groups don't get out of bed to go to work in the morning; individuals do." She started to move towards Janice, to really get in her face, but caught herself and leaned back against the jamb. "The only way a society can function is if individuals who are able to do so, largely carry their own weight." Janice started to reply, but Catherine held up a finger to stop her. "No one on the conservative side, including the Tea Party, wants dirty water, starving kids, or wants to push granny over a cliff, and you damn well know it. What we are debating about is how to achieve the maximum good. If anyone is selfish, it is you and your progressive pals, that want government to make everything better so that you, as individuals, don't have any responsibility for helping anyone yourself. Regardless of what Progressives say, the people you say you care about are suffering under inadequate programs while government types waste millions on themselves."

Truly outraged, Janice's mouth dropped opened, her face stunned. "That is ridiculous, Kate; your precious rich people only give what they are made to give, to help the poor."

"You are wrong, Janice, and I think you know it. Look it up, Reporter Girl, the left is the group that doesn't give to charity unless you count one of their socialist causes as charity. Hell, many of the most outspoken people on your side of the argument can't even manage to pay taxes that they actually owe, regardless of your media buddies trying to say otherwise. What's-His-Name that you were talking about last night owes billions, and he won't pay. Anyway, the fact is that government is incapable of supporting what you want. The only way this country works is for all of us, as individuals, to make it go."

Catherine could see her partner was so upset she was shaking. She didn't mean for her comment to lead to such a battle, but she decided that she was tired of giving in when Janice responded negatively to her point of view.

"You are impossible. It is like talking to a wall."

"I am sick of these fights, Janice. I think you are nuts, and you think the same thing about me. Neither of us is going to change the other's point of view, so why are we doing this? It is not good for our relationship and it is unpleasant, so here is what I am going to do. I need to let Maggie back in and go to work. You need to make your flight, and we both just need to calm down."

"Fine! Run away. I know that you are a good person, Kate, but you are sadly misguided. You and your Tea Party friends are so misguided, in fact, that they're dangerous. I have been reading up on the story that I am going to New York to cover, and it is clear that your friends are going to end up being the cause of one heck of a lot of violence because average working people are not going to just accept the greed of the rich that you are always defending."

"I give up Sweetie. Like I said, we are just not going to agree."

Clearly livid, Janice swallowed her vitriol. "I guess not, Kate." Fighting her emotions, Janice grasped for the door handle behind her. "I guess that we are going to have to make some decisions about our lives. I will call you when I can."

Disappointed and fatalistic, Catherine shook her head, resigned to what was likely to occur. "Good bye, Janice. Have a good trip."

❧

Catherine sighed loudly with exasperation as she considered her lunch, an uninspired taco salad as she endured Jack prattling on with his usual flair. What the hell, she thought. I guess it must be National-Argue-With-Progs-day. She laid her fork down, rubbed her eyes, and rotated her head to work out the kinks she had earned by staring at her monitor all morning.

"Come on, Jack, give me a break. For one thing, you brought the subject up. For another, you could care less what the facts are. You care more about your viewpoint than anything else. You don't want to talk about facts because you lose that conversation every time. Instead, you change the subject, make it a joke, or just denigrate data sources you don't like, even when it comes from your own side."

Leaning back, he ran his fingers through his slightly too long blonde hair and smiled at her, his blue eyes twinkling with mischief. "You make it pretty hard to take you seriously, Kate. If what you are saying is true, everyone in government would have to be participating in the biggest cover up in world history. Are things screwed up? Sure. But things are always screwed up. It will turn out just fine in the end anyway. Just wait, you will see that I'm right."

Catherine snorted and picked up her fork again. Taking her chances, she speared her salad, and was surprised to find that it wasn't as bad as she had feared it would be. Looking back at Jack, she noticed his smug expression and sighed.

Swallowing, she looked at her lunch partner. "What planet are you living on Jack? You can't drive across town anymore without running into someone whining about something. The Solidarity Protests are getting worse every day, or does this little fact elude you?"

"So? It is an American right to complain about stuff. People like you have been saying doom and gloom stuff for years, and somehow we are still getting by." Obviously feeling pretty superior, he took a sip from his soda, and nodded at one of an endless string of nurses who were always flirting with him. "I am not saying that things are good, but I think Washington is trying. Don't you think we should give the administration a chance? "

Catherine snorted. "You are assuming that things are, in fact, business as usual, and that the country has the time for what DC calls trying. Look, I have been out of work for almost a year now." She pointed at him with her fork. "I had a little over a year of food stored up before I got laid off. Regardless of what you think about politics, can't you see how that food was a benefit for me?" Even if you don't think we are screwed as a country because of all of the overspending, and stupid foreign policy decisions over the last few decades, you cannot deny that it is good to at least try to be prepared for hard times."

As he shook his head, she decided that talking to Jack was like talking to a child. She wondered why she even bothered.

Jack smiled. "I am not saying it wasn't a good idea in your case, but people like you aren't helping. Your side goes around trying to scare everyone, saying the end is coming, with your commercials and talk radio. I am just saying it is bad for the economy." He took a drink of his soda and smiled at her. "We would have probably already had a full recovery by now if your side would shut up, and let the bailouts do what they are supposed to. You have to admit that scaring people is not helping. People need to start spending if the economy is going to recover."

Catherine rolled her eyes. She was officially completely frustrated with him. She knew it was a pointless discussion, but, as with Janice, she hated the idea that he would think he had won the argument.

"You are insane, Jack. For one thing, too many people like me are out of work to have a recovery. For another, any extra cash I have is going straight to getting ready for what is coming."

"See, that is my point exactly. The President said last night that the signs of recovery are already evident. Once the recovery package is approved over in Europe, it will get better."

Looking him in the eye, she continued pushing. She decided if nothing else, it was good practice. One had to be verbally agile when talking to people who were indoctrinated.

"That isn't based on anything, Jack. Do you have any facts that you can base an argument on?"

"No, Kate, I don't, I have better things to do with my time. I actually have a life. I go out with friends and have a good time. I am actually living, not freaked out all the time."

"You assume too much. Just because I choose to be an adult, doesn't mean I don't enjoy my life. You can be aware of what is going on in the world and still enjoy your life. I saw yesterday that there was another record dump of treasury paper. Everybody around the world is selling our treasuries. Do you know what that means to us?"

Spearing another bite of salad, she noticed that he looked a little uncomfortable and shrugged, now clearly wanting the conversation to end.

"It means that people are questioning our ability to repay our debt. What do the pinheads in DC do? They keep right on printing money, selling the notes to themselves, all the while handing out cash, hand over fist, to the Europeans."

Jack shrugged. As he prepared to leave, he took a bite of his chicken and nodded. "It was a good debate, Kate. I hope I was able to give you some hope."

Well, she thought, at least she didn't give him the last word.

Taking a final sip of his drink, his phone beeped with a text message. Glancing at the message, he stood and gave Catherine his fool proof patronizing look as he prepared to exit the cafeteria. "I have to make a phone call. I will talk to you later." He smiled down at her and continued. "I hope I didn't distress you too much.

I know you have been taken in by all the scare tactics from the Tea Party. All I can say is to trust me. It really will be ok."

Catherine rolled her eyes as he walked away from her, wishing that his text would have come sooner. I have had it with talking to morons, she thought. I have done my best to encourage people to get ready. There is nothing to do for it, I guess. She took another bite of her taco and picked up her iPhone to see what she could find to read while she finished her meal. She was halfway through a story about a likely Israeli attack on Iran when she thought she heard someone calling her name.

"Catherine, Catherine Danvers, right? Turning around to see who was calling, Catherine noticed the woman from the funeral approaching her. She was wearing scrubs and carrying a lunch tray.

Trying valiantly to swallow, she gave the woman a halfhearted look of welcome, motioning for her to take a seat as she smiled. "Sadie..." Not recalling the woman's last name, she looked suddenly embarrassed. "I am really sorry, but I suck at remembering names. I am afraid I don't recall what you said your last name is."

"Don't worry about it. It's Cline. What brings you to Presbyterian? I hope everyone is ok. Lord knows your family has had enough trouble for a lifetime."

"Well, for the moment, I work here. I am helping out in your IT department for a couple of months."

"Really? It is a small world I guess."

"It really is. I don't know why, but I sort of thought you would be in hiding someplace."

Sadie smiled awkwardly as she began to eat. "I probably should be, but I still have bills to pay, and jobs are not exactly easy to come by, so here I am." Realizing she had selected the same taco salad as Catherine, she commented. "Is that any good?"

Placing her iPhone on her tray, Catherine gave up on getting to read and smiled at the woman sitting with her. "It is better than it looks, actually."

Sadie took a tentative bite and followed that with two more. Catherine could see that Sadie was really feeling awkward, and decided she would get to know her a little better.

"So, Sadie, have you and Janice made any headway on your situation, or has she just been a pain, 'trying to get her scoop' as they say?"

"Actually, I didn't want to presume too much, but I was just thinking about asking you if she had said anything to you about it. I haven't heard from her, really. She left me a voice mail saying she would get with me about a time to sit down and go through things, but I haven't heard from her since."

"Really, I am surprised. On the way home from the funeral she was pretty hyped up about getting to talk to you. I can ask her for you, if you want. She is pretty single minded sometimes. She picked up an assignment in New York, covering the financial meltdown mess. She flew out this morning." Seeing Sadie's face fall slightly, Catherine could see that this information was not what Sadie wanted to hear. "I am sure she will be bugging you more than you will care for, when she gets back. I am sorry she didn't let you know she was going out of town."

"That's ok." Her voice shook a little, and she smiled weakly. Catherine realized that Sadie was really depending on getting Janice's help. "I was just hoping she could help me figure out more about the connection to Iran. I really don't understand why someone is trying so hard to..." Her voice broke again and she looked embarrassed. "I don't get why they want to kill me," she whispered. "These jerks are making my life miserable."

"I am so sorry, Sadie, and I am going to call her about this. She made you a promise, and she needs to follow up. Have the cops learned anything at all about what this is about?" Sadie sighed and looked down. Catherine realized that she had just asked about something that she shouldn't have. Embarrassed, she slapped her head with the palm of her hand.

"Oh God, there I go asking stuff that is none of my damn business. I'm sorry, Sadie. I just hate the bastards, too."

"It's ok, really. I really can't talk to my friends here. It makes them nervous or they just don't understand." She looked into Catherine's eyes. "I know that you do though. I am glad that you asked."

"OK, but I am sorry for my bluntness. People always tell me not to be so direct. I just get really pissed off at the way Middle Eastern guys treat women."

Sadie grabbed for Catherine's hand. "Please, it's ok; I am having a tough time with all of it. If you want to know the truth, I have had it with people tip-toeing around it. I need to be able to talk through this stuff. I really appreciate you caring." Sadie sighed again, and closed her eyes before continuing. "Actually, after what happened to your family, I should be the one shutting up and being sensitive. I am the last person who should be dumping on you. I know you have your own loss to deal with."

Catherine returned her gaze. "Look, Sadie, you didn't do anything to my family. You need to stop thinking that way. The primitive bastard who pulled that trigger hurt my family, so just stop. I don't want you to own that, Ok? Please, I like to keep my anger pure and aimed at the right targets."

Sadie nodded gratefully. "Ok, Catherine. Sure. You are really kind to say that, and I appreciate it. I am usually better at holding it together than this, at least here at work. I guess seeing you and thinking about my problems instead of my patients broke down my shield."

Catherine squeezed Sadie's hand, placed her other hand on top of the pile, and looked straight into her eyes. "Sadie, you are in Texas, not Iran. People here will not put up with that kind of woman-hating crap. Are the cops giving you any kind of protection?

"I am afraid not."

Catherine gasped. "Please tell me you are at least carrying a gun."

"In my car, weapons are not allowed on hospital property. The security guard walks me out when I leave. The cops don't have any budget to help me very much, but I am staying at a hotel until they catch the other guy involved in this."

Catherine reached into her purse and took out her little note pad and a pen. "Look, Sadie, I have to get back to work, but let's exchange numbers, etcetera. I want you to promise that you will call me if there is anything I can do, or if you just need to talk with someone. I carry too, and one of my best friends is a cop. I would really like to help you, if you will let me. Besides, ask anyone, I need as many friends as I can make. I am told that I don't exactly have a winning personality."

She was pleased to see Sadie's smile following her self-deprecating comment.

"Thank you, Catherine, you are really very kind. I don't believe that you are personality deficient at all, by the way."

"That is only because I can fake being a nice person for brief periods of time."

Sadie chortled softly as she wrote down her number. "I am really glad I saw you today. I absolutely will give you a call, but you have to promise that you will not let me interfere with anything that you may have going on."

"You have a deal."

"Good. I am glad we ran into each other. For some reason, I thought you might be a reporter like your friend." She said you were partners, so I was thinking that maybe you were a photographer or something like that."

"Nope, that is Janice's thing. I used to be an operations manager at American Airlines, but I got laid off about a year ago. Since then, I do pretty much whatever I have to do to make a buck."

Sadie nodded as if she understood, and gave her a probing look. "Oh, well that sounds interesting, too."

Catherine took another sip of her drink and stretched. "Not that interesting, actually, but it paid ok until it didn't. Actually, Janice and I are a couple. At least we were this morning, when I left for work." She chuckled sardonically at her little joke. Catherine took a sip from her drink to see how Sadie was going to react to her frank admission. She couldn't say why, but she liked this woman. To her surprise, Sadie simply extended her hand in formal introduction.

"It is really nice to meet you again, Catherine Danvers."

She took Sadie's hand and shook it briefly. "Well, today is looking up after all. I made a new friend. Lord knows that I need as many of those as I can manage."

"Well, I think that is true for all of us, isn't it?"

Catherine noticed that Sadie hesitated, wanting to say something, but she seemed to be unsure how to go about it.

"Is something wrong?"

Exhaling nervously, Sadie took a cleansing breath and looked at her new friend, chuckling nervously. "Well, it's not something I generally lead off with when I meet people, but I guess this is a far cry from being a normal introduction. I am a lesbian, too Catherine. I guess you can rest assured that I promise not to throw any rocks at you or submit your name for immediate re-education. It's just that I am not seeing anyone, so I wouldn't want to make you or Janice feel weird or anything. I am just trying to get through each day at this point."

Catherine sat back in her seat, her expression brightening. "Thanks for telling me that. I will restrain myself from throwing any rocks as well, and I agree that it is always a good thing to avoid re-education camps. My friends all call me Kate, by the way."

Sadie chuckled and exhaled some of her uncertainty. "Really, you prefer Kate? That is a shame; I think Catherine is such a pretty name."

Chuckling again Catherine smiled at Sadie. "You can use Catherine, if you like. It isn't like I don't like my name; I guess I am just lazy."

"I don't believe you. You don't seem the type. You strike me as a pretty driven personality. After all, you are doing whatever you have to do to keep food on the table."

"I do what I can." Catherine smiled and got up to go. "I should get back to work. Nice seeing you again, Sadie."

"You too, Catherine, I will give you a call. Maybe we can have lunch occasionally."

Catherine smiled. "I would like that a lot, actually." Sighing, Catherine got up, grabbed her purse and her tray, and smiling her goodbye, headed for the tray return.

Chapter 16
Shadows

As the sun streamed through the less-than-spotless bedroom widows of the Spartan space that was Matt's bedroom, Megan rolled over to see her man was missing. Scowling past the crumpled mass of the well-worn comforter, towards the door, she sat up in bed. She really enjoyed a good night's sleep for once, regardless of having to make due with one of Matt's work-out shirts to sleep in. Megan realized she really needed to implement some redundancy around her basic needs in his apartment. Although she didn't stay here often, it could not hurt to have what she needed. As the word redundancy registered in her conscious mind, the thought brought a smile to her face, recalling what her father must have told her a thousand times. "Two is one and one is none." It is funny, she thought, how her dad's old saying had much more meaning now than it had when he first said it.

She padded over to the bathroom and turned on the hot water for a nice shower. Smiling, she snorted on the state of Matt's world. His apartment would have been right at home in the nineteen eighties. It was no surprise that he kept everything in good condition, and the apartment was generally very clean -- although dated.

Within a matter of minutes the steam was billowing out over the top of the glass partition of the shower stall and Matt's shirt lay crumpled on the tile floor. She stepped into the liquid embrace, luxuriating as jets of hot water worked to revive and awaken her body. Reaching for the soap, she rolled her eyes, and realized that today she was just going to have to cope with the deodorant soap and the all-in-one shampoo available to her in Matt's product caddy.

"Oh, my God, what am I going to do now? My job, my holdings, and maybe more, are all in play now." She worked the angles in her mind. Everything I am doing in my life, other than Matt, is dependent on my job and Sterns. If I leave the firm, they will definitely have every reason to be concerned with what I know, or what I may do, that could negatively impact them. If I continue on as I have, then I must accept some degree of risk.

Turning around to let the jets of water pound against her skull and neck, she tried to find a way to make the scenario work for her. Perhaps, she thought, staying the course would allow her to buy the time she needed to make arrangements. Pondering that thought further, however, she decided that it wasn't exactly true. She couldn't really wind things down without the firm taking notice. Actions like liquidating her positions and concluding the lease on her apartment would definitely register with security. They would definitely look at that sort of activity. Time would gain her additional cash, but only marginally so. She would have to continue her existing spending patterns to avoid raising the level of suspicion beyond what it clearly was already.

Almost without thought, she moved the bar of soap across her body, cleansing her skin as her mind worked to negate her problems. Enjoying the sensation of hot water coursing over her body, her mind continued to examine the facets of her situation from the firm's perspective.

The real catalyst, she decided, was the economy and the timing and speed of deterioration. If a collapse is really going to happen then my job will be of marginal value. Wall Street will definitely be a focal point for blame and people like Richard and I will make excellent distractions to take the brunt of the heat long enough to give the Board the cover they need.

Standing directly under the torrent of water, she blanked her mind, focusing on how pleasant the cascade of water felt, as she rinsed the suds out of her hair. Reaching back, she turned the handle to the off position, and reached over to the shower door for her towel. Bending over, her hair hung down almost to her ankles. She pinned her towel between her knees as she twisted her hair, wringing out as much water as she could. Grabbing for the towel, she put her hair up in a turban and stepped out of the shower. Taking a step to the counter across from the shower stall she smiled as she caught her reflection in the mirror as she wrapped a second towel around herself and turned back towards the bedroom.

"OK, it's time to make a move." With little upside and a ton of downside, she realized that the time to act was rapidly approaching. "The question is how to do that while at the same time appear not to be making a play."

She finished her morning routine and dressed quickly, not bothering to do much with her hair or makeup. As Megan entered the tiny apartment's living area, she savored the smell of sausage and eggs, and decided Matt was quite a catch. She walked up behind him as he sat eating at the diminutive little bar adjacent to his tiny little kitchen. "I hope I get some of that. Surprise, surprise, I am absolutely starved after last night."

Spinning around to face her, Matt gave her a wicked grin. "Good Morning, Babe, or should I say good afternoon?"

She kissed his forehead and smiled as Matt continued. "I figured that you needed the sleep after last week's drama, not to mention last night's exercise, so I let you rest." He stood, and she felt herself pulled into his embrace. Closing her eyes, she felt the caress of his lips, felt his tongue seeking hers. She sighed with pleasure as his hands took her face between them.

"I love you, Meg."

Releasing her face, he moved her onto the barstool next to him.

"Don't go anywhere; I will fix you up." A moment later, she took the cup of coffee he handed her through the pass through to the little kitchen. "I hope you can live with your eggs sunny side up. I am out of milk."

"Sounds perfect, thank you." Sighing, she relished the momentary contentment, experiencing it fully. She watched him cook, immensely enjoying the shape of his back, his athletic build, as powerful muscles moved under his t-shirt. Two minutes later, he handed her a plate filled with the sort of breakfast her father made for her every day before school.

"I went out this morning. I left through the fire escape on the fifth floor. Our friends were parked in a van just down the street in front of the bodega on the corner." He handed her a storage locker key.

She tilted her head questioningly as she toyed with the elastic band threaded through the hole at the top of the key. "Thanks, what is this, and what's up with the elastic loop?"

"I want you to keep it on you at all times. The loop is so you can wear it around your ankle. You never know when your pals outside might want to take you somewhere you would just as soon not visit. The key is to a storage locker I rented. It has a little cash, some clothes and things, as well as a purse with a prepaid cell and debit card." She noticed that he reached into the sack next to him for one last item. "It's a burn phone. You need to keep it with you as well. If anything gets hinky, you will have to jettison everything." He looked searchingly into her eyes. She returned his gaze and nodded that she understood.

"If you ever think that things are headed south, hit the number three to speed dial a text me with a 911. Do what you have to do to get some separation from your shadows, and go immediately to the locker. There is a gym next door. Go in there and change clothes, dump your cell, your purse, everything. You can't be sure if they have a transmitter embedded somewhere. They may not be that slick, but we can't take that chance. Also, here is an address and phone number to a small used car lot in New Brunswick. I served with the owner in Iraq. Ask for a guy named Booker. He can fix you up with a car for a few days. The other address is for a motel off Highway One, near Princeton. That will be our rally point. Memorize this stuff so that you can burn the note."

Matt got to his feet and took their plates to the sink, speaking over his shoulder as he went. "One other thing, you need to realize that they are going to be watching you very closely. You already know that you cannot deviate from your usual patterns, but you will need to be very careful about what you say to people at the office, in public, and even at home. Assume that you are being recorded at all times and do what you can to make them believe what we want them to believe. Also, don't forget to text me at ten, one, and at four, every day with the codes we talked about. Remember, send the emergency code if you get into a jam. And keep this device," he handed her a small transceiver, "on you all the time."

"Damn, Matt, you really went all out here. How much money do I owe you for all of this stuff?"

She noticed that he just smiled. "I will let you know. Maybe it is an investment. I love you, so what can I do? Besides, if the suits in all the big trading concerns think the party is over, then the likelihood is that things are about to get very interesting. We need to be as ready as we can. The next question is, what do you want to do next?"

Megan just blinked as she carefully laid down her fork. Turning to face him directly, Megan realized she really was getting scared. "I don't know. Matt. Living here and having this life was what I always wanted my life to be. I, I, don't know what to do, really. I guess I should go back home to Texas."

As she sat there blinking in her moment of realization, she felt Matt's arms encircle her as he stood behind her, enveloping her with support. "All this crap is nice, but it's just stuff, Babe. What I am asking you is if you want me to go with you to Texas? You are the smartest, most vibrant, strongest willed woman I have ever known. I want to be with you, but only if that is what you want too. I will get you safely home either way, but I am not the kind of man to leverage what is going on, by forcing you into something. You are a force of nature, Meg, and I know that hooking up with me hasn't been a good fit for your career, but all of that is about to change. "

Megan pulled back enough to look into his eyes. "I love you too, Matt, I always have. Do you want to leave New York? What about your family? I know that your mom and dad died during Nine-Eleven, but you have your aunts and uncles."

She felt Matt's lips caress her forehead. "I won't be staying here regardless, Meg. I have tried to get my people to see what's coming for a couple of years now. They just cannot accept it. There is a time when you just have to go, regardless of what others do."

Burying her face in his chest, she shuddered, overwhelmed with emotions. She was fully aware that, emotionally, she was grieving for the loss of her dream life. She was distraught over what she believed would be happening soon, and realized that the time had finally come for her to make a decision about what future she would have with Matt. She was amazed to realize he would so willingly discard his current life for her. Inhaling his scent as she cleared her mind, she knew with certainty what she wanted. She wanted to spend the rest of her life with him. The thought blossomed in her mind, and she crushed her face even tighter against his chest, as tears of joy threatened to overwhelm her. They remained motionless for several minutes, when finally, she spoke into his chest.

"Just so you know, I may make a terrible wife, and I don't know the first thing about babies." She felt as much as heard him chuckle. Releasing him, she smiled her contentment up at him. "Ok then, Matt Regan, if you are nuts enough to hook up with me, that's your problem. I guess Texas it is then!"

"Noted. Hooking up with you is one problem I will enjoy working through."

Megan smiled. "Good, that is one decision out of the way."

Matt nodded, but gave her a serious look. "Have you given any thought to how you're going to deal with your investments? What are you going to do about Sterns and Becker?"

"I have been, but that's a bit of a problem. I sort of need to have my cake and eat it too. I can't make a move without it being noticed. I guess the only angle that would work would be to make any moves after making our exit."

"It's no big deal to me either way, Babe. I love you for your body, not your money."

She stared at him in mock protest before responding. "I was just about to say something very much like that, so it seems we deserve each other."

❧

Riding the elevator up to her floor, Megan thought the same thing she always thought during her elevator ride. She hated Mondays. She didn't mind the weekend update briefing on Monday mornings, but she despised the weekly meeting with Ms. Tanner about her current projects. She realized that both of them knew full well what the game was. Barbara Tanner resented Megan and was determined to find any angle she could to sabotage her efforts. Megan, of course, knew that she delighted in making Tanner look silly with true, but misleading updates. "Oh my God, I hate that cow," she whispered. The doors opened, and she edged out from between two guys that were obviously annoyed by her need to exit before them. Crossing the foyer, she nodded politely to the receptionist and headed back towards the comfort of her corner office. As she progressed past where the cube dwellers lived, she decided the weekend really had made a difference in her day-to-day existence. Noticing Luther Sterling, she felt the tingle of fear pass through her as she moved past him on her way past the executive kitchen.

"Good Morning, Luther!" She smiled her most winning greeting at the man. "Did you have a nice weekend?"

Luther smiled in reply.

Megan noticed that his smile did not quite reach his eyes. "Why, yes I did, Young Lady. Thank you for asking. No doubt you were able to enjoy a nice weekend away from the office for once?"

"It was pretty nice, but too short, as always. I had a date with an old friend." She smiled warmly and moved on towards her office, hoping that he would not be able to perceive her real feelings. "Have a great day, Luther."

As she approached her office, she could feel a twitch behind her right eye. Fumbling to select her office key, she noticed the door was ajar. Taking in a breath, she felt a shiver run through her body. She was sure she had shut and locked the door when she left on Friday. Gathering her will, she dropped the keys back into her purse, and breezed into her domain. She realized immediately that someone was sitting in her chair with their back to her. She hung her coat on the coat stand as the large leather chair spun around to reveal the occupant to be none other than John David Sterns.

"Good Morning, Ms. Danvers." He smiled warmly at her. "I trust your weekend was a pleasant one, yes?"

She produced a look of surprise, thinking he already knew exactly what kind of weekend she had. She suddenly felt as if someone had just pored ice-water down her back, but followed the expression with a warm smile of her own. "It was a little quiet, but yes, it was very nice. Is there anything I can get for you, Sir? It is not every day that my chairman of the board comes to me. I am pretty sure I am supposed to make time to come to you."

She noticed that, even now, the man before her had a manner that was disarming. He made one want to follow his lead. From his cultured demeanor, to his background as a military officer in Viet Nam, he was the kind of man you wanted to follow. "Won't you come in, Ms. Danvers, and please shut the door."

She followed the instructions and took the seat across from him, the seat that Richard had occupied the Friday before. She reached into her bag for her note pad, as if to take dictation. "What can I do for you, Sir?"

She could see he studied her closely for a moment or two before speaking. "I have a matter of some concern, I am afraid. I would be very grateful if you could look into it for me." Once again she could feel his charm invade her senses. He was very, very good at this game, she realized. He obviously came to her office to reinforce the notion that he controlled everything about her life, and he wanted her to know it. At the same time he was almost overwhelming her with his personal charisma. "It concerns our young Mr. Blake, I fear. He has yet to come in this morning, and I have reason to believe he may present a problem for us." As Megan listened, she noted that Sterling steepled his fingers across his chest as he peered deeply into Megan's eyes. "He trusts you, I believe. Is that true, Ms. Danvers?"

"Yes, Sir, I believe he does. I am afraid I do not understand in what way Rich... Mr. Blake is a potential problem. Can you tell me what I should be looking for?" Megan decided her best play would be to go with an expression of ambition. After all, she was noted for that attribute.

Sterling nodded almost imperceptibly and moved a file over to her. "Please, Ms. Danvers, take a look, and tell me what you deduce. Have you any thoughts or insights on the matter? You have a keen and observant mind, Ms. Danvers. You may well derive something I missed."

Megan scanned the file to see that Richard had done just what she had been thinking about. He had sold his positions and moved his financial assets out of the market.

She felt as though she would shake apart, and was all but certain that she likely paled, her heartbeat racing, every neuron firing. Forcing her body to remain calm, she continued to read as she moved her right hand casually to her pocket, her fingers clutching her burn phone as she sat forward in her chair. Although terrified, her father's words came to her once again. She thought, Go big or go home.

A moment, later she looked up to face the old man, electing to stand her ground, one warrior facing another. "It seems, Ms. Danvers, that Mr. Blake seems to have grown wearisome of our company."

She looked at him thoughtfully. "You, of course, already know that I too thought to make a similar move, but then thought better of it. I took a regrettable loss last week as a result. May I assume, Mr. Sterns, that whatever intel we retrieved from the honorable Mr. Tibman had something to do with things not looking all that promising in Europe?" She tilted her head subtly to the right to project the image of trying to deduce what secrets the old man may be hiding.

"Astute, Ms. Danvers, have you a theory on how it is, exactly, that the two of you happened to have made such assessments without the benefit of hearing the conversations between Mr. Sykes and Mr. Tibman?"

"I would not presume to speak for Mr. Blake, as I had no idea that he was doing anything specific with his positions. For my part, I can say that I think the end game is upon us as far as Europe is concerned. One doesn't need to hear specifics to reach that conclusion. One merely need look out the window to see that events are beginning to reach a climax. Mr. Blake did relay that you, in fact, mentioned to him that Mr. Tibman had attended a secure briefing related to these matters. One need not know what was said, just that the meetings took place, and that the players surrounding the matter were taking things seriously. For this reason, I decided to go short."

Sterling leaned back, studying her carefully for several long minutes. "So, am I to understand that you, in fact, put in play approximately two thirds of your personal holdings on a hunch based solely on the reactions you witnessed from power players as they reacted to the events taking shape around us?"

She smirked, her mouth forming into a cocky grin. "Yes."

"May I inquire why you then reversed yourself by the end of the week?"

She looked embarrassed, but sanguine as she nodded out the window to the people on the street. "Because, Sir, we are the focal point for their anger. If things collapse, there will be no one who will be able to stop it." She looked forcefully into his eyes. "They will come for us with pitchforks, Sir. Politicians like Tibman will be happy to offer us up. I don't own an island to escape to, so I decided to think about it further."

Sterling chuckled as he rose from her plush chair. Megan followed his lead and also stood.

"Very well, thank you, Ms. Danvers. I am moving you onto my Board. You will report directly to me. I should like to have more of these conversations, as I do think you have a keen sense about things. I will have my assistant get with you about your new title." Sterling headed for the door, but stopped short before reaching it. "Ms. Danvers, do see what you may learn of our Mr. Blake. I rather fear he may be keeping company with some federal agents. Perhaps you can entice the young man to meet you somewhere cozy. Oh, one final thing, Ms. Danvers. Do move your positions into precious metals for the next few months, won't you? Yes. I think that might be most wise." She noted now that his enticing grin was, in fact, fearsome in its mildness.

As she closed the office door behind Mr. Sterns, her mind raced. Exhaling, she noted that the adrenaline was dissipating rapidly; leaving her weak kneed and light headed. She thought she had better sit down before collapsing. She could not be sure, but it seemed as if she had possibly just pulled off the most amazing coup of all time. Should she be willing to burn Richard, she would rise to a position that would allow her a great deal more flexibility, should things go south in the coming weeks. She knew she could check in with him on Nantucket to see if he was up there, but the reality of the situation was clear. Like Richard, she would have to make her move soon.

Reclaiming her chair, Megan sat down and stared out the window, thinking about what had just taken place. She wondered if he was trying to give her a message. If Richard was working with the Feds, that association could be another angle of escape. Regardless, the old man just gave her the green light to achieve the liquidity she needed, regardless of which scenario she chose to pursue.

Megan spun her chair around and again, using her portfolio as a foot rest, she opened her left file drawer, propped her feet up, and leaned back to rework the scenario in her mind. Pondering the problem, she realized that the key variable in this situation was no longer the timing of the collapse, but rather what she wanted for her life, and what consequences she was willing to accept for her decisions. The old man had just changed the equation, but whether or not he could be trusted was still indeterminate, regardless of her brand new promotion. Her new role changed what was possible, but her motivations were still unchanged. She loved the life she was leading, but this life was just not going to continue, regardless of factors under her control. She knew if she stayed it would be at the cost of her soul. Smiling to herself, she realized that she was deeply in love with Matt. She would miss the excitement of the deal, but the thought of making a life with Matt was intoxicating.

Sighing, she put her strategic thoughts aside for a moment as the thought occurred to her that she had some immediate concerns to ponder as well as the big picture. Her thoughts turning to tactical considerations, she suddenly laughed out loud.

"Well, Barbara, you are going to have a stroke when you hear about my new role. I would give anything to see the look on your face when you find out." Pulling her iPad out from her briefcase, she tapped it to bring the screen to life, and then tapped again to reach her assistant. "Liz, please send my regrets to Ms. Tanner for today's morning meeting. Tell her that I have another engagement and will not be attending."

She could hear the alarmed surprise in her assistant's voice, and it made her smile. "I will call her immediately. Who shall I place on your appointment calendar to cover you during the morning meeting?"

"No one, Liz, please leave it empty. You are quite right that she will definitely check, so when she calls, please decline the call. Tell her I am with someone."

"Of course, Ms. Danvers, I will take care of it right now." Megan tapped the device in her ear and smiled. Megan could tell in her assistant's voice that Liz was going to enjoy this little game also. Suddenly in an excellent mood, she reached for her remote. Time to see what the news is saying before getting an early start on Stratfor and the other tracking sites she considered as part of her daily regimen.

The screen came to life displaying Fox News just as it had on Friday when she left work. Megan started to change channels, but hesitated as the background showed an enormous European crowd that had apparently just managed to take over some sort of armored vehicle on the square in front of a parliament building in Athens. The caption below the reporter read:

"Greece Joins Cyprus - Expelled from the Eurozone – Other Nations expected to follow."

Megan turned up the sound to hear what was being said. "... Greece debt, like Cyprus before it, was downgraded to junk status by all of the major rating agencies. Greek debt was once again downgraded again this morning, from CCC to CC by Moody's, Standard & Poor's, and Fitch. Ministers meeting in Brussels confirmed that in accordance with last summer's bail out accords, actions meant to help Mediterranean nations avoid default were clearly not working as intended. Even last fall's confiscation of private savings accounts failed to stem the collapse. The Eurozone, led by Germany and France, voted overnight to remove Greece and Cyprus from the Eurozone in an effort to firewall the other Eurozone nations from the steadily mounting contagion caused by the utter failure of the appointed governments in both nations to stop the financial hemorrhaging."

Megan picked up her tablet again and tapped the icon for Stratfor. As the site displayed, she could see there was a special banner line that exclaimed:

"Eurozone crumbling. Greece expelled! Belgium, Ireland, Italy, and Slovenia downgraded by the major rating agencies."

Looking back at the television for a moment, she saw the images of rioters in Italy burning German Flags and their leaders in effigy. She immediately reached over and tapped her iPad to dial Dan Marley's personal phone number.

"Dan, are you watching Europe?

"Yes I am, as a matter of fact. Looks like this one could be pretty bad."

"Thank you, Captain Understatement. Look, I need to move everything into metal. I need you to do it right now; do you read me, Dan?"

"What do you mean by everything, Megan? Don't get me wrong, I am very happy to receive your commissions for recent activity, but are you sure? I agree that this isn't good, but I can assure you that the Europeans, and for that matter, our own Fed will not allow this to spread."

"Dan, you are a good guy, and I am telling you I need you to liquidate my positions as fast as you can. If you are smart, you will follow my lead and get out now before this sinks in."

"Um, ok, Megan, but you are taking one heck of a risk here. This kind of thing can change course for any number of reasons.

For one thing, the governments in Europe and the US cannot afford to allow this to happen. Do you want me to stay with the metal stocks you have now?"

"Actually Dan, I am glad you said that. I want actual metal. Send it to my folk's house in Texas. When you have a pen, I will give you the address."

Listening as he fumbled for the pen, she could hear his dismay, his whisper not sufficiently soft to avoid her being able to hear it.

"Unbelievable."

"Ok, Megan, go ahead."

"It's Route One, Box 30 H, Mineral Wells, Texas, 76068."

"Ok, I have it. I will do it right now. The shipping alone is going to be pricy."

"I don't care, Dan. In fact, why don't you overnight it and if you can, disguise it as something other than what it is. We wouldn't want it to go astray, now would we?

"You are freaking me out here, Megan. Do you have something you can share?"

"Give me a break, Dan; if my actions aren't enough of a hint, then I have no idea what to tell you. One more thing, I need a favor. Can you send over four or five one ounce gold coins and say a couple hundred in silver to my apartment this afternoon. I wouldn't mind at all, by the way, if you happened to misplace my folks address. My apartment here would be a perfect address for your filing."

"Sure, Megan, consider it done. I have to tell you, though; I think you just spoiled my morning. Now I am going to worry about whether you are nuts or not."

"Good Luck, Dan. You are always my guy for any investing I do, so take care of yourself." She tapped the device in her ear and went back to her websites so that she could give the old man her assessment with some actual data behind it. As she watched, she wondered if the buildings around her, and the cars parked outside the building she was sitting in would soon be burning. Would the people on the sidewalk below soon look like those on the television screen, fighting with security officers for control of military equipment?

Chapter 17
Mea Culpa

Annie sighed as she watched Mr. Davis get out of his car. She decided if she was going to have to talk to Russ's dad, she would much rather the conversation be outside in the parking lot than here inside, with everyone listening. She grabbed her purse, put a dollar bill on the table, and headed for the door. She barely made it out the door as he came up on her.

"Where are you going, Annie Girl? I saw your car, and, and, well Russ called me about an hour ago, and asked me to keep an eye out for you. Are you kids ok?"

"We had a fight, Mr. Davis. We both got pretty mad, and I had to get some air. Russ is so stubborn. Anyway, that's all there is to it."

"Ok, it ain't none of my business, other than I just want you youngins to be happy and all. You want to tell me who that black guy was that was in there drinking coffee with you?"

Annie rolled her eyes in exasperation, but knew she needed to keep it together. "He is a police officer here in town. He was investigating that murder across the street." She pointed to the apartments. "We went to high school together in Mineral Wells. He just happened to be here when I arrived." She thought that was a clever excuse. It was mostly true, at least. She knew full well that what she'd done was wrong, but she wasn't about to tell Jack Davis about it.

"Alright, Annie, like I said, it ain't my business, Girl, but you best be calling your husband now. You kids let me know if there is anything I can do for you. It's tough times these days, but my boy ain't afraid of no hard work. It'll turn out alright in the end."

"Yes Sir, Mr. Davis, I will call him."

"That's a good girl. You do that, and don't forget that you should be calling me, Dad. You are a Davis girl now, and I look after my own."

Annie smiled at him and waved good bye, as she mentally smirked. It would be a cold day in hell before she would call him, dad. By comparison, there was no way he came anywhere close to deserving that title. Annie walked over to her car, engaging the keyless entry when she got close enough. Fighting back her tears, she put the key in the ignition, and decided it was time to head for home, hoping that Russ would be in a better mood.

"Dear Lord, I really screwed up tonight. Can you please forgive me? I don't think that I would have betrayed my husband, really, but I know just thinking about it counts, so I am asking, in Jesus's name, that you help me be a better wife." As she turned right on to Van Buren, she thought about calling Russell, but decided that waiting until she got home was best.

"Also, Father, if there is anything you can do to help Russ and I get past our troubles, we could really use the help. It has been really hard, and we need to be together to get through it all. In Christ's name, I pray, amen."

Annie knew that it was going to be tough, but she decided that she felt a lot better after saying the prayer. After all, God could fix anything if you put your trust in him. She decided that she wasn't going to worry about their financial problems any more. She and Russ were doing their best and, one way or another, it would turn out ok for them. Her mom always said that God might not give you what you want, but he would absolutely give you what you needed, if you asked him with love in your heart.

With that thought, Annie turned into her driveway to find that the pickup was gone. Disappointed, she went into the house and let Bridgett out. Getting up her nerve, she dialed her husband's cell phone number. The phone rang once, then twice, and finally a third time. She sighed, thinking that he was screening her, but then she heard their truck pull up outside. Annie closed her eyes for a moment, gathered strength, and waited.

She stared at the front door, hoping that, somehow, things would turn out alright. OK, Annie, when he comes through the door, the first thing needs to be an apology about not talking to him about the baby before telling Megan. Her heart pounding, she heard Russell's key in the lock and watched the doorknob rotate.

Russ walked through the door. "Annie?" To her amazement she saw that he was carrying flowers. "Oh, you were waiting for me." He walked over and stood before her. Taking the flowers, she smiled weakly at him. She looked up at him through the bouquet, blinking in surprise at his gesture. Her heart jumped in her chest. She didn't know what to expect, but seeing him like this really was a blessing. He was calm and contrite.

"I'm sorry, Annie. I haven't been much of a husband lately, and I don't blame you for not trusting me about the baby or anything else, for that matter."

Stunned, she completely forgot what she was going to say, much less say it. "Russ, I'm glad you came home. I'm sorry too. I suck as a wife. I should have told you first thing. I know how hard you have been working to find a job to bring money into this house." She saw that his eyes were glistening with tears, unshed. Seeing his expression, she now desperately sought his approval as she peered up at him through dark lashes. "Are you happy about the baby?"

She found herself surprised once again as Russell rushed to her, taking the flowers back, and dropping them onto the coffee table. She could feel herself hoisted into the air as he swept her into his arms, kissing her deeply. She felt the wetness of his tears as they joined with hers.

"Of course, I'm happy," he whispered. I know the timing isn't the best, but I love you, and nothing could make me happier." He set her back on her feet and looked at her. "I love you, and I don't care what I have to do. I am going to find a way to take care of you and our baby. I will make that happen if I have to pick up trash or mow lawns. Whatever it takes, I will do it. Do you understand, Sweetheart?"

She smiled again, nodding that she did. "I love you Russ, and, I promise to never keep anything from you again. Let's just start fresh right here, right now. The past is the past, ok? What do you say? Can we just forget the last few months?"

"Done, Annie, but I mean it. I realized something tonight. I am my own worst enemy. I met a guy who made me realize how stupid I have been."

Annie blinked, not understanding. "I don't know what you mean, but can you tell me about it while I fix us something for dinner? I really need to eat something; I am getting light-headed."

"Oh my God, Sweetheart, sit down, Annie. I will bring you something. I had a hamburger at this little diner." Smiling more broadly, she watched him head for the little kitchen to see what he could find to feed his wife.

"Russ, just heat me up some of that soup from last night. I am a little nauseous anyway."

"Are you sure? I can make you a nice hoagie if you want."

"Really, the soup will be perfect; but you can let Bridget back in if you want."

She heard him move to the back porch. "Sure, Honey."

The sound of the back door opening was soon followed by the scramble of little paws on the linoleum floor. Within moments, she felt Bridget's front paws on her legs begging for attention. "Easy girl, get down." Smiling, she lifted her eyes to look through her ceiling to what lay beyond. "Thank you Lord. Thank you for helping us tonight." She whispered her thanks. As she sat there, she thought she could almost feel the presence of something good surrounding her. Suddenly, she felt the weight she had been carrying lift from her shoulders. She felt a little sick, but felt warm inside, regardless. She knew that, somehow, everything would be alright now. She decided right then that it was her job to make sure her little family stayed as close to God as she could manage. Smiling at her newfound hopefulness, she sighed, letting out another breath of tension as she heard the ding of the microwave, announcing that her food was ready. Russell came back to the little dining room with her best tray, atop of which was a steaming bowl of the home made beef soup she had made two nights ago. She smiled as she noticed he had carefully displayed some crackers on a plate under the soup bowl, and had folded a paper towel into a nice triangle with a spoon neatly laid on top of it. He placed a glass of ice water beside her. To her surprise, he even cut up a lemon, for her.

"Oh, Russ," she giggled at his attempt at domesticity. "This is perfect. You are very sweet." She picked up the spoon, but stopped herself. "Honey, can you say a quick prayer for us? I think we need to get better at that sort of thing."

She noticed a brief look of panic on his face, but he smiled almost immediately at her and nodded. "Dear Lord, please forgive us of our sins and bless this food and this house, that we may do your will, and be the people you want us to be. Amen."

Annie could feel herself smiling at her husband from the deepest parts of her being. "Thank you, Russ. I love you. We are going to be ok now."

He smiled back at her and laid out two twenty dollar bills on the table. "Here, Annie, we are going to need to start putting back some money to get you some clothes for when you get bigger. Let's put whatever we can into the drawer of your nightstand. We take care of us first, and then we can worry about student loans and truck payments. Maybe I can find a way to trade out of the truck and get something older."

"Where did you get forty dollars, Russ?"

"That was what I was going to tell you. When you left I wanted to follow you, but I ended up just driving. I had to clear my head, you know? I needed some time to think, and I was on Van Buren, so I just kept going. I don't know why, just that something kept me moving down the highway. Anyway, I ended up in Dover. I stopped at this little café to eat. I was really upset, Annie. I was mad at just about everyone and everything. Anyway, the people there were really nice. It really felt homey, so I guess I relaxed a little. Then, as I was about to come back home, this guy came in, saying he was in a real jam, and would pay one hundred and fifty dollars if anyone who knew how to weld, could help him out,."

"And you jumped up to help him?"

"I said I could do it, and we went down the street. He had a broken hitch. The guy really overloaded his trailer, and, I straightened it all out, and welded some scrap metal to stiffen it some. Anyway, the guy was telling me about selling just about everything to get out from under a big fancy house. He kind of did what we did. He bought more than he should have and got laid off. He said that he was mad at first, because he was old enough that it was tough to find work."

"Is he going to be ok, then?"

"Yes, I think so. He was really a pretty together old dude. He had to sell some sweet old cars and stuff, but he said that if he could get to OKC to sell what he had left in the trailer he would be good. A guy was going to give him enough cash to get him out of that house, so he could get something that he could afford." Annie felt Russell gently lift her chin to look up at him. "He said to know what was important in life. Girl, you are what is important to me."

"You are everything to me, too, Russ. I realized that while I was out, and that I was going to find a way to make it all work." Happier than she had been in months, she kissed her husband as she used her finger nails to roam through his hair, pulling him closer to her. "Actually, I will do the dishes in the morning. Let's go to bed." She stood smiling at Russell, and taking his hands in hers, she led him to the bedroom.

❧

As she came to consciousness, Annie realized that it must be at least eight thirty or nine o'clock, because the sun was already shining brightly. Content, she realized that the past week since their fight had been one of the best in her life, regardless of the challenges facing her family. Russell even earned another three hundred dollars yesterday, after going back to see if Mr. Dickerson needed any more work done.

Sitting up, she realized that not only was Bridgett on the bed again, and hogging more of her fair share of real-estate, but she was completely naked again. Embarrassed, she sighed with happiness as she recalled how her nudity came to be. Russell was back to being the husband she needed and she could not be happier, regardless of what was going on in the world.

She kicked aside the blankets and quickly moved toward the bathroom. Following a nice shower and now fully dressed, she looked over to see Russ and Bridgett still comfortably snoozing away. She smiled and moved into the kitchen to make breakfast. "Thank you for the day, Father. Please bless my hands to thy work, and this day to thy service."

It did not take her long before she had filled the entire house with the smell of fresh coffee and bacon. As she buttered some bread for toast she could hear Russell stirring in the bedroom. Humming as she reached for the carton of eggs, she heard Russell turn on the TV.

"Good morning, Beautiful. I love you! That smells really wonderful, by the way."

"I know that the bacon is really expensive, but it is Sunday, and I wanted to celebrate your hard work all week."

She reached over to fill up a cup with coffee, and turned the bacon again to keep it from burning. Noticing that the coffee was ready, she poured a cup and headed for the parlor to give it to her husband. Glancing at her, he smiled appreciatively.

She returned his smile with one of her own. "How many eggs do you want? Are you hungry?"

Flipping channels, he smiled up at her and took the cup. "Thanks, Honey. Two would be great. I am going to go out today and find some way to make a buck or two. Maybe tomorrow I can still get in over at the university maintenance yard."

"Whatever you do will be perfect. I will have your eggs in just a sec." With that, she moved back toward the kitchen to finish up their breakfast. She placed the bacon, toast and eggs on a plate and took them to the table. Returning for the glasses and a carton of juice, she heard Russell gasp at something on the news.

"Annie, come in here, Sweetheart. You need to see this."

She sat the glasses and the orange juice on the table and moved towards the sound of the solemn toned commentators.

As she entered the room, the first thing she noticed was the serious expression on her husband's face.

He looked up at her, his eyes wide with alarm. "It looks like Europe is done. They said something about more downgrades and kicking people out of the Eurozone. Rioters are taking shots at cops and stuff in Athens, Rome, and some other places."

"Oh my God, Russ, turn it up."

Looking from Russell to the TV, Annie was stunned at the grave expression of the commentator. "...the Fitch Rating system, much like the criteria utilized by Moody's and Standard & Poor's, are blaming their revisions today, on an unprecedented deterioration in the overall economic outlook in Europe, in general, and in the Mediterranean countries, in particular. Ministers in Brussels are pointing to the complete absence of any form of credible financial firewall against the contagion now engulfing Greece, Cyprus, and Italy. At this point, it really is a self-fulfilling liquidity crisis. Once confidence is gone, it is gone. People throughout the Eurozone are more than reluctant to part with any cash that they may have. Back to you, Cynthia."

"The situation sounds serious, Bill. Have your contacts given you any insight into what the ministry plans to do to restore confidence?"

"That is the key to things here, Cynthia. The rioters on the streets are saying they are through listening to platitudes from ministry officials. Protesters here are saying they will stop when they receive what they were promised by their governments. One economist I spoke to late last night had this to say..."

Annie and Russell sat staring at their television screen as the image of a reporter, standing on what appeared to be a hotel balcony, looking out over a massive riot below, was replaced with footage of an academic looking man in his late fifties, with a microphone thrust into his face.

"European leaders had hoped that an incremental, or shall we say, a gradual approach to defusing the crisis, would allow Eurozone governments to ease indebted populations into an understanding of reality, namely that unlimited government spending was just not going to be possible going forward." The man, now clearly nervous, shrugged. "Instead, what officials are learning, is that Europe will continue to face episodes of unprecedented financial volatility that is actually eroding the ability of those governments to repay debt, regardless of what policies they implement. Leaders are simply moving too slowly in reacting to the crisis, which started in 2009 when Greek leaders first admitted that Greece was in deep financial trouble."

Bill, standing on his balcony, returned to the screen.

Annie pointed at the television. "Are those military vehicles burning on the upper left part of the screen?"

Russell blinked and nodded that he thought they were.

Bill glanced over his shoulder, towards the sound of a loud explosion below where he stood. His voice shook when he continued. "Led by the Eurozone's strongest member, Germany, the EU is not budging on demands for the Mediterranean countries to cut spending. These governments are resistant to sweeping solutions, such as combining their assets and liabilities into one entity, with the ability to borrow via the issuance of Eurobonds. It is clear that the more prudent member nations have balked at increasing financing for further bailouts, and are, instead focused only on requiring the indebted nations to cut spending and reduce their budget deficits. The seventeen member states have also agreed to come up with a treaty requiring national law to limit deficits to levels agreed on during last June's accords. Cynthia?"

"Things sound very tense there indeed. I just talked to Senator Thorpe about Europe in the previous segment. He said the United States is in a position where we, too, should be taking action. He pointed out that with the Fed buying the vast majority of U.S. government treasuries, we may face similar problems here. Furthermore, he said that the current policy is just not working, and the inflationary impact is a concern. It seems we are failing to inspire international confidence in the full faith and credit of the United States. What are you hearing with regard to impacts here in the United States?"

"That is a very good question indeed, Cynthia. Most officials here are very much dealing with the crisis on a moment by moment basis, but they are saying when, not if, the contagion spreads, it will be global. I was with a very senior economist at the ministry last night. He said that the United States will definitely be impacted in coming weeks and months. Back to you, Cynthia"

Annie jumped when the screen suddenly went dark, as Russell turned off the television. She turned sharply to face her husband.

"Annie, I hate to say this, but it looks like Kate isn't a complete nut-job. She may have been right about all her doom and gloom crap, after all."

Annie looked at her husband, not knowing what to say. "We should eat Russ. Our breakfast is getting cold. We can decide what to do after that." She got up and went to the table, followed by her husband.

Finishing her eggs, she saw that Russell's mind had begun to function again. "Annie, I am thinking that we should sell the car. We should see what we can turn into cash before this thing gets going. I can probably get some good money for my welding stuff too."

"No way Russ, you can't sell your welding stuff, but I agree about the car. If this is what Kate has been talking about, you knowing how to weld will be all that we have to trade for food. Oh, my God, Russ what are we going to do? I'm pregnant!"

"It is going to be ok. We have each other, and we will find a way through this." She felt the reassuring squeeze of his hand. "Why don't you call your sister, Megan, in New York? Let's see what she thinks about all of this. She should know more about it than the idiots on TV. I would like to know what she thinks we should do." Annie nodded and got up to take the plate to the sink when the phone rang. Its tone suddenly more shrill than she remembered. She took two steps and picked up the receiver.

"Hello!"

"Annie, it's your pop. How's my little girl? Are you and Russ doing ok up there?"

"We are getting by, Daddy. Is Momma doing ok?"

"We are just fine, Pumpkin, she sends her love."

"We just saw the news, Daddy. It looks pretty serious overseas. Do you think it's going to be bad for us here?"

"That's why I'm calling you, Honey. I just got off the phone with your sister in New York. She believes the current system can't survive. She said she is coming home as soon as she can take care of a few things. I think you and Russ need to think about doing that, too. It might be a little tight here, but we'll have plenty of food. I sure would feel better having my girls where I knew they were safe."

"Oh, Daddy, is it really what Katie has been talking about? This seems really crazy."

"It is that, girl, it is that. Listen, I need you to put Russ on the line for me."

"Ok Papa, but I have something to tell you first." Annie looked at her husband and took a breath. "I'm pregnant, Daddy. We didn't plan it, but Russ and I are going to have a baby."

Annie thought she could almost see her father's face as he paused to process her announcement. "Congratulations, Baby Girl! That is wonderful news, just wonderful! You know I always wanted to be a granddad." She could hear him pull away from the receiver. "Beth! Your youngest is having a baby, so you better start getting used to the idea of being Grandma." Back with her now, her dad's voice grew serious again. "I am real proud for you Annie girl. Now you let me talk to your husband. Your mom and I want you kids to get here just as soon as you can, OK?"

"OK, Daddy. Here's Russell"

She handed the phone to Russell. A moment later, she noticed a change come over her husband, as his eyes hardened and his jaw set with determination from whatever her father was saying. As she scratched Bridgett behind her ears, she sat watching her husband in silence as Russell listened to her dad for almost ten minutes. She realized that she was getting more and more scared with each passing moment. As the conversation progressed, he blinked and nodded, obviously agreeing with whatever her father said.

"Yes, Sir, I understand. I can bring my welding gear. Annie and I were just talking about selling whatever we could, including your old Taurus." He listened for a minute more. "Yes, Sir, you can count on me, Mr. Danvers. There isn't anything I wouldn't do to keep my family safe. We will get moving on this stuff as soon as I hang up."

Chapter 18
Out With a Whimper

Catherine rolled her eyes and turned off the television. She decided that it was too early to be depressed. Besides, one could only stomach a certain amount of the steady stream of dismal news and remain human. Looking up at the clock on the wall by the front door, she saw that it was only seven-thirty. Thanks to the schedule change at the hospital, she had plenty of time to get ready for work now. Flopping back on the sofa, she put her feet on the coffee table. Staring at nothing in particular out the front window, she scratched Maggie's belly. Sighing, she allowed herself to relax. Glancing down, she noticed that Maggie, lying on her back next to her on the couch, watched her intently.

"The world can just go nuts without us for a few minutes, Huh, Girl?" The dog's clipped tail undulated in response.

Closing her eyes, she took in a deep breath in the silence of the empty house. Breathing evenly, she smiled as she realized that birds were chattering outside. "Ah, the benefit of being an underemployed loser, at least getting my hours cut at work gives me time to chill." Opening her eyes after a few minutes, she exhaled and stretched, as she sought the motivation to get dressed for work. She was just about ready to get up when Janice's ringtone, *Miniature Disasters* by Kate Tunstall, played on her iPhone. Her partner's smiling face displayed on the screen.

"Hello, Janice, Where are you now?"

"I am still in New York. Listen, Kate, do you have a few minutes? I know you are probably getting ready for work, but my time is just not my own, and we need to talk."

Sure, Janice. The hospital cut back on hours. They have me coming in at eleven now instead of nine. At least I get to avoid some of the protests and traffic. How are you doing? I have been worried about you. I have been watching your coverage."

"I am fine, Kate. Things are really getting bad here though. This story could earn me a Pulitzer"

"I am really proud of you, Janice. You look like you are doing really well on this one. I said this would happen like a year ago. Do you remember? You thought I was nuts, as I recall."

"Yes, I remember, but people are suffering in Europe, Kate. It's pretty tense here too since things went nuts yesterday. You can see it in people's eyes." Catherine, hearing the tension in Janice's voice, felt a chill go up her back. Looking down at her arm, she realized that she even had goose bumps.

"Look, I am not going to be able to come home anytime soon. It looks like the story I am working on is blowing wide open. I am really sorry about how things are turning out between us." Catherine recognized Janice's tone, and realized she was pretty sure what was coming.

"It isn't a big deal, Janice. We had a fight, and it isn't like it was the first time or anything.

"That is my point, Kate. I care for you. I know that you have a beautiful heart, but we are just different people. I have been thinking about this all week, but being here and seeing what is happening makes me realize that, as much as I love you, I just can't be with you anymore."

Catherine snorted. "Well, there it is then, isn't it? What the hell, Janice. You are probably right, for once." Catherine listened for several seconds as neither of them spoke. Biting her lip, Catherine broke the silence. "I know you kept thinking you would find a way to make me see the world the way you do, but I am just too grounded to buy it, I guess." She could tell Janice was suppressing laughter. "You do realize that your whole problem is that you always think you're right. You can't even consider that you are the one who is missing the point, can you?"

"Maybe not, but what can I do? I think I am right, so that is what it is, I guess."

"Actually, you may not believe it, but your determination was one of the things that attracted me to you."

"Thanks. I appreciate that, Janice. I really did want us to work out, because, in spite of being so misguided about the way the world works, you are probably one of the smartest women I know. I will also miss your optimism." Catherine listened to more dead air. She could tell that the conversation would soon be over, so she decided to change the subject.

"By the way, I ran into Sadie Cline the other day at work. She is a nurse at Presby so we have met for lunch a few times. She is really nice, and she has a lot of spunk. Anyway, she really needs help figuring out why that son of a bitch is chasing her. Is there anything you can do, or is that off the table now, since you are chasing the New York thing?"

"Crap! I really do want to help her with that, but I am twenty four–seven on this thing." She heard Janice's sigh. "Please tell her I will help her if I can, but I have no idea when."

"Sure, I will tell her. Oh, and by the way, you have some stuff here. Do you want me to just hang on to it for a while?"

"That would be great, Kate, if it isn't too much trouble."

"It's fine." Catherine listened yet again to another awkward moment before Janice continued. "Well, I have to go. I am really glad you are not too mad at me about this. It sucks to end our relationship over the phone."

"Don't worry about it, Janice. I know your heart. If you want to know the truth, I sort of knew it was coming. I have for months now."

"I guess that I did too. I just love you, so I didn't want to give up." Catherine listened quietly as Janice's voice changed back to that of a reporter. "I should hang up, but listen; I want you to know that although we disagree on how to fix what's going on in the world, the bottom line is that it is going to be really bad here in the US soon too. It looks like you are going to see some of what you have been predicting." Janice sighed. "I guess I was wrong about some things. There are some really serious rumors that we may be downgraded again here in the U.S. also. Unlike the last time, our interest rates will very likely shoot up if that happens. The chairman of the Central Bank of Japan, in Chuo-an made an 'off the record' comment to a reporter from Forbes last night. They don't think the US can make the interest payments if the interest rates go up for us."

"Really? Do you think the comment is going to carry any weight here?"

"Of course, Kate, it was an off the record comment, but it is out there, and enough people like me, know about it. Sooner or later, it will hit the news cycle, and when that happens, you are talking about it going viral in like hours. Just the mention of the United States possibly defaulting on U.S. Treasuries will almost certainly cause the value of the dollar to plummet."

"Thanks for the tip. Promise me you will take care of yourself. Be alert to what is going on around you, OK?" A final moment of silence passed between them.

"OK, I will be careful. You too, Kate."

"I will." Catherine paused. "Well, good bye, Janice. Take care of yourself, Sweetie. I will be looking for your reports."

Catherine set her iPhone on the coffee table in front of her. "So, Katie Girl, you can chalk up another stellar performance on how one can achieve love and success without really trying." She realized that maybe her dad was right when he called yesterday to get her to come home to Mineral Wells. It was going to get dicey, and she knew it. She ran through her supplies in her head. She had extra fuel, enough food for her and Janice for like eight months, and although it was probably scanky, she did have water in the dilapidated old well out back, and she had a water filter. She looked at Maggie, who was still staring at her, now with concern in her eyes.

"And they said I was nuts for buying a beat up old house in one of the oldest communities in the Dallas area." Catherine leaned back into her couch and grabbed a pillow to hug as she thought through what was coming. Man, I hope I don't end up having to try out that filtration pump. She stared at the ceiling fan for a few minutes, fighting her dark mood when she noticed Maggie roll over to lay her head in her lap. "I can always depend on you, can't I, Maggie? What a good girl you are. Don't you worry Sweetie, you go anywhere I go. It's not open for debate.

Well, what do you say? Let's tell Drake the good news. No doubt Ginny will be glad to know she is done with having to walk on egg shells." Catherine leaned forward to pick up her phone and dialed Drake's cell. The phone rang three times before she heard his voice.

"Hey, Drake, are you busy?"

"Been a little crazy since yesterday, but I know you already knew that. We have that Solidarity Movement group back over at Crawford Park again, so it is my turn to babysit them. What's up?"

"Just talked to Janice, and we are done this time. She is off chasing how the mess on the news yesterday morning could possibly have happened to such cultured and enlightened people. She said it is really going south there in a big way. I know I have been saying this was coming for so long, but now that it seems to be happening, I am really scared about what could happen next."

"I know what you mean, Kate. I hate seeing it every day too. We are just going to have to do our best and hold on. I am really sorry about Janice. Ginny and I figured it would happen, but I hate that you are hurting. She may have been nuts, but she was a nice woman with a big heart."

"Yeah, she is all of those things. Ah hell, Drake, let's face it, I am just a train wreck when it comes to people."

"Look, Kate, you are a pain in the ass, but you are my best friend and you are a good person. I guarantee you when the time is right, you will find someone." Catherine swallowed hard, thinking that she hated how her friends would indulge her now. God, it was too humiliating. "So, to change the subject, are you hearing anything local about contingencies to go with curfews etcetera? If things get ugly here, like they are in Europe, what will our leaders do?"

"We haven't been told anything yet. We are still being told the same stuff we have been told all year. I can tell you that the brass is meeting a lot more often though."

Catherine sighed. "I always just hoped that, somehow, all of this wouldn't really happen. You know, I hoped that one way or another, people would wake up and stop the craziness."

"I know, Kate. Ginny and I are the same way. Ginny took off from work yesterday afternoon and went to the grocery store, or should I say, grocery stores, to pick up some extra food. She also all but emptied our bank accounts and bought gold. Would you believe that it is over twenty-three hundred dollars an ounce?"

As Drake spoke, she casually scratched Maggie behind the ears, and stared wistfully out the front window. She knew that she was a complete mess. Emotionally distraught, feeling she was simply incapable of accomplishing anything lasting, she decided that she just wanted to quit trying. Nobody would give a damn anyway, she thought. She realized that she felt guilty because all of her warnings over the last two years were coming to pass, and people were hurting.

"Kate, are you ok? You got really quiet there."

"I'm fine. My mind just drifted, I guess. Anyway, I am not surprised about the cost of gold. I wish I had enough money to buy some. I bought some more silver awhile back but no gold. You guys should get some silver, too. You can't exactly use what might as well be a two thousand dollar bill to trade for food, etcetera, if this really goes into the toilet."

"You are right. I hadn't thought about that. I will see if Ginny can do that today." Drake sighed. "No, actually I won't. I am not saying we are there today, but at some point we will have to be a lot more careful about doing that sort of thing. I will go do it myself. That goes for you, too, Missy. We are in this together, do you understand me?

"Sure Drake." She rolled her eyes, but smiled, glad to have him in her life.

"I am serious, Kate. I mean it. I want you to promise to work with us on things if it gets bad. You know there will be jerks watching for targets who they think they can take down easily; and before you start, I am not saying you are an easy target, but you are a beautiful woman. Some gang banger will not think anything of taking a chance on you."

"Alright, Drake, alright, I am not a complete idiot. I am really grateful you and Ginny are here for me."

"OK. Good. We will get through this, Kate, and I really am very sorry about Janice."

"It's all good. We both knew it was inevitable."

"Would you tell me if you weren't ok? I'm serious, Kate. Let us be there for you, ok?"

"I'm good. I will miss her I guess, but I am tired of putting up with the political correctness anyway. It really is for the best. Besides, my dad called yesterday after the news broke. He wants me to come home."

"Are you going to do that?"

"Not just yet I think, but I might if it gets too ugly. My life is here, at least for now."

"Ok Kate, I am being selfish, but I am glad to hear it. Ginny and I can come by after work if you want. I hate to think of you hanging out in the house alone."

"I won't be alone tonight. I am doing a talk on prepping for Dennis, after work today. You remember him, right? He was the Tea Party guy that gave me grief at Country Day a few months ago. He asked me last week if I could do a presentation. I guess my speech will be timely enough."

"I guess it will be. Do you think that they will listen to you now? As I recall, they were a bit dismissive this time last year."

"I would think so. Janice said that big wigs in Europe and Asia are thinking the US is going to get downgraded soon if the interest rates go up, we could fold anytime. Besides he came to me this time, so I guess we will find out."

"Ok, if you say so. I am not sure I like that guy though. I wish I could attend tonight, but Ginny has plans for us."

"Thanks Drake. I appreciate it. I will be fine. I think they will listen now. I really wouldn't want to be in your job these days. Be careful, ok?"

"Tell me about it. Careful is my middle name, and my partner, Johnny, is even more cautious than I am. Besides, most of the people in Cedar Hill are pretty solid. I guess we will just see what happens next. You are the one who is home alone all the time. Keep alert about what goes on around you, and call me if you so much as get a funny feeling about anything, ok?"

"Aren't you sweet? My knight in shining armor."

"Come on, Kate, I know you can take care of yourself, but if it gets dicey, please call me."

"I will, Dumb Ass. I only look stupid. If it gets bad I will call, and you can bet I will stay armed. I won't be venturing out unless I have to, until the dust settles."

"Alright Kate, stay in touch. I have to go. One of the protesters is hassling someone. Talk to you later."

Catherine laid the phone down once more and patted Maggie affectionately on the head. "Well, Maggie Girl, I need to go to work. Leaving now will probably make me early, but you just can't tell how long a drive will take anymore. You just can't tell. No, you can't." She ruffled the boxer's ears and gave her a hug. "Are you going to miss me, Baby?"

Her response was Maggie lunging forward to lick her face. Smiling, Catherine pushed the boxer aside, stood up, grabbed her purse, and headed for the front door. Grabbing the door knob, she thought about what Drake had just said about being vulnerable and hesitated. Looking back at Maggie, who was still sitting on the couch, she grimaced, before finally arriving at a decision.

"What the hell! Better to be careful than sorry." Catherine went back into her bedroom, and took her nine millimeter Sigma out of the drawer next to her bed. After checking the magazine, she placed the weapon in her purse. She went back into the front room, paused to give Maggie another hug, and headed for the front door and another day in a rapidly changing world.

Chapter 19
Revelations

"Hey, Catherine, I missed you at lunch." Leaning into Catherine's cube, Sadie noticed that her friend was completely engrossed in her work, and did not even notice that she was standing there until she said something.

Startled, Catherine looked up, the surprise on her face quickly turning into a grin. "Sadie, hi there; you found me. I just ate at my desk today. I have been swamped, so I just worked though."

Nodding in understanding, Sadie smiled. "I won't keep you then; I just wanted to say hello."

"Wait! You don't have to run off, I just had to meet a deadline earlier. Actually, your visit will, no doubt, do much to prove to everyone down here that I do, in fact, have a couple of friends, after all. What brings you to my lair?"

"Nothing special. You have just been such a blessing for me the last week or so. I wanted to buy you dinner. I am betting that since Janice is out of town, you have probably been living on hot dogs and frozen dinners. Besides, most of the girls on my floor are married. They rush out the door the minute they clock out. I feel awkward going out by myself and where I am staying, I end up eating fast or frozen food, so here I am. Interested?" Sadie's question resulted in a warm smile. She noticed that Catherine's face was really pretty when she smiled. Unfortunately, the smile faded as quickly as it had appeared, overtaken by a look of regret.

"You bet I would, but I can't. I pretty much have to go straight home after work to let my dog, Maggie, out. After that, I am speaking tonight to a Tea Party group about preparedness."

"Really, that is a bit surprising, all things considered. I had no idea you were a Tea Party person."

Catherine smirked. "Actually, I am not really. I match up with them on some stuff, but obviously not on others. Since many Tea Party types are Evangelicals, and aren't exactly too keen with me being a lesbian, it can be awkward at times. Janice flatly refused to have any involvement with them at all."

"I bet."

She could see that Catherine was going to say something more when her phone rang. Sadie realized she should probably let her friend work. Smiling, she mimicked that she would call her, but Catherine stopped her with a gesture. Motioning Sadie to her guest chair, she pantomimed, just a sec. Looking over at the caller ID, and rolling her eyes, she turned back towards Sadie with a smile, ignoring the phone. The device rang once more and rolled over to voice mail.

"If they want me bad enough, they will leave a message or call back."

"Sorry, I don't want to be a bother, Catherine."

"Please. I didn't even stop for lunch today. Besides it is almost time to stop anyway. Now where were we?"

"You were telling me about your Tea Party involvement."

"Right, it is really closer to non-involvement. I really believe in the small government-low taxes part, but some people in this particular group just couldn't get around the gay thing, so it was weird. Also, I have sort of been a doom and gloom girl for the last few years, so I didn't really fit in, and I quit going to the meetings a year or so ago. Still, I occasionally get invited to talk about preparedness for disasters like tornados, or like last year during the Solidarity Riots."

"Wow Catherine, that is really cool. So, I guess that they want you to come back because of what is going on in the world?"

Catherine nodded. "Yep, that is pretty much the story. With the news in Europe the last couple of days being so grim, it is probably too late for them to do much, but I guess I will tell them to max out on food and what not, on their way home from the meeting."

Sadie noticed the guy sitting in the cube across from them sigh and roll his eyes, in response to her statement.

Grimacing with embarrassment, Sadie mouthed an apology about offending Catherine's office mate. "Sorry."

"Don't worry about it. We have covered the topic in depth and have agreed to disagree, right Jack?"

Catherine giggled, and shrugged as the guy gave them his back.

"You might be bored stiff, Sadie, but would you want to come with?"

"I would love to, actually. Are you sure that I won't get in the way?"

"I am positive. I would love to have you along, actually. Janice would never go to this kind of stuff. She thinks I'm a lunatic."

"I bet she doesn't think you're nuts, now. I am guessing that she is grateful you guys are prepared. Besides, I would think that, as a reporter, she would be fascinated."

"You would think so, wouldn't you? By the way, Sadie, I am afraid that Janice and I are done as a couple. She isn't coming back anytime soon, at least until things settle down."

Sadie could see the resignation on her friend's face, and gave her a sympathetic look.

"I am really sorry to hear that. You guys are a really cool couple. I was really looking forward to getting to know you both better."

Catherine looked up with a weak smile, waving off her sorrows. "It's alright, Sadie. This has been coming for a long time. Janice is really sweet, but she is just way too optimistic, and me, I am Chicken Little or Mary Sunshine or something. I guess that our world views were, finally, just too different."

Sadie nodded, noticing that Catherine suddenly appeared much more vulnerable than she had ever seen her before. Her friend clearly didn't even realize that she was fidgeting, unsure of what to do with her hands, as the conversation progressed. Smiling with sympathy, she was overcome with the need to comfort her, but unsure how to do so.

"Trust me Catherine, I really do understand. I went through something like that last year. I guess we are just a pair of misfits. In my case, I wasn't artsy enough."

Her friend nodded her understanding, rewarding her with another one of her heartwarming smiles, and she realized she really felt comfortable talking to this woman.

"Thanks for making me feel better, Sadie, I appreciate it. Lord knows that there is more than enough to be freaked out about in the world, without worrying about a busted relationship. Anyway, it is nice to see a friendly face. I really am glad you came down, and even more glad you want to hang out tonight."

"Who are you kidding? You have been so nice to me all week. Besides, sitting around my suite watching television every night is really a drag. When will you be done here?"

"Give me like thirty minutes to close this stuff out, and I will be ready. Where do you want to meet?"

"Is the lobby on the fourth floor ok? Security walks me out every evening after work, so I have been meeting them there, and then walking over to employee parking on the sky bridge."

"Cool, the fourth floor lobby it is, then."

Sadie smiled. "Great! I will go change into real clothes and I will meet you there."

⁂

Thirty minutes later, Sadie smiled when she saw Catherine step out of the elevator. As they headed towards the sky bridge and the employee parking area, she thought it really was too bad about Janice. She decided she would have to watch herself with Catherine Danvers. She was smart, self-reliant, and her fierceness was very attractive. Like her mom, Sadie thought there was very little that would keep this woman down for long. Still, nobody on the rebound was in a position to get right back into another relationship. As Catherine approached, smiling at her, Sadie thought she would really, really have to watch herself.

"Hi, Sadie, ready to go?"

"I am. I was just waiting for you and Dave, my fearless protector from security. He is normally here before I get here. Give me a moment, and I will go check on him."

Sadie pulled out her cell phone and pressed speed dial for security. Someone picked up on the first ring.

"Security, this is Mr. Decker."

"Um, hi, this is Nurse Cline. I just got off, and I was supposed to meet Dave at the sky bridge for an escort to employee parking. I was just ch..."

"I'm sorry, Ms. Cline. We have a situation down here. All of our guys are occupied in the ER. In fact, Dave and one of the other guys are getting stitches right now. You are going to have to wait until the police can get here to back us up."

"Oh my God! What is happening down there?"

"There was a food riot at Kroger's just north of Parker Road."

"Food Riot! That doesn't make sense."

"All I know is there was an altercation, and three people came in with gunshot wounds. Now we have their buddies down here trying to wreck the ER. Look, Sadie, I have to go. I will do my best, but it may be a little while before we can help you today."

"It's ok. I will be ok today, I think. I can walk out with a friend. I am really sorry about Dave. Give him my best, ok?"

"Sure, Ms. Cline, thanks." She heard the line go dead.

Looking to Catherine, she could see her friend overheard the conversation, and was clearly concerned as she had pulled out her iPhone to see what she could learn online.

"Do you see anything?"

"Just checking the news. Wait. There it is. A riot at the Kroger's, pretty much across the street, basically. Looks like it's still happening, actually. A bunch of food stores decided to limit bulk purchases by individual customers yesterday. People are starting to panic, I guess. It looks like a group is apparently going around town trying to buy more than the stores are allowing. Anyway, a huge fight broke out."

"Oh my God, what is happening to us?"

Catherine smiled grimly, shaking her head. “I wish I knew.” She returned her phone to her purse. “So look, do you want me to go out to my jeep, and come back to pick you up here at the entrance?”

“Where are you parked?”

“I am one level up.”

“That’s ok, I am really close. Let’s just go to my car. I can drop you at your jeep, and then follow you. Does that sound good?”

“Perfect.”

Sadie shook her head in agreement, and the women proceeded through the automatic doors, to walk across the sky bridge. Looking over at Catherine, Sadie noticed her friend was deep in thought. “You ok?”

“Sorry. I was just wondering how quickly this kind of stuff would escalate.” Seeing her friend look at her intently, Sadie cocked her head with interest, and motioned for Catherine to continue. “I was thinking it may be too late to easily get ready for what is happening now, at least for people who are just starting.”

“Tell me about it. I don’t even have my own apartment, at this point.” Pointing to her rental, she indicated her car. “This one is me.”

“Nice car, it looks new.”

Sadie used her key fop to unlock the doors and the two women got in the car. “It is a rental. My car is still in the shop after that asshole shot it full of holes. You would be surprised how much damage they found. Anyway, it has been three weeks, so I should get it back before too much longer.”

“Oh, right. I hadn’t thought about that. It was a Charger, right?”

Sadie pulled out of her slot and headed for the ramp to go up to the next level. “Actually, it is a Challenger. Do you like cars?”

Sadie could see that she did, as her face brightened. “Sure. My dad used to restore old cars when I was growing up. I drove a 69 Cougar in high school. You wouldn’t believe how the guys drooled all over that car. Unfortunately, my youngest sister, Annie, ended up getting it after I left home, and she ended up trading it in for something. Meg bought her own car. Like everything else with her, she insisted on doing everything on her own."

Sadie chuckled, recalling Catherine's tales of Meg's antics in high school. "Of course, what else would she do? Your sister sounds like a fireball."

Catherine shrugged. "I guess you could say that. Megan is just, shall we say, driven. She knows what she wants and God help anyone in the way." Catherine pointed out where she was parked. "I am up on the left. I am in the black jeep." Sadie noticed that Catherine's eyes shifted from her vehicle back to her. "I am glad you are coming tonight. It will make this much less onerous for me."

"Are you kidding? I am looking forward to it. Had I realized you were into this stuff, I would have been bugging you all week. My mom hated anything to do with politics, but with things the way they have been the last couple of years, someone would have to be nuts not to at least care a little."

Catherine nodded, but Sadie could see, she was clearly thinking about how they had both received object lessons in just how much the real world could impact someone's life.

A moment of reflection passed between them, and then it was gone. Sadie pulled the car to a stop next to the jeep. Catherine reached for the door handle, grabbed her purse and started to get out, but paused, to look back at Sadie.

"OK, so if you want, you can just follow me, but just so you will have a general idea, I will essentially head down the Tollway to I-35 and then south. When you get on I-35, move over two lanes to the left until you get past Woodall Rogers. After that, just stay to the right, and follow the signs for Waco. It will be a few miles before I-35 splits from Highway Sixty-Seven. When you see the Christ for the Nations building, stay to the right and take Highway Sixty-Seven. We will do that all the way to Cedar Hill. When we get there, take the Beltline exit. Turn right, on Beltline and that will take you into the old part of town where I live."

"Sounds good, I can't wait to see it. If I have any trouble I have your cell."

Catherine nodded, and got out with a wave, shutting the door behind her.

She watched Catherine look for her keys and then climb into the jeep. She smiled, and decided that just maybe things would be ok, after all. As she watched Catherine back out, her cell phone rang.

"Ms. Cline, this is Detective Reyes, are you in a position to talk?"

"Um, just a moment, Detective. Give me a minute. I am in the car and about to leave. I need to dig my blue tooth out of my purse." Locating the device, she pulled in behind the black jeep as she activated the little device and looped it over her ear. "Are you still there, Detective?"

"Yes, Ma'am, I just wanted to let you know that the FBI found out some information about the scum-bag who has been stalking you. Does the name Ahmad Tehrani mean anything to you?"

"I'm afraid not. Mom never mentioned anyone from her life before. Is he Iranian, like you thought?"

"He is, in fact. The FBI believe he is connected to their secret police, the MISIRI, or if you will, The Ministry of Intelligence and Security of the Islamic Republic of Iran. These guys are the muscle behind Iran's police state. Teharani is believed to be an enforcer for various government officials there."

"You have got to be kidding me. So you are telling me the asshole that filled my car with bullet holes, killed my mom, Darla Reins, and her son, is some sort of psycho spy."

"That is what it looks like, Sadie. Now that it is clear this is something bigger than a local thing, I am going to see about getting you into federal protection."

Stunned, she almost missed the on-ramp. Cutting over sharply, she made her way onto the freeway, almost side-swiping a pickup.

"Wait, wait, wait, what do you mean federal protection? I am not about to give up my life because of some terrorist." She could feel her anger rising quickly with every mile. "There has got to be a mistake. This is crazy. Why would someone from the secret police in Iran want anything to do with my mom now? Why would they want to hurt me? I have never even been there? Isn't there anything that you or the FBI can do?"

"I wish I knew why, Sadie. The thing that we can do for you now, is to get you out of view. You have to realize this information makes your attackers much, much more dangerous. It isn't safe for you to continue as you are. If this dirt-bag has state backing, he may well have found where you are staying." Sadie could feel tears coming hot and fast. "I have to think it over. I will call you back."

Chapter 20
Desperate Measures

Pulling up into the gravel driveway behind the black jeep, most of Sadie's trembling had stopped. Regardless of her puffy eyes, or what she now knew about the men who were trying to kill her, she decided she would put on a brave face. She decided she was grateful for the thirty minutes of drive time after hanging up with Detective Reyes. She needed every minute of that time to calm down. Getting out of her car, she followed Catherine up to the screened front porch, a genuine smile blossoming on her face at seeing the quaint little frame house. She thought that it could well have looked just like it did in 1950. The white painted, real wooden siding, the dark green shutters and the scalloped shingles on the gables harkened back to a more idyllic time.

"Oh, Catherine, this is adorable! It looks perfect for you. It has sort of the romantic feel of a house that belongs in Mayberry." Looking around the yard, she nodded with appreciation. "You even have a white picket fence around the front yard, and flowers in your flower beds. I just love this, but I don't have a clue how you have the time to garden."

"Thanks, I do like to work in the yard, but to be honest, I am not all that good at it. I figure it's hard to kill silk flowers, so I cheat. I just mix them in with the more durable plants that more or less take care of themselves." As Catherine spoke, Sadie realized that her friend was eyeing her closely. Sighing, it was obvious that her puffy eyes had been noticed. It looked like Catherine was going to ask about it, but then she turned back towards the house, acting as if there were nothing wrong. "I should warn you, that my boxer is very affectionate. Just give her a firm 'down' command, and use a "stop' gesture with your hands." Sadie noted the process as Catherine demonstrated the procedure. "Maggie is pretty sure she is human for one thing, and positive she is the center of the universe, for another, but she is a good dog. She more or less restrains herself from jumping up on people, except for when she doesn't."

Sadie exhaled some of the built up stress from her drive, and took the screen door that was held for her, following Catherine onto the porch, and then across to the front door. She watched her friend as she unlocked the door amid Maggie's frantic barks of excitement, emanating from the other side. She thought how charming Catherine was as her friend bent down to greet the boxer who was obviously beside herself with joy.

"How's my girl? Who's been stuck in the house all day?"

Soon Maggie's curiosity about the newcomer surpassed her delight that Catherine was home. Her head poked out from between Catherine's left arm and torso to peer up at Sadie.

"Hello there, Maggie. It is very nice to meet you." Sadie smiled, genuinely beginning to cheer up now. The acceptance in Maggie's dark eyes, and the enthusiasm expressed by the wagging nub that was her tail were heartwarming. As the moment passed, Catherine stood up, patting the boxer one last time.

"Outside, Maggie?"

The dog reacted instantly, bolting for the back door at top speed.

Catherine smiled, motioning for Sadie to come make herself at home. "I will be right back."

Sadie proceeded through the front room, into the little dining room as she watched Maggie's owner follow the dog to the back of the house.

"Would you like a diet soda or maybe some tea?"

"Some tea sounds really good, Catherine, thanks."

As she circled the little dining room table, she considered her surroundings. The little house was cozy and very homey. From the hardwood floors, and old fashioned but comfortable furniture, to the large windows with pull down shades, she loved it all. It was completely charming and she felt her tension easing as she took it all in.

Hearing the back door open and the dog scramble to get out, she reflected that she had almost called Catherine to cancel after the detective's call. Now that she was here, she was glad that she hadn't. Being alone would not have helped anything, and besides, although she wasn't sure why, being here in this little house felt nice.

"Maggie is really sweet, by the way. I always wanted a dog, but they aren't really a good fit for life in an apartment."

Looking at the pictures on a book case, she smiled. The faces of her friend's sisters smiled back at her as Catherine continued.

"Yeah, I like dogs better than people sometimes. Maggie is my best friend, really."

"How old is she?" Completing her examination of Catherine's pictures, Sadie hung her purse off of a dining room chair and sat down at the little table. As she relaxed, she heard the back door slam closed, followed by Catherine's footsteps as they brought her back towards the kitchen. Sadie watched through the cut-out between the kitchen and the little dining room to see Catherine take two glasses from the cupboard and fill them with ice.

"I have had Maggie since she was a puppy. My friend, Drake, got her for me as a birthday present a couple of years ago."

As her friend came around the corner of the kitchen into the dining room, Sadie could tell she was obviously a lot happier and more at ease here in her own domain than anywhere else. "Can I get you some nachos or something to hold you over till after the meeting? They will have cookies and punch where we are going tonight, but it won't exactly be all that tasty."

"Actually, I'm good. I would rather save my appetite for dinner afterwards anyway."

Perfect, we have a few places to eat here, so that will work. I can't imagine how they are staying open, but I guess, like everyone else, they are trying to make it all work."

Her friend handed her a glass and settled into a chair across from her.

Sadie sipped her tea, surprise creeping across her face. "Is this mint tea?"

"Yes, I should have mentioned that, sorry."

"Are you kidding? I love mint tea, but I am just too cheap to pay for specialty brews."

Catherine laughed. "It's plain tea. I grow the mint in the back yard."

"That is really cool, and it tastes wonderful."

Obviously glad to be home, Catherine stretched and sighed. Looking towards a cased opening that separated the public spaces from the bedrooms, she smiled, and waved her left hand expansively. "So, this is pretty much my little kingdom. It has two bedrooms with a bathroom between them. Unfortunately, it has tiny, tiny little closets, but the attic space is finished out, so I pretty much use that as a closet, too."

Sadie followed Catherine's hand with her eyes, as she spoke, and she took a long drink of the cold mint flavored tea. "I think your kingdom is just wonderful, Catherine. Thank you for asking me to come over."

"Seriously, Sadie, I appreciate the support. I suspect it will go fine, but you never know. It is always good to have a friendly face in the crowd." Finishing off her tea, Catherine set her glass down, and yawned.

"Ok, I guess I should change clothes and pick up my notes. I will be right back and we can head over to the church, just down the street, where we will be meeting." As she stood up, Catherine hesitated a moment, before looking her in the eye. "Sadie, for what it's worth, I can tell that you were upset when you got here. I'm here for you if you want to talk about it."

"Thanks, Catherine, but I really don't, not right now anyway. Is that ok?"

"Of course, just know that I want to help, alright?"

Sadie wanted to tell her about it, but just couldn't after what her problems had cost Catherine's family. Instead she nodded her acceptance and Catherine continued.

"By the way, can I ask you for a favor?"

Sadie Looked up. "Sure, what can I do?"

Catherine crossed in front of her, picked up the remote off the coffee table, and turned on the TV. "Can you scan for anything that I can use tonight? I listened to the news on the way home from the hospital. Most of that was about the food thing, but they said something about Governor Miller calling a special session to deal with the debt crisis. I didn't get much in the way of any detail though."

Sadie walked over to the couch and sat down, taking the remote from Catherine, as her friend headed for her bedroom. "No problem at all. I normally listen on my way home too, but ..." She hesitated, and saw that Catherine picked up on her hesitation immediately, and turned back to her.

Sadie took a deep breath. "Oh, what the hell, Catherine; you're right, I need to tell someone. Detective Reyes called me after we left the hospital with an update about the guy that has been stalking me. I am just sensitive about it, I guess."

Catherine retraced her steps, and sat down on the coffee table in front of her and looked into her eyes. She could feel Catherine's hands enclosing her own. "I can tell you are upset about it. If you tell me it's none of my business, I won't harass you about it; but you told me a couple of days ago that you appreciated having someone to share this stuff with. Nobody should have to deal with this kind of crap alone."

Her voice shaking, Sadie responded. "He said that the FBI thinks that the guys that are after me, and who mur..." she looked down, suddenly trembling again. Feeling a little nauseous, about her role in the loss of her friend's family members, she stumbled through what she was trying to say. "...murdered your family and my mom, are some sort of Iranian agents." She looked up at Catherine with tears in her eyes. "I am so sorry, Catherine. I have no idea what they want with me. I have never even been to Iran, and I don't know anyone from there. My mom left and never looked back before I was even born. None of this... nothing makes sense anymore."

Looking helplessly into her eyes, Catherine moved from the coffee table to sit beside her on the couch. She was grateful that her friend didn't say a word. Instead she felt herself being pulled into an embrace. She felt her body calming, and after a few moments she straightened back up as Catherine released her.

"I will be ok; I just get emotional about it sometimes. It is just so unfair. It is like they hate me simply because I exist."

She felt Catherine's hands clasp hers. "You are in Texas, not the Middle East, I don't have a clue why they hate women, or anyone different from them, but I can tell you one thing I do know. I don't give a damn. This is my country. If they don't like our culture, and don't want to play ball by our rules when they are here, I say we stick the bat up their asses. I would guess that you have a father out there who wants some sort of revenge. There is no telling why now, but does that really matter?"

Surprised by the coarseness of her friend's statement, she laughed out loud, and shook her head that it didn't. "What am I going to do, Catherine? Reyes said that the FBI wants me to accept protective custody. I am scared, but I don't want to live like that. I don't want to move somewhere else and start over. I may not have a perfect life, but what I have is mine. I have friends. I like where I work, and it isn't fair to have to give that up! He said the guy likely knows where I am staying. I am going to be a nervous wreck."

"Look, whatever this is, it is bound to be personal in some way. They will catch him, you watch. We just have to be careful until then." Catherine smiled encouragingly. "This really is probably just one guy. In this country, most of us all act like all Muslims are the same, but they aren't. Most of the Middle East guys I worked with at American Airlines were really great guys. Anyway, you are going to be fine, and the cops will catch the son-of-a-bitch, and you will get your life back."

Sadie took in a deep breath as Catherine reassuringly squeezed her hands.

"I don't think the Iranian government is hunting down individual Americans, even if they do have Iranian lineage, especially when they don't have a current connection with them. It has to be something about your mom's life before she came here. They will catch him and it will be over, ok?"

"Thanks, Catherine. You always make me feel better. I just don't want to give everything up, you know?"

"I understand Sadie. It is probably the safe thing to do, but I wouldn't do it either. I do hope you carry a gun with you though."

She nodded, wondering if she could really use it, should the need arise. "What I keep thinking about is why now? I agree, it has to be something about my mom's past, but why didn't this occur years ago?

Sadie was still thinking about what she'd just said when Catherine moved to the coffee table, where they had eye to eye contact again. "OK, Sadie, so I have an idea and I don't want you to think I'm hitting on you, but I have a spare bedroom. Why don't you stay here for a while? I could probably even adjust my schedule so that we could ride to work together in the morning."

Sadie felt her heart jump as she listened to Catherine's suggestion; then her mind kicked in, and she realized she couldn't put her friend in that kind of danger. Watching Catherine watch her, she realized she had just been read like a book.

"Don't worry about it. Drake is over here all the time, and he is a cop. Maggie barks her fool head off if anything or anyone comes anywhere near the house, and I carry a gun now, too, not to mention my shotgun. We are not exactly helpless." Sadie could see that Catherine was searching her eyes for acceptance. "Think about it. If the bastards had endless numbers of super ninja spies to chase you with, you probably wouldn't be here now. Whatever this is about, do you think they could afford to send an army of guys to accomplish their goals? Not likely. If you were to just disappear and they couldn't track you by credit card or whatever, they would have a pretty hard time finding you. There are like seven million people in the metro area after all."

Sadie realized that she desperately wanted to accept, but just couldn't put her friend in danger. She took a breath to say no, when again Catherine cut her off, again.

"OK, it's settled then. You are staying here for a while. Besides, think of the money you can save. That hotel suite has to be costing a bundle on top of your rent."

"Catherine, I can't..."

"Yeah, yeah, I know, you can't impose or put me at risk; whatever, but in case you didn't know, I am an obnoxious bitch, and I know you want to do it, so it is a done thing, ok."

"You are completely nuts, Catherine, and I will absolutely die if something happens, but OK. I am very grateful to you. Now go get ready, so I don't make you late."

Catherine had no sooner left the room when what she asked Sadie to look for, flashed on the screen.

"News Four has learned that Governor Dorie Miller has just notified members of the Texas State Legislature that they are being called into Special Session. The Special Session will begin on Thursday to address the profound challenges that are facing all Americans following the challenges that have transpired this week. This is unprecedented, as members are only being given two days to make their way to Austin. Governor Miller stated that issues transpiring this week are just too serious to wait, and that Texas government would face them squarely. He said that he expects that most, if not all other states, will do likewise. He stated that he would continue to call special sessions as often as needed to address the crisis, as events play out in coming weeks. In remarks to lawmakers in Austin this afternoon, Governor Miller confirmed that the latest downgrade of US credit was simply too serious a matter for the state of Texas to simply ignore. For this reason, the governor said he would be limiting the agenda for the special session to matters related only to the current financial crisis, and to actions that the state of Texas will need to take to ensure the wellbeing of our citizens. When asked what he meant by that statement, Governor Miller stated that although Texas has always had a long-standing policy of reducing its dependence on federal money, and the associated mandates, there are several serious issues to be dealt with at the state level, regarding certain federal shortfalls. News Four has learned that several bills designed to financially distance the state from the federal government are expected to be filed immediately, once the session opens in two days."

Chapter 21
Awakening

Sadie watched the faces of those around her, as Catherine led her through what appeared to be a recreation room at a Baptist Church near her house. She took a seat toward the back, and smiled politely at a very serious looking older woman sitting just in front of her. Catherine proceeded to the front of the room. The woman obviously appraised Sadie with skepticism, but returned her nod with curt politeness. Catherine chatted amiably with two men who appeared to be the group's leaders so apparently the men were over their issues with her situation. Sadie smiled and continued to observe those around her. As the room filled, she could see grim visages on many of those gathered. She realized the crowd was easily going to exceed the expectations of the group leaders who had just spoken to her friend. One of the men hastily tapped the shoulders of some of the guys who were already seated. Obviously the group leaders wanted their help, as they quickly got up to follow one of the men out of the room. The other man, with grey hair, hurried about the room, using additional chairs stacked along the wall, to set up more seats on either end of the rows of the existing chairs.

"Excuse me, young lady, are you saving a seat for anyone?" She looked up to see an elderly man smiling at her expectantly.

"No, Sir. Please sit if you like." She thought that he had nice eyes, but decided that he looked lonely. She wondered if there would be someone to take the seat on his opposite side.

"Thank you, Miss, I wanted to hear what they said tonight."

Sadie nodded. "I guess a lot of folks are about to get a lot more interested in getting ready for hard times nowadays."

The man nodded in agreement, as his eyes swept forward to rest on Catherine. "I rather expect that they will indeed, Young

Lady." Staring forward, he leaned slightly towards Sadie. "I heard this young woman speak last summer, but I thought that she was just another alarmist. Now I wish I had listened to her."

"Well, Sir, with the news being so bleak this week, I imagine you will not be the only one with that opinion tonight." She noted that he nodded his head slightly in agreement, as once again, she scanned the room. As she expected, the group of men returned with a push cart of additional folding chairs. Several men seated towards the front of the room jumped to their feet to assist in placing the chairs in neat little rows. As she looked around the room, she realized that today's news from Austin was apparently getting people's attention.

Finally, as the crowd began settling in, Catherine moved up behind the folding table at the front of the room. In the center of the table was a small wooden podium. Placing a hand on either side of the podium, she looked out at the crowd and smiled slightly, her expression earnest, as she looked across the faces before her.

"Good evening, folks. My name is Catherine Danvers. I appreciate you inviting me to talk to you tonight. I will do my best to help you in any way I can." Catherine took a breath and glanced down at her notes. "I guess I will begin tonight by telling you a little bit about myself. Although I recognize many faces, I am sure, for others, this will be the first time that some of you may have heard this message. I want to start tonight by saying that I am nobody special. I moved to Cedar Hill about three years ago. I don't have any fancy degree in preparing for the mess that appears to be headed our way. Most of what you will need to do is common sense, but it does require commitment. Anyway, I served four years in the United States Army as an intelligence clerk after I graduated high school. I got a degree in business from TCU, and worked for American Airlines doing schedule management before getting laid off a year ago. Now I do pretty much whatever I can to earn a buck." Pausing to take a sip of water, Catherine continued. "Obviously, none of what I just said has very much to do with why we are here tonight. I am giving you a brief background only to point out that we are all, more or less, the same." Sadie noticed that Catherine paused to make eye contact randomly through the crowd. Sadie realized that Catherine clearly knew what she was doing as she had them already. Looking at the faces watching her friend, she saw seriousness and a grim attentiveness as everyone was focused on the speaker behind the little podium and what she had to say. Surprisingly, as she watched Catherine speak, it occurred to her that she was proud of her friend. Blinking, she pondered that thought. She had only known Catherine a short time, but there was clearly a connection. Amazed at her revelation, she looked up, again focusing on Catherine's remarks.

"...Anyone here can begin to prepare, and everyone here should do so, to the extent that he or she can afford to. It isn't cheap, but it is important. Think about it. You are basically paying now for stuff you may not be able to get later. Hopefully, things don't get too bad, but who here tonight is willing to take the risk? It is nothing more than insurance, guys." Sadie could see a few heads nod in agreement. Some people were taking notes, but most simply stared grimly toward the lectern.

"I started buying extra food about six months before I got laid off. You might think that getting laid off would mean that I have probably gone through my stores already, but to be honest, I have managed, to more or less, keep things at least stable, even considering that I only work whatever temp job I can find. I don't care if you only get an extra week or two worth of food, anything you can put back is worthwhile.

Sadie saw that Catherine seemed to really be able to read the group. Catherine moved out from around the table and walked forward, just even with the first row.

"I don't know about you all, but I listened to the radio on my way home from work tonight. Raise your hand if you did something similar." Sadie watched Catherine's eyes scan the faces as she took in the numbers of raised hands. After a moment, she nodded. "For anyone who missed it, here are the highpoints. Both Moody's and Standard and Poor's downgraded the US credit rating again about three hours ago from AA to BB. Fitch is expected to follow suit any time." Catherine paused, as a teacher allowing the impact of her statement to sink in on her audience. Finally, pulling a note card out of her pocket, she continued. "Let me read what the definition of BB means to the financial world. It means that repayment does not pose a problem at present but may become problematic in the future." Again she looked challengingly at her audience as it occurred to Sadie, that regardless of her more pressing fears of being stalked, she realized what her friend was saying was very real, too. Her world was crumbling before her eyes.

Catherine continued. "On the way from my house, just now in fact, Channel Four said that Governor Miller has even called a special session to address the issues playing out before us. In a round table segment earlier today, a couple of the same Poindexter economist types that got us into this mess, said that the federal response to the disaster will likely cause the value of the dollar to plummet on the international currency exchanges tomorrow. Foreign central banks have already begun dumping their holdings in US Treasuries. The Japanese, foreign central banks, and international monetary authorities have dumped trillions of dollars' worth this week, and that was before today's announcement."

Sadie could see the shock on the faces surrounding her.

"In a couple of days," continued her friend, "I expect that our Treasury paper will be selling at some fraction of a dollar."

Sadie heard more than one gasp from a couple of rows in front of where she sat. Glancing to her right, she saw that the older gentlemen's steal grey eyes twinkled with moisture. As she watched him bear down to regain control of his emotions, he seemed to feel the weight of her gaze and turned to her as a tear traced the lines on his face. "It is a sad thing, Young Lady, but we will just have to find a way to get by." Patting her briefly on the shoulder, he turned back to listen.

Looking forward again, she could see Catherine was again on the move, this time to the left side of the room to call on a middle aged woman with her arm up.

"Yes ma'am, do you have a question?"

"I know that Europe has been having trouble, but I don't understand how this happened to us so quickly." Sadie could see that Catherine was exercising a fair amount of self-control as she looked down for a moment, pressing her lips together to avoid saying something snarky.

"This isn't a surprise, nor was it unexpected if you have been watching. Look folks, like I said, I am no egghead economist. I can tell you that I started getting ready a few years ago because I looked around and saw corporate leaders and our government taking the most ridiculous actions possible. George Bush, for example, in his "Ownership Society" forced lenders to put people in homes that no sane person thought they could afford. Don't get me wrong, I am not blaming any political party here. Both parties are guilty. His predecessor and his successors have done the same thing, or worse, with multiple bail-outs or stimulus packages." Laughing incredulously, she continued. "When China held most of our debt, you could see where their money came from. China makes things very cheaply and sells them. Now the Fed simply keystrokes cash into existence. Can anyone tell me what the Feds sell or produces to have such enormous amounts of cash to hand out?" She paused, to let someone answer but no one did. "Let me help you because it is a trick question. They don't make anything. They are creating cash out of thin air. The strategy only works when people believe in full faith and credit. My point, of course, is that our financial system is based on what is known as a 'fiat' currency. That means our currency is based on productivity and on our collective belief that our dollars have value. I believe our fiat system is likely ending now due to mismanagement and massive over borrowing. If you take nothing else away tonight, I hope you take urgency with you. Prepare as best you can, as quickly as you can. Work with family and friends. No one can survive alone..."

The woman interrupted her. "I watch the news. They were saying just a week or so ago that it was all going to work out. There was going to be an EU bailout."

Catherine nodded. "OK, and so what, you believed them? Regardless of what you can see plainly around you, with your own eyes, you went along with what they said because you are unwilling to face the truth. To put it bluntly, they lied to you. Ma'am, I am not trying to be rude or anything, but each of us here is responsible for this mess. The media and the political elites in both parties have been lying to us for a very long time, and we just let them, because we were too busy to be bothered." Sadie watched as Catherine approached the group seated on the left side of the room. "We are really all guilty." Speaking directly to the woman now, she asked her a question. "Can you honestly tell me that you spent the last ten or twenty years really paying attention to what those you elected did in your name, or did you excuse things as long as they were in your party?"

Sadie winced along with the woman. Her friend gazed at the woman expectantly, but she did not reply. After a moment, Catherine stepped back a step, and addressed the whole group again. "Regardless of party, we all said things like, 'Just wait until the next election; then we will get things right.' Let's face it, folks, the politcos played us against us each other, and stole us blind. Now we get to deal with the consequences. The good news, God willing, is if we work hard, deal with each other fairly, and mind who we elect to lead us, we should be able to rebuild our lives."

Sadie noticed a lanky man about her age and wearing a suit stand up indignantly and announce his outrage. "Screw that, Lady! You are talking about rebuilding and saying that we just have to accept what is going on." He looked out amongst the crowd. "I don't know about you people, but I have goals and things I want. If things really are going to crater, I want to find who is responsible and take back what is mine!"

"Sit down, Sir. This meeting isn't going to degenerate into a shouting match. If you want to know who is responsible, then look around the room, but begin by finding a mirror. Besides, it is too late for all of that now. What good will it do for you or your family to place blame? We are all going to have to pull together if we want to avoid being subjugated by the very same people that engineered this mess in the first place. Look at the people sitting next to you. It doesn't matter anymore what religion someone is, or whether he or she is rich or poor, or if he or she voted for the same person you did. All that matters are the following simple questions. Do you believe in God, regardless of what that means to you? Do you believe that individuals are responsible for their own behavior, and their own successes or failures? Do you believe that it is our individual duty to care for each other when someone needs a hand, or do you believe it's the government's job? I would like to suggest that if we support each other, and somehow avoid the trap of thinking that some Fed will ride in to save us, we can survive what is coming. This is a personal opinion, but I believe that the system is failing, and it is going to really be tough for all of us."

Sadie noted that the woman who had asked the question just sat there wooden-faced, but many other faces in the crowd were nodding in agreement.

Catherine moved back to her lectern and placed a slide on the projector. "Ok guys, we kind of got off topic a bit there. By now, you are motivated or you aren't, so I will move on. These are some pictures of what some good storage areas look like. Basically the main thing is to keep bugs and or pets or any other animal, for that matter, out of the food. You can use plastic tubs like you see here. Something like a linen closet is a good choice too. The next key item is watching your expiration dates. It doesn't do you any good if you buy food and have to throw it out. Obviously, freeze dried food is also a good choice if you can afford it."

A man in the third row raised his hand and Catherine moved a few steps in his direction and motioned for him to speak.

"How do you know what sort of food to buy?"

"Good question. I bought dry goods and canned items that I could use to make dishes that I like. It would really suck to only have powdered eggs, for example, although that would at least keep you alive. I recommend starting with having a lot more on hand of what you already do, but focus on things that will not go bad quickly." Catherine pointed at the picture of a food storage rack in a garage. "When you go to the grocery store, buy as much as you can afford and keep the expiration dates in mind, moving longer lasting items to the back and the older items forward. When you run out in your pantry you go to your storage for what you need instead of the store. The point is to rotate constantly. You can also do freeze-dried food, but keep in mind that with what is going on out there, time is very short now. I personally would not trust something to arrive via UPS, etcetera, if you wait very long to order it. When things go into a dive it will likely go very rapidly. With things getting shaky, I would expect to see prices move up sharply. Today we are already seeing that stores are limiting what they let you have at one time. If I were you, I might even consider going to buy some extra food tonight."

Sadie could feel the urgency and the fear growing in the room. A forty year-old woman just down from her was crying quietly into a handful of Kleenexes. She hoped that Catherine was seeing this too. It wouldn't be good to panic everyone.

Moving back to the projector, Catherine placed another slide on the viewer. "Food, water, and shelter are the most valuable things people must have, but it is also important to stock up on other necessities like toilet paper, gasoline and cans to put it in. Maybe consider getting extra garbage bags, matches, or laundry soap. One thing you can do is think about what you need on a day to day basis. If you start looking at your life with the assumption that it will no longer be easy to obtain things you need, any time you need it, what would you want to stock up on? Remember the goal here is to buy now what you will use later. That will require space to keep things in, and money to obtain it with, but, in the long run, it should not really cost you more than you are already spending, as long as you can avoid wasting food. If you factor in inflation, you will, in fact, likely save money." As Sadie scanned the faces in the room, she could see that people were actively accepting Catherine's message tonight. Several people were taking notes, or whispering to each other, and pointing at the screen behind her friend, as they discussed how they could accomplish what was being discussed.

Sadie observed that one of the serious grey headed men who was hosting the event tonight raised his hand from the side of the room where he was standing.

"Ms. Danvers, do you have any lists of items that a person wanting to take these steps could use to guide them in what to purchase and perhaps what to place a priority on. As you were speaking I made a few notes of key items, and I realized how extensive that list really is."

Catherine nodded and smiled at the man. "Sure, Dennis, I have copies of some useful lists and an outline of our talk tonight. People may take those with them as they leave. Something else you folks might want to consider is banding together. Let's face it; no man can be an island. Nobody will make it through all of this on his or her own. Each of us has family, friends, and people we know at church who can and should begin to work together. Think of how neighbors helped each other in the 1800's. People held barn raisings for each other. That is exactly the mental framework we may need to get back to. When we know a neighbor is in trouble, or needs something, we must be there for them."

To her surprise, Sadie saw that most of the heads were nodding in approval of Catherine's statement.

"One of the things I have mentioned to Dennis earlier, and I will reiterate for you all now, is that if you will add your email and contact information to the sign-up sheet by the door, we can begin working together tonight. Dennis can publish the list so that anyone needing help, or more importantly, anyone who can provide assistance to their neighbor, can reach out to address needs that may develop in the coming weeks and months."

As Sadie watched Catherine place her next slide on the projector, she saw that the lanky man who had spoken out earlier stood up again, holding his smart phone up as he spoke.

"This thing says that Fitch just revealed that they will be making an announcement in the morning about the US Credit standings. Some finance types in Tokyo announced they will no longer employ the U.S. dollar as a reserve currency. The president is going to speak to the nation." As Sadie looked around the room, she could see that people were blinking and looking at each other in disbelief. After a moment, another man brandishing his smart phone pulled a woman sitting next to him to her feet. "I don't know about any of you, but I am going to the store now. I suggest you people not wait too long."

The room stirred at his statement, and she watched as those in attendance became restless and abruptly got up and made their way to the door. Within moments, the room had emptied.

Sadie watched Catherine make her way over to her. "Well," Catherine said, "things are about to get interesting." Sadie nodded and followed Catherine out of the church.

Chapter 22
Men in Dark Glasses

Megan sighed to let off some of the stress from her week. All things considered, she decided that she had made it through another month, and even received a promotion from the old man himself. She smiled inwardly, at how appalled Barbara Tanner was at learning that Meg had been elevated to the boardroom. Still, the economic environment was all but impossible.

She noted that absolutely no one was in any way surprised that virtually all of the deals that had been in play were now de facto, on hold, if not formally in that status. As hard as it was to accept, she realized that Matt was right. It was time. She recalled that only two days ago, on Wednesday, the Asian markets opened, and then immediately began to melt down. It started off with a five percent drop, then six percent, and then seven percent. Each percentage point drop came faster and faster, until by lunch, the market was in an all-out free-fall. Anyone who was at all savvy knew right then and there, that it was over, she thought. In turn, the Asian market touched off an avalanche of selling. Markets around the world went into independent free-falls. Gold prices were rising hundreds of dollars every day all week, and regardless of her being in early on the rush, she realized that it was the most terrible thing she had ever seen.

Breaking out of her reflection, she reached into her purse for her burn phone, to enter in her text message to Matt, to let him know she was about to leave work. She carefully entered the day of the month, the 15th, followed by the number 13, which she found by looking on the fifteenth page in the book, Night of the Wolf, Tales of Blackwater, Texas that both she and Matt picked up at the book store in the building just down from her apartment.

She looked for the first letter of the word on page fifteen to see that the word began with the letter M, which she noted was the thirteenth letter in the alphabet. Alright she thought, that authenticates the message; now for my note.

Leaving now – see you at dinner.

Send.

Megan grabbed her purse, her brief case, and her iPhone off the desk and headed for the elevator. She was almost free from her work week when someone's left foot, clad in designer pumps, inserted itself into the elevator, just before it could shut. The foot was quickly followed by a hand with manicured nails as Barbara Tanner quickly followed her extremities into the elevator car. Megan noticed that she was about to apologize to whomever she had inconvenienced, until she saw who it was, and her mouth snapped tightly shut. Megan gave her colleague her brightest smile.

"Oh, Barbara, don't worry about it. I'm happy to hold the door for you."

"No discussion is really necessary, Ms. Danvers, and you may address me as Ms. Tanner. I am still senior to you, is that clear?"

"Sure, Barbara, our relative positions in this firm are abundantly clear to everyone. I think."

Megan cocked her head slightly to one side, and grinned mischievously as her former boss bristled with indignation and pointedly looked away. Oh, well, she thought, at least it will be a nice quiet ride to the lobby. Four minutes later, the doors opened, and both women stepped out. Tanner bolted from the elevator, walking briskly towards the parking garage. Megan moved off towards the front of the building and the oversized glass doors to access the street. She really didn't care to have to navigate around the already increasing number of protesters who were showing up in larger and larger numbers as the week progressed, but there was nothing to do for that. As with Sterns and Becker, other firms were actively laying off large percentages of their employees. The same people who last week occupied the buildings on this street, were now showing up to complain, after getting lay-off notices.

She was glad that she only had to go about a block to the Starbucks located just down the street to meet up with Matt.

As she walked along, she remembered Matt riding her to make sure that she constantly remained aware of her surroundings. It was clear, she decided, that most of the people on the street, other than those who were protesting something, were singularly focused on their own business and their own destinations. She stopped one time, as she pretended to examine a magazine cart for a moment. Briefly looking over the top of a magazine, she noticed the man she had nicknamed Moe, making his way up the street behind her. She was pleased with herself. It had only been a week, and she was already getting pretty good at spotting her watchers. She and Matt had talked about the coverage a couple of times. She agreed with him that it was odd that Sterling had put people on her that she didn't recognize at all. Matt just didn't believe that Luther was the type to outsource such a duty.

Reaching the Starbucks, she opened the door, and was immediately rewarded with one of her favorite smells, brewing coffee. It was busy but not too crowded. As she waited in line she looked up to see a television with the sound turned down, mounted on the wall near the counter. What looked like a panel discussion on the economy, complete with dramatic graphics was playing. Rolling her eyes with exasperation at what was likely a pointless discussion, she, instead, focused on the headlines crawling across the bottom of the screen.

"A real mess isn't it, Ms. Danvers?"

Startled that someone, a man with a whisky-smooth voice, was speaking to her, she turned sharply to face the man standing immediately behind her. He was tall and athletic, with dark hair and piercing blue eyes. Instantly on-guard and angry, her scowl demanded an explanation.

"How do you know who I am? I don't know you." She struggled to get control of her emotions after being startled as the man answered.

"No, Ms. Danvers, you do not know me, but I know you." His right hand slipped into his jacket to retrieve a plastic badge with his name and picture displayed under the initials FBI that was clipped to his shirt pocket.

Her mind racing, she responded. "Are you accustomed to stalking people, or am I special somehow Agent Ricks."

"It comes with the job, Ms. Danvers. We have been working with a friend of yours this week, Richard Blake. He thought that it was time that we should meet."

She eyed him thoughtfully, assessing as best she could under the circumstances, what manipulation might work best with him. "I haven't seen Richard since this time last week."

"No, you haven't. I am afraid that Mr. Blake became, shall we say, concerned about his associations there at Sterns and Becker. He has been with us this week, debriefing us on some of the activities that your firm has been up to." He smiled benignly and pointed towards the register.

"What can I get you, Miss?"

She smiled at the pale young woman. "Skinny Mocha, please."

From behind her, Agent Ricks chimed in also. "I will have the same." He handed the girl a twenty dollar bill, telling her to keep the change, which earned them both a genuine smile as she pushed the two drinks towards them a moment later.

Ricks motioned to a relatively empty spot where they could stand by the window. "We have been watching the honorable Mr. Tibman for some time now, Ms. Danvers. We noticed that you and your firm made some interesting moves in the market these last few weeks." He smiled graciously, and took a sip of his drink.

"I don't recall that trading in the market is the business of the FBI, Agent Ricks."

Watching him nod in agreement, she decided that this guy was good. He was likeable. She decided to tread very carefully with him. "It is, however, a bit of a problem when eavesdropping devices are placed under tables where people are trading insider information. Wouldn't you say?"

Her heart jumped. "If someone did that, I would say so, I guess." She smiled innocently and reached casually into her purse and appeared to look for something. She felt for the shape of her burn phone. Finding it, she felt for the button on the upper right and depressed it to let Matt know she had a problem, and then retrieved a small package of tissues. Blotting at her lips with a tissue, she continued. "Tell me what I can do for you, Agent Ricks, I am meeting someone soon." She saw that he smiled sincerely, again showing brilliant white teeth as he nodded in understanding.

"Of course, I am sure that the esteemed Mr. Regan will, indeed, be along shortly. Anyway right to the point then. We have you and Mr. Blake dead to rights, Ms. Danvers. You are both young and talented people, and to be honest, we are not all that interested in ruining your lives. Your boss and his board, on the other hand, are another story. They would be fish worthy of some considerable attention. I want you to join Mr. Blake in helping us out. I'm afraid Mr. Blake is hesitant to continue his employment, but you are an amazing woman." He considered her appreciatively. "You are attractive, and aggressive, yet still charming, and best of all, you have quite a nerve. You had no qualms whatever about going in this week, regardless of being well aware of the scrutiny you are under." He cocked his head slightly to one side, grinning with respect. "To be honest, I wish I had you working on my team. I mean it sincerely when I say you have quite a skillset for the type of work we do."

Megan adjusted her approach slightly, and subtly transformed her face into a seductive smirk as she took another sip from her drink. "Well, Agent Ricks, you seem to have made quite an impressive opening bid. With all that is going on in the world, it just so happens that I have been considering whether it was time to make a change. We will, of course, need to have another discussion on the merits of your proposal."

Ricks smiled warmly at her, his blue eyes twinkling brightly. "Excellent! Good choice Ms. Danvers. I will look forward to working with you. Well, I will leave you to your weekend then. I will be in touch." He flashed a grin, handed her his card, and headed towards the door, depositing his cup in the trash, as he held it open for a Hispanic woman with a child. She entered and he departed into the crowd with a small wave, moving along the sidewalk.

Matt materialized out of that same crowd moments later, and motioned for her to join him. Like Ricks, Megan disposed of her cup, and walked towards the door, now held by Matt.

"What was that guy about? I haven't seen him on you before."

Megan passed Matt a look of concern and handed him Rick's business card.

"Figures I guess. We need to talk, but it will have to wait."

Megan shook her head in agreement. "Sure. It's just as well, I guess. I really am done Matt. It is time, I think."

Matt considered her and nodded in agreement, his smile constrained and grim.

She mirrored his expression. "Are you hungry? I haven't eaten since breakfast, and I would love something really good."

"You will be glad to know that I made reservations at Sparks on Forty Sixth."

She smiled warmly at him. "You never miss a thing, do you?"

"I definitely try not to. Anyway, I am just up the block. We can talk in the car." They walked in nervous silence as she considered the angles of her situation, and Matt scanned the crowd.

She smiled at Matt as he held the door for her, and she climbed into the limo. Scooting over, she watched as he folded himself into the seat next to her. "Are you going to miss all of this?"

Matt shook his head slightly. "Actually, no, I really do not think I will. When I was a kid watching big black cars go by, I thought how cool it would be. Now I just want away from this place as soon as possible." To emphasize his statement, he motioned with his head, and his gaze, at a group of four policemen wrestling a man in a business suit to the ground, as the car moved slowly past in traffic.

Megan closed her eyes briefly and sighed. "I am done Matt. I am ready to get out. I just needed this week to take care of some things. I sent my favorite clothes to be cleaned. It is a completely normal thing to do right? Instead of them delivering everything back to my building, they will just ship it off to Texas. I also did the same thing with some of my favorite jewelry pieces. The rest, my super can ship later, I guess."

Feeling herself being pulled into his warm embrace, she relaxed for the first time that day. "We will get through this, Megan. What did the FBI say, by the way?"

She looked up at him. "It looks like they picked up Blake last weekend. He seems to have told them some stuff because Agent Ricks was talking about them having enough to make trouble for Richard and me."

"Hmm, Maybe, but they are also masters at manipulation with this kind of thing. What did you tell him?

"I told him the truth. I said I was considering a change, and would consider his request. I said we would have to discuss it further. He seemed pretty happy with that though."

"Ok, well, it doesn't appear to be a problem for now. I think that we are good." He looked down, and she could see the warmth in his eyes.

"Thanks for loving me, Matt. I know I have been really arrogant and all. I guess I sort of drank the Kool-Aid when I started to get some success."

As the car pulled up at Sparks, Megan felt her stomach rumble. Matt stepped out and offered her his hand. She felt his arm move protectively around her as they walked together towards the entrance. Surprisingly, there was not a line, considering that it was a Friday night. She saw that Matt handed the door-man a bill and they stepped inside, past the sound of a small group chanting. "Shame! Shame! Shame!" They were kept several feet away by a private security team, but their anger was palatable.

Thankfully, the sound of the chanting was cut off immediately, once inside the restaurant. It was replaced with light classical music. She saw that Matt handed the woman at reception his credit card. She nodded and smiled. "One moment, Sir."

Moments later, a young woman with a Jamaican accent guided them to a table and laid out their menus.

Megan looked around the room. “It is a light night tonight. I suspect people are holding their breath to see what will happen next. This is going to quickly kill all of the restaurants.”

Raising an eyebrow, Matt agreed. “Well, your friends should be along soon. Who is it today?

She smiled slightly. “Moe and Square Bob. However, I am thinking that some of these guys may actually be FBI, now that we know that they are watching too.”

She noticed that Matt made an ever so slight hand motion to caution her not to say too much here. “Keep in mind that we may not have identified all of them.”

“Oh, right. Sorry. I guess I am a little tired tonight.”

“Babe, after the week you have had, I would say that was understandable. What do you guys make of the events this week? Is it as bad as it appears on the news?”

She smiled weakly at him. She realized that, although he was talking to her, he was continually scanning the restaurant. “It isn’t good, that is for sure. There isn’t anyone who doesn’t believe that we are toast. Everybody is just positioning for what’s coming. Did you hear that Kaufman Brothers and Ticonderoga Securities both called it quits this week? We spent three days working out our layoff plans for Sterns and Becker. We were waiting for a Kodak moment of sorts. We got that two days ago, so heads rolling is a foregone conclusion for us.” As she realized the irony of her last statement, she giggled.

“What are you laughing at, Meg?”

She shook her head dismissively. “It’s nothing really, I just realized that I just referenced having a Kodak moment, and then it occurred to me that Kodak went bankrupt a few years ago.”

“Right, I guess that is just more of your investor humor. Besides, I thought they were still around, aren’t they?

“Sure, if by around, you mean that technically, they exist. They were forced to sell most of their key patents and assets. Still, you never know, maybe they can invent something new, I guess.”

"If you say so, Babe." Matt Smirked. "By the way, Moe and Square Bob just came in. They are sitting over by the bar. You really have to appreciate their consistency."

Megan covered a giggle with her napkin and smiled at Matt. "I really do love you, you know."

Matt began to respond when he noticed their waiter approach

"Good evening, I am Roberto. May I tell you about our specials tonight, or review our wine list for you?"

She looked on as Matt dealt with the waiter. She always enjoyed watching him translate his working class upbringing, and his military point of view, to more sophisticated social situations. She decided he really would be very comfortable in Texas.

"That will not be necessary Roberto. I believe that we are ready to order now. We will have unsweetened tea to drink. I'll have the sliced steak, medium with a baked potato and the steamed Broccoli. For the lady, she will have the filet, also medium, with the creamed spinach." She marveled at how much she adored the intensity in his hazel eyes, as he looked up from his menu.

"Excellent choices, Sir, if I may say so."

Megan handed her menu to Roberto, as did Matt. Roberto nodded his thanks and retreated with their orders.

Engrossed in his gaze, his voice brought her back to him. "You know what I would like to do after dinner?"

Surprised by the abrupt change in conversation, she was nonplussed, but only for a moment. Recovering quickly, she flashed him a curious smile. "What is that?"

Matt gave her a knowing grin. "You mentioned you had wanted to go shopping last weekend, and we never made it, really. I have something to show you I think would be fun. We can always attend that play tomorrow if that's ok with you."

"That is fine with me, Matt. If I am being really honest, I am not really in the mood for a play tonight anyway."

"So, shopping it is then." Matt smiled.

"Let's start off down the street from Macy's and work our way back. If we end up at Macy's where we will likely get the most shopping bags, it will reduce what we have to carry around with us."

Matt winked at her. "Always practical, I love it."

"I think that I am curious about what wonderful trinket of your affection I may end up with out of such a trip. I should warn you, however, that I will insist on my favorite weekend activity once we get back to my place." She smiled as he chuckled at her suggestion.

Taking a breath, she steadied her nerves, knowing full well that the shopping trip would put their plan into motion. Exhaling, Megan thought it was Matt who Agent Ricks should want to have working with him. She was really glad to have him in her life. He was such a natural. He adeptly kept up the conversation, talking as if they had the whole weekend ahead of them, just like any other weekend. She realized that someone looking on would never guess that his attention was firmly focused on the two guys across the room.

"You have a bargain Meg. I am of course hoping for just that very same conclusion to this evening's adventure."

❧

The limo let the laughing couple off on East 34th street, down the block from Macy's. Megan, portraying the effervescent girlfriend, looked down the street as Matt gave some instructions to the driver. A moment later, he joined her. Hanging playfully off of Matt's arm, she strolled casually down the street. She paused momentarily now and then to look at the various items displayed in store windows or step into a shop to see what they had.

Finally reaching Macy's, she led her man into the store, sure that their minders were likely being slowly driven crazy. "Matt, do you like this jacket? I think it really sets off my eyes and looks good against my dark hair."

He nodded that he did, but Megan realized he was more focused on searching for something else. He played the dutiful boyfriend as she moved, as a lioness on the hunt, through the name brand designer items, displayed on the open savanna that was the posh department store.

"I am going to get the jacket I think, and the hat to match."

"I think that you should. It will look great on you. Actually, while you are checking out I am going to go find a restroom. Can I meet you at, say, the Estee Lauder counter when you finish up?"

"Sure, Matt, that would be great. We can get some yogurt or something afterwards." She watched him leave with a grin on her face. As he turned and walked away, she studied him. She thought that he really had an amazing muscular butt. Cocking her head slightly, she smiled, loving the way he moved. Returning her attention to the merchandise before her, she browsed though some scarves and gloves, pausing momentarily at the jewelry. Impulsively she selected some earrings and displayed them next to her ears. Looking in the mirror she was pleased, not with the earrings, but that her two minders were across the aisle from the jewelry counter looking at watches. She knew it was important they were both still with her. As Matt had guessed, they did not follow him to the restroom.

Satisfied with her purchases, she checked out, placing her items in a large shopping bag, and headed for the designer dresses. Taking her time, Megan perused past several more counters, being thoughtful to make the experience as boring as possible for her shadows. A sardonic smile formed on her face when she considered getting her nails done, but decided that would take too long. Eventually, she made it to her destination, after selecting an amazing emerald green cocktail dress and three others, before heading towards the fitting rooms. As she entered the dressing room, she noticed the shopping bag that she was expecting, hanging off of a clothing rack next to the dressing room entrance. She grabbed it in stride as she entered the dressing room. Shutting the fitting room door behind her, she quickly unzipped her skirt and hung it up, along with her jacket on the store's hangers. Reaching into the bag, she extracted a pair of blue jeans, a jacket and hat, some reading glasses, and blonde hair extensions. Nervous, but excited, she felt pretty confident about obtaining a completely different look.

As she changed into the clothes, she carefully put her hair up, leaving only the blonde hair extensions, visible under the hat. Filled with anxiety at their ploy, she admired herself in the mirror for a moment. "Well, they do say that blondes have more fun." I just hope Luther's people are not as sharp as he is. Within moments, she was back out in the store and headed towards the department store's Broadway entrance, carrying nothing but her purse. She moved with purpose, but not in too much of a hurry, still casually touching an item here or there as she moved away from the bored men casually watching the dressing room. Leaving the store, she headed straight towards a knot of people who appeared to be waiting on a tour bus or something.

She scanned the street for Matt, in a taxi as they had planned, but, unfortunately, he was nowhere to be seen. Megan scanned her surroundings, pondering what to do next. She knew Matt would be kicking off his distraction any moment, so she decided there was nothing to do but wait. Noticing a large concrete planter near the drop off area, she decided she would look less conspicuous leaning against it checking messages, than just standing where she was. After about ten minutes her patience paid off, as a large number of people were briskly exiting the store amid the sound of a fire alarm. As she stood and looked back at the entrance to Macy's, she didn't notice the man emerge from the SUV that had just pulled into the drop off area. As she watched the chaos of the exiting shoppers, she felt iron hands envelop her, pulling her backwards, off balance, as she was dragged all but helpless into the waiting SUV. Time slowed to a crawl, and she felt almost as if she were merely a bystander, watching her body fight for her life. She could feel powerful hands grabbing at her, as they attempted to subdue her. Punching a man directly in front of her, she heard the plastic of the cell phone in her right hand crack as the blow landed. It was immediately snatched from her, and she felt the vehicle pull away from the curb and into traffic. She screamed in terror, as one of her masked attackers lowered the window and casually dropped her phone onto the street.

Chapter 23
The Measure of a Man

"...It is Monday, February Thirteenth. The time is: four thirty and that means it is time for the bottom of the hour update. Recapping today's top story, The New York Stock Exchange opened this morning, but closed again within minutes as world-wide, circuit breakers failed to keep pace with the avalanche of sell orders besieging the market. Finance leaders, both in and outside of government, have advised that mounting liquidity problems are at the center of the storm. The inability to raise capital is the key issue facing all of the major markets. Volatility is high, with indicators trending down sharply since last week's troubling announcements.

As a result of the latest downgrade, borrowing costs that had been oddly unaffected in previous downgrades, have now begun to rise sharply, as investors other than the Fed are unwilling to invest in US debt instruments. Corporate and Government leaders throughout Europe, Asia, and in the United States are actively selling bonds to raise capital. As yet, there appear to be few buyers willing to commit their dollars at any level. In an effort to help finance the rapidly growing gap facing federal government agencies, officials have begun digitizing larger and larger portions of the national debt, leaving private borrowers shut out of the market, as investors scramble to turn any capital they have into hard assets. The net result is that real interest rates on US paper are rising sharply today."

Annie sat exhausted on folding chairs in her empty living room, listening to the radio with Jana, as their men finished loading the U-Haul trailer Russell rented to get to Mineral Wells. Holding a squirming Bridgett in her lap, Annie stared blankly at Jana who sat across from her. "Oh my God! I have never been this sad in my entire life! You just never think that something like this can ever happen."

Jana put on a brave face, and smiled weakly back at her. "Just turn it off, Honey. I don't know what this world is coming to. I guess John and I are still hoping for the best, hoping that somehow they figure something out that can put things back to normal eventually."

Annie looked at her friend incredulously.

"You know I love you, but I have no idea how you can believe that, Jana. I keep thinking about that man who was killed here last Friday over at Holdings Food Store because he bought up the last of the canned soups, and wouldn't sell any of it. I am just glad we were able to sell my car last week to get enough money for the gas to get home."

Annie could feel herself tearing up and noticed that Jana was doing the same.

"I don't know where we would even go, Sweetie. My mom is in Colorado and John's family is in Iowa. Our home is here, so we will just do the best we can.

"I understand. I'm glad you took all the stuff we couldn't sell at our garage sale. You use whatever you like or give to anyone who needs it. Same goes for the house. I don't know how long it will be ours, but the taxes aren't due until the end of the year. I guess the bank will foreclose at some point, but if anyone needs a place to stay, please let them use it. I called a couple of churches to tell them, and gave them your phone number."

Annie sighed, watching her friend's tears, too heavy to be contained, running down her face.

"I will take good care of your place, Sweetie. You guys are too nice for your own good, but we have your payment book, and I will do my best to keep it occupied and paid for if I can, or just occupied if I can't." With nothing left to say, both women stood up. They looked sadly at each other, and then around the house one last time. Annie could see that, like her, Jana was reliving their good times here. When her friend's eyes made their way back to look at her again, she handed Jana her keys to the house and leaned forward to give her a tight hug.

"Annie, I am going to miss you. You are just about my best friend in the whole world. Please promise you will stay in touch, no matter what happens."

"I promise. You know I will send email or letters or whatever.

Jana did her best to smile, sniffling and blinking rapidly to ward off the emotions that had overcome them both. Annie could see that Jana needed to get going, to avoid breaking down completely. "OK, Girl. I guess I should grab John and get out of your hair."

Annie nodded to her friend, and they walked out to the front yard where the men were talking to someone. As she walked up to their truck, Annie realized that a dark blue pickup, parked on the street in front of their house, belonged to Nathan Jacobs. Stunned at seeing him, she looked over to Russ.

"What's going on, Russ?" She smiled at the two men, knowing that the surprise on her face was blatantly obvious. "Hello, Nathan."

Relieved, she saw that Russ turned from Nathan and smiled back at her. "Nathan is going to drive down with us."

Now, she was shocked. "Really, Nathan, are your folks ok? I mean you just started here a few months ago."

"Everyone is fine, Annie. Dad called last week. He asked me if I would come back home. Your dad mentioned that you guys were coming, so I was just asking Russ if I could convoy down with you."

Her husband gave her a smile. "I know I feel better with a group, not to mention having two vehicles in case of a break down or something."

Nathan nodded in agreement. "With things going into the toilet, Dad said that he wanted Lamont and me to be there. Lamont dropped all his classes at A&M and drove back from College Station last weekend, so I guess I should put my family first too."

Annie nodded. “Well, the more the merrier, I guess. I am sorry about you having to leave your job.”

“Yeah, well, Annie, you know how it is. My boss wasn’t really very happy about it, but with people beginning to riot, and gang types going after people with food, I really didn’t have much choice. I have to stand with my folks.”

Russell nodded. “You know what they say, ‘Strength in numbers.’ I am really glad you are coming along Nathan. Being a cop and all can’t hurt, right? I don’t think that we will run into any trouble, but you can’t be too careful.”

Nathan agreed and nodded to Annie, then turned to climb back into his truck. Annie put Bridgett onto the little pallet she fashioned with boxes and a blanket in the space behind the seats. Smiling at the puppy, she shut the door to keep her there. She watched Russell walk over to grab John’s hand, to say good bye. Again, she found herself fighting back tears, as Jana walked up for a final hug, after locking their front door.

“Love you, Annie. You take care of yourself and that baby. I expect pictures now, don’t forget me.”

“I love you too. I won’t forget.” She released her friend, and smiled as best she could. “When things settle down at some point, let’s get together. We can catch up, and you can meet the baby.”

“You have a deal, Girlfriend. I will look forward to that.” Jana stepped back, and Annie climbed into the pickup, moving Bridgett to the little spot they had fixed for her in the club cab area behind the pickup’s seat. Patting her on the head she scooted over past the steering wheel to her side of the truck. She watched Jana as John joined her on their front walk. Russ climbed in behind the wheel and started the truck. She smiled weakly at her husband, as Russell put the pickup in gear and pulled out of the driveway, returning Jana and John’s waves as they did so. Unable to repress her emotions, tears washed down Annie’s face, as they pulled away from their home. Feeling helpless, she wondered if she would ever see it or her friend again.

She felt Russell take her hand to try and comfort her. “Hard times can’t last forever, Sweetheart. We will see them again.

Besides, think how excited your mom is at having a baby in the house again." Annie smiled at her husband.

"I know you're right. It is just a lot harder than I thought it would be. I didn't mind quitting my job, but packing up the house and leaving like this just feels terrible." She looked one last time in the mirror, as her little white frame home fell away behind her. She felt Russ caress her cheek as the little convoy drove away.

"So Annie, Nathan and I were talking. We thought that we would stop for some dinner in Kingfisher. You can make it an hour or so can't you?"

Smiling at her husband, she placed her hand on his shoulder. "Sure, that sounds good. Besides, Kingfisher won't even take us that long. I just want to make sure we get home before midnight."

"I wouldn't think we should have any problem with that, but speaking of arrival time, you need to call your dad to tell him we're on our way."

Annie nodded and reached back to the space behind their seat. She rubbed Bridget behind the ears, then reached around the boxes of their belongings, to find her purse and her cell phone. She scrolled down to her parents' number and tapped it. She listened to it ring once, then again when someone picked up.

"Hello!"

"Hello, Daddy, it's Annie. Russ said to tell you that we are on our way."

"Good, Honey, I know you kids didn't want to have to do this, but it will be for the best."

"I know. We just hate imposing on you. You both have already done your part."

"We look after our own in this family; you know that. Besides, we are really excited to have you girls back at home again. Chet Donaldson and I have already started putting up new walls in the garage to give you and Russ your own little apartment."

"Daddy, you shouldn't be spending money on us now."

"Don't be silly, Annie girl; you have to have a place for my grandchild. I just wish that I could get your older sister to come home. Her problem is that she is too much like me for her own good. That girl is stubborn to a fault.

"You say that, but I think you like that she is just as stubborn as you are."

He made a "humph" sound, but she could almost hear the smile in his voice.

"Maybe you are right; still, I wish she would come home. Anyway, I'm going to let you go now, but I want you to call me back in a couple of hours to let me know you kids are ok."

"I will. We are going to stop in Kingfisher for dinner. I will call then. Oh, by the way, they probably already know, but Nathan Jacobs is driving along behind us. He said you mentioned we were coming to Mr. Jacobs. He might want to know that Nathan is on his way."

"I will do that, Annie. I am grateful for every one of you kids who come back here. We are going to need your generation, I think."

"I love you, Daddy. We will be home soon."

"I love you too, Pumpkin. I am going to hang up. Tell Russ to mind the road, now. Folks might not be as rational as they should be. We love you kids, and we are looking forward to seeing you both soon."

Annie turned to her husband as the two pickups drove south past Vance Air Force Base on Highway Eighty-One. "Daddy said to tell you to be extra careful in case there are crazies." She noticed that he was lost in thought and just nodded. She looked at him with sympathy in her eyes.

"I am really sorry, Sweetheart. I really wish your folks had come along. It is hard for us to leave. I can't even imagine how it would be for them." Annie patted her husband on the shoulder. "I guess that after living someplace for thirty years, they just could not see doing anything else. Just like Jana and John, they are hoping for the best."

"I know. My dad is a blowhard, and my mom makes me crazy, but I was just thinking. I hope they will be ok, and I'll get to see them again."

"I love you, Russ. I am sure we will someday. I will pray for them every day, Sweetheart." He turned to her and smiled.

"I know you will. You and our baby are my first responsibility though, and your folks have land and cattle. We are going to need to be near food. I know it is the right thing to do, and that is all that matters. Anyway, it is five o'clock. Do you mind if I listen to the headlines?"

"Sort of, the news is always so depressing lately, but I know you want to stay up on things, so go ahead."

Reaching back, she scratched Bridgett behind her ears again, and then turned back and looked out the window at the endless rows of young green wheat growing in the fields on either side of the road as the little truck moved down the highway. Her husband reached for the radio. She realized she really loved the way mature wheat made waves when it was tall and gold, just like the wind makes waves on a lake. Sighing, she wished it was later in the year so she could see that now.

"...As a result of the domestic reaction to the crisis, in a stunning show of bipartisanship, members of both parties in Washington, worked diligently to dramatically slash federal spending. Surprisingly, there are still a significant number of representatives that, even now, are unwilling to abandon entitlements for their constituents. A clear majority caucus, however, has solidified to reduce government spending by many trillions of dollars. The concern voiced by leaders today described the difficulty in making the needed cuts. In an interview with the Majority Leader an hour ago, ABC News learned that congressional leaders are finding it difficult to make needed cuts due to legally mandated interest payments and required spending for protected entitlement programs. Furthermore, regardless of the slim majority of members in the House and Senate who have agreed on a spending reduction plan, members are finding that the reductions are of marginal use with regard to reducing the deficits. After scoring this week's austerity plan, the Government Accounting Office noted that the savings achieved will be entirely consumed by dramatically increasing interest costs on the existing federal debt..."

After the last week of never-ending disasters, Annie turned from the wheat fields to look at her husband. The despair she felt listening to the report was overwhelming. She decided she hated listening to the news and never wanted to hear it again. Looking at Russell, she saw fear in his eyes as he stared down the empty highway. It occurred to her that, for now at least, he was as sick of the news as she was.

"Let's just turn it off, Russ. You know that they are not going to say anything good."

"In a minute, Sweetheart, we still need to know what's happening." She nodded dejectedly and looked back out the window at the never ending power poles as they passed them by. Shifting her eyes to the mirror, she was heartened to see that Nathan was still behind them. It cheered her to know he was there.

"...World markets are reacting to the close of the NYSE with volatility in a strong down trend. The United States Central Bank, along with other central banks around the world are forcing interest rate hikes to maintain liquidity. New York Federal Bank Chairman, Robert Gibbs, said that by sharply raising interest rates, the bank hoped to maintain investor support for their bonds. Global currencies, however, are still in free fall as gold, silver, and oil prices continue to rise as investors seek inflation protection. In addition, Mr. Gibbs noted that all of overseas trade balances are degrading rapidly with leading economic indicators declining."

Annie focused on a small herd of Herefords peacefully grazing on the winter wheat north of Hennessey. She loved cattle. They always reminded her of her childhood, and that made her feel safe. Russell finally reached over and turned the radio off, reducing the sound in the cab to that of the road and Bridgett's cute little snores. Grateful for the quiet, Annie kicked off her shoes to get comfortable, deciding she would follow her puppy's example and get some sleep. She pulled her pillow from behind the seat to prop against the window, and snuggled in as best she could in the cramped little pickup.

Sensing the truck slowing to a stop, Annie blinked her eyes open and sat up stiffly. She stretched, rotating her neck to work out the kinks she had earned by sleeping at an odd angle against the little pickup's window. "Ouch, this truck sucks for trips. Where are we, Honey?"

"We just pulled into Kingfisher a couple of minutes ago. Are you hungry? Nathan and I are thinking pizza if you think you can keep it down."

Annie yawned, glanced back at Bridgett, still sleeping peacefully, and smiled at her husband. Feeling a little better, she reached over to give his shoulder a loving squeeze. "That sounds good. I'll probably get sick regardless of what we decide on."

"You're probably right."

Her husband smirked at her, but she detected sympathy in his eyes. Playfully, she punched him in the arm as the cars moving through the intersection perpendicular to them began to thin out when the light turned yellow on their side. Annie yawned as a blue Ford dually, pulling a horse trailer, came to a stop to their left, across the intersection. The light turned green, and Russell started to go, but then stopped abruptly. Annie watched a gangly white kid, wearing a black flat brimmed baseball cap, with low-rider jeans, and a dingy jean jacket, complete with a skull embossed on the pocket, indolently lead a group of four boys, similarly dressed, across the street. Glancing back at her husband, she could see he was angry. Seething, he shook his head in disgust. "Punks like that are what's wrong with this country today. If I didn't have you in the truck, I would make them kiss my ass."

"I'm glad that I'm in the truck then. Our baby doesn't need to have her father shot by gang bangers." She could feel the anger radiating from her husband, and it appeared the boys slowly making their way past them could feel it too. Having just passed in front of them, the group's leader spun around to look directly at her. She chilled as the guy shot her an insolent smirk, accompanied by his making a pistol gesture with his hand, bringing his thumb down to mimic shooting at them. Noticing Russell's right hand going for their pistol between the split seats, she placed her own hand on top of his, restraining him. Staring back at the kid, she felt her own outrage rise as the guy next to the leader, poked him, pointed at her, and laughed.

The moment, the four were out of the way, Russell gunned the engine and they made their way through the intersection. Annie looked into the mirror as they passed and saw an older man yelling at the kids as he went by them. Again, they responded by making pistol gestures with their hands and flipping the man off. Watching in disgust, she witnessed the smallest of the four boys strike the man's truck with what looked like a tire iron or a piece of pipe. It was then that she noticed that Nathan's pickup was nowhere to be seen.

"Where is Nathan? I just realized he isn't behind us. Those kids just smashed a guy's tail lights out. I would feel better if he were with us right about now. "

"Me too, Annie. I should have said something, I'm sorry. He said he wanted to top off, so he stopped at a gas station as we got to town."

"Should we call him?"

"We better not. Your dad wouldn't want us sticking our noses into anything we didn't have to. Besides, Nathan told me to go ahead and order, so I'm sure he's hungry. He'll catch up to us at the restaurant, and we will be alright."

"Ok Russ, if you think so? Those guys just gave me the creeps. Maybe it's just that we had to leave our home, and being pregnant, and everything, but I just feel really vulnerable. I will be really glad to get home."

"Sure, Sweetheart I understand. We will be there in a few hours. "

Looking at him, she knew he was right, but she also realized that although she was constantly worried about everything, she was actually happy, regardless of the terrible news and having to pack up her home. The last week had been so stressful, but she thought that at least her husband was back to being the man she married. She decided there was no price that she wouldn't pay for that gift.

Russell smiled at her and patted her on the leg, then pointed to the Pizza Hut sign in front of a little restaurant on the right. "For now, we can relax and have some supper."

Annie nodded. "Good, I need to go to the bathroom. Remember, I shouldn't drink caffeine. Will you just get me some water and lemon?"

"You got it." Annie noticed that Russ turned right onto the street, just north of the Pizza Hut and pulled into the back of the parking lot, so he would not bother anyone with the U Haul trailer they were pulling behind them. Annie was still slipping her shoes back on her feet as Russell took the keys out of the ignition.

"Russ, will Bridget be ok here, like this?"

"We won't be too long, and I'll take her for a walk when Nathan gets here."

Annie looked back to see that the dog appeared to be content, and she reached for her handle as Russell rolled the windows down a couple of inches and hit the button to lock the doors. Annie got out and stretched, and then started toward the front door, pausing to wait for Russell, who was taking a moment to check the trailer.

Walking up behind her, he took her hand. "Wow, I didn't realize how hungry I was. The pizza really smells great doesn't it?"

Annie nodded in agreement, her spirits lifting a little. She noticed a young woman about her age trying to navigate her way out the door, pushing a stroller. Russell took a couple of quick steps and pulled the door open for her. She smiled her thanks as she exited the building.

Annie smiled down at the beautiful little infant swaddled in a pink blanket.

"You have a pretty baby. How old is she?"

"Thank you so much. She is three months old tomorrow. She is everything to my husband and me."

"Well, you have a nice evening."

"I will. Thanks again for the kindness. Good night."

Annie could see Russell had already headed for the restroom, so she did likewise. A few minutes later, she came back out to see Russell sitting in a booth on the other side of the little building, opposite the door. She realized he obviously wanted a good view of the parking lot. He waved at her and rose when she approached. She sat across from him, and she felt him take her hands in his. "You pick what you want, Sweetheart. I am hoping that you will be able to hold down your supper, so I am thinking..."

She smiled and held up her hand to stop him.

"Just get whatever you like, Russ. Just get cheese on my side. Pizza is probably not the healthiest option, but it will be fine for tonight. Actually, why don't you and Nathan just split a pizza? Look, they have a nice salad bar. I think I am just going to go for that, although I may steal a slice off of you guys."

Russell put down the menus and looked up as a pretty black teenager approached with their drinks and an order pad. "Hi guys, welcome to Pizza Hut, I am Chelease. Do you know what you would like tonight?"

Annie took a sip of her water as Russell smiled at the waitress, and handed her the menus. We just need a large supreme with extra sauce and a salad for my wife."

"What crust do y'all want?"

"Oh, right. Um let's just do like a pan crust if that's ok."

"Got it. I'll get that right out in like ten minutes." Looking at Annie, she motioned to the salad bar. "Go ahead and help yourself whenever you are ready."

Annie smiled at her and started sliding out of the booth. "Thank you, I appreciate it."

Chelease smiled, and walked off towards a tall skinny teenager with bright red hair, standing near the door, to put in their order. Watching her go, Annie wondered if she would be able to get another job any time soon.

"I will be right back, Sweetie." Annie walked over to the salad bar, selected a plate and began loading it. She decided that it would be weird living at home again, this time with a husband and in a few months, a new baby. Sighing, she realized that her mom was likely to drive her completely nuts with advice and her opinions on how to do everything. On the other hand she thought, at least she and Russ would have built in babysitters, and with just a little luck, maybe they wouldn't be as sleep deprived as Jana said she should expect to be. Noticing the hard boiled eggs, she added a few slices, then sprinkled shredded cheese liberally on top of her creation, topping it off with blue cheese salad dressing. As she walked back to their booth she saw that Russell was on the phone. She started to slide into the booth beside him to make room for Nathan when he got here, but her husband held up a hand to stop her, and got to his feet, to let her past him. Moving past him, she slid across to sit by the window.

Russell sat back down and put his arm around her. "...yes, Sir. I will have her call when we get on the road again. It shouldn't be too long. We only just ordered a few minutes ago, but I would think we would be moving again within the hour." She felt his fingers casually play with her curls as she began to pick at one of the cherry tomatoes. She giggled, realizing her father was giving him an earful. "Thank you, Sir, we will see you both soon." He laid the phone down and rolled his eyes, blinking away her dad's anxiety.

"Dad said there was some sort of riot in Dallas because a plant shut down and laid everybody off. Apparently, there was trouble, and when the cops showed, the workers started throwing rocks at them. Anyway, it sounds like it got out of hand, and the protestors charged the cops. People were getting seriously hurt, so the cops had to shoot some people. Then the rioters started shooting back. Anyway, your dad said that a bunch of people were killed."

Annie looked at him in disbelief. "Oh, my God, that sounds like Europe or Greece or something." She felt herself being pulled close as Russell gave her a reassuring hug.

"Don't worry, Annie Girl. Nothing will happen to us. We will be in Mineral Wells in just a few hours from right now."

"I love you, Russ. I really..." She didn't get to finish her statement as the door burst open on the far side of the restaurant. Annie stared in shock as a large pale unshaven man in his forties walked in and stood near the salad bar with a shotgun leveled as if he fully intended to use it at any moment.

Annie realized immediately that he was obviously drunk as he began to bellow orders. "Anybody even thinks about grabbing a cell phone they will wish they'd never been born!" Yelling back to the kitchen he motioned with the shotgun at their waitress and the cook to move into the dining room. "Get yo ass in here, Darrel. You too, you little black bitch!" Annie was terrified, frozen in her seat, as if glued there. She was unable to take her eyes off the large ugly man.

"Oh, my God Russ, what will we do," she whispered.

"Hurry up, Bitch! You still think it's funny, getting me fired, do you?" The waitress never got the chance to answer, before the drunken intruder, his eyes wild, locked on a young man making a run for the door. A deafening boom echoed through the dining room, the shotgun belching fire from the muzzle. The man fell in a heap and didn't move; his blood sprayed across the windows and the door he had so hoped to be through by now.

To Annie's horror, the man whipped around, looking directly at her, the ominous smoking barrel trained right at her head. It was then she realized she had screamed, drawing his attention. Suddenly nauseated, she could taste the acrid taste of her terror.

"Please don't!"

She felt Russell stand, moving in front of her as best he could, constrained by the proximity of their booth to the table in front of her. Awkwardly, he tried to pull her behind him with his right hand, extending his left hand to the ugly man in a placating gesture. Through her tears, she saw his gaze focused like lasers on the wild man's drunken bloodshot eyes.

"Look, Buddy, we got no quarrel with you. She only screamed because you scared her. I just got laid off myself. I know how you feel, ok?"

Shaking uncontrollably, she realized that she might not ever get to see her folks again, never get to hold her baby or even see tomorrow. She felt herself shrinking into a small little ball, as her eyes moved from Russell to the dirty alcohol sodden man.

"My name is Russ, let's work something out here. You don't want to hurt anybody else, there's no point to it, you know? You want folks to think you had your reasons, right. Killing a bunch of people now is just going to get you written off, Man."

Annie saw the man's head tilt as he considered what her husband had just said. Russell was subtly shaking his head no. "Come on, Man, you need to be thinking about what you want to say when the bastards show up. Look, you're in charge here; nobody else is going to move. I just really need you not to hurt my wife. She is all I got." Annie realized through her terror that whatever else was happening, the man was at least thinking about things. She had never seen Russell so focused. His eyes darted from the people staring in shock at the ugly man, to the body lying in the red pool, glistening under the restaurant's pot lights, then pausing briefly on a heavy glass beer mug on the next table, and finally back to the ugly man.

Annie watched as the man blinked at Russell and considered what to do. In a slow motion nightmare, the restaurant door behind the man opened to reveal Nathan moving forward with his pistol leveled.

"Police, drop the weapon! Drop it now! Drop it! Drop it! I'm not telling you again! Do it! Do it now!"

The man was clearly shaking now, and Annie thought she could see his resolve weaken. He bent down at the waist, laying the shotgun on the floor.

The ugly man began sobbing. "I'm sorry, Man, I ain't got nothing now! They've ruined my life! You don't understand, Man."

Nathan approached the man cautiously, having to sidestep briefly to avoid stepping in the spreading crimson pool. "It is going to be ok, now. You will get through this, Pal."

Gasping in a deep breath, she thought it was over, when again, she heard three sharp cracks. Staring in horror, Annie saw that the ugly man had just pulled a pistol from where it was concealed in a holster inside his pants, near his spine. He fired at Nathan at point blank range. She saw her friend spin around from the impact of the bullets hitting him.

"No!" She heard her voice screaming. The man was now as wild as any animal she had ever seen as he struggled to get back on his feet. Terrified, she saw Russell sprinting towards him, grabbing the heavy mug off of the next table as he went past.

Frozen in place, she watched as he slammed the mug against the man's head like he was swinging a club, golden droplets of beer racing in an arc behind the glass. She heard another loud crack, this time from the impact of the mug slamming against the man's skull. Stunned he just stared, confused, not realizing what had just happened to him. Russell swung again, the second time, a backswing, coming from the other direction. The glass smashed this time as it impacted on the man's nose, dropping him like a rock, his blood now joining his victim's on the restaurant floor.

Chapter 24
Valley of the Shadow of Death

Instantly furious, and more than a little stunned from being man-handled, Megan struck out hard with her right foot. She felt her heel connect with the ski masked man attempting to gain control of her flailing legs.

"Relax, Bitch. This will go a lot easier for you if you don't fight it!"

She realized that the iron grip that held her arms was desperately working to slip something past her hands, as another man fought for balance as he tried to adjust his position in the moving vehicle. Feeling her skin prickling with unmitigated terror, she realized she was in deep trouble. From the very core of her being, she knew that not fighting was not what she was about. Adrenaline surged through every fiber of her body as she fully committed to the battle. Desperately, she squirmed with all her strength. In the struggle, she managed to pull a third man's ski mask askew, temporarily blinding him. She caught his jaw with a knee, after which he removed his ski mask and lunged at her anew. She wrenched causing him to miss grabbing her. Again, her foot connected with the man trying to control her feet. She was gratified to hear something snap when her kick connected.

The man controlling her arms stank of sweat and beer. She could feel his anger and frustration mounting quickly. "Get her under control, damn it! We don't need anyone noticing this commotion!"

Still wildly resisting, Megan knew she needed a strategy and needed it quickly. Her eyes wide and flitting around the vehicle, she desperately looked for any advantage. From the front seat she saw the driver's face, turned half towards her for a moment. My God, she realized that it was Luther's assistant, Ron something. Though watching the road, he momentarily made eye contact with her. "Calm down, Meg, or we will have to hurt you." In that moment, she knew she was fighting for her life. Ron driving, along with the man in front of her removing his mask, could only mean one thing. They did not plan to let her live.

"Fuck you, Ron!"

Fighting even harder, she head-butted the man behind her but she immediately felt the bite of zip ties binding her arms tightly behind her. She felt his response to her aggression, as he vainly grabbed a fist full of her blond hair extensions. To his surprise, the hair extension came away in his hand with no effect on controlling his prey.

She barely had time to process her little victory, when she saw the other man's knuckles rushing at her. She tried to move her head and avoid the blow, but she felt the bone jarring shock of his fist impacting the side of her face. She rocked back, head slamming into the van.

❧

"Ugh." Megan opened her eyes, but realized her vision was less than optimal. She groaned and blinked, hoping to clear her vision. Disoriented, she realized that she hurt everywhere, but the worst was the right side of her face. She tried to reach up to touch where it hurt, but discovered that she was, in fact, unable to lift her arms, as they were tied behind her. She was propped up on a folding chair, with her right ankle zip tied to a radiator. Petrified, she looked around the dingy room at her surroundings, trying hard to remain as calm as possible. She felt like screaming, but knew that it would not do any good. She could picture Matt telling her to be cool and methodical. "There is almost always something in the environment to use, Meg. It is critical that you always look for you opportunities," he would say. She realized then she had ignored his advice about not resisting and wasting energy when overwhelmed. She wondered if she should have saved her strength in the van and watched for an opportunity like Matt told her to do.

"Oh God, I am in a real jam here. I knew I was not being who I should have been, but I did it anyway. Please forgive me? I am sorry for putting money and prestige above honor and integrity."

She knew her words sounded hollow now, but she also knew that she meant it. Her surroundings were dilapidated, but appeared to be a room in a residential apartment building. As she looked around the small room, she sighed as there was just nothing she could use, other than the chair she was sitting on, a short piece of pipe under the radiator next to her, and the battery powered light across from her, by the door. There wasn't any sign of life that she could hear, so she decided the building must be empty or under renovation. Grimacing, she thought maybe Matt would find her before the apes who took her showed up again. They had no way to know that Matt had given her the tiny transceiver that she had slipped into the waistband of whatever she wore each day. Dear God, she was grateful he knew what he was doing. She just hoped he wouldn't take too long. Wherever the bastards were, for now thankfully, she was alone in her grimy prison.

As her eyes darted around what was once probably someone's tiny bedroom, she realized that even though the room's window was boarded up, it existed. Therefore she must at least be above ground. "Dammit! I just wish I knew what time it was." Finally, she decided it must be dark outside, because there were not any pinprick's of light between the boards on the windows. She wondered to herself how long someone who was knocked unconscious typically remained out of it. Without her phone, she had no idea. "Come on, Matt, where the hell are you?" she whispered desperately under her breath, as tears streaked down her swollen cheek. Struggling in vain, she pulled desperately at her bindings. "Get me out of here!"

OK, ok, ok, I have to just calm down. "Think, Meg, think." She thought that maybe the apes aren't here because they are dealing with Matt right now. Oh God, what if something happens to him? It was that thought which made up her mind. Her best chance of escape was to work out the angles calmly, like she always did. She knew she had no choice but to have faith that he would be ok, and that he would find a way to get her out.

Taking a deep breath, she let it out slowly and worked the situation in her mind. They went to the trouble of getting me here. They must need something, or they would have already killed me. Finally, her mind functioning again, she decided that her primary goal was to buy Matt some time. She shivered as she turned over what would come next. Whatever they wanted, she realized that it would not be a negotiation she wanted any part of.

The thought of what was probably going to happen next brought more tears to her eyes. Her head dropped in despair. "Please, God, let Matt find me before they come back." As she sat immobile, in miserable anticipation of the unknown, she began to cry harder. Despondent, she reached out with her mind and her senses to find something, anything, that could give her what she needed more than anything else; hope.

As the moment turned into two, she dropped her head to pray. As she began to speak, she saw what she needed. There on the floor, between her feet, was a small crucifix, broken, where a chain had once been attached. She smiled weakly, and her courage renewed, she again began pulling against her restraints. It then occurred to her that the radiator next to her was really rough where it had been poorly repaired. Immediately, she began to rub the zip ties binding her hands against the rough spot on the exposed metal of the radiator. Feeling the heat she generated, she knew that she was making some headway. She worked on her restraints for several minutes, when she slipped, and felt the metal cut into her wrists. Biting off her scream, she took a breath and resumed her efforts. After a few minutes, she tried to break free, but her arms were just too stiff from being pinned behind her to have the strength to do so. After a few more minutes and another cut on her wrists, she felt the plastic give way. Gasping, she immediately attacked the tie holding her ankle immobile. Unfortunately, her time was all but expired as she heard people entering what was likely the front door to the apartment-prison. Panicking, she recovered the broken zip tie and picked up the crucifix. She put her arms behind her as they had been, locking her fingers to help her maintain the ruse.

The door to her prison opened as Ron from her firm entered. To her surprise he was followed by John David Sterns himself. Megan was so stunned; she almost revealed that she had the use of her hands. She knew, of course, that he would have authorized her current predicament, but her mind reeled that he was here in person.

Feeling the broken crucifix biting into her palm, she raised her chin in defiance to stare reproachfully at the man who had clearly come to personally witness her death. "I would have thought this was the sort of thing you would have had outsourced, Sterns." His visage reflected his discomfort at seeing her bound, her face battered, but she also saw the resolve in his eyes.

"Good evening, Ms. Danvers. I truly regret that matters have progressed to this juncture, my dear. You are an exceptionally bright and beautiful young woman. I am quite afraid that you have become a serious liability, however." Appraising the dingy surroundings in disgust, he grimaced slightly. "I am afraid that you agreeing to work with Agent Ricks this evening made this result inevitable. Whether you would have gone through with assisting them, I cannot say, but it is of no consequence, as I simply cannot afford such a risk."

"Of course! You have someone on Agent Rick's team. That is the only way you would know anything about what I may or may not have said."

"Just so, Ms. Danvers, A costly operative, to be sure, but a necessary one, all things considered. Bravo, your analysis is always spot on. I will miss your keen insights."

Megan rolled her eyes, but said nothing, and did her best to stare him down with disinterest.

Acknowledging her scorn with a smirk, he continued. "Yes, well, to answer your question, Ms. Danvers, regardless of how our association together is concluding, you are not a mere pawn to be sacrificed. I learned as a young military officer in Viet Nam that a leader must never give an order he is unwilling to carry out himself. I have always conducted my affairs with honor and dignity, even when, like today, they are distasteful. I personally placed you on my board of directors. That is something you earned as a result of your hard work and your intelligence. For this reason, Ms. Danvers, it is my unhappy burden to personally oversee what takes place here tonight.

Surprisingly, Megan heard herself laughing. "Do you honestly expect me to think any better of you, Sterns? You are an elitist bastard, and you will end like all elitist bastards, when the peasants revolt! Do you know what makes me the sickest out of all of this? I was just as guilty as you are, until a couple of weeks ago.

"Well said, Ms. Danvers, well said, indeed. As I noted earlier, I find you to be a remarkable young woman. Regardless, you are no doubt wondering what is to happen next. Allow me to explain. Our Mr. Blake has been somewhat hesitant about sharing what he has explained to your friend, Agent Ricks. My operative arranged our reuniting with Mr. Blake, but he has proven surprisingly reticent about divulging what exactly the noble Agent Ricks is privy to. I would like your assistance in tying up that particular loose end."

Megan watched in horror as an understated smile emerged on his face. She knew that smile to be his tell, which meant that he held all the cards. "May I ask why I would be willing to assist you in this?"

"Of course, Ms. Danvers, I would expect nothing less of you. Why you should participate in my little query is at the heart of our negotiation, is it not?"

Megan could feel her hands beginning to tingle. She realized that she needed to move her fingers, but doing so risked giving away that she had the use of her hands. Watching Sterns pace back and forth before her, she realized that while repulsed by the man, she was delaying a more unpleasant negotiation tactic.

Moving in closer to her, Sterns squatted down to look her in the eye, a serpent examining its prey. "Sadly, Ms. Danvers, you are far too intelligent to realize that, although it wounds me, I cannot let you live. What I can offer you, however, is a quick and painless passing, as opposed to leaving the task to the imagination of my employees. Furthermore, should you choose to be of assistance, I will personally see to your family's well-being in the coming crisis. Conversely, should you choose not to assist me in this, I am afraid that I will visit upon your dear sisters the same fate that will befall you, should our negotiation conclude unsatisfactorily."

Again, Megan found herself stunned at the old man's utter ruthlessness. She now realized that this man was the most evil person she had ever known or imagined.

The old man stood again, sadness plainly displayed on his face. "I will give you a few minutes to think it over. I should emphasize that if you do not choose to assist me, I promise you that your sisters will pay quite dearly for your failure to see logic in this matter."

Staring at him with horror, she watched Sterns motion to Ron to withdraw. He gazed upon her sadly, and then grimaced, before turning to follow Ron out of the little room, shutting the door behind him.

Megan's mind raced as she watched Sterns and Ron leave the room. "Oh my God, I am never going to see my family again, never see Matt again." Shaking and a little nauseous, she could feel her fear mounting with every passing minute. "Please, God, please, God, please, God, help me. I don't want to die here. I want to see Kate and Annie. I want to hold Annie's baby and..." Her voice trailed off, her tears overwhelming her. Desperately fighting her panic, she began coaching herself through the nightmare. Ok, Megan, you've got to fight for a way out. She decided that her first priority was mobility. Looking down, her ankle was so tightly bound to the leg of the radiator she could barely move her leg. She noticed a short length of pipe under the radiator but knew it was too thick to be of any use in freeing her leg. Then it hit her that the end of the cross that she picked up would fit into the end of the zip tie. She thought that maybe she could shim it loose, using the metal end to block the teeth of the tie from catching. Encouraged, she was able to loosen the bond slightly but her hope was immediately dashed as she heard the front door open again and footsteps approaching the door in front of her.

Paralyzed with fear, she again clasped her hands behind her as Ron and a Hispanic guy that she vaguely recognized, entered the room, holding Richard between them. Like her, he had been beaten, and in his case beaten savagely. Recognizing her, he shut his eyes with grief, as hope left him. The Hispanic guy immediately ducked back into the other room and returned with another folding chair. Megan watched in horror as they dumped Richard on the chair and zip tied his ankle to the other side of the same radiator she was lashed to. As they were finishing, Sterns entered again and motioned with his head for his employees to leave.

When they were gone, his face took on a sad but concerned look as he gazed down at the two of them. She saw that Richard just looked down as he licked his bleeding lips. Trying to stop her tears by force of will, she looked up at Sterns. He returned her gaze with an imperious look to emphasize she had better play her role as they had discussed moments ago.

Chapter 25
The Contest

Glancing down at his iPad where it lay on the seat beside him, Matt sighed, grateful that the red dot representing Megan was finally motionless. He knew that this part of the city was notorious for dilapidated buildings, which if not abandoned, were only occupied by the most desperate of drug addicts. He nosed the restored green 1972 Ford pickup with matching camper forward, just enough to look down the street. He did not see much in the way of human beings, but as expected, the black SUV he had been tailing for the past forty minutes was parked down the block under a street lamp. It sat in front of a heavily tagged brown tenement. A large man, with short cropped blond hair wearing a dark blazer, leaned against the vehicle as he smoked a cigarette.

He decided that whatever the bastards wanted, this was going to be the place where it went down. As he looked on, he noticed that a second black SUV pulled up. Reaching down for his binoculars, he brought them to his face and adjusted the focus to see that four men were getting out. The shortest of them held the door for someone. A moment later, he saw John David Sterns step out of the vehicle. "Holy Shit, you don't see that every day." Son of a bitch, that makes nine jack-asses to deal with, he thought. "Not exactly the odds I prefer." Sterns and two of the men from his vehicle, along with the man who had been waiting by the first SUV went into the building, leaving two from Stern's vehicle out front.

Matt sat back considering Agent Rick's business card that Megan had given him earlier. Maybe it would be best to just call the FBI. "Damn it!" He slammed his palm on the dash, thinking he just did not have the time to wait on the Feds. As he fumed, he noticed the three men who jumped Meg right in front of him back at Macy's exited the building. As he watched, they got in the first SUV and drove away.

"I swear to God, if you dick-wads hurt her, you are going to regret it." Matt reached for the gearshift and put the truck into reverse. He edged it back the way he had come along a metal-clad chain link fence that shielded a small empty lot. Matt opened the door and got out. Pulling the seat-back forward to reveal an assortment of tools and weapons that lay behind in the small cargo area, he exhaled and selected a pair of bolt cutters. Walking quickly to the gate on the fence next to where he had stopped, he made quick work of the lock. He pushed the gate aside and trotted back over to the pickup. Putting it in gear, he relocated the truck out of sight from the street as he hastily decided what he wanted to do next.

Again he got out, this time grabbing the shoulder strap to an AR14, a 12 gauge Mossberg with a pistol grip and a canvas satchel. Matt could feel his pulse racing with the knowledge that he had to get to Meg quickly or things could go badly. He reached down and took the old school colt 45 automatic from its holster which was clipped to his belt just to the right of his spine and pulled the slide to chamber a round. Looking around quickly, he pushed his head and arm through the shotgun sling, so he could carry the Mossberg on his back. He grabbed knee pads, his tactical gloves out of the bag, and then, as he did with the shotgun, he slung the canvas satchel over his shoulder as well. Methodically, he then pulled the slide on the AR14 and combat-slung the rifle on his right side to use as his primary weapon. Finally, he pulled his iPhone out and tapped the screen to bring up his tracking app. Although tense and more than a little angry, he was pleased she hadn't moved. "Hold on, Baby, I'm coming."

Moving off at a trot, Matt headed to the back of the empty lot. Climbing atop a rusting 1980's Caprice abandoned there, he jumped the two feet between it and the brick wall that separated the lot and the back of the building, adjacent to the tenement where Megan was being held. Once on top of the wall, he could see that the building in front of him had what passed for covered parking. Fortunately, the parking structure was only one story. He decided he could run along the roof, to gain access to the fire escape on the building he needed to reach. He started to jump the almost five or six feet to the roof of the parking structure next door, but he decided against it when he noticed a discarded section of painters' planking, leaning up against the wall, just a few feet down from where he was standing. Knowing it would be foolish to take unnecessary risks, he pulled up the board and used it to bridge the gap. Quickly, he then made his way along where the tenement joined the parking structure.

Gaining access to the second floor fire escape, he glanced at his watch and sighed that it had only been about ten minutes since he had pulled the old Ford onto the abandoned lot. Matt knew he was rushing things. He could not afford any mistakes. Forcing himself to calm down, he paused to take in his surroundings, and to listen to the environment. As his breath began to even out, he could feel the icy remoteness that had kept him alive in Iraq and Afghanistan descend over him.

Again, he checked the iPhone to validate Megan's position relative to where he was at the moment. "Third floor eh boys; I guess you assholes are too lazy to walk up any further." Ready now, he cautiously peered into the window next to him. He could see that the room beyond was once a bedroom. He reached down and tried the sash. Figures, he thought, its painted shut. Laying the assault rifle down for a moment, Matt pulled his canvas bag around in front of him and took out a roll of duct tape. Tearing off several strips, he placed all but a couple of them on the glass in a star pattern. Returning the tape to the bag, he took the butt of his rifle and tapped sharply on the upper right corner of the glass to break out a small piece. Using the remaining strips of tape to fashion a hand-hold where the glass was broken away, he leaned in hard on the pane breaking the glass with relatively little noise. Using his makeshift hand-hold, he lowered the broken glass panel to the floor of the room.

Carefully stepping into the darkness of the building's interior, his frustration was palatable as again, he had to pause to let his eyes adjust to the darkness. He strained to listen for any sound that could be a scream, but heard nothing. Again calming himself, he moved to his right, into an empty living room. Padding lightly across the floor, Matt moved to the apartment's front door. As he listened for movement at the door he scanned the room. Noticing the window in this room was already broken out, he rolled his eyes and sighed, pissed off that his previous efforts were pointless. Looking through the peephole was worthless due to the low light, and the filth making it all but opaque.

Taking a breath and moving his finger near the trigger guard of the AR14, Matt carefully opened the door in front of him and peered out. The hallway was dark and empty so he moved down the hall in a crouch, staying about 8 inches from the wall with his rifle pointed into the darkness ahead of him. He made it to the stairs in seconds and paused to again access the canvas bag. Putting a red lens pen lite in his mouth, he shuffled through the contents of the bag. As he searched for what he needed, he felt a cold fear that he would not be in time nagging at his heart. He had executed this type of operation many times but never before with the life of the woman he loved depending on him. Finally, his fingers located the canister he needed. Pulling it out of the bag he reached into a zippered pocket on the outside of the bag for the small roll of fishing line stowed there.

Working quickly, he duct-taped the flash bang to the banister. Looping the fishing line through the pull ring of the canister, he strung the line across the stairway at ankle height and tied the opposite end to a pipe that went up along the wall near the corner of the stairwell. Judging his efforts, he decided it would work well enough. He didn't care for surprises behind him.

He smirked. "With my luck, I will forget about this and trip it myself, on the way out." Matt sighed and carefully stepped over his trap, and headed to the third floor. Proceeding carefully, Matt was conscious of the placement of where he stepped on each tread. He was careful to stay close to the wall, to avoid the sound of the rubber soles of his boots on the treads. He decided that Megan was resilient and smart. She would know he was coming and would hang tough. He just hoped he could get there before hanging tough was a challenge for her.

~

"Well, Mr. Blake, Ms. Danvers, here we all are. I must say that I am deeply disappointed. I had such high hopes for you both." Megan clamped her mouth tightly shut, her mind racing with the thought of the sociopath before her possibly harming Katie or little Annie. She realized that she was literally shaking with fear as he spoke. Time was quickly running out, and she knew that the son-of-a-bitch was all too capable of keeping his promise regarding her family.

Eyeing Megan closely, Sterns continued. "I was just explaining to Mr. Blake how we could work through our little impasse. How the situation could be managed, if we cooperate. I need him to tell me everything that he has shared with his recent hosts. I am afraid, Ms. Danvers, that Mr. Blake has been a bit reticent to explain exactly of what his new friends are aware, and of what they are not."

Shaking so badly, it would be hard to discern any intentional movement, Megan nodded to indicate to Sterns that they had an agreement. She saw that he acknowledged the gesture and smiled slightly.

"I am going to retire to the other room for a short time to let the two of you discuss your situation amongst yourselves, free from any undue pressure my presence may inspire. If you elect to be helpful, then I will arrange for you both to walk out of here. If not..." She observed his gesture of helplessness. "I will have to turn our negotiations over to my associates." He smiled and turned on his heel, closing the door behind him.

Richard glanced over at her, regret evident on his face. "I am really sorry, Meg. I never thought that..."

She cut him off, mouthing to play along. "Richard, we are going to have to cooperate. We simply have no choice." As she spoke, she revealed that she had freed her hands and quickly resumed her attack on the zip tie holding her ankle.

Surprised, Richard smiled, amazement lighting his eyes. "You cannot possibly believe him. Why would he let us go? That doesn't make any sense, Meg. We can't trust him, you must know that."

"What choice do we have, Richard? We are out of options, as I see it." Achieving victory over the zip tie, Megan slipped her foot out of the loosened restraint and went over to free Richard as well.

"You know that the Feds will prosecute us if we do this. Do you want to spend the rest of your life in prison?"

"At this point, Richard, having a life, period, is what we are talking about. You do get that, right?"

Megan worked quickly, and a moment later Richard was rubbing his wrists and moving his ankles to restore the blood flow. Megan pointed at the section of pipe she had noticed earlier.

Smiling weakly at Richard, she whispered. "I am sure that Matt should be here soon. We have been really careful for weeks now. If he's not, I would still like to take one of them with me."

❧

Matt grew very cautious as he approached the third floor landing, and paused when he reached the top. With his head at an angle close to the floor he carefully leaned out, so that he could just barely look down the hallway. As he had assumed would be the case, a guy stood about halfway down the passage. As he watched the man, he recognized that although his opponent was obviously not expecting anyone to challenge him, neither was he inattentive. He decided it was at least thirty feet from the stairway to the apartment he guarded. There was no way he could take the guy out quietly. "Damn it", he whispered to himself. "I wish I knew for sure how many targets are in that apartment." Withdrawing slightly to run through the math, he decided that the likelihood was that he would be facing three guns and Sterns. With the two out front, that meant there would likely be three targets to deal with once he got into the apartment. Better three than what he was figuring on earlier, he decided.

Gripping his assault rifle tightly, psyching up for what he had to do, he paused with a last minute thought. Pulling out his burn phone, he typed out a text message for Agent Ricks.

If you want Sterns, get here quick.

Send.

He then redialed Agent Rick's number and set the phone down on filthy stairs near his right knee.

With the phone ringing he peered around the corner, this time down the sight posts of his AR14. He steadied his breathing and softly exhaled, pulling the trigger three times in quick succession. He was up and sprinting down the hall, almost the moment the last round left his barrel. The man had a look of shock on his face as he registered the sharp reports of an automatic weapon being fired in a confined space and spun from the impacts of the bullets. The man fell in a heap, just to the left of the door.

Hugging tight to the jam on the right side of the door, Matt went to one knee as he turned the door knob with his right hand and pushed it hard, quickly withdrawing behind cover as he brought his rifle tight into his left shoulder. Four shots rang out from inside, effectively covering the entrance. Matt calculated that the interior would be much like the apartment through which he had entered the building. He snapped around the door jamb sending a three shot burst in the general direction of the corner near the kitchen which he would have used for cover, had he been on the defense. He could hear his shots impacting but did not hear any cries of pain, so he remained in his crouched firing position.

From inside he could hear a commotion and was gratified that he had indeed achieved surprise. "Get Sterns into the bedroom, now!"

"Harper, we got Regan! Get your asses up here and take the fucker out!"

Knowing he only had a few minutes, he peered sidelong into the apartment and responded. "Already called the FBI, jack-ass;

they will be here shortly. This isn't going to end well for your boss if you don't send me Meg, so we can all get out of here."

Relative time slowed to a crawl as he noticed the just barely visible barrel of his target's pistol coming into a firing position. His rifle, already pointed into the interior, he moved his aim point slightly to the left and fired a burst through the wall, level with where his opponent's pistol was quickly coming to bear on him. He was rewarded with a grunt of pain as the man fell backward, his pistol, clattering to the floor.

"God please keep her safe for just a little longer."

ൟ

Richard shook his head in agreement with Megan's comment. "I would at least like a fighting chance to get out of this too," he whispered. "What should we do now? I am not too confident in taking out Sterns security types with a piece of pipe." She nodded in agreement and then froze, hearing the sound of someone shooting somewhere in the building. Her eyes locked with Richard's, in terror, as her heart jumped into her throat. "Get in your chair; it's got to be Matt," she whispered. More shots rang out, and they could tell that Stern's security goons were now returning fire from the next room.

Ron began shouting orders. "Get Sterns into the bedroom now!"

"Harper, we got Regan. Get your asses up here and take the fucker out!"

She heard the movement as feet pounded across the floor outside her dingy prison. Richard, she noticed, had picked up the pipe and laid it against the radiator just behind him.

Looking at him, she could see the determination displayed on his face. "We are going to get through this, Richard. We can do this."

The door slammed open as Sterns charged into the room, pulling a 9mm automatic. One of Sterns's security detail, a Hispanic man, positioned himself to the right of the door jam, his pistol trained on what must be the entrance to the apartment.

Matt called out to them, making her heart jump in her chest, adrenalin flooding her veins.

"Already called the FBI, Jack-ass. They will be here shortly. This isn't going to end well for your boss if you don't send me Meg, so we can all get out of here."

There was another burst, and she heard someone crumple to the floor. Looking at Sterns, she could see that his eyes were wild with a calculating madness. The man guarding the door fired several times. Again, shots from the hallway danced all around him.

The security guy fired again and turned to Sterns. "Get behind the girl, Sir; we need her as our hostage. We are way outgunned here, and I don't know how long the numb-nuts on the street will take to get up here.

Boom!

"Fuck! That was a grenade!" The guy with Sterns yelped.

Rattled by the roar of an explosion, Sterns opened the closet next to him, looking for cover as he tapped his earpiece, shouting orders to the men below. "Take Regan out! Time is short and extraction is now paramount."

Megan's eyes drilled the guard by the door, looking for an opening. Clearly scared now, the Hispanic man fired again. "Come on in, you chicken-shit mother f..."

His movements a blur, Richard's pipe connected with the Hispanic gunman's head cutting off the man's taunt with a loud and sickening crack. As the man fell, his blood sprayed like modern art across the wall beside him. Richard immediately scrambled for the man's gun.

"Matt! It's just Sterns now!" Megan called out.

His eyes were wild. "Unacceptable!" Sterns screamed.

Jerking her head back to the closet, and her former boss, she saw Sterns rushing towards her, firing at Richard as he came. Flame leaped out of Sterns's muzzle in the dim lantern light. She screamed and charged forward also, like a runner leaping forward at the sound of a starter's pistol. She slammed into Sterns, driving him back and onto the floor like a linebacker. She could hear quick steps outside the room and was shocked at Stern's strength as she fought desperately for control of his pistol. On top of him, she screamed out, as she struggled to pin his arm to the floor.

Enraged now, Sterns roared with indignation. "Enough! I - will - not - be - beaten - by - you!" His knee connected with her ribs, knocking her off of him. As she regained her balance she saw that he was rolling onto his side, his arm coming down, to bring his pistol to bear. Again she screamed, but to her amazement, he suddenly dropped the pistol.

Shaking uncontrollably, she looked up to see Matt standing over her, his barrel aimed directly at Sterns's face, his finger almost pulling the trigger.

Matt smiled at her. "Enough, indeed, you sociopathic bastard! Sterns, you even twitch and you are one dead mother fucker." Looking briefly at Megan, he kicked Sterns's pistol over to her. "Kill him if he moves or does anything; got it? We have two more, on the stairs, that I have to go deal with." Megan nodded and picked up the 9mm and aimed it center mass, as Matt sprinted out the door again.

Looking Sterns in the eye, she was stunned by how dispassionate he was, even now. He really was a sociopath. She considered just pulling the trigger, when Richard moaned painfully behind her. Stealing a quick glance in his direction, he pulled himself into a seated position.

Richard smiled weakly and nodded at her. "Meg, I can cover the old man. Matt may need help and I can't move. He got me in the hip." Her eyes going wide, she glanced over her shoulder to see Richard sitting up with the Hispanic man's pistol in his hands.

"My God Richard, we have to get you to a hospital."

"I agree completely. That actually is the very first thing on my agenda once we get out of here."

Laughing now, Sterns pushed himself back a foot or so from where he lay, so he could lean against the wall. "You two will not be leaving here, I fear. Ms. Danvers, my people will kill your soldier friend, and then come up here and kill both of you."

Megan scowled as she gathered the will to pull the trigger. "That was always your problem, Sterns; you underestimate people. Matt will hold off your people and the Feds will show up, and you will go to jail."

He looked at her mockingly. "I guess that we shall see soon enough, My Dear. Trust me when I say that, even if you are correct, I will have influence you cannot imagine on the matter. I will never see a prison cell."

Behind her, Richard moaned again as he fought to stay conscious. "You know what, Sterns? I think you might just be right, and I don't think I want to take that chance." Megan jumped as Richard's pistol barked twice behind her. Looking on in horror, she saw Sterns jerk with the impacts, blinking in disbelief at what had just happened. She could see he was trying to talk, but all that came out of his mouth was a line of blood. Behind her, she could hear the footsteps now, carefully coming through the apartment's front door.

"Harper, you cover, I will check inside." She spun to face the door as did Richard, when two bursts rang out from the direction of the hallway."

Chapter 26
The Burning Phoenix

Although Catherine believed what she was seeing on the screen in front of her had been building for a long time, it was still hard to watch. Sitting in the front room of her little house with her dog in her lap, she was still unprepared for the shock of seeing what was being played out in front of her on television. Glancing over at Drake, she noticed that he, too, seemed to be in a similar mental state. His features were hard and set as he witnessed the destruction of a culture play out before them.

'My God, Drake, I just don't want to believe that this is happening." His head moved subtly in agreement. Looking back at the screen, the correspondent in Miami tossed the coverage back to the anchor in New York. Catherine rubbed her arms to alleviate the goose bumps that appeared there. The segment ended, and the latest sensational Fox News graphic displayed across the screen.

The World in Crisis! – Day 6

"...Thank you for your report, Randal, stay safe." The pretty blonde woman's serious expression tightened as she continued. "As with all major events, you can trust Fox to provide you with the best wall to wall coverage of the situation around the world, as it happens. Next up, we are back with Eric Nunez on the ground, covering the rioting in Missouri. Eric, this is Tina White in New York. What is the latest in Saint Louis?"

"It's touch and go here, Tina. Talks overnight not only failed to resolve union complaints about the mass layoffs here at Darco Manufacturing, but in fact, things appeared to have been exacerbated by management negotiators' insistence that the company could not continue. The company's position is that due to the cancellation of seventy five percent of its current orders earlier this week, as a result of the Eurozone implosion, it simply could not continue. Tina, company officials confirmed an hour ago that they filed for bankruptcy protection Friday afternoon. This action caused a backlash, resulting in the protestors behind us. Workers immediately aligned with the Occupy and Solidarity movements here in the Gateway City to hit the streets. Darko employees, along with other union sympathizers, have been out in force since late Thursday. They are claiming they will stay as long as it takes. Employees are claiming that Darco officials failed to comply with the law, violating the Warren Act, with the mass layoff announcements coming so abruptly."

Catherine rolled her eyes as the report continued.

"Company officials, however, noted that layoff notifications were delayed at the request of the President."

Catherine shook her head in dismay as she watched police in riot gear, reinforced by National Guardsmen, trying to hold a shield wall against thousands of screaming protestors. Several vehicles were burning along the street, and the cameras were unable to cut away quickly enough to avoid showing the bodies of those killed in the skirmish. The scene appeared to be escalating quickly when a Molotov cocktail exploded at the feet of a group of Guardsmen, splattering them with burning gasoline. As Catherine watched the scene, the reporter took a couple of quick steps towards a burly middle aged man with grey hair and a sign.

"Eric Nunez, Fox News! Can I ask you why you're here today?"

"Damn right, you can! I am here because Fascist Bastards have taken over this country. The jack booted Nazis over there have my son! They came right to my house on Wednesday. They just barged in and took him! They slammed my wife against a wall and just took him away. He's a college kid, dammit; he wasn't involved in this stuff."

"Can I ask you what your son was charged with, Sir?"

"Charged with? Charged with? He wasn't charged with anything! Them DHS bastards just came into the house saying they had reports on him. They said he was a terrorist. They said they could hold him for as long as they wanted, and if I didn't stay out of their way, they would arrest me and my wife too. They took our computer and a bunch of boxes and left."

The reporter and the man ducked as some rocks thrown in their direction impacted the wall next to them. They took a few steps to one side to get out of the way from a scuffle taking place just behind them.

Catherine again looked over at Drake to see what he was thinking. "I can't believe we are seeing this. The Feds aren't even trying to hide it now."

Drake shook his head in dismay. "The National Defense Authorization Act makes it legal, but I agree it shouldn't be. So much for the Feds only using NDAA to combat terrorism. The kid was probably on some chat room and got himself mixed up with the wrong group."

"This is going to be bad, Drake. Americans won't put up with this sort of thing once they finally wake up and get a clue about what is going on."

Putting his hand up to quiet her, he thumbed the remote, to turn the TV up a little. "Just a sec, I want to hear this."

"...Greedy corporations are running things into the ground, and then laying everyone off, and they think we are just going to take it? Well, we're not! We aren't standing for it. Screw them - the cops too! They have my son, and there isn't anything I won't do to get him back."

On the far left side of the screen, almost off camera, Catherine noticed a line of several men and a woman tied together, their hands zip tied behind their backs, being marched over to police vans, prodded forward by DHS agents in riot gear and combat helmets.

"It just doesn't look like America any more, does it?"

"Nope, but then you sold me on this crap a couple of years ago."

Catherine scooted Maggie's head off of her lap, and stood up to stretch. "Sadie will be off work soon. I should go fix her something. Can I get you a beer or a snack?"

"I'm good, Kate, thanks."

She saw that his eyes were just as drilled on the news now as they were an hour ago. She smirked as Maggie's eyes followed her into the kitchen. The dog didn't stir, apparently deciding there wasn't a shot at a treat. "Did Ginny say when she would be back from her mom's house in Houston?"

"Not really. She knew she was going to get laid off, but she still took it pretty hard. I guess she just wanted to be with her folks for a few days."

"I understand that. I am really sorry, but we will all get through this. As long as I have a roof, you guys do too."

Taking his eyes from the screen, he turned and smiled at her. "I know, Kate, same goes for you guys."

"I know. Thanks."

Catherine put some ham and pepperoni on some hoagie bread and sprinkled mozzarella liberally over the top as the smell of the little toaster heating up made her think that she needed to clean it. "You do know that we are not a couple, Drake. We barely know each other. I like her, but we both agree that it is too messy right now for that sort of thing. I am just helping her out while they find the Iranian bastard that killed her mom."

Drake rolled his eyes and turned back to the television. Catherine noticed that Maggie had stolen her seat and was now getting her head scratched, as Drake watched the disaster unfold.

She finished up the sandwiches and licked the ranch dressing off her fingers. Within moments, the smell of melted cheese and toasted ham made her stomach rumble. Putting a cover over one plate, she took the other to the front room. Drake turned to her and smiled as she set his hoagie in front of him.

"What is this?"

"You know you're hungry. Shut up and eat it."

He smiled. "Thanks Kate. About the couple thing, you two go ahead and think whatever you like. I think you are a great fit. Ginny and I were just saying the other day that you guys looked great together, or should I say sounded great together. Trust me, not having to listen to the constant arguing is a nice change of pace."

"Stop it. Janice was nuts on some stuff, but you know as well as I do, that she really does care about people. She ..."

"Just a second." He cut her off with a hand gesture. Turning his head sharply back to the television screen, she noticed that he leaned in as he watched.

"What is it, Drake?"

"The crawl just reported that the Israelis are cancelling all leaves and passes for their military. Apparently, they are having some sort of alert; something about Iranian warships harassing a cargo vessel headed for Tel Aviv. Just what the world needs, more heat."

Catherine watched the crawl to see if she could learn anything more when she heard a car slowing down in front of the house. She looked out the front door as a black Dodge Challenger drove up into the driveway.

"Speaking of heat," Catherine got up and headed for the kitchen. She heard the car door slam shut as she placed Sadie's hoagie on to the metal tray, and slid it into the little oven. "Wow, it looks like Sadie got her car back from the body shop."

Drake took a bite and leaned over to look out the window at the sleek black machine, as Maggie got up and went to the front door, her stubby tail beating wildly.

Catherine, too, peered out the window in the kitchen, to get a better look at the car as the screen door slammed shut. "What do you think, Drake? Nice wheels, right?"

The front door soon opened and a tired Sadie, still wearing scrubs came through the door. Maggie immediately pounced on her with an abundance of affection.

"Down, Maggie, down, Girl." Hitching her purse back onto her shoulder, Sadie reached down to scratch the dog's head. "Hey, guys."

"Hi there, Roomie, are you hungry? I will have a hoagie for you in just a bit," Catherine said.

"Oh, my God, Catherine, you are a life saver, I am starved, and it smells terrific."

Catherine peeked in to check on the sandwich and put some chips and a pickle on a plate. Drake patted the sofa beside him and smiled up at their weary friend. "Good morning, Sadie, have a seat. We were just watching the news, but I think we have had enough for a while. How was work?"

"Long and busy, I hate overnight shifts. It started off with a suicide. Some guy lost his house and just checked out. Then we had a lady who was knifed at an Albertson's for her grocery cart, but the worst one was a teenager who came in after she was attacked by some boys for, if you can believe it, being Jewish. It may be some sort of new gang thing, I don't know. She told the police that three boys made some racial remarks, and then they grabbed her. They took her into an alley, poured gasoline over her head, and proceeded to light her hair with a lighter."

Catherine's hand went to her mouth, and she could see that Drake was furious. She knew the stuff he was seeing every day was wearing on him.

"Oh, my God Sadie, that's inhuman!"

Sadie sighed loudly and continued.

"Tell me about it. The cops said that apparently these guys had exchanged comments on Facebook prior to the attack. They all had Facebook profiles that had anti-Jewish statements. Anyway, there was a guy that was walking his dogs where it happened. He saw them take her off the street, and followed them back into the alley. He was able to put her out just as they were lighting it, so she only sustained minor burns and the loss of her hair." Kate shook her head in horror as the oven dinged. She took the sandwich out, cut it in half, placed it in a nest of potato chips and pickles, and took the plate, along with a soda to the front room.

Drake shook his head in disgust. "Son of a bitch! I'm glad the guy was there, but I am surprised that the little pukes didn't attack him too."

"They started to, but the guy had a concealed carry permit. I guess they took off when they saw the weapon."

"You act like our guys knew who they were. Is that right? Do we have these pukes in custody?"

Sadie looked up, and smiled brightly as Catherine set the plate in front of her. "You are being far too good to me, Catherine.

Seriously, you are going to spoil me terribly." Sadie pushed aside Maggie's inquisitive inspection of her food, and turned back to Drake and smiled weakly, shaking her head yes.

"It sounded like the cops got them, but I am not sure."

Catherine sat down on the recliner next to the sofa and leaned back. "Is there any way this isn't attempted murder, Drake? We get to really nail these little assholes, right?"

"Yep, should be an easy enough case to make, I think. They have the victim, an eye witness and the Facebook posts. I don't see any way they are not toast."

Sadie took a bite of her sandwich. "Hope you're right," Sadie sighed. "I see stuff every day that is just insane, so it makes me wonder."

Catherine exhaled, releasing some of the stress. She was about to speak when Sadie's eyes went wide as she took a bite of her hoagie.

"Catherine, what did you do to this? It is amazing."

"Nothing special, smoked ham, pepperoni, some jalapeno, and a ton of mozzarella. Oh and some ranch dressing and tomatoes. I'm glad you like it."

"I don't like it. I love it. Thank you again."

"No problem, Sadie that is what friends are for." Catching Drake's attention, she nodded towards the television and gave him a questioning look. "So what did I miss?"

"Not much. They switched to the financial stuff at the bottom of the hour. They recapped yesterday's thing about the NYSE finally opening two hours after it was supposed to, and about world markets gapping down from yesterday's close, whatever that means. I have always sucked at finance stuff, so I sort of tuned out."

Sadie took a sip of her soda and looked at him. "Aren't you worried about your 401K? That is all the guys at Presby are talking about lately."

"Thanks to Mary Sunshine here, I stopped contributing to my 401K like two years ago."

Catherine stuck her tongue out at him.

He smiled his appreciation for her acknowledging his efforts to tease her. "Anyway, from what I did gather, they are hoping that maybe the worst is over, but that our dollar will likely stabilize at like half of what it was only a week ago. Supposedly, when the weekend is over, we will see if this is the bottom or not. The treasury guy says it is, but the reporter types were giving him a pretty hard time."

Catherine rolled her eyes and was about to comment when Sadie sat forward a little.

"Whatever!" Sadie said. "Those idiots in D.C. couldn't find their collective asses with both hands."

Drake looked over his shoulder at Catherine and smirked. "It is about time, Kate, that you started hanging out with someone with some brains."

Sadie grabbed her plate and empty soda can and stood up with a yawn. "Well, guys, I am beat. I think I am going to take a shower and turn in for a few hours. I want to thank you both again for helping me go get my stuff from my apartment this week."

Catherine smiled and waved away her appreciation. "It is no big deal, really. I think that Maggie likes you better than she does me, in fact."

Drake nodded in agreement. "Seriously, Sadie, I was really glad to help."

Glancing up to meet Sadie's eyes, Catherine continued. "They will catch the guy that is terrorizing you, but until then, you really do have to be very careful."

Sadie sobered a little, nodding in agreement. "Anyway, you have both been just great to me, and really, I just appreciate it a lot. Drake, please pass that on to your partner for me, OK?"

He nodded and smiled as Sadie headed towards the kitchen with her dish.

"Catherine is working so hard on food storage and preparation. I really wanted to get what I could from Mom's house and my apartment to help out.

"I'll tell him, but he really wanted to help too. We all hate what happened to you, and there is no cop I know of, that wouldn't jump at the chance to help you."

Coming back out of the kitchen, Sadie nodded and headed for the guest room as Maggie jumped up on the couch to take her place next to Drake.

"Well, Drake, with Ginny at her mom's, we have a Saturday to do what we want with, I guess. Do you want to hang out and watch movies or maybe go shoot a few rounds?"

"I could go for either one, but sitting on my butt has a certain appeal if you know what I mean."

"Sounds like a plan then. You get to make the snacks after the first movie though."

"What are you talking about? That be woman's work." He smirked, glad that Catherine didn't have anything to throw at him. "Besides, I have a dog in my lap, I would hate to disturb her."

"Whatever, and people wonder why I am a lesbian." She smiled and leaned the recliner all the way back, as Drake started scrolling through the available movies. After several minutes of debate, they agreed to watch *Ghost Rider: Spirit of Vengeance* which had come out on pay per view not too long ago. The movie was off to a good start with a kid getting taken by the bad guys, when Catherine saw someone approaching the house out of the corner of her eye.

As she sat up to see who it was, the doorbell rang. "Damn it."

Maggie jumped up, and ran to the front door, barking in alarm.

"Who is it, Kate?" Drake peered out, but made no effort to move.

"Looks like Dennis Cob and his buddy, Chase something, I can't remember his last name."

"The guy who took over the Tea Party group after they told you to get lost?"

"That's him, and thank you, Captain Courteous. I appreciate how you delicately considered my feelings just now."

"Sorry, Kate. I just don't know that I care for that guy. What the hell could he want with you this morning?"

"I have no idea." She pushed the recliner forward and pulled herself to her feet. "Oh crap, we were going to meet to talk about the phone tree stuff I have been pushing, but I thought that was tomorrow." She pushed Maggie back with her foot, and stepped out on to the front porch, shutting the door behind her.

"Hey, guys, what's up? We were getting together tomorrow, I thought."

Chase and Dennis looked at each other, confusion apparent on their faces. "Sorry Kate, I was pretty sure we said Saturday but," Dennis looked a question to Chase, "we can come back tomorrow after church if you want."

Exasperated, she sighed. "What the hell! Come on in, guys. For all I know, I may have been the one to screw it up. We just need to hold it down because my roommate just got off work after pulling an all-nighter, so keep it down, ok?"

The guys both smiled and agreed enthusiastically. "No problem, Kate, we can keep it down can't we, Chase?"

"Sure, no problem."

Catherine moved forward a step and undid the latch to the screen door. "Don't worry about Maggie; she will pester you, but she is a good dog. We can sit in the dining room." The guys followed Catherine into the front room. Drake stood and shook hands with both men, as Catherine coaxed Maggie into the back yard to keep her from barking at the visitors.

Coming back, she ducked into the kitchen from the back porch and turned the fire on under the kettle. Picking some mint leaves from the plant in her kitchen window, she put the leaves in a pitcher along with a couple of tea bags. "Can I get you boys some chips and hot sauce, or ranch dip maybe?"

"Seriously, Kate, thanks but we just had a huge breakfast about an hour ago. No need to make a fuss over us."

"Fair enough, let me at least fix everyone some tea. We can talk about the way I think we should organize things. Then you guys can decide what you think will work." She could see they passed a look between them, but could not imagine what it may have meant. Waiting for the water to boil, she remained in the kitchen, leaving them to themselves. She reached up, and grabbed four glasses, as Drake and the two visitors at the dining room table recapped the headlines. Setting the glasses down, she opened the freezer, and reached in for ice, as Drake commented on the riots in Missouri. After a moment, she saw the pot was about to begin whistling, so she took it off the burner and sent ice tinkling into the glasses. As she poured the hot water into the pitcher, she noticed that Drake was relaying Sadie's story, and she smiled at him for putting up with the intrusion. Shortly, the aroma of freshly brewed mint tea filled the kitchen as Catherine set four glasses of ice on the dining room table along with some packets of Splenda.

"I will be right back with the tea."

"I appreciate you folk's time, and we absolutely do need to talk about the phone tree, but there is something else Kate." She noticed that Drake's brow wrinkled with suspicion as Dennis spoke, but he appeared to be withholding judgment for now.

"Ok, Guys, so what are the furtive looks about?"

Blushing, Dennis placed his hand flat on the table and took a breath. "We want you to lead the group, Kate. You know more about preparing, and what is happening than anyone, and you obviously saw this coming a couple of years ago. We want..."

Drake stood up and leaned into Dennis's space a little. "Are you kidding me, Dude? I seem to recall that you guys all but called her crazy for saying this stuff was going to happen. Now you want her to just forget that you told her to get lost?"

Dennis leaned back and moved his arms out in a palms-up expression, showing his acknowledgement that they screwed up. "Look, Drake, you're right. We didn't see it. Come on, though, you have to admit that what is going on now is crazy. Nobody could see this coming."

Obviously genuinely angry, Drake pointed at her as she returned with the pitcher of tea.

"She did! She saw this coming a couple of years ago. You just didn't want to listen because she doesn't fit your Ozzie-and-Harriett world view."

She set the tea down and placed a hand on her friend's shoulder, squeezing slightly.

"Guys, keep it down, Sadie is trying to get some sleep."

The men acknowledged her admonishment. "Kate, we are really sorry about what happened in that meeting a couple of years ago. You were right, are right about what was going on. If we hadn't had our heads up our asses, and were doing what all Americans are supposed to do, we would have known things were messed up. I guess it is a hard thing to realize that your whole way of life is screwed."

Drake was about to reply, when Catherine put her hand over his to stop him. "So who exactly are you talking for? You can see now that this isn't going to be fun or easy. It is going to take a real commitment to have even a hope of holding things together." She probed Dennis's eyes for signs of understanding and commitment.

Looking down, his head nodded slightly. When he looked up, she knew. She could see the sincerity on his face.

Studying him for a moment, she continued. "We are going to have to do more than just keep a phone tree together, Guys. I am talking about really helping people out. We are going to have to take people in, share food, do work for each other, whatever it takes to keep the community together. The government folks at all levels are going to have their hands full." Catherine's eyes darted to Drake who sat there with his jaw clenched as she spoke. "My point is that we are not going to be able to depend on anyone other than each other. There is no way to know how bad it will get, but if people are hungry, it could get bad and get bad very quickly."

Chase started to comment, but Dennis beat him to it. "We talked it through at Thursday's meeting. The last couple of weeks made everyone realize what the truth is, Kate. We voted, and while I won't say that it was unanimous, I will say that it wasn't even close. The idea to ask you to do this won easily. We need you. We were getting pretty good at politics, but seeing further out is not something we have a feel for. It is why you are the one to take over. You are focused on the big picture, and that is what we need now. It is different today. You know that, Kate. If our group is going to have value to the Tea Party, or anyone else, it has to mean something more than winning an election. You can do a lot of good for people. Please say yes."

Catherine looked over at Drake, who simply shook his head in amazement, and shrugged. "It's up to you, Kate. If they will listen, you can probably do some real good. If they don't, you will be wasting time you don't have to waste."

Catherine got up from the table, thinking about what this would mean for her life, and what she had to do to keep things going. As she paced through the dining room and front room of the little house she realized she was emotionally spent. Although she wanted a good ending she just didn't believe one was possible. As she turned to head back through the dining room she realized their eyes were all on her.

Dennis eyed her closely. "You are thinking you are struggling to make ends meet now and that you can't afford the time. I don't know if you realized that although it isn't a lot of money, the position is funded through our dues. Please say yes, Kate. Look, we know it is going to be tough, but you really are the one person who can make it work."

Kate stared at the three men as she pondered what Dennis said. She could use the extra money, but the idea of facing the same people, who rejected her before was terrifying. Standing there, looking at Dennis at her dining room table, she could still hear their homophobic comments as she fled the building two years ago.

Chapter 27
Home Again

Exhausted and emotionally spent, Annie held Bridgett in her lap as Russell turned off the highway. The familiar jarring sensation, as they drove over the cattle guard, filled her with relief. Although tired, Annie smiled at seeing Danvers Ranch displayed on the sign that she and her sisters had placed at the entrance to their property when she was a child. It was made up of rough-hewn oak planks with the letters painted a dark red. The sign, attached to two six foot tall posts, was located just to the right of the entrance to the ranch. As always, her mom had the flower bed around the base of the sign planted in brightly colored flowers and bushes.

Looking down at the clock on the dash, she saw that it was almost noon. After staying up all night with the police in Kingfisher, and then going to the hospital this morning to check on Nathan, she was exhausted to tears. She was honestly amazed that Russell was still able to drive at all. She still thought it would have been better to just get a room and rest for a day, but both her dad and Russell had agreed it was best to push through when they finally got a chance to call home.

Looking at Russell, she could see his face was hard, his eyes glued to the road leading up to the house. Noticing that he was being watched, a weak smile crept onto his face.

She returned the gesture and reached over to caress his cheek. "Are you ok, Honey?

"Yeah, I'm fine, just tired. I still just can't believe that what happened yesterday really happened. You should call your dad and tell him we're here, that we just turned off the highway."

Nodding, she placed Bridgett back onto her pallet behind them. "Right."

Reaching over to the cup holder, Annie picked up her phone and dialed the number. As Russell drove up onto the little rise that led to the Danvers's home, the phone rang.

"Hello."

"Hi, Mama, we're here; we are just pulling in now."

Annie could hear the tension leaving her mother as she exhaled with relief. "Thank God, Annie, we are both just so grateful that you are safe. How is Nathan doing? Did the surgery go alright?"

Russell pulled up to the adobe fence near the rough wooden gate outside the old mission style house. Annie smiled, seeing her father already coming out the door to meet them.

"Daddy's coming up now, Mama; I will tell you everything inside." Annie hung up the phone, hooked Bridgett's leash to her collar, and opened her door as did Russell. She stood and stretched. The dog jumped from her perch onto the seat and then to the ground.

As her dad approached, Annie realized just how much she appreciated the powerfully built man who was her father. Even now, his full head of hair was only beginning to turn a dark shade of grey. "Alright then, glad you kids made it. I know it was a hard thing pushing through, but you're home now, and we're going to take good care of you."

Grateful, she smiled at the way her father firmly shook Russell's hand, and pulled him into a hug. It seemed her father had finally put his misgivings about her marriage to rest. His reaction was as unexpected as it was genuine, she thought. He eyed her closely as she came around the front of the truck, with the little Pomeranian in tow. "Come give your old -man a hug, Annie. I guess that I am getting old, but you still look like my little girl to me." She was pleased to see him smiling broadly, as he began guiding them toward the house. "Now, you don't worry a bit about unloading just yet. We will take care of all of that, once you both have had some rest."

Russell held the gate open, as the little group proceeded into the Spanish styled courtyard and garden in front of the house. Annie's spirit brightened as she took in the sweet smell of the lavender bushes growing along the adobe wall separating the front garden from the gravel parking area of her childhood home. It was now, as it always had been. The house was an adobe mission styled house that reminded her of the Alamo, except that it had a large garage framing the yard on her right, and an extension on the left side of the structure that contained a guest room and her daddy's office. On the right side of the home, near the garage was a swimming pool, its water a cool blue in the early afternoon sunshine. All along the front of the house was a rustic porch made of timbers, covering a terracotta tiled patio which was overflowing with her mom's potted flowers and herbs.

The front of the house held six sets of French doors set in heavy timber door frames. She loved this house, with its eighteen inch thick walls and the snug comfortable feeling she always got when she was home. The house's natural tendency to maintain a constant seventy three degrees, regardless of the time of year, due to the back two thirds of the home being dug into the gentle slope of the hill just made it feel permanent and solid to her.

Stopping for a moment, she bent down to Bridgett, who was following along. She looked up at Russell who turned to see why she was pausing. "I thought I would let her explore the yard. You don't think she would jump into the pool do you?"

Russell blinked at the unexpected question, but shook his head no. "I don't think so. She should be all right, I think."

Looking up at her dad for his approval, she saw him nod, and give her his famous wink.

"Thanks, Daddy. She really is a good little girl, and she really loves people."

"She is your dog, Honey. What else would she be? I have no doubt she will have your mother completely spoiling her inside of a week." As if on cue, her mom appeared from the centermost set of French doors, a smile, lighting up her face. "Anyway, we should get inside; your mother is beside herself. She made a late breakfast, so I hope you kids are hungry.

"We figured she would do that, so we skipped eating. I just wanted to get home." Annie unhooked the leash and stood up as the little puppy charged off towards the flower beds along the front wall. Turning back towards the house and her mom, and now free of Bridgett, Annie ran to her mother. She jumped into her arms as Russell and her dad followed her at their own pace.

"Oh, Momma, I can't tell you how good it is to be home. I really have missed you guys so much." As she hugged her mom, she felt the tears come, and felt as if a huge weight had been lifted off her shoulders. "It has been so hard, Momma, and last night was just the end. Nathan saved our lives and ..." Choked up, she realized she couldn't go on. She just stayed right there on the patio and held her mother tight, afraid to ever let go.

"You're safe now, Sweetheart. I'm so sorry you kids had to go through that, and we have been praying real hard since you kids called. Bob even called Pastor Glenn at the church, so we could get everyone praying for Nathan to pull through." Annie felt her dad's presence behind her, patting her on the shoulder, but she just could not stop her tears.

"Your Mom is right, Honey. You got yourself a strong man for a husband, and you're home now, so you're going to be just fine. It's going to get pretty tough for a few years, but we have our faith to guide us. I know that Nathan's family is the same way. Our family and friends will sustain us, as we will them. Now, let's take this inside, and eat some breakfast before it gets cold."

Her mom squeezed her tight and then pulled back. Placing a hand on each shoulder, she then physically turned her toward the house. "Your father is right; come on now. It's going to be a whole new start for all of us." Annie hadn't realized how relieved she was. Fighting valiantly to stop her tears, it felt like her emotions were running away with her now that she was home and safe.

Going inside the house and into the dining room, Beth Danvers handed her daughter off to Russell, who guided her to a chair and eased her into it. "It will be ok, Annie, it has been a rough night, and you know that the hormones are making it all worse." Although the comment irritated her, she knew he meant well. She placed her hand on his to indicate that she would be ok.

Looking up at her husband, she patted the seat next to her. "Sit down, Honey, I'm fine. I'm just tired, and it's so hard to believe how crazy everything is. It's just insane." Putting her napkin on her lap, she smiled at her husband as he sat down next to her at the wooden plank dining room table. She saw that he exchanged looks with her dad, as her mom brought a platter of scrambled eggs, sausage, and bacon to the table. Scooping some of the steaming eggs onto her plate and stabbing a couple of sausage links to accompany them, she finally got her emotions under control. She passed the platter to Russell as her mom returned to the table with a basket of fresh biscuits, hot out of the oven.

Annie began to eat with relish, as Russ dished out a large helping onto his plate. Nodding, he handed the platter off to her dad. She could see her dad clearly wanted to know what happened the previous evening, so she decided to break the ice. "Look, guys, we're fine now, I'm fine. Like Russ said, it's just the hormones. I will probably be crying about the color of my nail polish an hour from now. I'm just so grateful that Nathan's surgery went well. God was really looking after him. The doctor said that only one of the bullets was serious." She looked at her husband. "Why don't you go on and tell them what happened."

Russell's face grew serious, and he took a breath and put down his fork. "We were just getting ready to eat our pizza after I hung up with you guys. The next thing I knew, this really sauced guy came in waving a shotgun. The cops said he had just been fired for messing around with a couple of the waitresses there."

Watching Russell's face, her mind went back to the trauma of the previous evening as chill bumps spread across her arms. She could almost taste her fear anew. As she watched her husband, she realized that as strong as he was trying to be for her and her father, he shook slightly as he retold the story.

Pausing to take a sip of orange juice, Russell continued. "Anyway, he was ranting and raving. Then, when a guy made a break for the door, he just blew him away. After that, he was just out of it. He turned on us next. I thought he was going to shoot, so I started sort of talking to him, you know?"

Annie felt her heart start to race and took a couple of deep breaths, taking up the story. "We were in a booth across from the door. I was on the inside by the window. Russ stood up, leaning in front of me, pushing me down. He was really amazing. Even the cops said that he did just the right thing to try and calm the guy down."

Rubbing her arms to alleviate the goose bumps, she saw her mother cover a gasp with her hands. Her father lowered his head, his mouth tightly clamped, as he, too, dealt with his emotions, having come so close to losing his youngest daughter. Seeing her husband's ears turning red, she felt his hand over hers as he again took up the story.

"I just knew I had to keep things cool to have a chance at the guy. I could tell by his eyes, that nobody was home, and that he just wanted to hurt someone. Anyway, Nathan showed up and I thought we would be ok. Nate made him drop the shotgun and then out of nowhere, the guy went for a pistol from his belt and started shooting. With Nathan hit I knew I had to do something or we were all screwed. I grabbed this big beer mug from the next table and nailed him with it a couple of times. He went down, and I grabbed his gun. Then the cops showed up, and almost freaking shot me. Thank God for everybody yelling at them that I wasn't the bad guy!"

Looking at her Husband, she could see that he was uncomfortable, as his voice shook a little now. Glancing back at her dad, he was shaking his head with approval at Russell's actions. She thought, for the first time, that Russell was finally part of the family.

Her mom was doing all she could not to cry, her face ashen from living her child's nightmare. She got up and came around the table to take them both into her arms.

"My dear God, what are we coming to? Russ, I can never do enough for you for taking care of my Annie. I just couldn't have recovered from something like that." Beth Danvers kissed Russell's head and Annie realized how proud she was of her husband.

Like her mom, her dad, too looked taken aback. "That goes for all of us Russ. In Nam I saw some good men in combat unable to react when it counted. You brought my little girl back home, and I won't ever forget that, son." Astonished, Annie saw that her dad had a tear in his eye, something she had only seen once or twice in her entire life.

Annie smiled weakly. "They took Nate to Kingfisher Regional. We followed once the police were through with us this morning. He was just out of surgery when we got there. They said he was hit three times, but only one of the wounds, a collapsed lung was life threatening. One bullet hit him in the thigh and the last one was a graze, on his opposite shoulder. The nurse at the hospital had already called Mr. Jacobs, so his parents were there when we arrived."

Russell shook his head in agreement as her mom sat back down, her face still pale from the story.

Russell took a breath, and looked at her father. "Annie and I called you guys next, but as you know, we thought we should stay until the doctors came out to tell us how the surgery went for Nate."

Overwhelmed with emotion, she could feel the tears coming again. She rubbed her face vigorously to keep her composure. Her voice shaking, she continued. "He was still unconscious when we left. It looked like he would be ok, though, and Mr. Jacobs said he would call when they knew something."

The table grew suddenly quiet, and Annie took a biscuit and smeared butter on it and then reached for the honey. Appreciating the taste of fresh biscuits and honey, and not wanting to think about last night any more, she decided to change the subject. "How are things here, Mom?"

"Oh, Honey, everyone here is just really upset like they are everywhere. After the President's latest speech, most folks are doing what they can to get ready for hard times. Even Wal-Mart is having a hard time keeping some things on the shelves. We are just really fortunate that your father keeps all of those plastic tubs full of food, and the shelves in the tornado shelter are stocked. We will be just fine here." Annie realized her mom was unsettled, as she watched her pick at what remained of her eggs, a look of concern forming on her face. "Your father and Bart Tillman have been working to expand the garden all week."

Her father leaned forward, folded his hands and looked at Russ. "I'm hoping that maybe you could help us put in some fencing around the new garden. It is going to be almost half an acre for vegetables and what not. We are going to repair that old chicken coop, too, so your welding skills will be a big help."

"You bet, Sir, it will be good to do something useful. I was thinking as soon as we got settled, I could look for a job too. Annie and I want to contribute."

"You won't have any problems contributing, Son. Between what we need done here, and what some of my neighbors will need, you will be staying busy and going to bed exhausted. Some of us have been working out a system to trade out what we all need."

Annie was down to picking at what remained on her own plate. She knew she would continue to worry, but took comfort from being home with her family again. Her dad's request for Russell's help caused her husband's face to light up like it was Christmas.

Smiling, Russell nodded solemnly at her father. "That sounds real good, Mr. Danvers. Thank you, Sir. You know I will gladly do whatever is needed of me. I have my own tools and a pretty decent rig for anything that needs welded. I haven't done much of it, but I know a little about how to run a backhoe or a dozer too." Her husband was smiling and had a zest in his eyes she hadn't seen in some time.

Annie pushed her plate back as her father nodded, pleased with Russell's response. Placing his palms flat on the table, in what she knew was his pronouncement pose, he replied.

"That's good, Russ. The news this morning said the NYSE finally opened this week only to close two hours later. The egghead traders may have thought they were done, but it looks like losing fifty cents on the dollar is only going to be the beginning." Her father sneered as he spoke of the so-called experts. "Just yesterday, the TV pundits were telling us about the dollar falling right along with Europe. They are finally figuring out that the only thing keeping it from collapsing overnight earlier this week was the circuit breakers and regulations on automated trades. This is it for real, this time, and there ain't a damn thing the pointy-headed morons in those fancy suits can do about it." He clamped a hand on Russell's shoulder. "We are just going to have to make due on our own. We have our neighbors and although the folks in town are still hedging a bit, they know inside what is coming, and I think they will work with us. There are a lot of folks still willing to listen to what the Feds have to say for now, but that won't last if this keeps going."

Annie picked up on her mother's tension immediately, following her daddy's last comment.

"Let's not go into all that right now, Bob. They just got here; there will be enough time after they are settled in."

Alarmed at her mom's tone, Annie's mouth dropped, fearing the worst. "What is it, Momma, what's wrong?" She shivered a little, looking from parent to parent. "The mystery that I will worry about is going to be worse than whatever it is." Resigned, her mother acquiesced, with a look towards her husband.

He father sighed, pushed his own plate back, and responded. "It is just a fool waste of time and money is what it is. The EPA has declared that a bunch of my land over by the Brazos is now a wetland. We have been back and forth on this stuff for a few months now. In a nutshell, the government wants to tell us how to produce food. This wetland thing is just their latest move. Bart's family is being told he can no longer have his kids driving tractors. They are requiring a commercial license to operate any of their own equipment, and the teenagers aren't old enough for that."

"Not to mention how much all of that costs," her mother interjected.

Her father nodded his agreement. "It is all of this ICLEI stuff from the UN about reducing greenhouse gas emissions and creating so called sustainable communities. It is part of something called Agenda Twenty One."

Her mother frowned. "It is nothing more than communism." As she spoke, her mom speared one last piece of sausage. "These people have convinced, or tricked our local leaders to putting this stuff into our building codes and regulations at all levels. They think if they can regulate us enough, or make our land worthless, we will have to give it up for pennies on the dollar. They need good food producing land, so they are doing what they can to force it out of the hands of individual land owners."

Annie saw that Russell was just as shocked as she was. He started to speak, but she asked the question first. "How can any of that be legal? Doesn't the Constitution or something say they can't do that?"

"In a nutshell, they assume that ordinary people aren't good stewards of the land. They think the government will do a better job if it runs things." Her dad smirked. "Anyway, I told them they could go to hell. We have been continuing to do what we have always done. Needless to say, guys in suits have been out to talk to us several times."

Seeing her mom tremble as her dad spoke, Annie decided that her sister really was right and that the world was upside down. Her mom's face was grave now, as she spoke.

"They are fining us thousands of dollars every day, kids. We aren't going to pay it, obviously, but you can imagine how upsetting it is. Your uncle is our lawyer, of course. He is fighting it and says that we should win, but that it will take time."

"Oh my God, Momma, what are we going to do?"

Her father interjected. "We are going to fight them any way we can, Annie Girl. That is what we are going to do! What they are trying to pull isn't right, and it isn't constitutional, so we are just not going to take it. I had a conversation with Martin at the sheriff's office a few weeks ago. He agrees completely with those of us that the government is going after. They went to him last week to evict us off or our land, and he told them to get lost. He said that they could think of it as an Occupy-Your-Own-Land-Movement."

Russell burst out laughing at the sheriff's comment. "I bet they were not too keen on being talked to like that. Wow, this really is getting to be like a Twilight Zone episode."

Her dad smiled at Russell's reference. "It is that, Son; it is that indeed. Like I said, a few of us have been meeting for a while now. We have God, our families and we got good solid neighbors. We are going to get through this just fine. You kids just be aware of what is going on around you. I don't expect any trouble, but with all the people moving about these days, we don't take chances. We make sure that someone knows where we are all the time, ok?"

It was that moment that Annie realized that her father's pistol and gun belt was hung off of a peg by the door, and a rifle was propped up against the door jam.

Chapter 28
On the Road

Her eyes floating open, Megan was momentarily disoriented, her mind not yet catching up to the fact that she and Matt drove non-stop through Saturday night and Sunday to crash with Matt's close friend, stationed at Fort Knox, Kentucky. Looking around at the efficient but comfortable décor, typical of an apartment inhabited by a single NCO in the United States Army, she suddenly found herself questioning her life since leaving college. Until this weekend, she had a great job, made a lot of money, and had the so called "good life." The problem was that a lot of money in New York City didn't necessarily mean all that much. Their host, Glover, had new leather furniture, a nice flat screen television, and she decided she would not be at all surprised if he even had more square footage in his apartment than she did in New York, and he didn't have to compromise himself. Staring at the ceiling, thinking things over, she realized that she was ashamed.

Incredibly, it was only Monday, early Monday morning to be exact. As she lay next to Matt on a pallet, on the floor of Staff Sergeant Glover Washington's living room, it occurred to her that she was incredibly lucky. Thinking through the angles of the previous weekend, it truly was a miracle that she was still alive. It was only a couple of days ago that Stern's assholes had taken her from where she stood outside of Macy's. Closing her eyes for a moment, she willed herself to stay calm. She knew she was fine now, but every time the memories of her experience entered her thoughts, her anxiety spiked anew. As they made their way out of the building that night, she was completely overwhelmed, not only by having to leave Richard wounded on the floor, possibility dying, but also by the idea of being arrested for what had just taken place with Sterns. With the sound of sirens drawing closer with each passing minute, her nerves were stretched past what she could endure. She remembered almost breaking down when she saw the empty lot with his pick up sitting there waiting for them. She had no idea how Matt kept his cool, but he had, and she was grateful. Thinking back, she knew the police were almost on them and they would take care of Richard, but Matt was right when he shut her down after she began to protest about leaving her boss behind. He had her open the gate to the lot as he pulled onto the street. Only moments after she climbed back into the truck, and they started down the street, several police cars zipped past, headed for the empty tenement building.

Taking a deep breath, Meg rolled over so she could watch the early morning sun through the patio doors of the apartment. They decided on Sunday, somewhere in Ohio, that they were going to lie low for a couple of days. Stretching, she smirked. They must be going nuts at work this morning, with Sterns dead, she decided. So much for Barbara's sucking up, she thought. Lying here in the quiet stillness of the morning, the lingering smell of coffee brewing from Glover's morning routine was beginning to make her think about crawling out of bed.

On the other hand, fighting for her life over the weekend, and driving eight hundred miles, much of it in the dark, as they escaped the city, was exhausting, not to mention frightening. Matt said, as they passed the airport on their way through Newark that it would probably take them an hour or two to react to things, but Agent Ricks struck him as being pretty competent. Matt decided he would have an APB out on them the minute he realized they were in the wind. She smiled to herself, impressed by the man next to her. It was Matt, not her, that had all of the aspects of their escape thought out ahead of time. The FBI had no vehicle description, no electronic footprint, and no credit card trail. She knew they would be fine when Matt pulled onto a dirt side road, the first time they were running low on fuel. She thought it was obvious now, but Saturday night when she asked, he explained that the Feds would really be focusing on gas stations if they really wanted to find them. Matt said he had ten five-gallon military jerry cans in the back, in case fuel got hard to come by. His planning turned out to be a life saver, allowing them to get west without being noticed.

Watching another morning begin, she realized that she was content in spite of the legal mess with which they would surely have to deal. She had been arrogant and shallow, only caring about money and prestige. Lying here with a man she knew and loved deeply, on her way home to her family, her life seemed richer. She now looked forward to the kind of life she couldn't wait to get away from just a few years earlier. Knowing Matt and she had some real challenges ahead, she closed her eyes to softly whisper a prayer. "Dear Lord, I don't know how this will work out, but please watch over Matt. He had no choice about killing those men."

Smiling, Megan sighed, feeling hopeful as she felt Matt's arm reach around her.

"Good morning, Babe. Did you sleep ok?" Meg flopped over onto her back again, looking up into Matt's hazel eyes. His head propped up on his right hand, his left traced the outline of her collarbone, smirking at her, as he lay there.

"I did. Who knew a couple of sleeping bags would make such a great mattress?"

"If you are tired enough, sleeping on rocks feels like heaven. Still, this was pretty great, I think. Glover is good people. Smells like he made coffee before he left. Do you want some?"

"I do, in fact. A shower would be nice, too. You may not want to be around me much longer, if I don't.

Matt made a derisive grunt, and threw back the blanket. "Fat chance of that, Meg, you are stuck with me now." Getting to his feet, he stretched to loosen the kinks, and moved off towards the kitchen, wearing nothing but his boxers. She marveled as the muscles of his back rippled smoothly under his golden skin. Even the pale line of a past scar crossing his right shoulder only accentuated his appeal. She was certain there was not another man like him alive. He was amazingly good looking, a marvelous lover, a powerful and skilled warrior, and yet, almost completely unassuming.

Lying there watching him pour their coffee, she felt guilty for not having told him how much she cared a long time ago. Getting up herself, she walked over to the kitchen and leaned against the dish washer taking the steaming cup offered her.

"Matt?"

He smiled at her with a question on his face at the tone in her voice. "Yeah, Babe, are you alright?"

She shook her head that she was. "Matt, I am an idiot. I love you desperately, and I have loved you for a long time." Holding back his cocky grin, his eyes were alight with amusement.

"I know Meg. I've known how you felt for a long time."

"Why did you put up with it? My arrogance, I mean. You could have any woman you wanted. I was terrible to you, not acknowledging what I felt, not saying that I was yours with the pride that I should have."

He smirked again and took a step towards her. She could feel his strength, as he pulled her up against his chest, kissing the top of her head.

"Nothing to put up with, Meg. I love you and I knew you felt the same way. I could care less what any Harvard boy thought." Feeling his fingers playing with her hair, he continued. "I knew you were not really one of them. I knew you would figure it out sooner or later."

Breathing in his scent as she buried her face in his chest, she could almost feel his heart beating. "If we can somehow avoid prison I want to be your wife Matt. I want to have your kids and grow old with you if you will have me." She felt him twitch with surprise.

"Well now, I didn't see that coming, but I do like to think that I am not a stupid man. I accept." Looking up into his eyes, she began to respond, but instead found his mouth covering hers, his tongue, seeking her soul. Light headed, her knees weak, she kissed him back, wanting nothing more than to be with him. Finally, pulling back slightly, he smiled down at her.

"Meg, marrying you would be the best thing that ever happened to me. I love you and there is nothing I would not do to make you happy. What happened is a complication, but it was self-defense really. With things this messed up as they are, the state of New York will likely have much larger issues to resolve than coming after us."

Feeling like she could float away, she realized she had never felt so alive. Her tears ran down her face, wetting Matt's chest. Clinging tightly to her man, they just stood there in their embrace for what felt like an eternity, neither of them wanting to move away. Content, she relished the feel of his arms enveloping her until finally he kissed her again and smiled down at her.

"Ok, so now that our future is settled, how about some chow, Woman?"

Laughing, she popped him on the butt and moved towards the fridge.

"Let's see what, Dear Glover, has to eat?"

A few minutes later, she placed scrambled eggs and ham in front of her man and sat across from him with her own plate. "So, what do we do today? You said we shouldn't go outside or be seen? I guess we will just have to come up with something we can do right here." She beamed a sultry look at him.

Returning the look, he smirked. "Now, that does sound like an excellent plan."

Grinning, Matt took another bite, never taking his eyes off of her. "I think we have, in fact, earned a couple of pleasant days away from the world."

"I couldn't agree more."

Finishing their breakfast, Matt picked up the plates and headed for the kitchen. You know that the FBI will reach out for your folks. If you can think of someone you really trust in Texas, we might be able to get a message to them. I'm sure they are going to be worried. You can bet that the Feds are listening in on their phones, so you need to think of someone who can talk to them in person."

"Oh, right. Still, wouldn't they need a warrant for something like that?" Seeing the sardonic expression on his face, she winced. "Ok, so I'm gullible. I am young, remember?"

"I might be taking this too far, but I prefer not to take any chances. I am thinking we can call someone they won't listen in on, who can drop in on your folks without appearing out of place, to let them know you are ok."

"Tina, my best friend in high school teaches with my mom now. I could give her a message."

"Perfect. Glover said he would go fill up our gas cans and get us some new burn phones when he gets off duty later on. With ten five gallon cans, we should be able to make it to Texas before we have to grab fuel again, but I think we might be ok to buy gas if we can find some little spot off the beaten path. I don't think we want to risk getting too low on fuel, in case gas gets scarce."

"Works for me, Sweetheart, but honestly, I would like to go back to the previous agenda item if you don't mind. "

Nodding his head in agreement, he stepped into her, pinning her against the counter, his lips again, seeking hers. "Good enough, I second that motion to go back to the earlier idea of how to spend our day."

Smiling, she hooked a leg around his, running her fingernails through his hair, and kissed him passionately.

~

The smell of baking enchiladas filled the apartment as the sun began to set. When Glover returned from duty, the three of them decided it would be safe for Matt to ride along to fill up the fuel cans if Matt stayed in the car while Glover paid. He brought them new cell phones and even thought to pick up some lunch meat, chips, and snacks to eat on the road.

Opening up the refrigerator, she took out an onion and a tomato, after checking the clock again for the third time in the last half hour. The guys left almost two hours ago when Glover showed up after work. She was beginning to worry a little, thinking they should be back by now. On the other hand, she knew they had 10 cans to fill up. Matt didn't want to stand out, so that meant going to multiple gas stations. Megan had to admit he really was pretty good at this cloak and dagger stuff. She realized that she would not have thought of half of the things Matt just did naturally.

She took three plates out of the cabinet and placed them on the table, alongside of the silver wear and napkins. She studied the table to discern if she was missing anything. Returning to the kitchen, she forced herself not to look at the clock, instead putting the shredded cheddar cheese in a bowl. Picking up the onion, and the tomato, she chopped them up and shredded some lettuce for the guys to add as desired. Glover didn't have much hot sauce left, but she decided that there was enough in the bowel next to the sour cream to give each of them enough for their meal. Not seeing anything that she needed, she walked back into the kitchen, opened the oven door, and looked in to see the cheese bubbling. Sighing, she turned off the oven and glanced at the clock before she could stop herself.

"Well, nothing to do until they get back. Looking at her burn phone on the counter next to her, she considered calling to check on them, but opted to wait a little longer, choosing instead to see how bad things were on the news.

Sitting on the sofa, Megan picked up the remote and tapped the power button. Rolling her eyes as the history channel came on, picturing something about monster trucks. Keying the remote, she surfed channels until she found a news channel. Exasperated, she saw they had the usual pundits going back and forth about the meaning of today's dramatic news.

"What dramatic news? Can't you morons assume that just maybe people might not just sit in front of their televisions all day?" The discussion wore on for a few minutes about the necessity of some sort of asset backed global reset. Frustrated, Megan almost switched the television off, knowing that the guys would be aware of whatever the latest development was when she noticed her name crawling across the bottom of the screen.

...S&B senior executive Megan Danvers is currently unaccounted for and is sought for questioning in the matter in an ongoing FBI investigation.

"Oh crap!" I'm glad that I was able to get a message to mom and dad this morning.

Now truly alarmed, Megan impatiently waited for the crawl to recycle through the headlines back to the story about her.

Agitated beyond imagining, time seemed to literally slow down as a commercial came on followed by one headline after another crawling across the bottom of the screen followed by three little dots or the Fox logo. Megan was ready to throw something at the screen when it finally came back around a few minutes later.

"...S&B's chairman, Billionaire John David Sterns, along with his security detail were shot and killed late Saturday night, following an unexplained altercation in an abandoned tenement house. S&B senior executive Richard Martin Blake was also wounded. Senior executive Megan Danvers is currently unaccounted for. Authorities fear that she may have been taken against her will. The FBI is investigating."

Leaning back into the sofa, she gasped as the front door opened to the apartment. Turning sharply, she realized that the pistol Matt told her to keep on her at all times was still on the kitchen counter, next to the tortillas.

"It's us, Beautiful." Glover came in smiling broadly, his white teeth contrasting sharply with the dark coloring of his skin which was quite appealing. "Sorry it took so long. Gas is already starting to get a little scarce, so there were some long lines. Matt is right behind me with some beer." Glover threw a fatigue jacket across the back of his recliner and headed for the kitchen to take a look. "Wow, that smells great, Megan!"

"Thanks, Glover, have you guys been listening to the news? They are looking for us in a big way." Hearing Matt shut the door, she almost ran to him. She buried her face in his chest. "What do we do? They are acting like I have been kidnapped." She could hear Glover getting the enchiladas out of the oven as Matt held her.

"We are going to be fine." Matt motioned for her to sit down at the little table as Glover approached with the enchiladas.

Matt smiled grimly. "You know, Meg, it is possible that your FBI friend is just trying to smoke us out. If you recall, I did call the guy right as things were going down."

Megan nodded as she took a seat next to her man. Glover began dishing out the food. "Well, the FBI will know that Megan was there from her fingerprints," Matt said. "They also know that she had agreed to help them out. Unless they're morons, it's pretty clear that a guy like Sterns doesn't hang around deserted apartment buildings." Matt looked at Megan, confidence apparent on his face. "I'm sure they would like to have us in their pockets, but even without Richard saying so, they will be able to tell you were being held by Sterns. If I were them, I would want to know how Sterns got Blake away from their tender care."

Glover put another bite in his mouth. "These enchiladas are really great, Meg." Wiping his mouth, he turned to Matt. "I think you guys should probably hide out here for a few weeks." His face growing suddenly serious, he continued. "Think about it. It just doesn't track very well, does it? Not just anyone walks away with an FBI witness like that. I bet you anything that they are going through their own people in a big way, looking for anyone that might be dirty."

Megan nodded. "Actually, that night the arrogant bastard as much as said he did. Whoever it was, he or she has to know they're toast. They just need to look for whoever didn't show up for work."

"Maybe, but either way, I don't plan on finding out if I can help it. I am thinking that the Feds are about to be really busy with bigger fish to fry in the coming weeks and months. Things are really going into the toilet in a big way this last day or two." Dishing up another enchilada, Matt looked at Glover and continued. "While you were paying for the last of the gasoline, I was listening to today's big announcement. It looks like anyone dumb enough to still be screwing around with equities or currency is finally panicking." Matt took a drink of his beer before continuing. "The market is in a complete free-fall. It looks like all trading has more or less stopped. They said that there are no new factory orders or housing starts of any kind. Companies of all sizes, both here and around the world, are now, or soon will be, laying-off their workforces. The newscaster said that unemployment could hit fifty percent by the end of the week."

Looking at Glover, Megan noticed that the scope of the disaster was starting to really register in his mind.

He took a breath. "Son-of-a-bitch! There is no way those kinds of numbers will go well."

Megan nodded. "That will happen really quickly, too, I think. Last week Sterns and Becker finalized our own layoff plans. We thought we would have a month or two, but now that things are spiraling down, the board will not wait. They probably already pulled the trigger on that this afternoon."

Glover shook his head in dismay. "Damn, I wonder what this is going to mean for the military?"

Finishing off his beer, Matt looked Glover right in the eye. "You may not be too happy about things, in a week or so. Think about it. With things getting this bad, you may find yourself right in the middle of some stuff. Like you said, people are going to go ape-shit when everyone gets laid off, and food gets tough to come by. If you aren't on alert by the end of the week, I will be amazed."

"Aw, crap! I bet you are right. You think they will have us backing up the cops, huh?"

"Look, Glover, the wheels are coming off, and nobody is ready for anything like this. People are going to be really scared. Some of them are going to do some stupid stuff. Worse, some of those stupid people are in DC, and you are going to see some crazy orders coming down."

Megan watched as Glover's eyes grew larger and larger as Matt talked. He could tell that the wheels were turning now about what he would and wouldn't do. Matt continued.

"Every leader up and down the chain, will have to make decisions every day, regarding what is legal and what isn't. You guys will be handing out MREs and guarding key facilities. Just pray they don't try to use this stuff to justify some sort of power grab. If I were you, I would print off some key bits of the US Constitution and hand them around. The political folks are going to have to declare martial law; they have no choice. The question I have is, what happens after that?"

"Damn Matt, why do you always have to be two steps ahead of everybody? I was in a really good mood. Now it feels like the time we are about to roll in on Fallujah for the second time."

Megan realized she was shaking as Matt spoke. Watching the conversation, it was clear that Glover was pretty shaken up too. They all three fell silent, each clearly thinking about what was said and about what they should do. Megan had a plan and was already doing what she could to get home, and then she had another thought. Even with Sterns dead, that didn't mean her family would be safe. He could still have someone else who would come after her family. Megan set her fork down and pushed her plate away and looked over at Matt.

"Matt, we have to get in touch with my dad. Sterns threatened my sisters if I didn't cooperate. He always keeps his promises. They have to know there is a risk Matt, they have to." Seeing that Matt was thinking about how to get them a warning, she got up and took her dishes to the sink. Glover, too, began clearing the table. She rinsed off her plate and began putting dishes into the dishwasher as Glover brought them to her. Feeling a hand on her shoulder she turned to face Glover.

"Don't you worry about any of this stuff, Meg. That man knows what he is doing. There isn't anything I wouldn't trust him with. Hell, after what he said about us having to ride herd on Americans here at home, I have half a mind to go AWOL and join you guys. If it wasn't for my duty to my troops and needing to make sure that military guys don't get used to violate the Constitution, I would absolutely say to hell with it."

Meg gave him a hug and smiled up at him. "Well, you know you are welcome any time. If you get to a point where you have done what you can, and you need a place to go, we are just west of Mineral Wells, off of Highway One-Eighty."

"You got yourself a deal, Little Lady."

As Megan put the last of the dishes in the dishwasher, Matt walked into the kitchen and leaned against the counter opposite Glover. "Here is what I came up with. We will just have to get another burn phone and call them. We can dump the phone after that. The only down side is it will give our location at the time of the call to anyone who is looking. Not close enough to do them any good with regards to picking us up, but it will reduce the places that they have to search for us. They have probably already figured we are headed for Texas, but they cannot be sure what roads we are using. We need to not be where they think we are."

Frowning, Megan knew it was a stupid risk, but she had to let her folks know. As she thought through the angles, she saw Glover's face light up.

"I got it, Matt. I am in the motor pool doing maintenance on our tracks anyway. I will power up one of the command tracks. I have the frequencies to hit a military satellite. I can make a satellite call to you from the command track and then conference in her folks. I can't give you very long, but long enough. They could trace things back to Ft. Knox, too, of course, but it will take them a little while, and, like you say, it is likely they are going to have bigger fish to fry. Also, I am thinking the army will not just bend over backwards for some FBI witch hunt especially if we get busy with relief efforts."

"You are a genius, Glover." Megan hugged him tightly, and Matt patted him on the back.

"Really, Glover, thank you; I think I am going to be able to breathe again," Matt said. "I just couldn't stand it if something were to happen to Meg's family. Good call, Buddy. I always said you were fast on your feet."

Megan grabbed both men by the arms and guided them into the living room, determined to finally relax. She had just turned on the television to find a movie when the phone rang.

"Be right back, Guys. Pick whatever looks good." Glover went to the kitchen to answer the phone. "Staff Sergeant Washington."

"Aww crap, a couple of us were just talking about that being a real possibility." Meg looked into the kitchen as did Matt. "Yes, Sir. I am already packed, Sir. I can be there in fifteen." Matt looked at Megan with a resigned expression.

Megan let Matt pull her into a hug. "It's starting, Babe. We are going to have to be more careful now, and I mean it. I really do want you to keep that pistol on you, not in the next room, ok?" He winked.

Glover walked back into the living room. "Sorry guys. Looks like things are moving pretty fast. I have to be back on base by twenty hundred hours. I am going now though. I am going to start warming up equipment and running maintenance tonight. I should be calling you guys in an hour or so to try your folks."

"Thanks, Buddy; Meg and I owe you one. You watch your back, all right?"

"You can count on it, Brother. Let me know you guys are safe when you can, ok? I guess we all just have to do our best to keep things together at this point."

"Yeah, I just hope there are more NCOs and officers out there who are smart enough to keep things from getting too out of hand."

"Me too, Matt, me too." Glover smiled grimly.

Megan could see the bond between the two men as they hugged. Glover then turned to her, and whispered into her ear. "Take care of him for me, will you?"

"I will, Glover. I don't plan to let him out of my sight ever again."

He put on his field jacket and headed for the door. "God Speed, Brother. Talk to you soon."

Chapter 29
Proclamation is Policy

Walking up to the door, Sadie concluded that, although she hated the drive, she loved staying with Catherine the past week or so. As terrifying as her life had become over the past five or six weeks, she found the suburb of Cedar Hill to be relaxing, and she felt safe somehow, not to mention how much she really loved Ginny and Drake. Acknowledging that her impression of Catherine's life as idyllic was a groundless illusion, it was still very appealing. As always, she was tired after her shift, but she smiled contentedly, as she opened the door, knowing that Maggie was just on the other side, to welcome her home. Entering the front room, Catherine's friend, Dennis, waved, as Maggie pounced, requiring immediate attention.

Dennis stood and smiled.

"Hello, Sadie, Kate is in the restroom. We are just working on organizational charts. Is your morning going ok?"

Setting down her purse and collapsing onto the sofa, she looked over at Catherine's Tea Party colleague. "Not too bad, I guess. Don't get me wrong, it is getting crazier every single day. At least we didn't have any suicides this shift, so I think that counts as a win." Moments after sitting down she had to readjust to accommodate Maggie as the affectionate boxer jumped on the couch to lie beside her.

"I heard about some of that on the news, but I guess I hadn't realized it was an everyday sort of thing."

"Well, it isn't an everyday thing, but it happens way too often. We had like almost a dozen over the last ten days or so."

"Wow, Sadie, that is terrible, but now that I think about it, I'm not surprised. People are really edgy."

Sadie nodded in agreement. "So, what are you guys working on, so early in the morning?"

"Kate wanted to tighten up the group roster, and work on the organization a bit, to give us better redundancy in case folks leave for whatever reason. She is thinking we are going to have to be really flexible now that things are going bad so quickly. All of the central banks have been sharply raising interest rates on their bonds all week, but nobody is buying. Anyone with any cash is spending it, or if they are less than bright, they are just sitting on it."

"I wouldn't have thought about it a few months ago," Sadie said, "but its groups like yours, that will get us through this if anything can. It really makes me mad that the Hospital cut the funding for Catherine last week. It really sucks not being able to eat lunch together, but she is doing what she needs to be doing. I think."

"Well, she really is good at this stuff. We are all grateful that she agreed to take over the group. I am not too proud to admit I am out of my league with things being what they are."

Hearing the water running from the bathroom, Sadie reached down and picked up the remote.

"I will let you guys work, I don't want to interrupt." She turned on the TV, but turned the sound almost all the way down, and began surfing for the latest news.

"Actually, I am about to leave. We have been on this for a couple of hours, and I need to get to the office anyway."

Sadie acknowledged the comment as Catherine came out, and looked over at her. "Hungry? I can make you something if you like. We are pretty much done for the moment."

"No, really, Catherine, I ate at the hospital before I left." She selected the channel she wanted, but muted it until the commercial was over. Leaning back, she closed her eyes for a moment while letting the stress from her shift begin to loosen its grip on her body and soul. She could feel Maggie creep a little closer, as the boxer sought a comfortable lap to lay her head on. Sighing, she relished the comfort she felt in this moment. Vaguely aware, she listened as Dennis and Catherine wrapped up what they were working on, and then hearing Dennis moving towards the door, both of them speaking softly, she focused on getting her anxiety to dissipate.

"I will call you later, Kate," he whispered.

Catherine closed the door behind him, and made her way to sit in her recliner. A moment turned into two and Sadie considered just letting go, and falling asleep right where she was, when she heard Catherine sit up abruptly.

"Oh, my God Sadie, can you turn it up for a moment?"

Opening her eyes, Sadie sat up blinking, trying to force her mind to comprehend what her eyes were seeing, to make sense of the bodies she saw falling out a tall building before her. The first appeared to be a man, his tie fluttering behind him as he fell. Behind him was another, this one losing his jacket in mid fall.

"Catherine, what's happening? Where is this? Why are they jumping? It looks just like 9/11."

"Tokyo, I think. I am not sure, but the graphic said something about our dollar collapsing." Sadie heard a gasp and then realized it was she who made the sound. Clumsily thumbing the remote, the sound came up as the image on the TV switched to the floor of the New York Stock Exchange. People were just standing around with shocked looks on their faces, as they watched their status boards. They just stood there in an eerie silence, as there appeared to be nothing further for them to do anytime soon.

"... Ted, we are here at the heart of Wall Street, and the mood is one of stunned disbelief. Traders have just been milling about since the announcement came across the intercom here about fifteen minutes ago. A few of them are talking in small groups, but already several have begun to wander out of the building. Like the other major finance centers, today's complete collapse of the US Dollar impacted markets immediately."

"Ted, this is Stuart in the studio. Have you talked to anyone who has any ideas related to a solution?" Sadie noticed that the expression on the reporter's face was one of complete unabashed incredulity, but he answered, regardless.

"I spoke to a trader a few minutes ago who told me it would be impossible to restart because there was just too much debt, and no way to validate fair values on the assets that back up that debt. The bond market expert who I spoke to..." The Studio anchor cut into the report.

"Just a moment, Ted, I am getting a response in from the White House. The President will be addressing the nation any time now. I am being told he is on his way over to address a joint session of Congress within the hour." Stuart James then looked directly into the camera, mustering all the sincerity his training allowed him. "Obviously, this is a grave time for all Americans, indeed for all people everywhere. We will, of course, go directly to Washington when the President enters the chamber." Refocusing his attention, the anchor again addressed his attention to Ted on the trading floor. "Are you still with us, Ted? You have my apologies for the interruption, please continue." The anchor gave the camera a look of grave concern as several seconds passed. "Ted?" Stuart looked off screen, seeking direction and then focusing again on the camera, he began to adlib. "We have momentarily lost contact with the trading floor, but we will go back there as soon as the connection is reestablished."

Sadie turned to Catherine who was watching the report, but sensing her stare, Catherine turned, their eyes meeting. The moment passed between them. Her eyes wide with uncertainty, Sadie spoke first. "Do you think this is it? Are the things you have been warning people about finally beginning?"

Catherine looked completely miserable. It was clear she was every bit as frightened as Sadie. "I think it started months ago. I guess historians will pick a date someday, but it was inevitable once more than fifty percent of our population became dependent on the government for a pay check or assistance. The politicians sold us out by buying votes with money we didn't have..." As Catherine's spoke, her eyes flashed with anger, her face hard.

Seeing the fire in Catherine's eyes, Sadie understood that regardless of her friend's fatalistic attitude and hopelessness, this woman was someone who would never give up on what she believed in, no matter what was in her way. Moreover, Sadie knew that regardless of what happened, she was really attracted to Catherine. She didn't care if they had only known each other for less than a month, or that their world was falling apart; she was going to find a way to be in her life long enough to find out if they could have a future. She was old enough to know it was too soon to go gushing about her feelings, but, her own resolve hardening, she had decided she would do whatever it took to make it work.

In lecture mode now, Catherine continued as images of distraught traders repeated continually on the screen. "...In the end they will likely blame the politicians since they have done almost nothing of substance since the two thousand eight housing crash. Anyway, do you think I need to activate the call tree?"

"Yes, Catherine, I do. Think about how you are feeling right now, and you are the girl that everyone in your group is looking to for answers. If nothing else, it will let everyone know that they matter, and that someone is looking out for them. Besides, there may be someone that needs help, or just needs to be with someone." Catherine's expression softened upon hearing her suggestion.

"Thanks for that, Sadie. I think you are absolutely right. Everyone will be looking for something to hang on to. You really are very intuitive, you know? Let's come up with a quick message to send out." Both women got up to go into the dining room where Catherine's laptop was still open, when Fox News's dramatic tone associated with the financial collapse, alerted them to an update. The graphic displayed, and this hour's anchor, Stuart James announced the president.

The World in Crisis – Breaking News!

"The President is said to be about to enter the chamber."

Catherine walked over to stand beside Sadie, as the Sergeant at arms prepared to announce the leader of the free world.

"Mister Speaker! The President of the United States!"

"As you can see, the president is very serious this morning as he approaches the podium. Obviously, many of the Congressional members have only recently arrived, clearly a result of the historical urgency of today's news."

"You are quite right, Stuart. For this kind of emergency, one would have to go back well over a hundred years, if not further. It is clear that these members of Congress are nothing if not grim faced as they await the President's remarks."

"I notice, Chet, the President is hardly pausing to speak with any of the members, as he makes his way to the well. If this were a State of the Union, for example, he would typically take several minutes to make his way down the aisle."

Sadie looked at Catherine, who was standing beside her, staring at the screen. "Catherine, I want you to know that whatever happens, I am here for you. I will help anyway I can. I believe in you."

Turning to Sadie, her eyes wide with anticipation, Catherine blinked, returning her gaze. "Thanks, Sadie. I hope you know I really do appreciate your support. Here we go, I guess."

The reporter's face was replaced on the screen by the image of the President behind the podium as he stated the obvious.

"The President is about to speak."

Looking grim, but resolute, the President looked across the room, and then into the camera.

"Mr. Speaker, Mr. President Pro Tempore, members of Congress, and fellow Americans:

In the normal course of events, Presidents have repaired to this chamber to report on the state of our Union, or to speak to matters of great import to this great nation. It is my sad duty this morning, to discuss with the American People that our Union is sorely challenged by the press of events that have befallen us.

As many of you may have seen in news reports overnight and into this morning, markets around the world are experiencing unprecedented difficulties. Americans have seen and endured difficult times before, and as great nations always do, we will overcome our challenges as Americans have always done, by working together. As seen in the courage of our warriors who have defended this nation in its many wars to protect freedom, as is witnessed when our first responders rush into harm's way to save those in need, as written about in our history, when Americans set out to settle this great land, we will persevere as we always have. Americans have brought freedom to millions, we have set foot on the moon, and we have freed entire continents from the ravages of war. Now, we have a new challenge we must overcome, and we will rise to meet this challenge."

Her eyes again shifting from the screen to Catherine's face, it was clear that, like Sadie, her world almost looked like it had stopped spinning, as they waited for what the President would say next.

Catherine already began to shake her head in disgust, not even waiting to see what the man would say.

"Watch how he will play victim here. They are all going to act completely amazed that such a thing could happen to them."

"My fellow citizens, for the last eleven days the entire world has experienced unprecedented financial challenges. I am here to say to every American, that a nation is more than just its check book. We are a people willing to share and sacrifice for the good of others. We are the acts of kindness, as we help each other through hard times. We are the resilient pioneers that settled this land, and for which, no obstacle was too great to overcome. For these reasons I am here to state clearly to the American People and the world that the state of our union is strong regardless of the challenges we face today."

"Whatever. Just get to the part where you plan to steal from the American people to pay off your friends," Catherine said. As Sadie watched Catherine watch the President, she could see her friend's anger building. She felt hers doing likewise.

"This morning, we are, as a country, facing grave financial challenges. It is clear to all that our nation has pursued policies that have resulted in a troubled dollar. Mistakes have been made, but we will implement the needed changes to our policies, and we will recover from this challenge, to once again rise to be a nation that others can depend on. Our shock will turn to anger, and that anger to resolution. With the help of the Congress and other leaders at all levels, the federal government will, with your help, forge a path through these challenging times. All of America is touched by the events now transpiring. I can tell you that Republicans and Democrats are already joining together to face this tragedy as one nation, together. They are facing the challenge as we always do, as Americans. On behalf of the American people, I would like to thank these leaders, as well as leaders in Europe, Asia, and around the world for their willingness to work with us, to resolve the issues confronting us all. I can tell you that already, world governments are actively working to finalize a plan that has been in development by a bipartisan committee for almost two years...."

"Son-of-a-bitch, the bastard just proved that both parties have known this was coming all along and have been planning for this day for years. They steal from us to pay off their elite friends, and then when it all finally goes down the drain, they are all suddenly willing to work with everyone." Sadie mirrored Catherine's look of revulsion as Catherine continued. "Watch him throw the Constitution out the window. I bet you anything he is about to tell us how only more government assholes can fix this, and they can't be bothered with the pesky Constitution."

"...As soon as some of the final details are worked out, my government, in conjunction with other world governments, will announce a recovery plan that our partnerships with the global community have produced. This plan will secure the futures of citizens around the world. My administration is working closely even now with key members of the House of Representatives, the Senate, and the Judiciary, to identify ways and means to effectively implement needed reforms quickly. This effort will require that we all work together for the common good. For this reason, I am announcing that I have appointed a bipartisan group of experts, consisting of our best economic minds, to work closely with legislators and to craft regulations that will quickly help us to begin the recovery process. I regret to say that during an interim period, some of the current guarantees that underpin our way of life will simply not be possible to observe until the economy begins to recover. The issues plaguing our economy are complex. While free markets and private ownership of our key industries are the hallmark of the American way of life, the urgency of the crisis, requires the immediate and coordinated response of economic experts, not the haphazard approach of profit seekers. For this reason, my administration will work closely with your representatives in the legislature and with private industry to ensure Americans continue to have necessities of life available to them. The federal government has expended vast sums of taxpayer money to support private industry over the years. In this time of crisis, we will be asking for the same consideration from private industry, in support of seeing the American people through this hardship. I know this necessity will trouble many Americans, as I, too, am troubled, but our first priority must be saving American lives. I want to emphasize these measures are temporary, and will be rescinded when possible. I want to remind all Americans their deposits are all insured to two-hundred-thousand dollars, and your government will stand by this commitment."

Seeing that Catherine was shaking with rage now, she moved closer and placed her hand supportively on her friend's arm.

Catherine snorted with derision, screaming at the screen. "So what? Two hundred grand won't mean much by the time you finish talking, and you know it. The dollar is worthless, you feckless ass-hole!" Turning to face Sadie, she had tears in her eyes. "This is it. Right here, right now is how freedom dies. My God, Sadie, we just witnessed history being made. The son-of-a-bitch just trashed the Constitution of the United States with a press conference." Almost in shock, she turned back to stare in horror at the television screen.

"...In the interim period of time, I want to encourage all Americans to do their best to continue in their lives as they always have. I know that there will be challenges, but together, we, along with all of our partners and allies around the world, will set things right again. In times of great challenge, Americans have always shown the world the meaning of courage. I am confident that we will do so again in this challenge. It is my hope that in the months and years ahead, life will return almost back to normal in many ways. We'll go back to our lives and routines. Each of us will remember the moment the news came, remember where we were, and what we were doing the day that our lives changed, but we will also remember the greatness that is America. Together, we will not yield; together we will not rest; together we will not relent to rebuild an economy even more robust than what we have lost. We will build an economy that can guarantee security, not only for some Americans, but for all of the American people. The course of our work is not yet certain, but the outcome of our work is assured. Prosperity and freedom from want are the outcomes that, together, we will achieve.

Fellow citizens, we will meet this challenge with firm resolve, resilience, and collectively, we will overcome this challenge. In all that lies before us, may God grant us wisdom, and may He watch over the United States of America. Thank you."

"I am so sorry Catherine. I know you have tried to avoid this, and I am scared too, but do you want to hear something?"

Catherine faced Sadie, tears now streaming down her face.

Sadie took Catherine's hand. "I couldn't care less what they say, I believe in you, and Drake. I believe in Dennis and the rest of the guys. I also believe there are thousands, or actually, probably millions, of people, like you, who will get us through this with our freedom intact."

A weak smile flashed on Catherine's emotionally stricken face, and Sadie felt herself swept into her friend's arms, embracing her more fully than she had been held in years. Lost in emotion herself, she wanted to remember every sensation, as Catherine's left hand cupped the back of her head, and as Catherine's right hand pulled her close. Tuning out the commentators shocked reactions, they just stood there comforting each other, not knowing what the future held, but knowing they would face what came, together.

After a moment or two, Catherine released her. "Thank you for being here, Sadie. I know I'm not a lot of fun some times."

"Who are you kidding? It's you who are helping me, remember?" Sadie said.

"This would suck to face alone." Shaking off the emotion, Sadie could sense resolution flowing into Catherine, replacing the hot anger. "We should get that phone tree going. We need to make sure we get help to anyone who might be in trouble."

"What can I do, Honey?" Sadie asked.

Catherine smiled sardonically. "You can get some sleep. It isn't like there is going to be anything to do about any of this in the next few hours. I am going to see about getting some of the group leaders together a little later. I will call Pastor Tom, to see about meeting over at the church. If you want to help with things later, that would be good though. You are off for a couple of days, right?"

Sadie nodded that she was and picked up her purse to head to her room. "I am off until Monday, actually, so I am your loyal assistant for whatever you need."

"Thanks, Sadie, you may regret saying that, but I am grateful for the help. See you in a while." Catherine smiled, more confident now that her rage was cooling to a manageable level. Sadie realized that, although she knew that she should be afraid, somehow she wasn't.

Chapter 30
Power Play

Catherine took a sip of her diet soda and sat back while she waited on Pastor Tom to return with his folder of people in the community who needed help. Sadie went to look for a restroom, leaving her momentarily alone with her thoughts. Leaning back for a moment, she assessed the little meeting room. It was intimate, without being cramped. It had durable blue carpet and walls painted in a pale grey. The center of the room was dominated by a large wooden table surrounded by eight padded office chairs. Four more chairs were arranged along the wall. She sat facing the door which was located in the corner of the room on her right. Working through the priorities before the group, the idea occurred to her, that this wasn't all that different from working through the priorities that she learned after high school while serving in the army. She really was using the skills she learned in her leadership development courses. Facing the situation before her, she had resources, and a team of people. All she had to do, she theorized, was work with the guys to best utilize what they had, to help as many people as possible. At least waiting for the disaster to unfold was over now, not that there wasn't always room for things to get a lot worse, she decided. Catherine took another sip from her soda as the door to the little meeting room opened. Drake stepped into the room, wearing faded jeans and his bright yellow Gadsden T-shirt, with a coiled snake prominent on his chest. He was smiling slightly, but she could see the stress lines around his mouth, and although freshly shaved, he looked tired.

"Hey, Kate, are you hanging in there ok? Ginny wanted to come tonight, but her mom called and was pretty upset after watching the news today, so I am 'representing' - if you know what I mean."

"I am glad you could make it, Drake. Tom will be back in a sec. Dennis and Chase just got off work. They said they will be here in like fifteen."

Drake acknowledged her comments with a gesture, and took a seat across from her. "Is Sadie working tonight?"

"No, she's here. She just stepped out for a bit. She'll be right back."

Drake stretched and hung his jacket over the back of the chair as he took the Dr. Pepper Catherine offered him. "Crazy stuff today, you would not believe the calls. Would you ever think that on a given day, people would all just loose it? I had to arrest an eighty-four year old man this afternoon. He was heading to Dallas, to the Federal Building with a rifle. His daughter called in, asking us for help. She said he was going to make them pay. 'Them' being the federal government, I guess."

Catherine snorted. "What did you arrest him for? It doesn't sound like he had done anything yet."

"That was the weird part. He was really pissed. Johnnie was talking to him while his daughter filled me in. He flat out said he was going to take them down for what they did to the country. We tried to calm the guy down. You know, tell him that we would get through this together, but he wasn't having any of it." Drake took another drink and shook his head. "I guess that he was just scared and really angry. Anyway, he said the minute we left, he was going down there. He didn't even try to hide it. He gave us no choice, really."

The door to the little room opened again, and Sadie entered followed by Pastor Tom. Catherine could hear Dennis and Chase talking further down the hall so she began passing around the typed up bullet points she wanted to cover, so that they could get started as soon as they were all present. Sadie resumed her seat beside Catherine and Tom sat at the end of the table on the opposite end of the room from the door. Catherine's eyebrows shot up in surprise at how calm he looked. His sandy hair and strikingly green eyes sparkled, as they always did. He opened his folder and made a couple of notations on the list there. After a moment, he gave Catherine a look to indicate his readiness to proceed as the other two men entered the room and took seats on either side of Drake.

Catherine made eye contact with each of them and placed her elbows on the table, clasping her hands together. "Well, guys, it looks like it's finally happening. I thought that we should get together briefly, to make sure our organizational structure is working. I wanted to be sure that we are off to a good start in identifying needs in the group, and to begin trying to figure out how to help the community, if we can." She sighed as she considered how freaked out the people she had seen today were. She wanted to jump right into Pastor Tom's list, but realized she was missing something. She looked at Sadie with a question on her face. "What am I forgetting?"

Sadie giggled subtly. "Recruiting; you wanted to see if we could get some more people involved, now that things were really happening out there."

"Oh, right, thanks Sadie. Ok, so first things first. Did we have any problems with the call tree today? Have we reached everyone in the group?"

Chase leaned forward. "It took a while for a few of our people, but as of about an hour ago, we have reached out to everyone except the Richards. Not sure where they are, but we have tried to call them several times today. That was a good idea, Kate. Most of the folks I talked to really appreciated that someone had their backs."

"Thank Sadie. She encouraged me to go ahead and do that, sooner rather than later."

Highlighting the two names on her list, Catherine turned to Drake. "Do you think you and Johnnie could look in on them tomorrow? Dean Richards was always pretty loud with his opinions. I wonder if they are out of town or something. Still, I would think he or Dana would answer their cell phones."

"No problem, Kate. We will be glad to."

"Did you guys have anyone from any of your groups that were losing it, or that had any real issues today?"

Dennis, Pastor Tom, and Drake began to speak all at once. The three men looked at each other and, by unspoken acclimation, motioned for Tom to go ahead.

He inclined his head, thanking the men for their courtesy. "I can say that, for my part, the people I talked with were pretty concerned. There are a number of people who are pretty upset, here in the church, and in the community at large, for that matter. I have been telling people we have already made arrangements with the food bank, and along with the local Tea Party we'll do all we can to help. I am telling people to have faith in God and in their neighbors. We will be ok." Catherine noticed the others were shaking their heads in agreement.

"So is that pretty much what everyone is hearing? Is that about right?"

Everyone nodded their agreement. "OK, I think Tom is right. We just need to keep reassuring people that together, we are going to get through this." She turned to Tom. "Can you start a list of what the people we talk to need? Obviously, we can't really promise anything right now, but we need to at least have an idea of what the pain points are." Examining her team, she could see the tension on Chase's face. "Chase, are you ok?"

"I'm fine. Like everyone else, it has just been a long day."

Drake patted him on the back, as Tom and Dennis nodded their understanding. She smiled at him, making a note to herself not to forget the needs of the planning committee.

"Ok, so I know we talked about reaching out to people so they know someone cares. We want folks to feel like they have friends trying to help out. Along those lines, I think we should also ask them how they can help their neighbors. It will help to keep people calm if they are busy doing something. With all the layoffs that are coming, we don't want the community feeling helpless, and of course, we can use the help."

Dennis raised his hand, with an agitated expression on his face.

"Go ahead Dennis, do you have a concern?"

"Look, Kate. I think that everything you are saying is good to go, but we have been over what we have in the group. I don't see how we are going to open up to the broader community, without spreading ourselves way too thin. It isn't that I don't want to, but we just don't have enough supplies."

Catherine tapped her pen on the portfolio as she thought about the scope of the problem, and how it would only get much worse in the coming weeks. Looking at her predecessor, she knew he meant well, but she also realized this was just the reason he asked her to take over.

"I understand what you're saying, Dennis. I am not saying that we burn through our stocks, but the key dimension of the problem, especially now, is not about our stores, but about the psychology of the problem. We have to include as many people as we can, because anyone not working on solutions, will be part of the problem. If nothing else, we are selling hope here, guys. If we do nothing more than act as a clearing house between what is needed and what folks have, that will be better than nothing."

Subdued, but acknowledging her point, Dennis sighed and nodded his head in agreement with the strategy.

"Thanks Dennis, can I get you and Chase to work with Tom to try and address issues for people as best we can from within the group? That way, you can feel good about what we are doing with what we have. I am thinking we should start making lists of what people have extra of, and what they would be willing to share or to trade for something they may need. For things we cannot help with, we can see what the government types can do."

Her face furtive, she continued. "The biggest thing we can accomplish for the community immediately is just to communicate. I don't want anything happening to anyone and someone on our team not know about it. I think our primary challenge will be to keep people calm and get them to work together. I heard this afternoon that layoffs were already starting. It wasn't an hour after the President's speech that American Airlines announced it was ceasing operations, and would be laying off most of its work force until it could access what actions the company should take. I know also that the GM plant in Arlington started showing people the door."

All of the men in the room were grim but resolute.

Chase raised a finger.

"Maybe we can set up a group to look into things like power, and making stuff we are going to need on our own. Spring will be here soon. For sure, we are going to need to get a bunch of gardens going. We need some people who can show others what to do. We can get some people who know what they are doing to mentor others."

"That is a great idea, Chase," Catherine said.

Drake raised his pen to catch her attention.

"Drake?"

"Regarding the recruiting, I think all of us should be talking to our neighbors and people we run into throughout the day. If you like, Kate, I can send out a spreadsheet for everyone to send me with any names they collect. I will manage the lists, if you want me to. I am thinking the more people we have with us, the more resources we will have to help out."

"Thanks, Buddy, that's nothing but goodness. I appreciate it. Let me know if you get swamped, and we can split it up. In fact, with any luck, we will hopefully have enough going on we will all have to have help with that." Writing down the notes, Catherine caught Sadie's eye. "Sorry, Sadie, I didn't see you. Did you have something?"

Sadie looked at Drake. "Let me know what you want me to do, Drake, I want to help too if I can."

Drake smiled broadly. "You don't have to ask me twice, Girl. I think between the two of us, we have things covered for no..."

The door to the meeting room opened suddenly, as two men in slacks and dark blue polo shirts with black windbreakers bearing the DHS logo above an embroidered badge entered the room, their eyes appraising those sitting at the table.

Startled, Catherine noticed Pastor Tom began to rise with a stunned look on his face. She noticed the taller of the two men, a guy with a sharp face and blond hair, reacted automatically, his right hand reaching for his side arm.

Giving the agents a placating hand gesture, Tom spoke. "Can I help you, gentlemen? As you can see, we are having a meeting here."

"I can see that," the dark haired agent said. "Your meeting is part of the reason for our little visit." The man smirked, his face cocky and arrogant. "We have been monitoring some of the activity from your little group for a couple of months now. It seems several of you seem to be stockpiling quite a bit of ammunition and supplies. Isn't that right, Mr. Cob?"

Dennis cocked his head towards the dark haired agent, his eyes cold. "I'll tell you what, Friend, what I buy or don't buy is none of your damn business as long as they are legal purchases."

Catherine's eyes looked an unspoken question to Drake, who was clearly nonplused at the intrusion. Her eyes then moved to Tom, the outrage on his face overtaking the kindness that usually resided there. Obviously gathering his thoughts, Tom, took a deep breath. With all eyes on Tom, Catherine unobtrusively began to slide the pages in front of her, under her portfolio.

"Gentlemen, I am the pastor of this church. We are in a private meeting, and I am afraid you are intruding. I must ask you to leave."

The sharp faced blonde agent responded, never taking his hand off of his side arm. "Pastor, unless you have something to hide, I am sure you will agree it would be in everyone's best interest to comply with our questions. It shouldn't take long, unless you are doing something you should not be doing." The two men sneered at the group, sitting around the table, but continued pleasantly. "First of all, I will need your names, and we will need to see all of your driver's licenses." The agent looked briefly at Catherine, then back to Dennis. "Then, Mr. Cob, I would like you to ask your secretary here to make me a nice copy of that membership list she is so subtly trying to hide from view. As the leader of this little so-called Tea Party, Mr. Cob, we, of course, know who you are. We just need you to have your friends jot down their roles as well."

Drake blinked, recovering from his momentary surprise. Reaching over to his iPhone, where it lay on the legal pad in front of him, he casually, began to scroll through his contacts.

Feeling Sadie's hand grab at her from under the table, Catherine rose from her seat, she extended her left hand to forestall Tom's coming outburst. Her face, radiating irritation and her voice quiet, but venomous, she froze the blond agent with an icy glare. "First of all," she held up her right index finger, "I don't have a clue who you two numb-nuts are, as you seem to have neglected to announce yourselves at my meeting. Any dumbass can buy a DHS windbreaker." She held up her right middle finger. "Secondly, I am in charge of this so-called little Tea Party." Kate held up her right ring finger. "Finally, unless you two dip-shits have a warrant, you need to leave, now!"

The dark haired agent turned on her, surprise obvious on his face, but Catherine cut him off before he could retort. "What? Don't tell me that you arrogant, inbred, over educated, constitutionally ignorant, morons with delusions of grandeur, made a mistake. Oh wait, of course you did, because your whole agency couldn't find their collective asses with both hands and a flashlight."

Drake interceded. "That's enough, Kate."

The dark haired man, fury evident on his face, started around the table towards Catherine. "Kate is it? Congratulations on your new position. You see, Kate, it's like this. We have a memo that came down this morning, instructing us to pay real close attention to you little Tea Party types. It seems that there is a real threat from Tea Parties working on terrorist plots against the federal government."

She noticed the blonde agent was now beaming with amusement as his partner continued, exaggerating his slow and careful diction, as if talking to a child.

"Fortunately, the Congress, in its considerable wisdom, had the foresight to pass a little provision in the National Defense Authorization Act a couple of years ago that allows us to deal with American terrorists you see. It is a beautiful thing, really. We get to send them away for as long as we want. How does that sound, Cupcake?"

Her eyes blazing, she began to retort, when Drake cut her off, speaking into the cell phone, now in his left hand, his right hand on his own pistol which was holstered at his waist.

"Officer needs assistance, Baptist church, conference room off of Houston Street." Looking daggers at the two agents, he turned to face them squarely. "Ok, guys, I am a police officer. You don't have a warrant and you have been asked to leave. Do so now or you are both under arrest." His hand gripped his Glock. "I would suggest we all just back away from this, ok?" Catherine's eyes went wide, as Chase, too, stood up. His hand moved his shirt away from the pistol he always carried. Thankfully, she could hear the sirens coming.

Drake smiled coldly. "What's it gonna be, boys?"

Clearly furious, both agents traded looks. Several breathless moments passed, before the dark haired agent turned on his heels and stormed back out the door, followed by his partner.

Catherine followed Drake and the two men down the hall and through the double doors onto Houston Street. By the time the two agents got to their SUV parked on the street, two CHPD units had rolled up. A uniformed sergeant stepped out of the nearest cruiser to cautiously survey the scene. As the second cruiser came to a stop behind the SUV, two more officers in the second vehicle got out, serious and focused expressions on their faces. Both new arrivals were taking no chances, with their gun hands hovering very near their weapons. She could see that Drake's eyes never left the federal agents, as he headed toward the other cops. She could tell that the sergeant was looking them over carefully.

"What do we have here, Sabol?" the sergeant asked.

Before he could answer, the blonde agent interjected. "You have yourself a discipline problem sergeant. I am a federal..."

The sergeant held up a hand cutting him off in mid-sentence. "I will be with you in a moment, Agent." Turning to the officer standing next to the other cruiser, he gave an order. "Roenfeldt, validate those two's credentials and get their story."

"On it Boss."

Drake walked over to where his sergeant stood. "We were holding a meeting when they just bust into the room with hands on their weapons, and started going off on everyone. The gist is they don't seem to have any sort of warrant, and they don't care much for our Tea Party affiliation." Looking over at the group standing in the door way, Drake motioned for the Pastor to join them. "Pastor Tom, can you come give Sergeant Harris your statement?" Tom nodded and headed his way, as the sergeant grasped Drake by the shoulder, and turned him away from the little group in the doorway.

Catherine turned to Sadie, her eyes flaring in amazement. "Well, that wasn't an inordinate amount of fun was it? I am so freaking pissed off. The bastards aren't even pretending to give a damn about the Constitution." Watching Sadie's expression, she realized the dark haired beauty seemed to have a temper. Suddenly, realizing that her friend was really angry, and not just at the federal agents, she grimaced.

"What were you thinking, Catherine? That guy was really mad. You knew they could arrest you without recourse! Why in the world would you antagonize them like that?"

Turning to face her, Catherine replied. "Maybe I went too far, but if we don't stand up for our constitutional rights now, they won't exist to be stood up for later. Things are going to only get harder from here. Freedom isn't free, Sadie."

Her own eyes flashing, Sadie went on, not calming down in the least. "I am not saying we shouldn't stand up for what is right. I am not saying we should have given them what they wanted, but you really pushed him. I am just saying we need you," she hesitated a moment. “I need you, Catherine. You won’t do anyone any good in a cell somewhere.”

Catherine just stared into Sadie’s eyes, her head tilting to one side as a slight smile crept onto her face. Sadie started to reply when Catherine noticed her friend’s eyes widen. She turned her head sharply, following Sadie’s gaze. Making eye contact with the driver of a non-descript car, who was watching them closely. Catherine realized instinctually who the man was as the Middle Eastern man returned her gaze, his eyes cold.

“Drake!” She saw her best friend look up from his conversation and pointed at the Middle Eastern man’s car.

Chapter 31
Tools of Tyranny

The sun filtered, sparkling clean, through the row of glass blocks that made up the window of Annie's bedroom. The window was set high on the wall inside, but was only inches from the ground on the outside of what was largely a below ground space. Annie giggled softly to herself regarding her husband's reaction to her bedroom. Like many of her friends in high school, Russell thought it was a little weird that her parent's house had all of the bedrooms arranged along the back of the structure, and were like seventy five percent below grade level. The glass block provided light, but was not prone to breaking. The front of the house, in contrast, looked perfectly normal, opening out onto a Spanish style courtyard. She reflected that he was more impressed, however, when her father mentioned how low their power bill was.

Lying in bed, she stretched luxuriously, trying to touch the footboard with her toes. She looked around the room and realized that Russell was already gone. Reflecting on that, she was really glad about how happy he had been the past few days as they settled in here. He and her dad really seemed to be enjoying each other, as they worked on the space that would be their apartment in the garage. Recalling the week, she thought they had accomplished a lot. The walls were already framed when they arrived, but the two of them had done all the wiring and were now putting up drywall. She was proud of her husband, she realized. They had accomplished all of that in the three days they had been home since arriving on Monday.

She knew she needed to get out of the bed, but it was just so very comfortable. She was in heaven, snuggled into the pillow soft mattress, her Indian patterned blankets pulled up around her neck. Gathering her courage to get up, she watched the patterns of light shining through the glass blocks of her window as they danced along the terracotta colored walls of her bedroom.

As she poked her feet out from under warm blankets in search of the rug under her bed, she sighed, grateful to be home. The President's speech yesterday and Katie's phone call last night were just unbelievable, especially on top of what Megan's friend, Tina, told her mom. Then there was the call from the FBI dude a couple of days ago, who was looking for her sister.

Annie grabbed her robe off the chair and headed for the kitchen. As soon as she opened the heavy wooden door, and the familiar squeak of the iron hinges announced her presence while bringing the smell of frying bacon to her nose. Smiling, she delighted in how the great room was still just as it was when she left home. The worn but comfortable leather sofa, her mom's favorite rocker by the fireplace, and the three paintings of her sisters and her, hanging over the mantle touched her heart. Walking across the great room and past the plank dining room table, she saw that Bridgett was lying on her back in the middle of the yard, squirming in delight. She smiled. Approaching the kitchen, she saw her mom was mixing up batter for pancakes.

Her mother smiled warmly at her. "Good morning, Sleepy Head, do you feel like eating?"

"I am always hungry, at least until I am not. What can I do to help?"

Beth Danvers smiled. "Why don't you set the table and put out the butter and syrup and what not. Also, tell your father and his new side kick that breakfast is ready, if you don't mind."

"Sure, Momma." Annie went to the cabinet and took out the plates. Opening the drawer to her left, she placed forks and knives on top of the little stack of plates and looked back at her mother. "Have we heard anything new from Meg?" The look on her mom's face became instantly strained, but she replied.

"Not since they called on Monday night, Sweetheart. I just hate that she is mixed up in something. I knew she had no business going to New York."

Annie nodded. "That FBI agent said she was just a witness, right? They can't make you testify if you don't want to, can they, Mom?" Her mother sighed, wiping her hands on her apron. She smiled helplessly at her daughter, and Annie took the assembled dishes to the table, setting them in their usual places.

"I wouldn't think so, but your sister said her company may have done something wrong. Your father called his friend in Washington. She said she would look into it. Obviously, he also called your Uncle Jerry. We will just have to sort it all out, that's all."

Annie went to the fridge for the butter, as her mother handed her the syrup on her way back to the table. "Who do we know in Washington, DC? I didn't know we knew people there."

"Your father and I hosted a get together here at the house during the election. Your father supported the woman who became our representative in Congress, so he is hoping that she can tell us what is going on with your sister." Her mom dolloped two circles of batter on the electric skillet, and was about to start a third, next to the two sizzling pools now becoming pancakes. Looking up into her daughter's eyes, she smiled hopefully. "Why don't you go get the men, dear? I don't want to talk about these things while we eat, if you don't mind. It isn't good for your father's digestion."

"Sure, Mom, I'm sorry, I just want my family back home again."

"I do, too, Sweetheart; I do, too."

❧

Needing a break, Annie looked up from pulling weeds to watch her husband on the tractor twenty feet away. Russell wiped his forehead with a handkerchief and rested a moment before climbing down off of the small tractor he had been using to till under the half acre of grass her father wanted ready for planting soon. As he approached Annie and her mom, he grinned. Happy to have a break from the weed pulling, Annie's mom sighed and looked up, blowing out a long breath. "Has anyone heard from

Bob yet? It will be dark in an hour or so. I would have thought he would have called in by now." Annie handed her husband a bottle of iced tea out of their cooler and gave him a saucy look. She thought he looked like the guy she fell for five years ago. She realized that a guy like Russell really just needed to be useful. He had to know he worked hard every day. She realized, to her surprise, that her mom also had a look of admiration on her face.

The grin on her husband's face changed to a guilty grimace.

"I talked to him a couple of hours ago. He was still talking to your Uncle Jerry, about Megan. He said they were watching something and would be home a little late. I'm sorry, Mrs. Danvers, I should have told you."

Looking at her mom, Annie gestured towards the house with a nod of her head. "Can we call it a day, Mom?"

"I think so, Dear. We need to get dinner, after all."

Cued by his wife's comments, the two women and Russell turned towards the garage. They were almost to the driveway, when they heard the crunch of gravel from the pickup pulling up out front. As the truck approached the storage barn off to the right of the house and garage, Annie looked with concern on her face towards her mother. Her father slid to a stop and climbed out of the truck, approaching them with a really serious look on his face. Watching him, Annie saw that her father was almost seething with anger as he crossed the space between them.

"Russ, I need a hand with some supplies." Turning to Annie and her mom, he forced a weak smile onto his face. "You girls need to get back to the house. Some things happened today, and we are going to need to sit down as a family and talk them through. Beth, why don't you and Annie make up some sandwiches, if you don't mind?" Patting Russell on the back, he continued. "Russ and I will be along as soon as we unload the truck."

Concern on her face, Annie's mom reached out for her father. "What is it, Honey?"

Her father grimaced. "The news isn't good. Not good at all, and for the duration of this mess, we will need to be open and straight up about things, but it can wait until we get inside."

Annie traded glances of apprehension with her mother, but they mutually decided to let it wait, and started towards the house. They walked in silence until they reached the opening in the chain link fence leading to the driveway near the entrance to the garage. Annie started to close the two oversized four foot wide gates, but her mother motioned at the tractor, still sitting in the garden. Annie realized what she was indicating and nodded her understanding. Gathering her courage, she decided to ask her mom what she was thinking. "If something were going on with Meg, Daddy would have said it straight out, right?"

"Yes, Dear, it has to be something to do with our legal problems with the government people, or maybe something to do with the mess the country is in these days." Crossing the driveway, Annie held the small wooden side gate for her mom, and they crossed into the front yard to Bridgett's happy yelps of joy.

"Down, Girl. No jumping on people."

"I am going to heat up some of the left over vegetable soup. Why don't you start shaving some ham off for the sandwiches? We can just put the platters on the table, and we can all make our own."

"Sure, Mom, I wish Meg and Katie would come home. The world is really getting weird."

"I know, Honey. Meg will be here soon, I hope, but I don't know about Kate. She said that she is leading a group of some kind that is trying to help people get by. She said she will come if it gets too rough."

Annie rolled her eyes. "Like she would admit that. She has been saying all this depressing stuff forever. You know, she is probably eating it all up."

"Annie! All that means is she was ahead of the rest of us. I am very proud of what your sister is doing, and you should be also. I wish she were here too, but you should give her credit for trying to help people." Taken aback, Annie just nodded demurely but didn't say anything further as they moved towards the house, each of them thinking their own thoughts. Her mom smiled at her again and gave her a hug as she opened the door into the kitchen.

They both jumped right into their tasks, as they shuttled their dinner to the table. After putting the soup on the table, Annie finished up by putting out the condiments and a bowel of chips as the men came in through the twin French doors nearest the kitchen. Her dad gave her his best reassuring smile, but more telling was the hard expression on Russell's face.

Her mom spoke first. "Bob, I want us to eat first, and then we can go into the living room and sit by the fire to talk." Her dad considered her comment for a moment as he sat down. Annie felt Russ's arm encircle her with a hug before pulling out her chair. She looked a question at him as he followed suit himself sitting next to her as she scooted up to the table.

"Beth, I am going to give the blessing, and I am going to go ahead with what I have to say. In this case, it won't be any more stressful than waiting." Annie saw him give her mother a look, and her mom's mouth snapped shut on her retort. Her dad gave her mom a nod of thanks, and then he turned to make eye contact with his daughter, and then his son-in-law. Clearing his throat, he began.

"Our Father in heaven, hallowed be thy name. Please bless the bounty that you have provided us this day. Please guide our hands in thy work and bless this home to thy service. Please forgive us our sins and help us to forgive those who sin against us. Please watch over Megan and Catherine and keep them safe, and if you will, bless this nation that we may return to righteousness and once again be a light for the world. Amen."

Annie's mother looked up after the family prayer with questions on her face that Annie wanted answered as well. No one even made a move toward the food, so it was clear that everyone was on edge.

"Alright, Dear, what is it? Is Megan in trouble?"

Bob Danvers looked around the table. "I am not sure about Meg, exactly. Uncle Jerry talked to the FBI today to let him know she was represented, and that she was not to speak to them without him being there. He spoke to an Agent Ricks, who said she agreed to work with the FBI about something to do with that firm she was working at." Annie noticed that he visibly had to gather courage to finish what he had to say. "It seems there was a shooting which resulted in her boss being killed. It seems Megan and another executive were working with law enforcement to expose whatever was going on. The FBI hasn't seen them since an incident in New York, however, and they to want badly to talk to them. He believes Megan's company may be trying to stop her."

Annie heard her mother gasp. "Bob, we have to find my baby. You are telling me that she is out there being chased by killers? Is that what you are telling me?" Her dad closed his eyes and sighed. "Beth, Agent Ricks said her boyfriend is a very capable man, with extensive military experience. We know that is true because of how they contacted us a day or two ago."

Annie's eyes, too, were wide in horror. "What if these men catch them?"

"Look, Girls, none of us likes being in the dark, but if the FBI can't find your sister and her boyfriend, I do not see how some thugs, hired by her firm, will be able to do so either. We know she is trying to get home, and I am sure we will hear from her soon." Taking a breath, her dad continued. "We will pray for Megan and her young man, and hope for the best. Because of your sister's situation, and with what is going on in the world, we are going to make some changes around here."

Her eyes wide, she held her breath, waiting for the other shoe to drop.

"To begin with, from now on, we are all going to be armed, especially when we are out on the property." Annie could see her mom shaking, and realized that she, too, was feeling pretty jittery. Feeling Russell reach out for her, she relaxed into his arms. Her dad looked at her.

"Annie, have you picked up a weapon in the last year or two?"

She shook her head that she had not.

"Ok then, after breakfast in the morning, I am going to take you and Russ to the shooting alley out back, and let you get familiar again. I don't know if we will have any problems, but we are not taking any chances if these men bring trouble to our door. Are we all agreed?"

Looking around the table, she saw that everyone was shaking their heads that they understood.

Her father took a breath, smiled grimly, and took some ham from the platter and began to make a sandwich. Likewise, her husband followed suit. Russell passed her the soup, and she ladled some into her bowel as her mom put her own sandwich together. As soon as she had her sandwich together her father continued.

"I am afraid our problems are not the only concerns we have. Things are looking pretty grim out there." Placing his hands on the table, he sighed. "The Israelis began attacking Iran's nuclear facilities approximately an hour ago. The reports are saying they had credible information that the Iranians were preparing a preemptive strike on Israel, so they seemed to have little choice. After the initial attack, the Iranian Revolutionary Guards announced they threatened to attack any country supporting Israel, or which allows its territory to be used by their enemies. In other words, they mean us."

Her eyes wide with fear, Annie interjected. "What does all of this mean, Daddy?"

"It means, Honey, that on top of everything else, we will likely be at war soon. The Iranians are also launching a military strike against Saudi Arabia, as we speak. They, of course, say that they were responding to the Israeli attack. Iran is saying if the West becomes involved, they will stop the flow of oil permanently. The US Navy is saying they will keep the Strait of Hormuz open, but it appears that Washington is hesitating to act, so our guys are just sitting around waiting on a decision out of DC."

Annie and her mother spoke at once. "My God, what is this world coming to? This couldn't happen at a worse time?" Annie could feel her husband's grip on her tighten.

"It will be ok," Russell said. "Your dad and some of the folks in town are already working on things if it gets bad here." Looking slowly from her husband to her father, Annie realized she was terrified with the world literally shaking apart before her. She could not stop trembling, and the world suddenly felt unreal. Russell reached over to comfort her, but she was getting sick.

"Let me go!" Annie stood abruptly, knocking her chair over as she ran to the bathroom.

She barely made it to the toilet before her soup came up. She threw up twice, as Russell came in behind her. She felt him gently pulling her hair back, to hold it out of her face. "Are you done, Baby?" She nodded that she was, but she was still shaking from what she had just heard.

"Can you get me some water?" Annie asked.

He stepped to the left of his wife, and took a Dixie cup from the dispenser and then filled it for her. After handing it to her, he disappeared. Moving to sit on the tub, she flushed the toilet and leaned head back against the cool stone of the tub surround, as Russell returned with a larger glass a moment later.

"Oh Russ, please don't ever let anything happen. Do you realize it has only been a few months since things went to hell? The whole world is going crazy, and it is happening so fast. I just can't believe it."

Russell crouched down in front of her, making eye contact. "It is scary, Hun, but do you want to know what I think? I think it is going to be rough, but we will come out on the other side as stronger and better people." Annie felt him take her chin, perching it gently on his curved right index finger. "The country is a wreck, because we all got greedy and selfish. I think the world is just like us, Annie girl; it is all screwed up, just like I was. People are making one mistake after another." He gave her a gentle smile. "Look at us now though, we are right with what we should be doing, and things are better. It is going to work out. You just wait; you'll see."

She looked up at him as she got to her feet. "I love you, Russell Davis. Don't you ever take any chances with yourself, ok? I need you to keep on telling me this kind of stuff." She buried her face in his chest and instantly felt much better.

"I'm not going anywhere. We are really lucky here. We have all we need, and we are going to be just fine. Now, let's go back to the table."

Leaving the bathroom, Annie smiled sheepishly. "Sorry. It just creeps up on me like that."

Her mom's eyes were alight with sympathy. "Don't worry about that, Sweetheart, it is just the way of things." Russell held her chair for her again and she resumed her seat.

She glanced at her parents, embarrassed. "So, what did I miss?"

Her dad looked at her, concern evident in his gaze. "That was the majority of it. I just told your mother that folks are hitting the grocery stores and banks pretty hard. Uncle Jerry said the stores are already having a hard time keeping anything on the shelves."

Studying his face, and then turning to her mother, she realized that she was missing something. "What are you not telling me?"

Her dad sat up straight in his chair, an exasperated look on his face. "Not everything your mom and I talk about is any of your business, Young Lady. It has nothing to do with your sisters or world events so just leave it at that."

Narrowing her eyes at her father, she pressed the issue. "I thought you said we had to be really open with each other because of the crisis."

Her mother sighed and explained. "Some government people are telling us that we can't plant or put cattle on our land down by the river this year. A few months ago they sent us a letter saying that part of our land was being classified as a wet land, and we could not use it for food production anymore."

"What? That has been our land since we got it from Grandpa. How can they tell us something like that? Daddy, how can that be legal?"

"That is what your Uncle Jerry and I have been working on. There is no way it should be legal, but that isn't stopping the EPA from coming in to tell us what to do with our own land."

Looking alarmed, Annie's eyes moved from face to face. "What does that mean? Are we in trouble with them?"

Her dad stood up. "It doesn't mean a damn thing -- that's what. This is my land, and it was my father's land, and his father's before him. My taxes are paid, and I don't owe anyone, so I will do with my property as I like. I am not about to let some socialist from Washington tell me any different. Those EPA boys can take their fines and shove them where the sun doesn't shine."

Annie sat with her mouth open, as her dad struggled to get his temper back under control by leaving the table. Looking at her mother, she felt the tears coming. It was all just too much.

Chapter 32
Strong Measures

Megan sat up in her seat. She decided she was simply unable to tolerate the kink in her neck that had developed over the ridiculous number of hours on the road, since they left Glover's place at three AM this morning. Rotating her neck and stretching various parts of her body, she looked over at Matt who was sitting like a robot staring out at the highway in front of the old pickup as they zipped past the highway stripes one after another. Opening her eyes wide and blinking to wake up, she focused on the radio, wondering what the latest disaster would be. Reaching over to the little round knob on the dash, she turned up the volume.

"...thus Iran extends the hand of friendship to any nation or group that confronts the 'cancer' Israel," General Hossein Salami said on Thursday.

Addressing worshippers at prayer, and later that day on state TV broadcasts in Tehran, the Islamic Republic's Supreme Leader Ayatollah Ali Khamenei stated that the country would continue its nuclear program regardless of Western pressure. He said that military strikes by the little Satan only make Iran stronger. He further warned that any U.S. or European involvement in this matter would result in immediate strikes in those nations' homelands. 'It is Allah's will that we finally confront the Zionist regime, and in so doing, remove it from the face of the earth. We have no fear expressing this,' said Khamenei."

Dismayed, she looked again to Matt to gauge his reaction to the news. "Well, that is encouraging, isn't it? Do the Israelis even have a chance?"

"I wouldn't want to mess with them, but it is going to be tough sledding, I think, no matter how it turns out. I am really glad we got out of New York when we did. Mayor Blanton declared martial law there a couple of hours ago while you were asleep. The governor is calling up the National Guard to try to keep a lid on the rioting. We were almost too late getting out."

Megan swallowed hard, thinking about it, deciding it was enough of a mess as it was. She really hoped her friends would be alright. She realized she had goose bumps.

Looking back up at Matt, she replied. "If it wasn't for you, I would probably still be there, if not dead. I love you more than you'll ever know."

"I know you do, Meg; I love you too." He gave her a knowing smirk. "We are coming up on Springfield in a little bit, by the way. Are you hungry yet?"

"Springfield! Are you ok, Baby, why didn't you wake me up?" I should have taken over the driving hours ago. I thought we were going to swap places at the Mississippi River."

He rewarded her with another sly smile. "You were just too cute snuggled with your pillow against the window. Besides, I was doing fine. I would have said something if I was sleepy."

Megan looked out at the passing trees and fields, looking for a road sign to give her some clue about just how far away Springfield was. "How long did you say it would be? I need to go to the restroom in the worst way."

"We are just past Rogersville, so Springfield is just a couple of miles ahead."

Megan smiled back at him, and decided perhaps he wasn't a robot, after all. "I am officially sick of peanut butter and crackers, or anything else that resembles road food." She looked hopefully at her man, knowing he did not really want any contact with anyone if they could help it.

Matt smirked. "Anyone seeing us could be a problem, Babe, but on the other hand, I suspect if they are still looking, they are likely focusing on the highways leading into Texas. We are finally far enough north of where I suspect they are looking for us, we should be good."

Megan gave him a tired smile. "I will survive, I guess, but you did say we should fill up the gas cans at some point, right? We don't want to be anywhere close to empty with things getting out of hand like they have been, do we? After what the President told us yesterday, that we were all screwed, however you slice it, people are going to go nuts about grabbing whatever they can."

"Fair point, I agree. We really do not want to get anywhere close to empty with things like they are now." Looking at her again, he nodded. "Ok, so I'm sold. We can poke around town here for a bit to fill up our gas cans. Maybe can score a decent meal, while we are at it. That is, of course, assuming one counts junk food as decent food."

Megan snorted as she noticed that Matt took the off ramp for a street called, Republic Rd. / Gladstone Blvd. Pulling up to a stop sign, she saw him toggle the blinker and pull into the far right lane. Looking for a place to eat, she rolled her eyes. "Looks like hamburgers or Subway."

"You pick, Meg, although I wouldn't mind eating some fries."

Pulling up to the light, to turn left into a shopping area, Megan looked at the little town, wondering what the people here were thinking about the state of the world. They appeared to be going on with life, but she realized it was impossible to gauge what they thought, what they feared, or what they hoped for. Looking out the window she noticed a man in his forties who pulled up next to them at the light. He was wearing a dirty baseball cap, and he just stared at them with an odd look on his face.

"Matt, look at this guy."

Looking over, Matt nodded to the man. The man returned the gesture and gave them an appreciative nod before proceeding through the light when it turned green.

"What do you think that was about?"

Chuckling, Matt pulled into the drive-through. "It is likely one of two possibilities, Meg. He thinks I rock because I have this sweet old truck or because I have you sitting in it. Could be, that I am all that, for both of those reasons."

"Pretty sure of yourself there, aren't you?"

"I sort of am, I guess." His smirk morphed into a look of arrogance, and then he smiled at her with a wink.

"So Matt, I'm dying here. I really have to make a restroom run. Can I go first? I will hurry right back and then you can go, ok?" He nodded as she got out of the truck. Looking back at him, she saw that his face was all business again, scanning their surroundings.

"Ok, Meg. I will hit the drive-through. Text me if it will take you more than, say, ten minutes. We take no chances, right?"

"Right, I'll be careful."

Walking back outside a few minutes later, Megan found the pickup parked in front of the McDonalds, next to a tree. She climbed in to find Matt staring across the parking lot at a commotion that seemed to be developing across the street, on the other end of the shopping area, next to where they had stopped. Climbing into the truck, she followed his gaze. She realized there was a large crowd in front of a Wal-Mart, and it was apparently growing fast, as it wasn't even there minutes earlier. "What's going on?"

Looking through binoculars, Matt replied, not taking his eyes off the activity across the street.

"I think those SUVs are DHS. The people over there started streaming out of the Wal-Mart just after you left. I have been watching them for a few minutes." Matt handed her the box containing her hamburger, and continued.

"They have a bunch of what look like normal folks, including women and kids with their hands cuffed behind their backs over to the left of the Garden Center." He handed her the binoculars and pointed at a small group of people, guarded by a guy with the assault rifle. Megan could see he wore a wind breaker with the letters DHS emblazoned on the back. Two other DHS men, covered by a third agent, with a rifle at the ready, forced a middle aged man to the ground, to cuff him. Even at this distance, Megan could hear a woman screaming, comingled with indistinct male voices, shouting orders. One of the DHS men roughly shoved the screaming woman out of his way, as he grabbed what was probably her teenage son. A moment later, two additional DHS agents, decked out in full combat gear, emerged from the Wal-Mart dragging yet another terrified teenage boy between them. He struggled, his face horrified, as the agents shoved him roughly to the ground.

Megan stared in disbelief. One of the men in full combat gear knelt on the boy's back while the other cuffed him with plastic ties, before dragging him over to their other prisoners next to the garden center. Her face tightened, her body jerking with emotion when one of the agents kicked one of the teenagers. "The son of a bitch just kicked that kid in the head. I can't believe I am seeing this." Feeling a repeat of the cold chill she had felt when held by Sterns, she realized she was shivering. "They are treating American citizens like animals, pushing women and kids around like they are nothing."

Eating her lunch, disgusted at what she was seeing, it was clear that the crowd continued to grow. It only took a couple of minutes before two more black SUVs showed up to the store followed by several police cruisers. Megan was too far away to hear what was being said, but it was obvious that the scene was rapidly deteriorating. The police immediately began working to set up a perimeter, as they pushed the onlookers back away from the federal agents making their arrests.

"Oh, my God, Matt, what do you think they did?"

"Hard to say Meg, but we can't afford to stick around to find out. I would guess some sort of protest although this response seems a bit heavy handed to me for that. Maybe they were going for weapons or ammo."

"Let's get out of here Matt. I don't want to see this happen. It makes me want to throw up."

Matt turned the keys in the ignition, looked over his shoulder, and carefully backed up. Changing gears, they were soon headed for the exit. Matt turned left on Gladstone Avenue instead of turning right. Megan turned towards him, confusion evident in her voice.

"What are you doing? Aren't we getting back on the freeway?"

"Like you said, we still need the fuel. I am thinking that anyone associated with law enforcement will be preoccupied for a bit, so let's take the risk and get it over with."

⁂

Megan sighed as she drove past the golf course and the University, glad to finally be in Enid. It was a shame, she thought, that Annie had already headed for Mineral Wells. She knew that it was probably for the best that she had done so, but she desperately wanted to see her family now. She looked at her watch and realized it was almost five o'clock. Chuckling to herself, she was amused that, for all of Matt's protesting about being wide awake, he was out cold within minutes of trading places. The four hour drive from Missouri was uneventful although she realized it really affected her when she passed two large conveys of military vehicles on I-44, east of Tulsa. She almost woke Matt up, but decided not to do it since there was nothing he could do about it anyway.

She had been working the angles of what was taking place in the country ever since getting behind the wheel. The incident in Missouri resolved any doubt she had about what was coming. It was a new game now, without any doubt, and she knew it. The foundation that America was based on for the past hundred years was being swept away by economic fact. Regardless of anyone's wishes, the country would change to accommodate a new paradigm.

What was critical now, she decided was getting through the transition to whatever reality would assert itself, and hope like hell the new paradigm would still allow for personal liberty, with something like the ability to make individual decisions about one's own life. After what happened in Missouri, she was no longer confident about a positive outcome. She was still shocked that news reports confirmed that three people were killed, including a teenaged girl who had tried to free her brother when she thought she wasn't being watched. It had all been about a church group that was attempting to buy weapons to protect themselves. It shouldn't have happened she thought. They apparently had the legal right to do what they were doing, but ATF and DHS didn't like the idea. She, in no way, bought the assertion by the DHS spokesperson that the group was on a domestic watch list.

Turning right on Van Buren, she decided Matt would have to wake up soon, so she turned on the radio to catch up on the news.

"...IMF representatives, along with leaders from the G20 are diligently discussing options as Central Banks from Europe and the US reconvened yet another emergency meeting in Davos, Switzerland. Ministers are strongly hinting that the consensus from its members is that the only way to revive the markets is to completely restructure all debt. This action would have to be done internationally, at one time in a knife edge cutover." Glancing over, she saw Matt's eyes were open, and he was looking around.

"Are we getting close, Babe?"

"We're here. Welcome to Enid."

"Nice little town."

"If you like small and quaint, it really is. Still, these people will do better than New Yorkers by a long shot I think."

"Probably, but New Yorkers will surprise you. They are a resilient group of people once they have no choice."

She smiled at him as the news continued.

"...a complete reset of the system globally, requiring massive land transfers by debtor nations. The debtor nation repayment plans will mandate that all countries submit to terms set out by a new global Finance authority which is quickly being formed out of the G20 nations..."

Matt turned it off. "Holy crap, this mess is going to be really ugly." He looked at Megan as she turned into a cute little neighborhood. "Do you ever feel like you have just been sucked into the movie *Alien*?"

Megan sighed, and smiled weakly.

Matt snorted.

"Well, Babe, You were right; you called it right on the nose. The big money guys really did have it all figured out from the jump."

Ashamed of whom she had become, she pulled into Annie and Russell's drive way, put the vehicle in park, and turned the keys, killing the engine. "I was part of it, Matt. I helped to cause all of this. I can never hope to fix..."

Raising his hand in a halting motion, accompanied by a scowl, Matt cut her off so fast, and with such vigor, she jumped when he turned on her.

"Enough of that, Meg, I mean it! You screwed up. So what! You give yourself way too much credit. What is happening now has been building for a long time, and you damn well know it. I know you think that you know everything, and you are brilliant, but it isn't a crime to want to make money. The point is you corrected yourself when you realized what the score was." She saw the fierceness in his eyes faded some as he continued. "There will be enough recriminations in coming months. I want you to leave your mistakes in the city. Nothing good will come from any of that. *Capishe*? Just do the right thing from here on out, ok?"

Stunned, she shook her head meekly, in compliance.

"Thanks Matt. I'm sorry. I guess the last couple of weeks have just given me a lot to think about. Anyway, what do you want to take in to the house with us tonight? I called Annie's friend, Jana, with the burn phone, when we started getting close to Enid. She said she could get there between five and five thirty, so she should show up any time."

"Just the sleeping bags, I guess, and the coolers with our drinks. We will need a couple of cans of stew unless, of course, you would like to have Spaghettios again."

"I swear if we ever get home, I will never eat those again, if I can help it." She grinned as Matt chuckled at her discomfort. Smiling, they both got out and walked to the back of the truck. She waited while Matt opened the camper and climbed in to grab the sleeping bags and his duffle bag. Appreciating the view of Matt straining to free their gear, she giggled at his struggle. Her reflexes were all that saved her from catching Matt's duffle bag with her face. As he tossed their gear back to her, she set what they needed on the tail gate, as a dark haired woman in her thirties drove up in a dark blue SUV. Megan nodded as the woman parked the car on the street and got out, waving at her. She noticed that the woman then proceeded to the opposite side of the car to the passenger side door. Turning her attention back to the pickup again, Matt handed Megan her backpack as he climbed out.

"Is that your sister's friend?"

"I think so, I only met her once, a couple of years ago, but who else could it be?"

Smiling politely, her heart leapt as she realized that the woman had a couple of pizzas in her arms, when she straightened up from the open car door.

As the woman approached, the smell of pepperoni and melted cheese was overwhelming.

"Oh, my God, you are a lifesaver. Thank you so much for thinking of dinner. We were just contemplating what we were going to do about supper."

"Your sister is my best friend; it was the least that I could do. Come on in."

Matt stepped forward and took the boxes from Jana as she led the way to the house.

"I had forgotten how much you look like Annie. Your folks are beside themselves worrying. I hope you don't mind that I called them when you reached out for me. Annie had got a message to me through your minister, Pastor Glenn, that you were coming. I am not sure what that is about, but I called him back. I was careful not to be too specific though. I just said that I had a renter for the house."

Alarmed at Jana's admission, Megan cringed a little and looked at Matt. He shrugged, but just smiled at Jana as she inserted her key into the lock.

Seeing the resulting tension on her sister's friend's face, she tried to lighten the mood. "I'm sure it will be fine. By the way, this is my fiancé, Matt."

Jana turned and regarded Megan's guy as she opened the front door. "It is nice to meet you Matt."

"It is nice to meet you too, Ma'am."

Jana giggled. "Oh my, you do have an accent, don't you? Well, if you are around Annie and her folks, I know they will have you talking like a Texan in no time."

Megan shrugged and handed the door off to Matt, and they entered the little house. "It was kind of you to bring food and to let us use the house, Jana. Matt and I really appreciate you going to all of this trouble."

She smiled back at them. "It really is no trouble, it is your family's house anyway, and with the President coming on the TV talking about how bad things are, I was more than happy to be able to help. It is really bad all over, I guess. There was a commotion on the news yesterday because some government people were going around to all of the grain elevators. They are locking everything up and putting military people on all of our food stores. There was even some shooting. It was just terrible." She nodded toward the pizza boxes. "The pizza place even said that they would not be open much longer. They are apparently not getting their supplies after this week. They said they will close when what they have on hand is gone."

Megan nodded grimly and noticed that Matt, too, looked very solemn.

Jana reached over and adjusted the thermostat, giving her and Matt a slight smile.

"Anyway, I just know Annie and your folks will be so excited to see you both."

Megan walked into the modest front room with Matt right behind her. She was surprised to see basic furniture inside. "I guess Annie and Russ had to leave all their stuff behind. We weren't expecting any furniture."

"Oh, Honey, your sister sold most of what they had, and took the rest with them." Sweeping the little house with her hand, she explained. "All this stuff came from church folks. Annie said to try to do what we could for folks until things settle down again."

Megan dropped her gear on the cheap little sofa, and went over to Matt taking the Pizzas from him so he could go back for their other items. She followed as Jana crossed into the little dining room table. “You just sit down and relax Hun. We have plastic cups, plates and utensils in the kitchen. I will be right back. I know you both must just be worn-out.”

“A little bit, true enough. We drove in from Kentucky today.”

Jana returned with a six-pack of Dr. Pepper and two plastic cups, filled with ice. “Oh wow, that is quite a drive. Well, then I won’t stay, you must be exhausted.”

Megan could hear Matt was returning from outside. Reaching into the pizza box she put a couple of slices on a plate and poured soda into the cups.

“Come eat, Baby; we can unpack in a little bit.”

Janna headed for the door, smiling at them both. “You have electricity and water, so you two just settle in and make yourselves at home. You will find necessities in the bathroom so you can get cleaned up, and I have marked the house as unavailable at the church until you tell me different.

Matt smiled and set his load down on the couch. “We will likely only be here a few days. We just want to get some rest before heading to Mineral Wells.”

“Well, you are welcome to stay for as long as you need. There are two sets of keys on the bar. Don’t hesitate to call me if you need anything.”

She waved, and she disappeared through the door, closing it behind her.

Turning to Matt she looked up at him, smiling tiredly into his hazel eyes, her fingers sliding over his chest, and up to interlace behind his neck. “What do you think of eating some pizza, taking a nice shower together and crashing?”

Matt bent down and she felt his lips on hers, as he pulled her in tight. Electricity shot through her, as his tongue met hers. She felt his hand grasp her head as he massaged the back of her scalp. He kissed her tenderly on her earlobe. “Now that is the best offer I have had all day,” he whispered.

Chapter 33
Random Acts of Panic

Opening her front door to go out to search her Jeep for her cell phone which she hoped she'd left there, Catherine was surprised to find a newspaper on her front step. Her surprise was caused by the fact that she didn't take the paper. She decided that having just had breakfast, her mood had actually improved this morning. Regardless of a few of her neighbors demanding that the city somehow do something about the lack of food in local grocery stores, she was still able to reach many of the people at the previous night's meeting. Her message of pulling together to get through the crisis was beginning to resonate. Even her outrage at the two federal agents, who almost arrested her two days ago had largely subsided.

The world was spinning out of control, but at least she knew now just what she could do to try and make things better. Grinning, she thought sleeping late this morning hadn't hurt her mood either. Regardless of the reason, she was hesitant to take the newspaper out of its plastic sleeve, lest it spoil her rare moment of contentment.

Returning to her front room, Catherine plopped down on the couch and, after a moment's hesitation, pulled off the plastic to read the front page. She knew she would not like what she would see there, but she also knew well, that one had to stay up on the insanity, especially now that others were depending on her. Closing her eyes and blowing out a long breath, she gathered her strength to emotionally deal with the stupidity that awaited her.

"Global Bail Out!

While addressing journalists, on Friday, following the initial meeting of the President's joint economic taskforce, Senator Maynard Krugman, announced that the consensus of the bipartisan committee was in complete agreement with the President and their counterparts from the European and Asian central banks. The only way to revive the markets is to fundamentally restructure all debt at one time. Senator Krugman's committee was appointed late Thursday, following the President's address to a joint session of Congress, in response to this week's earth shaking financial developments. The senator went on to outline that a complete reset of the system was the only way to avoid a deep and prolonged economic catastrophe. The plan will require massive work arrangements and land transfers by debtor nations, to compensate creditors, similar to the various bailout programs already being implemented in Europe over the past two years. Repayment plans will require these steps as a precursor to a universal debt forgiveness event, the result of which will mean a fresh start across the board for all nations. To ensure that this sort of crisis can never again recur, a new Global Finance Authority is quickly being assembled from G20 member nations. The Global Finance Authority, (GFA), will establish mandates that all countries will be required to submit to, under terms now being ratified by the governments of member nations. Once governmental approvals have been finalized over the next few weeks, GFA members will convene in Brussels, and upon due consideration, will publish global guidelines to be implemented in coming months. The senator noted that contingency planning for the events such as what took place this week have been discussed and agreed to amongst our European colleagues for years. The United States government, in conjunction with major corporate leaders from around the country, are substantially in agreement, that working with the international community is the sound and responsible approach to this unimaginable disaster. It is critical to achieve market liquidity and confidence in the briefest amount of time to avoid a prolonged and painful global depression. Although leaders here and internationally recognize these changes represent an abrupt departure to the way things have happened in the past, it is necessary to avoid an unprecedented upheaval in populations here and around the world. The very lives of citizens everywhere are at stake and leaders around the world know all too well that it is our collective responsibility to defend our populations from starvation and loss of life. Global guidelines outlined by the GFA have been discussed at length by leaders that have had to face the harsh realities now before all of us. Senator Krugman noted that the President was even now formulating an address to the nation, to inform the American people what to expect and how the federal government will proceed in coming weeks and months to insure we all come through this calamity together."

Putting the paper down on the coffee table, she realized her hand was shaking and that she had goose bumps. "Oh my God, this cannot be happening so fast -- so much for my good mood."

Catherine noticed Maggie's intent stare and smiled scratching the dog behind her ears. She realized that Maggie seemed to have picked up on her anxiety. As she stroked the boxer's head, Maggie inched forward, placing her front paws and head on Catherine's lap with the back portion of her body still on the floor next to the couch

Sighing, she hoped that Sadie would return soon from the hospital. She really needed the company. Unfortunately, Sadie said she had no idea when she would be back because she had to stay for a mandatory meeting after her shift ended to discuss this week's events.

Feeling resentful that her good mood was suddenly stolen, she decided to fix herself a cup of tea, only to be thwarted when Maggie chose that moment to climb up and lie beside her on the couch. Exhaling, Catherine changed her mind and leaned forward to take her cell phone from the table. She pressed a number on the cell for Drake while petting Maggie's head.

"Officer Sabol."

"Hi, Drake, I didn't realize you were on today, are you busy?"

"I wasn't supposed to be, but they added shifts after Thursday's speech. Things are pretty messed up. I am over at Kroger's now. We have a couple of guys at all of the food stores. People are really freaking out. Looting has become a real problem at the grocery stores, and you can forget the banks. Kate, are you and Sadie ok?"

"Sadie had to stay late for some sort of mandatory meeting this morning, so she isn't here yet. She said that she would call before she left though."

"I am glad you guys are staying aware of your surroundings. It is dangerous to be out right now. You are better off staying put if you don't have to be out. Dallas just had some gang bangers get into a massive shootout at DFW Gun Club. The morons didn't fare too well, but several people in the area were also injured. Four of the gang bangers were killed and two more are critical at Parkland."

Catherine snorted. "I bet; everybody working there is a weapons expert, and they are all packing. What kind of idiot does it take to think that will turn out well?"

"Yeah, it sounds like Darwin at work to me."

"You said some bystanders were hurt? Were the guys at the store ok?"

"They got lucky, mostly. A two year old was grazed, but not seriously; and another gentleman was hit in the arm. The guys in the store had one guy hit when it started, but they were all wearing vests. It sounds like they had already talked it over, and realized this sort of crap was likely."

Moving the phone to the other ear, Catherine replied. "No doubt. It is a good thing we all stocked up on the ammo we need because it is already nonexistent. I hear you have to know someone to find any. Anyway, I just read a story about how the Feds are magically already set to step in and protect all of us from the evil world. I was wondering what you thought."

"I don't know, Kate. They read a memo at roll call this morning. It said we will need to be prepared to support the FBI, ATF and other agencies as needed. We all agreed that we think they are really going to shake things up in a big way. We will just have to see what it looks like, I guess. I will drop by and check on you guys when I get off. We can talk more then. I really need to get back to work here, ok? I would appreciate it if you guys just stayed in for a few days until we see how people take some of what is going on."

"Sure, Buddy. I don't have anywhere to be, really, that is, anywhere that I will be going without you or the guys from the group."

"Good. Ginny is on her way back from Houston with her mom. I will be a lot happier when I have my people where I can see them."

"I know what you mean. I want you to know I really appreciate it. Talk to you later Drake, stay safe, ok?"

"You got it, Kate. Talk to you tonight."

Kate sighed and began to replace the phone on the table when it beeped with a message. Looking at the screen, she saw it was from Sadie.

Leaving in 30 mins :-)

She tapped the screen to delete the text.

OK, so an hour and a half from right now?

Send.

Beep - *Yes. Just have to change clothes and get my check.*

"*See you then... Be careful.*"

Send.

Finally, laying the phone on the table, she glanced again at the paper with disdain when the doorbell rang. Maggie instantly rolled over and raced to the front door barking.

"Enough, Girl, it's ok, I have it." Moving the dog away from the entrance, she looked out the peep hole to see her next door neighbor, Mrs. Dillard standing at the screen door. She smiled, thinking she liked the elderly woman even if she did have a tendency to be a little fussy. Taking a breath, she put on her most pleasant expression, opened the door, and stepped out onto her front porch.

The little woman looked uncomfortable, her snow white hair not as well kept as it usually was. "Hello, Dear, I hope I am not intruding by stopping by."

"No Ma'am, not at all. Won't you come in?" Catherine undid the latch and pushed it open to allow the little woman to enter.

"I won't take much of your time, Dear. I was just speaking with Pastor Tom at the church about..." Catherine's eyes softened, realizing the little woman was embarrassed. "Well about maybe working at the church part time. I thought I could help out with the food kitchen they set up." The woman's gaze dropped just a bit. "Anyway, he said the local Tea Party was running the kitchen. He said you were in charge, so I wanted to ask you about getting involved."

"Of course, you can help. Lord knows we need all the help we can get. I was just about to eat a little soup. Will you join me? We can talk about where you can help out. I can heat us up a little snack."

The little woman's eyes brightened, and she nodded her acceptance.

"You remember Maggie, right? She is a good girl, just tell her down, and gesture with your hands. She gets excited when we have company."

"I remember, Catherine, thank you. It is very kind of you to feed me like this."

Catherine smiled. "Don't be silly, you fixed me a beautiful cake on my birthday, remember? My roommate is still at work, so I appreciate the company." Catherine opened the door and stood between Maggie and her guest. Mrs. Dillard patted the dog on the head and headed for the dining room.

Catherine followed, motioning Maggie back over to the sofa. "You know, Mrs. Dillard, if I recall, you used to work at a bank, didn't you?"

Half turning to face Catherine, she smiled. "Why yes, I did. I was a bookkeeper before retiring. You have quite a memory, Dear."

"Sometimes I do, but I do well to recall what day it is some days. Please, make yourself comfortable."

Catherine motioned to the dining room table, and moved on into the kitchen. Taking the large pot of soup she had been eating from, out of the refrigerator, she placed it on the stove and turned on the fire.

"Anyway, I don't know if Pastor Tom mentioned it or not, but we absolutely have everyone we need for the kitchen operation. I would be really grateful, though, if you could help us keep track of what we have coming and going with regards, to our barter program." We are really trying hard to feed as many people as we can, and take care of the most urgent needs by matching up what people have extra of, with what folks need."

"I would be happy to do whatever I could to help. I am afraid I'm realizing that with the prices as they are now, I'm not going to have enough money each month."

Catherine moved from her Fridge to the counter with some left over potato and carrots to add to the soup. Smiling through the pass-through between the kitchen and the dining room, Catherine began slicing a potato.

"Most of us are not going to have enough nowadays, I think. We will just have to look after each other, won't we?"

"Yes, I guess that's right. I just don't know what to think anymore."

"You have been a good neighbor to me, and you have always been kind. One way or another, we will be fine. Anyway, this will be ready to eat in a few minutes. Why don't we talk about getting you going with the group, and after that, we can eat. I will send you home with enough soup for dinner, too. Would that be alright?"

Returning to the dining room with two glasses of water, she noticed that the woman was dabbing her eyes with a handkerchief.

"God bless you, Catherine. You are a nice young woman, and I'm grateful for your help. I promise to work really hard."

❧

Waving goodbye to her neighbor, Catherine resumed her seat next to Maggie on the sofa, and looked at the newspaper. She considered reading about the fighting breaking out across Europe but decided it could wait.

She figured that if she wanted to wallow in the news of the day, she may as well do so with pictures and full color. Picking up the remote, she tapped the power switch, bringing the television to life.

"... as Riot Police and National Guard Units are deployed throughout the East Coast, police and military units find themselves being attacked by the very people they are there to protect. This morning, Baltimore Police Lieutenant Cheryl Reins confirmed fifteen officer fatalities resulting from a riot at an SEIU Protest."

Catherine looked on in disgust, as the images before her showed police in riot gear falling back under the pressure of a large mob. Two officers were using their riot shields to cover a fallen comrade as the officers on either side of him pulled him along as they retreated.

The correspondent continued. "...desperate people, trying to withdraw their funds from their local banks and the increasing incidents at the nation's grocery stores have law enforcement nationwide on high alert.

"Overnight in Dallas, Texas, four men were killed by..." Catherine gasped upon hearing the story Drake had just relayed to her. "...the owners of a local gun store defending their business from looters. In Chicago, police and National Guard soldiers are standing shoulder to shoulder with fire fighters, to protect them from being attacked after three first responders were killed by snipers, as they worked to quench fires started by Solidarity Movement protesters in that city. It is bad, Sheila, and it is happening in virtually every city nationwide. Back to you in New York."

The images of looters facing off with the firemen while police, and soldiers stood guard with assault rifles was replaced by the ashen face of this hour's anchor, Sheila Burckhardt. Catherine decided it was obvious the anchor had not slept in some time.

"Thank you for your excellent coverage, Roger. Do you know if law enforcement arrested the sniper? Also, do authorities there have any hope of restoring order?"

"I'm afraid not, Sheila. Chief Jaden Darnell pulled law enforcement out of the area after the engagement. He said, and I quote: 'Let them burn their neighborhood down.' He said that the risk of civilian casualties, a heavy response would pose, isn't worth it. The benefit is outweighed by the cost of providing them coverage. For the moment, authorities are staying out of the area."

Dismayed, Catherine shook her head, profoundly sad at what she knew lay ahead. Unable to contain her emotions any longer, tears rolled down her face. She had never wanted to see this actually happen, regardless of its inevitability. Now that it had begun, she felt the weight of all the destroyed lives pressing in on her. As if to emphasize the impact her emotions were having on her, sirens screamed nearby as they raced past on Beltline Road.

"I'm afraid it is just too early to tell, Sheila. The President is scheduled to speak tonight during primetime. Officials here are hoping that, somehow, he will be able to do something to calm things down. The key challenge that economists are talking about is that workers who still have jobs, are realizing that their wages are quickly being consumed by the sharply rising inflation rate. The Fed announced today they were preparing to make good on the thousands of bank closures that have taken place this week. Workers are well aware that their deposits will be reimbursed with money that will likely be worth very little by the time they actually receive it. Many workers are now demanding daily inflation indexing of their salaries, and in some cases, are even demanding to be paid daily. However you want to look at the situation, the President has a very large task in front of him."

Catherine rolled her eyes and angrily stabbed at her remote to bring up channel four to see if the local news had insights that were not quite so patently obvious. Unfortunately, for the state of her mood, the local coverage was almost identical to what was airing nationally, with the exception, that as a whole, things locally, were not anywhere near as far out of control. She was thankful that although Dallas, Austin, and Houston were experiencing riots, they were not as large or as destructive. Smirking at the image of a white teenaged guy with a bat smashing car windows, she could not help but comment, even if only Maggie would hear.

"What's the matter, Loser? Are you using a bat because you're worried you will get yourself shot?" Angry, she knew that Texans being armed was exactly why rioting in the state was less extensive. Actually, now that she thought about it, she realized she should be better prepared, even if she wasn't going out. Moving Maggie aside to stand up, she went to her bedroom and took her holster out of her dresser, and her pistol out of her night stand. After inserting a magazine into the weapon, and the pistol into its holster, she clipped it to her belt. When she returned to the front room, Maggie was lying on her back on the sofa, her feet in the air. Deciding if she should just take the recliner or move the dog, she just stood there motionless, as a new headline flashed on the screen: *Texas Takes Action*!

Chapter 34
Hatreds Crucible

Thinking she was wasting her life glued to the news, Catherine sighed and decided to just turn it off. Glancing up at the clock, she wondered where Sadie was, thinking her friend should have been home by now. Pondering whether or not to call, she reached for her phone, when Fox's tone signaled that an urgent update was about to begin. The accompanying headline simply read, *Texas Takes Action*!

"News Four has just learned that Governor Dorie Miller has requested time to make a statement to the people of Texas. Dan Stark, our correspondent at the Press Briefing Center in Austin has confirmed that Governor Miller, accompanied by Lieutenant Governor Denise Chandler, Speaker Paul Logan and what appears to be seven of the nine justices of the Texas Supreme Court are to come out momentarily to make an announcement. With that, we are tossing it to you, Dan. Have you been given any clue regarding the governor's remarks? This kind of address is highly irregular, isn't it?"

Dan Stark's face replaced the News Four anchor. "We have not been given anything of any specificity, only that the governor, along with key members of the state government will make an announcement."

Pausing, Catherine felt her heart catch. Suddenly, she felt more than a little apprehensive about what they would say. She more or less thought well of Governor Miller, but knew that he had to be under an unprecedented amount of pressure. As he had consistently spoken out about the unconstitutional overreach of the federal government since his election, she could not imagine what this announcement would be. Whatever this was, she did not believe that the governor would be a part of anything that would curtail freedom or violate the constitution, but she also knew that the world was nuts, so she remained frozen in place awaiting the announcement. As the minutes passed and the pundits discussed back and forth about what the state of Texas could possibly do to affect a financial collapse, a sardonic expression formed on her features. She liked the governor, but she also knew there would be little he could do to make things any better given the train wreck in which the nation, not to mention the world, found itself.

As she watched, Catherine rolled her eyes as the image on the screen, now focused on the Press Briefing Center in Austin, changed back to the studio and the pundits.

"We are getting word that the governor's party has been delayed but will be making their address shortly. Stay with us for the latest coverage, and we will go right back to the briefing center in Austin the moment we hear that Governor Miller is about to speak.

Exasperated, Catherine muted the television and stood up. "Come on, Girl, I think it's about time for you to go outside." A mention of outside was enough for Maggie. The boxer twisted and jumped from the couch so fast she all but bowled Catherine over on her way to the back door. Catherine followed to let her out. Returning to the front room, she saw Sadie's Charger had pulled into the driveway.

Opening the front door, she could see her friend really looked beat. "Hey, Roomie, so was it terrible?"

Sadie returned her greeting with a grimace. "It was about the same as last night, or Thursday, for that matter. People are really losing their minds, but that isn't the weird thing." Catherine stood aside to hold the door for her friend, and then followed her into the house.

She smiled, noticing Sadie looking for her four-legged roommate. "Maggie is in the back yard, I assume?"

"Yeah, it is a nice day, at least if you are a dog, and she needs to get some exercise."

Sadie sat on the couch and promptly kicked off her tennis shoes. "You will never believe what the mandatory meeting was about." Catherine thought that it would be disaster related, but shrugged. "A lot of the docs got together to pretty much demand we all get paid weekly, and that our wages be cost adjusted for inflation. There is a huge uproar at work concerning how they are even going to manage that. Obviously, they don't have extra cash coming in, so it's tough to pay it back out."

Catherine leaned against the cased opening between the dining room and the living room, thinking this sort of discussion would be going on nationwide, with employees and employers everywhere. "Wow, that does sound ugly. What are they going to do?"

"Not much choice, really. They are going to start paying everyone in cash every week and are transferring money around to make it work for now. They laid-off a bunch more people, and the hospital will be reducing service, so they can at least try to pay those who were staying as much as possible to try and keep up." Catherine shook her head in dismay.

"I can't even imagine how you guys can keep up with it all."

"Well, I won't be finding out, I'm afraid. I was one of the ones canned."

Catherine moved over to sit next to Sadie reaching out to give her a hug. "You know you have a place here as long as I do." Catherine lifted Sadie's head with a finger to look into her eyes. "It is going to be ok; things will work out somehow. Taking care of each other is what we do."

Catherine felt heartened at seeing Sadie's smile. "I guess it will be ok. Besides, can you believe that I got a severance? Who knows? I may be better off this way, getting paid something up front."

"You know, you really may have gotten the best deal." Several moments passed between them before either woman spoke up. Finally, Catherine patted her friend on the knee and stood again. "Are you hungry?"

Sadie looked up. "I ate at the hospital. I think I will just take a hot bath to wash off the stress. Um, Catherine? I really appreciate your generosity. I don't know what I would do without you.

Still, I want it to be really clear that I am going to pay you back for this. Agreed?"

She smiled and nodded. "Agreed."

"OK, a tub of hot sudsy water awaits for me then." Sadie picked up her tennis shoes, stood and headed for the bathroom.

Catherine headed for the recliner. She knew she should feel bad for Sadie, but secretly, she thought it might actually be a blessing. The world was getting really crazy, and if she were being honest, Sadie's help with the group was going to be sorely needed. She started to pick up the paper, but opted for the Kindle app on her phone to pass the time, until the governor came out. She had been trying to read the same book for almost a month, and just hadn't made the time. Leaning back in the recliner, she tapped, *Dark Night of the Soul: Tales of Blackwater, Texas.*

Stretching out, she thought this was just the thing she needed. With Sadie home, her Tea-Party work done, and nowhere to go, she decided the afternoon would consist of some well-deserved rest and relaxation.

She knew she should get out into the backyard and work in the garden, so it would be ready to plant in the spring, but she decided it was just too comfortable lounging to worry about that today.

Reading for twenty or thirty minutes, she sighed with contentment. Turning a virtual page on her reader, she looked up, thinking she saw movement out of the corner of her eye. She turned her head, and seeing nothing, she continued reading. Looking back at her Kindle, she heard a crash coming from the front porch. This time there was no doubt. Someone had just kicked in her screen door.

Sitting up abruptly with the sound of her screen door being smashed open, her mind took a second to register as the sound of the splintering wood of her front door impacted her consciousness. Reacting on instinct alone, Catherine jumped to her feet with adrenalin pumping into her system. Two dark haired, olive skinned men burst into her front room. One of the men glanced at her, but kept moving towards the dining room. The other man looked first towards the kitchen and then directly at her. Seeing the man process his surroundings, he abruptly stopped his rush towards the kitchen, turned and charged right at her, a pistol menacing in his right hand.

Scrambling desperately for the first thing she could lay her hands on, Catherine threw a snow globe that was sitting on the side table next to her chair.

The glass sphere struck the man in the face allowing her to sidestep his charge as she scrambled to put the coffee table between them.

It was then she recalled the pistol at her side. Taking another step to her left, she drew the weapon, and almost had the slide back to chamber a round when he landed on her, driving her hard into the couch. Frantically struggling, she was stunned by the man's strength as his left hand immediately gained control of her gun hand. The pain in her wrist was unbelievable as he twisted the weapon from her grasp, smiling with pleasure as he did so.

She heard herself scream, as his right hand brought his pistol into her peripheral vision.

"Shut your mouth, Whore!" His breath stank of onions and cilantro, his teeth stained with tobacco; it felt as if time had all but frozen as she writhed to free herself from his grip.

Flailing and blind with anger she grasped blindly for any weapon. Her fingers finding the TV remote, she struck at his face, smashing it on impact. This time the man yelled out in Arabic, obviously cursing her. Unable to restrain her left hand and retain his weapon, his eyes went wide with unbridled fury, his yellow teeth bared like a wild animal. Trying to claw at the man's eyes, she was too late to block the pistol in his right hand as it impacted on the left side of her face. The impact jarred her as she heard something snap and her vision narrowed. Woozy now, Catherine felt him twist even harder on her captive wrist. Sure that her wrist would snap, she fought even harder, desperately wanting to hurt him as well. He leaned in so hard on her she could barely breathe. With his face directly over hers, blood from the cut she just inflicted above his right eye dripped onto her cheek as the barrel of his pistol came into view. Terrified and nauseated, her strength seemed to evaporate. She glanced from the maw of the barrel to his face. Looking into his eyes and seeing only contempt and hatred, she relented in her struggle.

Upon her surrender, his smile grew almost maniacal, a trickle of blood running down the right side of his face from the cut. He gritted his teeth in a tight lipped sneer as he repositioned his grip on her right hand, twisting it sharply, thus introducing immediate and unendurable pain. Pinned awkwardly between the couch and coffee table, she hardly noticed that he tossed his pistol onto the arm of the sofa to her left, as the other man came momentarily back into view from what must have been a cursory search of her home.

Catherine's mind raced to find a weapon or to think of something she could do. Sadie had to have heard the fight. She probably called the police, but if so, where were the sirens? "What do you want from us?"

The second man, his demeanor implacable and cold, stared down at her dispassionately. "Where is your friend?"

She returned his gaze, with her teeth gritted, her disgust unmistakable. "Fuck you!"

Her assailant reared back, slapping her bruised face with all his strength. He sneered at her again, his loathing as palatable as his breath. "From you, nothing, Jew; other than what I shall take from you for my troubles before casting you into Hell."

"Screw you, you primitive asshole."

The second man cocked his head to listen, but was clearly frustrated by Maggie's urgent barking as the dog desperately scraped at the back door.

The man scowled. "I think you will tell me everything I wish to know." He brought his pistol up and pulled the slide to chamber a round, but hesitated at the unmistakable sound of movement emanating from Sadie's bedroom.

Catherine's eyes fixed, reflecting her horror at what the sound would mean for her friend and herself. The man on top of her motioned with a nod,

"She is that way."

A feral smile descended on the second man‘s face. Heading again towards the bedrooms, he looked over his shoulder at his friend. “Take your pleasures quickly, Amhed. We cannot stay long.”

Now speechless with terror, and overcome with grief, her eyes went wide to see that her assailant had replaced the gun in his hand with a large knife, pulled from a sheath at his side. She briefly struggled yet again, only to almost lose consciousness as another blow landed on the left side of her face. She screamed soundlessly when the gleaming blade descended to her throat. As the knife bit into her, she felt the man readjust his position, as his left hand released her wrist to grasp the front of her top, ripping it open. He then grabbed her throat, almost crushing her wind pipe, thereby freeing his knife hand.

“If you so much as move, Whore, I will cut you like a pig and fuck your lifeless body!”

She could feel the tears running down her face as she heard Sadie’s terrified scream followed by two sharp cracks, as the bright blade cut through the front of her bra.

The stinking man laughed. “It seems your friend, the apostate whore, is no longer...”

Pop! Pop! Pop! The stinking man never finished his thought, nor would he ever have a thought again. The blade clattered onto the hard wood floor, and blood burbled out of the man’s mouth, and from the ragged bullet hole just created above his collar bone.

Exhausted and barely able to move, Catherine could feel the sticky wetness of the man’s blood all over her. Screaming, she vomited, and then pushed the lifeless man off of her, as she slid out from under him. In shock, she looked up to see Sadie standing in the doorway to the little hallway, just beyond the dining room, wet, horrified and half naked with only her open robe partially covering her. Catherine realized she, too, was in shock, the smoking chrome revolver still leveled in her direction.

“The gun, Honey; it’s ok now.” Sadie lowered the weapon as Catherine got to her feet. Crying in relief, she ran to Sadie, pulling her close, grasping her head close to hers. Now, she realized, she could hear sirens.

Chapter 35
Reunion

Megan was glad to be on the road and was even a little surprised to admit that she was really looking forward to getting home again. The sun was shining brightly while she watched barren trees and freshly plowed farmland pass by her window, just south of Chickasha, Oklahoma. If nothing else, it really did smell better than New York City. Reflecting on her childhood, she was forced to admit it wasn't all that bad. She was really glad they were finally on I-44 after driving down US Highway Eighty-One for the past couple of hours. Smiling out at the country-side, she decided that today would just have to find a way to be wonderful. It was only a short drive now, at least as compared to earlier in the week. Staying at her sister's house had been nothing short of wonderful. Refreshed and hopeful, she sighed. Yes, she decided, today she and Matt both deserved a pleasant trip after all they had been through since New York. Thinking back on her life since leaving home, she worked her way through her decisions. She realized that although she adored the culture, the bright lights, and the excitement, she had to admit the constant battle that was her work life was draining. Moreover, it had cost her some of her soul. Reflecting on that thought, she realized that, regardless of Matt's assessment that she needed to move past her actions over the last few years; she knew she owed a debt.

Exhaling, she decided that she was alive. God spared her that awful night in New York. Coming to a decision, she committed to herself to becoming a better person going forward. The only way she could begin to make up for decisions that she knew were wrong, would be to focus on helping others. It then occurred to her that she had no idea what Matt would want to do with his life now.

Noticing a lonely tractor moving across a field, she realized that although she had only been in New York for a couple of years, she had really lost the feeling of what open space really meant. Looking over at Matt, she wondered what he thought. For him this would be a much larger shift in culture than for her. She at least had her upbringing to rely on.

On the other hand, she thought, he had spent a lot of time in Afghanistan and Iraq, so she decided he would be fine. After a moment, Matt turned to regard her with curiosity raising an eyebrow as he did so.

"What are you thinking, Meg?"

"Nothing really, just looking forward to getting home, I guess." Caressing his arm, she returned his gaze with a new contentment. "I'm just hoping that you don't absolutely hate it in Texas. It can be pretty mundane compared to New York."

"Who are you kidding, Meg? You are thinking about it through the perspective of the college girl looking to make it in the big city. Don't get me wrong, there is a lot to like about New York, but I have always liked a more straight-up existence. Besides, depending on how things play out, I suspect the city may soon be more like Fallujah than I would ever care for."

"Yeah, you're probably right, but it breaks my heart. There are just so many really great people, and the art and..."

Matt cut her off. "It is what it is, Babe. We will just have to make things great in Texas, right?"

She nodded. "Yes, we will. No doubt you will have me barefoot and pregnant in no time."

He gave her a sideways grin at the thought. "I might just try that, actually." Stifling a yawn he stretched a little, rotated his head a bit, and rolled his shoulders. "Can you reach down and grab me a Dr. Pepper and find us a station? It's noon, and I want to hear what's going on out there."

"Sure." Doing as he asked, she handed him the soft drink and began spinning the antique knobs of the truck's radio, scanning for a news report. After several minutes of hissing and abbreviated chips of music and snippets of conversation, she landed on a useful station.

"...were shocked as stunning developments continue to pour out of Riyadh. Reuters confirmed this morning's report of the assassination of King Abdullah, and his heir apparent, Crown Prince Nayef, along with a number of their personal guard. The coup d'état took place overnight and was reported to have been a suicide attack ordered by Shi'a extremists headed by Cleric Nimr al-Nimr, who have long pursued a confrontational approach in dealing with the Saudi Royal Family."

Matt's face grew serious instantly. "Son-of-a-bitch!"

"...This report follows yesterday's assassination of Khalid bin Sultan, head of the Saudi Royal Air Force, in a shoulder launched missile attack. Independent reports have indicated that supporters of the ruling family and militants continue to fight in Riyadh as Iranian ground forces stream west. Invading forces are reported to be meeting only sporadic resistance, regardless of deep historical animosity between Saudi Arabia's Sunni population and the Shi'ite invading force from Iran."

Megan began to ask a question, but it died on the tip of her tongue in response to Matt's upheld hand.

"A military spokesman in Tehran stated that the current operation is a part of what Iranian officials claim to be the beginning of the creation of a Grand Caliphate which will extend from Turkey in the Eastern Mediterranean into Western Asia and throughout all of North Africa. In follow up questions, there were even hints that this, empire, if you want to call it that, will extend into Pacific Rim countries, including such nations as Indonesia.

Furthermore, the statement threatened an immediate nuclear retaliation on Saudi population centers if Saudi military officers chose to resist.

Iranian military units continue to move west along the Riyadh-Qaseem Expressway, bypassing Saudi oilfields. Analysts are speculating that the Iranians are heading for Medina. BBC reports indicate that IRGC commanders approached US Military officials in Kuwait earlier today and are offering a working relationship with The United States, but only if US forces do not attempt to intervene in their ongoing operations. As of this morning, although US forces are on extremely high alert, pool reporters have confirmed that American units have not left their bases..."

Wide-eyed, Megan gasped. "Oh my God, Matt, are our guys there in trouble?"

His face hardened suddenly. "It isn't good. Our people can take care of themselves, and the bastards in Tehran know damn well we have two carrier strike groups just off their coast, but this is definitely a game changer. The intelligence community began looking into this possibility years ago, but until the Arab Spring began shaking things up, it was considered highly improbable." Matt began to explain further, when the anchor switched to the Palestinian fighting with the Israelis. "Hang on a sec, Babe; I want to hear this."

"...Following Friday's initiation of kinetic hostilities, Israel began bombing Iranian air defense sites, military sites, and nuclear facilitates. Hundreds of missiles from Palestinian controlled areas continue to fall on Ashdod, Beersheba, and even Tel Aviv. Today IDF elements continue to make arrests of suspected terrorists. Their armored formations continue to storm into Gaza and Judea, accompanied by punishing airstrikes and close air support, amid threats of nuclear strikes and counter strikes as both Israel and Iran seek to intimidate the other into submission. When asked whether the United States would be committing troops to defend Saudi Arabia or to defend Israel in the two day old war, administration officials deferred, saying only that the United States stands by her allies, but that no immediate response is being taken, pending a thorough review of the current situation."

Seeing the anger on Matt's face, Megan reached over and turned off the radio. As she did so Matt turned his head sharply in her direction. "What the hell did you do that for?"

Returning his fierce gaze, with a sympathetic look, she explained. "What can we do about it? We have another four hours of driving in front of us, and you are about to tear that steering wheel from the column."

Matt exhaled sharply and shook his head, clearly realizing she was right. "Sorry, Meg, it just pisses me off how the bastards in DC are so spineless. They pissed away the lives of my friends for more than a decade and now when it really is going to count, they're just going to sit on their hands."

She reached over and placed a hand on his shoulder. "You are probably right, but there are more angles to consider now, aren't there? For one thing, the idiots in DC are going to have their hands full keeping people here from going hungry, or just keeping us from killing each other."

"Yeah, you're right, damn it. We just need to get our people home and figure out how to hold onto what we have."

She saw him relax slightly, but only briefly, as she noticed they were rapidly approaching a long line of parked cars, stopped on the highway. "What do you think this is about? There must be a bad wreck or something."

As the truck came to a stop, she noticed he was clearly frowning with concern.

"I don't think so, Meg. Can you reach my binos under the seat?" Unbuckling her seat belt to do as he asked, she noticed that he grabbed his pistol out of the side caddy in his door, as he opened it to get out. Putting the pistol in the holster to the right of his spine, he stepped onto the door jam and climbed up, to stand just forward of the windshield. Finally getting the binoculars out of their case, she handed them up to him.

Matt nodded his thanks and brought the field glasses to his face. "Stay put, Meg. I will be right back."

She leaned over to the left side of the truck. "What are you seeing?" She yelled up at him.

"Looks like a military checkpoint of some sort. They have Hummers and a couple of five tons barricading the interstate. All I can guess is that they are being really careful about who they let through. Fort Sill is here, so I guess they are taking no chances."

Megan rolled her eyes. "Chances with what? We are on an interstate highway not the road into Fort Knox."

"Actually, now that they let that last truck through, I can see better. Just a sec." Straining to look up at him, she could see he was scanning the road block. "Crap! They are actually searching cars and asking questions. I don't think this is something I want anything to do with."

"What do you want to do?" Seeing him climbing back down, Megan scooted back over onto her own side and pulled out the map to look for a way around. She looked at him once he was back in the truck and had shut the door.

She noticed he was in operator mode, as he turned the ignition. "Since the military reservation is federal property, I guess they are going to show everyone who is in charge."

"Welcome to America, Sweetheart."

Matt snorted in derision, as he looked behind them. Considering the options, he pulled into the passing lane, and then turned onto the median, to head back north again. "I need you to help me look behind us. Let me know if you see anything coming up on us. Look for radio whips and if you can, glance around at the sky. I doubt they have air support, or even care about us, but it would be nice to know, right?"

Nervous now, she nodded. "Right, nice to know. What do you think they're looking for?"

"Who knows? Since they are actually searching vehicles, they either have actionable intelligence, or some officious bastard is making a point about people doing what the hell they are told to do. Either way, I sort of doubt they will much care for us having our little arsenal."

Truly nervous now, Megan scanned the sky on her side and the highway behind them, as she felt the truck's v-eight accelerating smoothly.

"Nothing yet."

Matt nodded. "How soon can we turn off?"

"Just a couple of miles. Take Two-Seventy-Seven east through Elgin. We can turn south again at Rush Springs and take Eighty-One into Texas. From there we just take state Highway Fifty-Nine from Bowie to Jacksboro. From there, it is under an hour down Two-Eighty-One to Mineral Wells."

"Good work, Meg. We probably should not have done the interstate anyway."

Meg smiled at her man and looked at the approaching highway sign. "There is still nothing behind us that I can see, and we are coming up on Two-Seventy-Seven."

Matt drifted to the far right and on to the exit ramp, which curved around to the east in a lazy curve past a traditional looking red barn, and an even more typical farm house. As they pulled up to the stop sign, a string of east bound traffic streamed past as Megan spotted a Humvee closing in from behind them.

"We have company. There is a military truck behind us."

"I see him. Stay frosty; let's see what he does." Finally getting an opening, Matt accelerated into traffic, and past a weather worn sign which read, "*Welcome to Elgin, Oklahoma, Population 2,156.*" Looking back, Megan noted that the Humvee was stuck waiting on traffic, just as they had done moments ago. She then realized Matt getting ready to stay to the left as the road split.

"Matt! Go straight! Sorry, the road name is changing, we need State Highway Seventeen." Checking the mirror again, she saw the Humvee turn into a Sonic they had just passed. "And you might like to know your soldier pals were just hungry. They pulled into that Sonic back there."

"Thanks Meg. I'm sure we are fine. There is no reason for them to chase us, really. Sorry about the drama there, Meg. I was just being careful."

Megan blew out a long breath. "No problem. I much prefer you being careful, than me ending up murdered in a seedy tenement. We are like three or four hours from home, and I just want to get there in one piece.

❧

As the pickup approached Mineral Wells, Megan found herself looking for the Citgo at the edge of town, where Two-Eighty-One would become North Oak Avenue. She decided that seeing that gas station would mean she was officially home again. Despite having spent the last week playing hide and seek as they made their way across the country, her anticipation was mounting at seeing her family and feeling truly safe again. Her heart swelled as she watched the familiar frame houses pass and realized although the Norman Rockwell feel of her little town wasn't glitzy, it was a clean and decent little town. Looking over at Matt, she realized he was watching her experience her homecoming. Blushing, she gave him a know-it-all look, but smiled none the less. After another couple of blocks, they drew nearer to what was considered downtown, and she smiled, seeing Wendy Everett walking into the Church of Christ with what was probably her husband, a man Meagan didn't recognize.

"Does it feel good to be home, Meg?"

Laughing a little, she replied. "I could not wait to get out of here a few years ago, but it really does feel good. Do you see the tall tan building on the left, a few blocks down?"

His gaze followed where she pointed, and he acknowledged seeing her point of interest with a look of surprise. There towered over the small Texas town an impressive sky scraper.

"OK... You don't see that every day. It is sort of out of place for a small town like this, isn't it?"

"Yeah, I guess that it is. That is the Baker Hotel. It is abandoned now, but back in the day, guys like Clark Gable, Judy Garland, and Glenn Miller, along with a few politicians stayed there during World War Two. It was quite the health spa once."

"Really? You said that it's abandoned. What happened to it?"

"Modern medical practices, more or less. Various people have talked about fixing it up again, but so far the idea hasn't really gone anywhere."

"Well, I suppose I will just have to get familiar with all of the local lore if this is going to be home." Mat pulled to a stop as the light at Hubbard Street turned yellow, and then red. Megan pointed to another red brick building a block down from the intersection. "That would be the Mineral Wells Police Department on the right and ..."

Abruptly changing subjects in mid-sentence, Megan pointed at her father's pickup parked in front of the Hayes Station. "Matt, pull in over there." She pointed to the front of the charming little soda fountain. "That's my father's pickup. He and my mom may be in town for some reason."

Surprised, but blessed with excellent reflexes, Matt pulled into the parking space she indicated. He looked over to her, and took in a sharp breath, his eyes flaring.

Megan laughed. "What are you worried about? You met Dad before, a year ago at Christmas. Remember? Besides, you are my knight in shining armor, and I am going to marry you, whether anyone including you, likes it or not."

Watching him, as he reluctantly made his way to the quaint sidewalk in front of Hayes, the difficulty containing her amusement at her man's expense was overpowering.

"You're pretty sure of yourself there, Babe. How do you know I won't get cold feet?"

"I just know. You love me and have loved me for some time." She grabbed his hand, and they made their way into the little fountain. "Besides, you are not anybody's fool, and there is no way you would have put up with my crap the last couple of years, not to mention risk your life to keep me alive, unless you loved me."

Joyous, she felt him stop momentarily, and pull her in close, wrapping his arms around her. Hugging her for a moment, she looked up to see his smile as he released her, and they continued to the entrance of the historic old building. Taking a quick step towards the entrance, he reached out to hold the door for her. Stepping inside the building, the nostalgia hit her full force. The little tables and booths, the antique stained wooden counters, and her favorite, a mirror framed by an ornate light bridge, located just behind the soda fountain hadn't changed at all. Sighing, she breathed in the magnificent smell of the custom blended coffees that were the shop's specialty. She stood with Matt just inside the doorway looking through the various knots of people gathered around tables, no doubt discussing the current disaster. After a moment, she spotted her dad sitting with his back to her at the back of the building, near the corner of the dining area. He was sitting around a table with a few of his friends, and of course, her Uncle Jerry.

Smiling broadly, she walked across the floor, Matt trailing her. As she approached, it was obvious that the men were deep in discussion with her dad. Uncle Jerry, and another man she didn't recognize seemed to be exasperated, as they tried to make old man Davis see their way about something. As she approached, her dad reached for his almost empty glass of tea. Without breaking eye contact with Martin Davis, he handed it to her for a refill. Uncle Jerry was about to say something, but Megan beat him to it.

"I haven't worked here in a really long time, Daddy, but I'll go get you some tea."

Her father's response was startling. Dad was on his feet and turned to face her, so fast that he almost knocked Martin Davis out of his chair.

"Oh my God, Megan, you made it! I have been praying and worrying myself sick over you, your mother, too for that matter." He breathed out an enormous sigh of relief, and she felt herself pulled into a crushing bear hug. Unable to speak, she felt her father's tears on her face amongst the grey whiskers that were scratching her. The moment turned into two, as he seemed incapable of releasing her. When he finally let her go, she realized that Matt was shaking hands and introducing himself to the other three men.

Pulling back from her father, she smiled. "I really am very grateful to be home, Daddy." Turning to pull Matt away from Mr. Davis, she presented him to her father. "I know you remember Matt from last year when you and mom came to visit me in New York. What you don't know, is that I have finally recovered from being stupid, and we are getting married."

Matt reached out, and grabbed her dad's hand with gusto, and shook it, nodding his head in greeting. "It is nice to see you again, Sir."

Her father blinked, but a smile quickly emerged on his face. "Well, Son, I am in your debt for bringing her home to me. It is more than I can ever repay, but I owe you. You have my thanks, Matt." His eyes shifting from Matt, to gaze upon both of them, she saw approval in his countenance.

"No, Sir, you don't owe me."

Meg beamed with pride as Matt stared into her father's eyes.

"There is nothing I wouldn't do for her. I am lucky that she said yes."

Megan giggled. "Whatever!" Looking at the men, she smirked. "I proposed to him."

Every one chuckled, and Megan thought that this might just be the happiest moment of her life.

Beaming, her father looked them over. "Engaged, is it? I was hoping you would come around someday, Girl, and I think from what I know about Matt, you picked a fine man, Honey. I am real proud of you both."

Realizing that all four men were still on their feet, Megan spoke. "Matt, we are interrupting their meeting; we should probably head on over to the house."

Uncle Jerry passed a look to her father. "Actually, amongst other things, we were talking about the two of you. If you both are not too tired from the road, maybe you could sit for a bit." Megan looked back to see what Matt thought, as Mr. Davis and the man she didn't know, reached for their jackets. She began to say that she and Matt could wait, but Mr. Davis waved off any protests and picked up his check. "Reggie and I will look into some of what we discussed. I think the rest of this discussion is a family matter. You know where to find us. Come on, Reggie, we should give these folks some time." The man referred to as Reggie, touched his right thumb and forefinger to the bill of his stained Dillard Feed Store baseball cap, and the two men headed for the register.

Her father pulled out her chair and Megan sat down. Matt sat opposite her, next to her uncle. The waitress brought them both water and handed them menus. "I am afraid all we have to drink is tea. We are not getting our delivery trucks like we are supposed to, so I am afraid we are out of a few things. We can still fix you anything that doesn't have tape over it. That doesn't mean the tape on the prices though. We had to start adjusting menu prices when things got bad." She could see her dad grimace, but he said nothing.

"It's ok. Will you check on what you can do for us if we pay in silver? We have been on the road, so we don't have much left, but I think we can make a fair trade."

"Sure, Miss. A lot of folks are doing that sort of thing nowadays. I will find out what the rate is and be right back."

Her dad snorted. “I never thought I would see the day that folks would be bartering in Hayes for a meal.”

Matt nodded. “I know, Mr. Danvers. Things are really bad in some places. How about here? I am guessing you have had visitors asking about us?”

Her father gave Matt a sharp look, two adult men, sizing each other up. “We did, as a matter of fact. A fellow by the name of Ricks asked us to call him if we heard from you.” Turning to look at Megan, Bob Danvers eyed his daughter closely. “Would you care to tell me what this is all about, Meg?”

Jerry Danvers put a hand on his brother’s sleeve. “Not here, Bob, we can finish lunch and head over to my office.” He smiled at Megan, shaking his head to reassure all concerned. “Megan, you should know your dad hired me to represent you in any of these matters that may cause the family trouble. I would like to get your story on all of this, but I can tell you that the main thing Agent Ricks seemed to be interested in is what happened to you after you terminated your dealings with Sterns and Becker. He stopped by my office a couple of days ago. The day our fearless leader gave that stupid speech that has everyone in an uproar.”

Realizing she was holding her breath, she exhaled, looking down. “The firm was into some shady deals. I agreed to help the FBI.”

Her father frowned. “Well, I never liked you going off to New York, but I am proud of you for trying to stop them from doing wrong.”

Tears formed in her eyes, and she looked up at her father. “Don’t be proud, Daddy. I was part of it, wasn’t I? I helped them. I mean, I stopped when I realized what I became, but I...”

Jerry interceded. “That’s enough, Meg. We are not going to discuss this here.” Her uncle looked hard at the family, and they acquiesced.

Chapter 36
Declarations

Sitting on the soft powder blue sofa next to Sadie, Catherine stared out the large bay window in the front room of Ginny and Drake's house. Their friends were both still out front, after walking Dennis, Pastor Tom and his wife out to their cars. They seemed to be having quite a conversation.

Sadie exhaled. "They were nice to come by, but I am glad they finally left."

Although the endless stream of well-wishers stopping by to check on her and Sadie was gratifying, she was grateful that they were gone. She just wanted to forget the experience. She wanted to be able to sleep at night again, without reliving the nightmare.

Reflecting on the aftermath of the attack, she could still see the panicked look on Drake's face, as he arrived only minutes after the first officers on the scene rolled up. She and Sadie were both still splattered with blood from the ordeal. Maggie sounded like she was about to rip through the back door to get into the house. Much of the rest of it almost felt dreamlike, in a way. With the exception of the ache she felt emanating from the cut and dark blue whelp under her bruised left eye, and the fact that she jumped at every sound, it could almost have been only a nightmare.

It wasn't a dream, though, and she knew it. It was very, very real. From being pistol whipped and slapped repeatedly, to having her attacker shot to death, while on top of her, she relived every detail, over and over. Glancing at her bruised and swollen wrist, she shook involuntarily and again tried to force the memory from her mind.

She recalled still being in the bathroom with Sadie when the officers stormed into the house. Sadie held her, as she repeatedly vomited, when the first officer, his weapon drawn, burst in on them. In a detached sort of way, she found it odd that she felt numb to the horror then, but was having a tough time shaking it now, two days later.

Looking through the pale cream sheers in Ginny's front room, she felt Sadie's hand reach for hers. Turning back to look at her friend, she realized that Sadie was staring at her, an odd expression playing across her face.

Although she sustained the physical damage, she knew her friend was suffering too, having been the one to kill two men. "What is it, Honey? Are you ok?"

Sadie shook her head to indicate she was fine. "I guess. As ok as one could be after something like what happened to us, happened." She looked down at her feet, the red nail polish on her bare toes contrasting brightly with the off white carpet. "I was just thinking how crazy it was that the FBI believes an Iranian political leader wanted my mother and me dead because of what's going on overseas." Catherine shook her head in dismay. "Who knows, Honey? I guess their politicians are subject to the same lust for power as the elitist bastards in DC. Your father apparently saw your mother and you as obstacles to his shot at leading whatever this new caliphate turns into."

Sadie swallowed hard and shook her head slightly to try and wipe the thought from her mind.

"Catherine, there is something that I'm going to tell you now; I think. It probably isn't smart, and the timing isn't right, but I can't, not say this, if you know what I mean."

She looked up and into her eyes. "It's like this, Catherine; I am in love with you. I knew to keep it to myself, at first, because it might just have been an initial attraction, and of course, you just broke up with Janice, and the world is all messed up and, and, I..."

Her voice trailed off as Catherine smiled. "You don't have to explain."

Scooting closer on the sofa and pulling her close, Catherine moved in until their lips met in a gentle, but stirring kiss. "I love you, too. I think you can do better, but I am not about to argue with you about it."

Sadie giggled softly. "Really? I hoped that you did, but there has just been so much happening and it really is way too soon for..."

Catherine smiled. "I know, but what the hell. Janice and I were together for quite a while, and we never connected in the easy open way that you and I do. I honestly didn't know what to do with what I feel. It's obvious that I'm nuts, hard headed, and difficult to get along with. Like I said, you can do better"

Smiling now, Sadie ran her right hand through Catherine's wavy brown hair. "Are you insane? Catherine, you're beautiful; you're smart, and you are unstoppable. I don't know how I would have gotten through the last few weeks had I not met you." A drawn look appearing on her face, she continued in nothing more than a whisper. "I might not be here today, if you hadn't been there for me."

Catherine leaned in for another kiss, and lifted the hair away from Sadie's face. "Well, we can start fresh now. The bastards following you are gone. We can go to Carrollton tomorrow, to see what your buddy, Detective Reyes, can tell you about what the FBI found on them. Then I guess if you want to, we can talk about what to do next."

Catherine felt Sadie take her hands as she smiled. "I can tell you right now what I would like to do. I want to dump my apartment and live with you, permanently. I have no idea what is going to happen with all that is going on, but if things ever get anything like normal again, I can sell my mom's house, and we can do ok, I think. Please say, yes, Catherine." Sadie smiled imploringly. "Please say, yes."

"You do know we have only known each other for like a month, right? It has been an intense month, I grant you, but I'm not sure that you really get what a pain in the a..." Sadie cut her off.

"Look, Catherine, I agree it hasn't been long enough, but I think with what we have been through the last month or so, I have likely seen all there is to see with you."

Giving her a skeptical look, she began to reply, but Sadie interrupted her.

"I'm not finished yet. Unless you are hiding some deep secret or something, I think we can put your ill temper aside. You may have noticed I have my own foul moods."

Catherine smiled and began to speak, but again Sadie cut in, this time with a look of panic on her face.

"Oh, my God, I am rushing you. I am putting pressure on you and putting you on the spot when you aren't ready for that level of commitment." She visibly paled, as her hands went to her mouth.

"Sadie! Take a breath, Sweetie. You are not rushing me. I feel the same way about you. I just don't want you to realize later, that I am too difficult to live with. I have not had a great track record by any stretch of the imagination. Don't forget, eventually we have to go back to my place. Are you sure you can be comfortable after what happened there?"

Sadie exhaled, and closed her eyes, relief obvious on her face. "I don't know how it will feel, but I am not letting anyone, especially the evil bastards that attacked us, ruin how wonderful I found living with you here in Cedar Hill. I love your house. I have loved every second of the time we have had there, and I love you, especially when you are a total bitch."

Sadie smiled hopefully, and Catherine realized logic didn't stand a chance. Rushed or not, she didn't really care. She wanted to go for it.

Sitting there with Sadie, Catherine realized that she had just made a decision, and having done so, a sense of strength surged through her. It was true, she thought, that she'd screwed up everything she'd ever tried, but she also knew her father didn't raise a quitter. She realized she had purpose now. Looking into Sadie's warm brown eyes, she smiled, thinking if she had Sadie's love, nothing else mattered. Maybe she could she make it work this time.

Her heart melting, she smiled weakly at Sadie. "Well, the guys said they cleaned up the house and got rid of the sofa. I guess we could paint, or whatever. If that is what you want, we can make it like it was again."

"That's right, we can. Maybe it will be tough at first, but worth it. I told the guys to go grab the sofa from my mom's house. It will look just fine, I think."

Sitting with Sadie, listening to her talk about a future, Catherine realized she could see her life opening up again. She knew it felt right, and she was doing the right thing to reach out and grab the dream, but whether from exhaustion or habit, she realized she was still afraid.

Looking into Sadie's eyes, she felt the tears coming again. This time the emotions welling up were about joy and hope, but she couldn't quite shake the doubt she still felt. Like Sadie, she was exhausted. Neither of them slept much following the attack.

She hoped her emotions were associated with optimism, but taking a breath, she decided to be sure.

"Ok Sadie, I need you to listen to me. I love you. You have to know that I want nothing more than to have some kind of a life again, and a life with you would be a dream. I just worry about you making a decision when things are so screwed up for both of us. I am a complete wreck, and I know that you are, too. You were more than brave the other day, but I couldn't live with myself if you ever regretted a decision made when..."

"Enough Catherine!" Sadie grabbed her head as if to keep it from exploding. "Dammit, you are the most stubborn creature on God's earth! Let me make this clear for you." Like a Drill Sergeant, Sadie pointed at Catherine's chest to emphasize her point. "Too late! At this point, I am not asking you, really; I am telling you that I love you, and I know for sure you love me now too, so that's it. We are moving in together, and I don't want to hear any of your second guessing crap."

Taken aback, Catherine blinked and smiled, speechless for once. Exhaling loudly, she reached out yet again and pulled Sadie into an embrace, as a returning Drake opened the door to their home for his fiancée.

"You know you're nuts." Catherine glanced from Sadie to the front door. "Ask Janice, or Drake, or anyone else for that matter, who knows me well. They will tell you what you are in for, but you have just made me very, very happy."

Drake smiled as curiosity played across his face. "Ask me what?"

Both women looked up at their friends, embarrassed. Kate dabbed at her tears with her sleeve and beamed at her friends. "I somehow suckered Sadie into moving in permanently. We are officially an item."

Ginny clapped enthusiastically. "Now that is the first decent news that I have heard in a while! I am so very happy for you both."

Standing behind his soon-to-be bride, Drake grinned broadly. "Keep it down, Honey; you will wake up your mom." He drew her into his arms and continued. "I am really glad you guys finally figured it out. It took you long enough. You know of course it was patently obvious to absolutely everyone from the moment you guys met."

With her own tears of happiness now threatening to overflow, Sadie stood, smiling. "Thanks guys. You all have made me feel so welcome the last few weeks. I can't tell you how much you all mean to me."

Visibly shaking, Sadie continued, as Catherine, too, rose to hold her protectively. "Saturday was the worst day in my life, but I can honestly say if the attack was what it took to make today possible, it was worth it." Turning to face Sadie, Catherine saw the joy on her face reflecting her own feelings. She felt Sadie's hand encompass her own. "Catherine, I love you, and today is one of the best days of my life."

Hugging her close, Catherine nodded in agreement. "Me, too, Sadie, me, too. I actually almost feel guilty now. Things are so horrible. I was just feeling completely exhausted and depressed, and now I think I have never felt happier or more alive."

As Catherine again dabbed at her eyes, Ginny moved in to hug them both. "Don't even think about feeling guilty, Kate. You both have been through hell. You deserve to be happy. To hell with the world! You guys need to enjoy this."

Seeing that Drake wanted his turn, Catherine smiled at him, as Ginny moved back to let him get in on a group hug as well. Feeling her friends surround her, not letting her go, she sighed, mentally reaching out to God with her mind. Thank you, Father, I know I don't deserve what you have done for me, but I am grateful. I promise to do my best this time.

The moment passed, and everyone, now smiling, released each other. Catherine's eyes followed Ginny and Drake as they moved back to sit on the matching sofa positioned at a right angle from where she and Sadie were sitting.

Sitting back down, Catherine looked at her friends, sitting in front of their bay window, across from them. It suddenly occurred to her that the sun was shining, its light splashing Drake and Ginny's front room with hope. Even with her aches, she could feel the knot of tension she carried around, begin to loosen.

Always the chipper one in the group, Ginny sighed happily, as if she were about to suggest baking cookies. Catherine decided it was time to go home. She knew that she would not feel any better by waiting, and the sooner she faced it, the better.

Catherine glanced at Sadie, giving her a knowing look. Smiling with appreciation, she looked at her friends and made her announcement. "Well, not to change the subject after all of the fuzzy bunny stuff, but we should probably go home now that Dennis and the guys have the place cleaned up."

Ginny grimaced, shocked at what she just heard. "Don't go, Guys. I know your folks are coming in from Mineral Wells, but you can just have them come here. We can have a nice dinner in a little while."

Catherine saw in Drake's expression he immediately understood what she was thinking. He patted Ginny's thigh, and gave her a look of his own. "They are going to have to work through things with the family, Sweetie. If I know Kate's dad, she will have her hands full not being kidnapped and taken back to the ranch."

Catherine shrugged. "Yeah, he won't like it, but it will be ok. Sadie and I are still mostly in one piece, and what I need to do with the group hasn't changed. If anything, it is more important than ever, that we all pull together. We can show that when decent people work together, nothing can stop us."

Catherine gave Sadie a nod, and they stood. "We should go get Maggie from the back yard and pack up."

Sadie smiled. "I will take care of packing our stuff."

Catherine nodded her thanks and Sadie headed off to the guest room. Catherine smiled and took a step to hug her friends again, when Drake's cell rang. Catherine settled for hugging Ginny alone, as Drake stepped away to take his call.

Wiping an errant tear of gratitude, Catherine sighed, squeezed Ginny a little tighter, and whispered her thanks. "Thank you both for letting us stay with you guys for a couple of days." Ginny returned her smile, but hearing the tone of Drake's voice change, they both turned towards him as he hung up.

"I have to go in to work, Guys, looks like trouble."

Chapter 37
Fall of the Phoenix

As Catherine and Sadie approached their front door with Maggie tugging at her leash Catherine realized that the guys from the group had not only patched up her splintered front door, but had actually replaced it. Trading a significant look with Sadie, they made their way onto the porch with Maggie determined to beat everyone into the house. Catherine opened the screen door and passed it off to Sadie as she struggled to avoid tripping over Maggie. Catherine took a deep breath and took out her brand new house key as she made her way up to the front door. Feeling Sadie's hand pat her comfortingly on the back, she turned the key in the lock. She exhaled and pushed the door open, almost afraid of what she would see. As expected, her favorite sofa was no longer there, but to her surprise, the one that took its place was almost new. She reached down to let Maggie off the leash as Sadie crossed the threshold behind her.

"Oh, my gosh, they did a great job, Catherine. Do you like the couch?"

Catherine sat down on the jewel toned, wine and dark blue sofa, and leaned back into the sumptuous cushions. "It's good. Who would have thought your mom's sofa would match colors in the drapes so well?"

Sadie exhaled. "True enough. I kind of like the stripes overlaid with the subtle gold paisley pattern. They give it a sort of elegant look. I am almost afraid to go look at my room though."

Catherine stood up and took her new partner's hand again. "Well, first off, I'm sure that they did a good job in there too, but you do realize, Honey, it isn't your room any more. As soon as my folks leave, what do you say we make soup and sandwiches, and decide what we want to do with our bedroom?" Her heart leapt at the sparkle of excitement in Sadie's eyes as she stepped forward to kiss her. Feeling Sadie's soft lips caress her own, she pulled her in tight. The embrace only lasted a moment, yet Catherine felt as if her soul was completely fulfilled with a lifetime of support. Releasing Sadie, she smiled with contentment.

Sadie took both of Catherine's hands into hers. "It's going to be fine now. We will find a way with our friends and family to get through things, regardless of what comes. I was a little afraid I would relive last weekend when you opened the front door, but I'm not really. Actually, I feel like a weight has been lifted off my shoulders."

Catherine nodded empathetically. "I can only imagine, Sweetie. You have been living under the threat of being killed for over a month. No one would find that comfortable. You did what you had to do, and you saved my life, as well as your own. I say let the bastards rot in hell."

Catherine glanced over at the clock on the wall, and realized that her mom and dad would be here soon. Not wanting to spoil the moment, but knowing she should let Maggie out, she sighed. Shrugging, she took in a deep breath and blew it out slowly. "I guess I'll let Maggie out, so she can terrorize the squirrels, and I'll go with you to check out your old room."

Sadie smiled. "Your mom and dad will be here any time. You should go make some tea after you let Maggie out." Sadie nodded reassuringly. "I'm ok. I'm glad I don't have to sleep in there, but I really am good."

"Are you sure?"

"I'm sure. I think I'll just go sort through some of the stuff in my room." Moving towards the bedroom, she gave Catherine a sidelong glance. "Maybe I will see what I can get moved into our room while we wait for them."

"I would like that." Blushing, Catherine headed for the backyard, and patting Maggie on the head, she opened the newly-painted back door. Maggie bolted out into the yard. She smiled after the boxer, as Maggie charged around the yard smelling her favorite spots to make sure all was well. Watching a moment, Catherine smiled with tepid contentment and then turned to head into the little galley kitchen. Preparing her argument for her dad, she filled the tea kettle and turned on a flame underneath it. Telling herself that she was a grown woman, she began filling glasses with ice and put them on her serving tray along with some packets of sweetener. As she set the tray on the table, she realized Sadie was actually singing softly to herself from the other room. Her partner's joy brought a grin to her face as she returned to the kitchen for chips and dip.

Soon the table was ready, and she was pouring the boiling water into a pitcher as she heard the sound of car tires crunching on the gravel driveway.

"It sounds like they're here, Sweetie! Prepare to be smothered." Catherine walked into the tiny dining room and set the pitcher of cooling tea on the table. As the women gathered near the front door, Catherine glanced nervously at Sadie. Taking a breath, Catherine opened the door and walked out onto the front porch and waved, followed by Sadie.

Watching her family get out of the car, she felt Sadie's breath on her neck. "Do you think they will like me well enough?"

She realized not only her mom and dad had come, as her baby sister emerged from her dad's truck, along with her sister's husband, Russ. Rolling her eyes, she replied to Sadie in the same low tone. "I would think so. What's not to like? They got used to Janice, and she had absolutely nothing in common with them, other than being with me." She frowned. "What I hate is they brought my sister's dumb-ass husband. I guess I should have expected it though. He's such a tool, but I guess we'll just have to endure."

As the small group approached, Catherine took in a sharp breath as her mom rushed ahead of the others, pouncing on her daughter as Catherine opened the screen door.

Seeing her mother's expression, she was reminded how bad she looked.

"Oh, Katie, your face!" Her mom looked back to her dad, her face stricken. "Do you see what those monsters did to my little girl?"

Facing Kate again as the others drew nearer, her mother gasped. "Honey, I am so very sorry about what happened. Your friend, Drake, called and told us about it, of course."

"I know, Mom." Looking at the little group, Catherine stepped back a little to make room for everyone, and pulled Sadie up next to her. Her eyes traveled from her father to her mom, to her little sister as they filed onto the front porch.

"I want you guys to meet Sadie". She pointed at her family members, each in turn. "This is my mom, Beth Danvers, my dad, Bob, and my little sister, Annie." Pausing a moment, she realized she had overlooked her brother-in-law. "Oh, and my sister's husband, Russell Davis."

Looking at her mom, she could see that her mom was horrified by her bruised and swollen face, as well as the reason for it being so. "Well, come on inside. I made mint tea and some snacks." Smiling as best she could, she turned, winced at Sadie, and led her family into the house. As she crossed the threshold, she could hear her sister's comment which mimicked her mother almost exactly.

As they all filed into the front room, Catherine turned to see her mother appraising what she saw. "The house looks wonderful, Sweetheart. I was afraid of what I would find after what the news people were saying about how terrible it all was." Her mother stepped up to her, and she felt her mother's hands grasping both of her arms to pull her close enough to examine her daughter's injuries.

"I'm ok, Mom, really."

Catherine gave her family her best smile, knowing it would have little effect, for she realized that they too were dealing with strong emotions. Even Russell looked more sympathetic than she expected.

She glanced nervously at Sadie. The smile on Sadie's face was forced but sincere. Her partner's tension was obvious on her face and in her body language as she got up the courage to say something.

"It's very nice to meet you all."

Surprised, Catherine blinked as her mom pounced on Sadie as she had just done with her, pulling her into a fierce hug. "It's so good to meet you, Dear. You girls were so terribly brave. I have been praising God for watching over you both. I'm so grateful to both of you for being so very strong."

Dad pulled Catherine into a restrained version of one of his overpowering bear hugs. He didn't say a word, but she realized he was trembling with emotion, as his massive hand cupped the back of her head, crushing it into his chest. When he finally released her, she smiled up at him.

"It really is ok, Daddy. Come on into the dining room. I just made fresh tea. I know we need to catch up." As she turned towards her dining room table, her eyebrows raised as Sadie held her mom's hand, already leading her towards the kitchen to get two more glasses for Annie and Russ.

Winking at her little sister, she motioned for everyone to sit down.

As her father took a seat and she reached to take her dad's jacket, she noticed that he had his old army forty-five caliber Colt 1911 in a holster under his arm. Even Russell, she noticed, had a pistol in a holster clipped to his belt. He pulled out her sister's chair before sitting himself. Pausing only briefly, she blinked and began pouring the tea, surprised at his courtesy towards her baby sister. After filling the two additional glasses Sadie brought in from the kitchen, Catherine sat in her typical seat at the end of the table, nearest the window, with Sadie in the seat next to her on her right. The small talk faded away, and her dad leaned back and gave her a serious look.

"Well, Catherine, I know you have already probably figured what I would have to say to you girls. I want you both to come out to the ranch. Your sisters are already there, and Russ and I are finishing out more living space in the garage. We will be painting your sister's apartment next week, so she will have room for the baby. Megan and her fiancée are taking have a room and you girls could move into your old room."

Catherine smiled. "Megan is home from New York? Why didn't they come with you guys? I have tried to reach her a couple of times, but it always went to voice mail."

"Think about it, Katie Girl. You know why. We can't afford to leave the ranch unguarded. She and her fiancée stayed behind this time. We basically decided we will have someone at home for the duration, so to speak. That is another reason that you really should come home. We need you."

Catherine blinked. "Wait a moment. Did you just say, and her fiancée?"

Her father looked at her smugly. "If you called more often you'd know these things."

Sighing, she realized she should call at least weekly when it dawned on her that he had also just said -- you girls -- obviously meaning Sadie as well as herself. Furthermore, looking around the table, she observed in the other faces that nobody even looked surprised at the ease at which the pronouncement came out of his mouth. Processing that thought for a moment, she realized that everyone was looking at her expectantly. Annie even smirked at her disorientation.

Catherine stammered and glanced at her partner. "Daddy, I don't even know how to tell you how much I appreciate the gesture." She took Sadie's hand in hers to emphasize that they were, in fact, a package deal. "I know you are, well, let's just say you are dealing with things about my life as best you can. I know you love me." Looking around at the sincerity displayed on the faces around the table, she smiled slightly. "I know you all do. Still what happened over the weekend is not an everyday thing. We have Drake and the guys, and we are both typically armed most of the time now. We are going to be fine."

Feeling Sadie squeeze her hand, she paused to let her interject. "Mr. Danvers, I am not going to say that what is going on with the world doesn't scare me to death. It does, but I also know that what Catherine is doing, what we are doing, is making a difference in people's lives. Our Tea Party group is feeding people. We are helping with shelter and doing real good for a lot of folks who need it." It is true, anything can happen, and nobody knows how bad it will be, but your daughter is doing what's right. A lot of us here depend on her leadership."

Catherine exhaled, embarrassed, but before she could talk, Sadie put a finger in the air to quiet her. "I just have to say that I worked in an emergency room, and I have seen some really horrible things, but I have never witnessed anyone fill the gap, and reach people in a crisis like Catherine has. Our group has more than doubled; in fact, it has almost tripled in size in the last few weeks. She..."

Catherine raised her hand in surrender and smiled gently at her better half. "They get the point. You keep going, and I won't be able to get my head through a door." She looked seriously at her dad, placing her hands flat on the table, with the same air of finality that he practiced all his life.

"The bottom line is, I'm not going to Mineral Wells, Dad. I love you all dearly, but I have things to do here. I need to stay and do them. If it gets untenable, maybe that will change, but you yourself said there are times you can't run from a fight. Maybe this is not exactly a real fight, but leaving now would be running away from people that I made a commitment to. Unless something makes staying impossible, that is what we are doing, ok?"

She eyed her mom and dad carefully. Her dad's jaw was set and firm, his eyes hard, and she could see her mom was doing all she could to hold back tears.

Catherine smiled sympathetically. "Come on guys, it is bad, but the cops and National Guard here in the southwest have really done a pretty good job. If it gets too rough, we will head home. I promise."

She could see her dad turning things over in his mind. "Catherine Danvers, you are still young. I really do respect what you're doing. It's the kind of thing I raised all my girls to believe in. Still and all, I haven't said much about my army days. You know I was nineteen and in Saigon when the VC kicked our butts out of there. You cannot know what something like that is like, unless you have seen it firsthand. I am not saying we are going to have that sort of thing happen here, but I am not, not saying it, either." Shifting in his chair, he placed his hands down flat on the table. "You both have seen what can happen when evil men are unconstrained by any sort of civilized behavior. Violence can happen very quickly and you don't always win. If something like that were to happen to one of my girls, I couldn't live with it." Her father eyed her seriously. "Do you understand me? I couldn't cope with it. It would kill me, or make me into something I haven't been since I left Vietnam." Catherine could feel his eyes bore into her soul.

Her father leaned forward, took a breath and clearly made a decision. "I want you girls to know something. It may well affect how you look at things." His face grim, he continued. "It isn't public yet, but your uncle is talking daily with some of our guys at the State House." Catherine and Sadie glanced to each other, and then back to look at her father.

"I know you're already aware that Governor Miller called a special session a couple of weeks ago, right?"

Catherine nodded she was.

"Good. Well, since then, our legislators have been working around the clock more or less, crafting and filing legislation about what, if anything, we should be doing at the state level about this disaster. What I should say is they were working on contingency planning until the President's speech last Thursday."

Catherine could feel a lump forming in her stomach. She realized she was pretty sure what her father would say.

Her dad took a sip of tea and frowned. "Up until that point, most of what was getting heard in committee, was about cutting programs and dealing with the federal spending shortfalls from Washington."

Deciding that the suspense was killing her, she decided to push her father to the bottom line. "Daddy, I don't know the guys you do, but our group is aware of all that. That's why we're working so hard to help our neighbors. The State is going to have to quit spending money, too. What does that have to do with Sadie and me staying here in our home? If anything, you are making my point."

"Let me finish, Girl! That is the sort of thing they were working on until Thursday. Friday morning Senator Anderson Ellis filed a bill which more or less nullifies the actions that the federal government is now taking with the UN and Europe. Speaker Thomas fast tracked it through committee. Governor Miller will have it on his desk any time now. It isn't exactly what happened in 1832 when the South first nullified federal law, but it will be taken that way."

Sadie gasped, all of the blood draining from her face. "My God, are you saying that... Are you saying that Texas is talking about secession, like what started the Civil War?"

Catherine patted her arm. "It isn't exactly what started it but, it was definitely a precursor. That was about the Feds of the day imposing taxes that basically only the South had to pay. The South claimed states' rights and said no thanks. The Civil War was almost thirty years later, but it was still a real sore point."

Her father smiled in spite of himself, but held a hand up for them to let him finish.

"What the bill says this time is Texas will be staying true to the Constitution of the United States of America. It says, in fact, the federal government has over-reached and has become so overbearing over recent decades that state leaders around the country can no longer responsibly continue to permit that intrusion to the detriment of our citizens. They basically quoted right out of the Declaration of Independence saying, that whenever any form of government becomes destructive, it is the right, and in fact, the duty of the people to alter or abolish it and to institute new government."

Catherine realized that her mouth was open, but then she noticed that so too was her little sister's, so this was obviously news to her, as well. Her mother just sat there almost looking ill. Russ was almost stone-like as he held on to his wife.

"Oh my God, Daddy, are they really going to pass it? I mean, will Governor Miller sign it?"

Her father shrugged. "Don't know, but your uncle believes he will. What choice do we have? DC is pretty much telling everyone that they're going to just hand over large tracts of land and property to this new international body to make good on our debt. The word is they're going to do wage controls and tax the crap out of everyone to pay back the very jackasses that borrowed and spent the money in the first place. That's what I'm telling you Katie. This is likely to get really bad, very quickly. I want my girls at home where we can defend each other. The sheriff is already deputizing people to keep order."

Catherine could see that her mom had tears in her eyes, and Annie just sat there with big eyes, terrified and speechless. Glancing at Sadie, she could see ghosts in her eyes as well. She realized that her partner's mind had already gone to a place where she would be tending the wounded in some terrifying conflict.

Kate stood abruptly, her hands flat on the dining room table. Startled, everyone looked up at her. She stared back at each of them for a second or two, her jaw set, her eyes hard and unyielding.

She held up her right hand, extending a finger for emphasis. "First, I love you guys, and we are going to get through this. It will get rough, but we don't have it in us as a family to do anything other than what we are doing." She extended a middle finger. "Second, everyone at every level is broke, and the Feds first priority should be to get our guys home from overseas. We have been fighting since nine-eleven. Even with the billions of rounds the government has purchased in past years, do they have the stockpiles of equipment and munitions on hand now for any real conflict? Now that the bubble has popped they can't pay anymore. Who knows how all of that will go?" She extended a third finger and looked a question to her dad. "Finally, if I heard you right, what they are legislating is in full support of the Constitution that they all freaking swore to defend in the first place. I am sure it will be a mess, but they are right about the federal government abrogating its obligations. As citizens, it is not only our right; it is our solemn responsibility to do what is right."

Her eyes softened, and she smiled sympathetically at her mom. "I love you all. I really do, but I can feel it in me like I never have. I am meant to do what I can for my neighbors, and I intend to do just that. I hope you can understand."

Her mom lowered her head in resignation while looking down at the glass in front of her as Annie began to cry openly. Looking to her dad for support, she saw that he too was fighting to keep back his tears. Bob Danvers jaw was now clenched tightly shut, but she realized that he was with her on this, even if he didn't like it as he jerkily nodded his head ever-so-slightly in approval.

Sadie rose to stand next to Catherine and she felt her partner take her hand. "I love your daughter, Sir. There is nothing I won't do to keep us safe."

Still shaking his head, he responded. "I know, Young Lady. I know what you did, and I am grateful to you for that." Turning to face Catherine, Bob Danvers stood and took a step towards his daughter, grabbing her by the shoulders. "I am proud of you, Katie Girl. You are everything I ever wanted you to be. You understand what I'm telling you? You go do what you must do then, but don't for one minute take on something because you are trying to gain my approval. Am I clear, Young Woman?"

"Yes Papa."

Chapter 38
Birth of the Phoenix

That Matt was on edge was obvious in his posture as he sat on the edge of the leather sofa with his fingers steepled and his elbows supported on his knees. It was early, and the women were working on breakfast as the guys got ready for another day of preparations around the ranch and caring for the livestock. The smell of ham cooking filled the Danvers home as Russell sat down next to him with Bob Danvers across from them in his favorite club chair. The twenty-four hour coverage of the financial crisis was now sharing time with the disaster taking place in the Middle East, and Matt realized he felt guilty for being safe in Texas when his friends and colleagues were in harm's way.

"...Tensions continue to remain extremely high as the President and Congressional leaders in Washington continue to debate overall strategy in dealing with the continuing escalations now occurring throughout the Middle East on a daily basis. For the sixth straight day, United States Forces have largely remained neutral in the conflict playing out across the region. Israel's IDF continues to pound enemy targets in Gaza and Judea, and are providing close air support for ongoing operations there, and now in Lebanon as well. In addition, Israeli missile frigates began what was described as an extremely heavy assault on Beirut, in retaliation for missiles fired from there at Nahariyya and Ma'alot."

"Regarding Tehran, the debate continues as to the effectiveness of Israeli attacks on Iranian nuclear enrichment facilities."

Russell looked at Matt askance. "It looks like Israel is doing pretty well."

Matt exhaled loudly, his skin crawling with apprehension. "They are for now, and the Israelis are going all in, but they just do not have the reserves of material or the human capital to win in the end. They will run out of ammunition and missiles, and their population is only equal to like say that of Dallas Fort Worth. Most Israelis are trained, to some extent, to fight, but the warrior business is a young man's game." Matt saw that Bob just stared silently at the coverage with a scowl on his face. Turning to face Russell, Matt continued. "Russ, the bottom line is if the United States doesn't help them, they will eventually be overrun. Of course, they do have nuclear weapons which they will absolutely use before that happens, but they simply cannot hold out on their own without logistical resupply."

Russell paled, his mouth hanging open. "Why did they attack, then, if they knew that they would lose?"

"There is a lot of intel that says Iran was going to attack them either way. They cannot afford to absorb a first strike, so they threw the first punch. They are depending on their allies. They are depending on us to help. The problem is the spineless politicos in DC have their hands full dealing with the mess they made here. We have the ability to provide support with gear we already have, but I would be willing to bet the Feds are thinking that they may need the equipment and what munitions we have to keep control here at home." Russell blinked and turned back to the report when Bob looked over at Matt. As Bob gathered his thoughts his anger mounted.

"Sons-a-bitches! I will tell you what I think. We have been mostly sitting on our hands for a week now, ever since they had that little get together in Kuwait when this thing kicked off. The Jihadists had to have promised the bastards in Washington they would continue the flow of oil if we stayed out of it."

Matt nodded. "That is a solid assessment, Sir."

Bob snorted. "Don't be calling me, Sir, Son. You have earned your place in this family. You can use Bob or Dad. I won't have it from a warrior and from the man who saved my daughter's life, not to mention all the work you are doing around here. I would not have even thought of digging spider-holes to over watch the house."

"Yes Sir, um, no problem, Bob; I appreciate the gesture."

Whatever Bob Danvers was going to say next was lost, to a dramatic tone on the television and its accompanying Fox News Alert graphic. *American Strike!*

Bob turned up the television before Matt could make the request.

"...culminating with a strike force from the carriers USS GHW Bush and USS Abraham Lincoln. There is a mystery about the operation, however, as our sources in the Pentagon have confirmed that the strikes appear to have been initiated outside the chain of command."

"This is Tina White in New York. Jason, are you saying that commanders on the scene are acting without orders in carrying out these missions."

"That appears to be correct Tina. We are of course continuing to seek further validation on that. What we are being told is that Fifth Fleet commanders took the actions to secure the US Naval base in Bahrain, and extract US personnel that were under immediate threat in the region. We are being told that the actions are being taken following the capitulation of Saudi Arabia and the alleged unsanctioned killings of US personnel supporting the Saudi Air Operations Center in Riyadh. Sources within the Iranian Government, speaking for the IRGC have stated unequivocally that the killings were undertaken by Jihadist extremists, and were not acting under Iranian control. Our embedded journalist aboard the USS Bush said Admiral Foxglove was said to have remarked that he would not abandon Americans to the savagery taking place there. Furthermore, he stated he would do whatever he had to do to protect American lives..."

Matt slammed a fist into his hand, his head nodding in admiration, as the anchor went to a commercial announcement, sponsored by the United States Government.

Again, Bob muted the government sponsored announcement before Matt said a word. As the Federal Communications

Commission began sponsoring official messages on the major networks, following the cancellations by commercial clients under the economic pressure, Matt's patience with commercials evaporated completely. Not only were these messages really getting repetitive, but he considered them outright Goebbels' style propaganda.

"Thank God somebody in this mess has a head on his shoulders and brass ones large enough to do what's right." Matt stood up and headed to the kitchen to help Megan and the women put breakfast on the table.

❧

Wiping his face with his sleeve for relief from the late afternoon sun, Matt noticed the dust trail behind a rapidly approaching vehicle. Pulling the tractor to a stop, where he had been plowing manure into the soon to be planted garden, he squinted to see if he could make out who it was. Unable to tell for sure, he decided to err on the side of caution. Ignoring the pungent smell, he dismounted, grabbing his AR-14 from where it was stowed to the left of his seat. Running in a crouch toward the corner of the garage, near the fence, he pulled the slide on his rifle, chambering a round. He quickly climbed the rickety old painting ladder that he placed there several days earlier, and crawled over to the sand bags he had placed on the edge of the roof for his makeshift Sniper's nest. As he turned the bill of his Dallas Cowboys cap around to face the rear, he hoped Bob would recall their signals indicating friend or foe, and if he needed help or not. He also realized that he really needed to zero in the sniper rifle that he brought with him, so that he would have a more appropriate weapon for this sort of task.

As he peered through his scope, he exhaled; glad the vehicle pulling to a stop in front of Bob on the gravel drive out front was Megan's Uncle Jerry. He flipped the safety switch on the left side of the AR-14 to the safe position, and stood up to climb back down again.

As he approached the two men, his rifle slung, he saw that even with the world as crazy as it was, Jerry Danvers was clearly surprised by the assault weapon on his shoulder.

"I am very sorry if I startled you, Mr. Danvers. We are just being careful."

"Call me Jerry, Young Man. I would say you are doing just what you need to be doing. I was just telling Bob here that Governor Miller went public with what they are calling the "Constitution Movement" in a prepared address in front of a joint session of the state legislature and a majority of the state supreme court about an hour ago. The President put out a statement saying he would be communicating with Governor Miller to work out any misunderstandings, but Natalie called me just before I came out here. She said DC is in an absolute uproar."

Matt realized that Uncle Jerry read the confusion on his face. "Natalie, or I should say Congress Woman Natalie Chafee, is a friend of the family. She said she and her staff have been on the phone all morning about this. Governor Miller notified the President before the speech to give him the courtesy of not being surprised, but things are heating up fast."

Bob kicked a large piece of gravel with his dusty boots and spit tobacco off to his right and sighed. "Well Boys, we knew it would happen. I just damn well hoped it wouldn't come to this. Is anyone telling folks what we are supposed to do? Everyone is already on edge about the war in the Middle East, and all our trouble here at home. One more thing is likely to push some people over the edge."

Jerry shrugged. "Yep, about thirty of our senators walked out in protest during the official vote, along with a little over twenty-five percent of the house members. Two of our justices, who were opposed to the measures we have to take on behalf of our citizens, have resigned as well."

"Hell, Jerry, I am surprised any of the Democrats stayed. Cowards is what they are."

"I hate to tell you, Little Brother, but there were several Republicans in the group who walked out. All hell is breaking loose at every level. The key point we are trying to make clear around the country, is that what we are doing here in Texas is not secession. He and other leaders will be traveling around the state over the next few weeks, explaining what this means in real terms. The core of the discussion is that if anything, leaders in Washington DC are the ones who have abandoned the Constitution and not just as a result of the President's speech last week either. If we're all honest about it, we got away from what we were supposed to be doing years ago."

Matt rubbed his face with his sleeve again as he listened. He knew damn well that no sitting president, regardless of party, was about to let something like this stand. There would be trouble, and it would come fast. If the people here thought they would make this stick without a fight, they were kidding themselves. "Guys, you do know that, legal or not, the President will use military force to prevent this from happening. I think the idea that Texas is not talking about seceding, but rather is in full support of the existing constitution is a key point legally. That will buy some room especially with public opinion and with media coverage, but make no mistake, he will use military force to oppose this." It was obvious in their expressions that both men were well aware of that likelihood. The three men stood and stared at each other for several seconds before Jerry Danvers spoke.

"Well, gentlemen, the bottom line here is there are changes coming from top to bottom. The Governor immediately approved a bill that passed the legislature last night that rescinds EPA restrictions within the state of Texas to ensure that we have power and fuel for vehicles. There are several similar bills in committee as we speak, establishing some sort of emergency currency and establishing a temporary credit system based on physical assets."

Bob sighed. "I'm glad I don't have to figure any of that out. I hope you, wearing your hat as my lawyer, have made sure that my accountant is withholding any payments towards federal taxes."

Matt had to suppress a smile at the dirty look Jerry gave his brother. "Obviously, Bob. The Governor has already called another special session, to begin immediately following this one, to begin work on the mountain of details that will be required to basically operate independent of the federal government."

Bob patted his brother on the back. "Well, as they say, we are where we are. Let's plan on talking at least every other day. Things are going to move pretty fast I think."

Matt nodded and added his point of view. "I think it would be a good idea to take a page out of your oldest daughter's playbook and make sure folks are looking out for each other. We need to get on top of a community network to make sure folks are all staying in touch with and supporting each other."

Bob nodded his agreement as his brother climbed back into his pickup. "I've been talking to people about that already, but I will step up the urgency of that sort of thing. I've heard of several incidents this week from around the state, where the DC folks have already stepped up enforcement of various federal laws. Natalie mentioned she got an anonymous tip that the President basically turned all of the various agencies loose on Texans following Governor Miller's courtesy call on Monday."

"Bob, what I'm trying to say to you is that we have had EPA all over us. Don't talk to them if they come around and call me immediately, alright? You let Russ or Matt here do the talking. I don't want you shooting your mouth off. I know they piss you off, but now is not the time for a shoving match."

Matt watched as Bob reluctantly agreed. Jerry started his truck and headed out towards Highway One-Eighty, passing the Danvers home, waving good bye as he left.

Bob exhaled, shrugged and started to head back towards the rusting metal out-building that the family used as a barn when his cell phone rang. Reaching for the phone clipped to his belt, he took a deep breath.

"Hello."

Matt paused to make sure things were alright before heading back to the tractor. He studied Bob's face, and not seeing any stress reflected there, nodded, adjusted the rifle slung on his shoulder and started back to the garden, only hearing the end of Bob's call.

"Sure, Honey. Might as well."

Raising his voice, he yelled after Matt. "The women want us to go ahead and eat since we were more or less at a stopping point anyway." Matt turned back to face his fiancée's father as he continued. "Why don't you go get cleaned up first while I drive out to the back forty and pick up Russell? Beth said he must have his radio off again because she couldn't reach him."

"I can go get him, Bob, you go ahead," Matt said.

Bob smiled his thanks and smirked. "You don't have to tell me twice, son. I appreciate it though. You make sure to box Russ's ears for me for not having his radio on him. We can't afford to be lax with this stuff anymore."

"You got it, Bob. I was already thinking just the same thing, actually. We will be back shortly." Matt watched Bob head for the house, rotating his head to work out the kinks in his neck, stretching, and rubbing the small of his back as he went.

Matt turned and walked over to Bob's favorite toy, a mostly restored Willys Jeep 4x4. He chuckled. He thought every soldier he knew would have loved to have one of the old classics. Climbing into the dull partially green, partially primmered, vehicle he set his AR14 just behind the seat on the passenger side within easy reach and leaned over to the center of the console and depressed the start button.

The four cylinder engine protested for only a moment before coming to life. Matt depressed the clutch and pushed the long gearshift up and to the left, moving the little jeep forward. Instead of heading out on the road to highway One-Eighty, Matt circled the long metal barn to the right of the garage and the garden where he had spent much of the afternoon. As he drove past the barn and up the slight rise, he then proceeded through the grove of trees separating the house from a small section of wheat the family grew to offset the cost of feed for the livestock. He continued west down the dusty trail towards the Brazos River which bordered the Danvers Ranch not only to the west, but also bordered their property to the north and south as well, as the river snaked its way back and forth across the Texas landscape on its way to the Gulf of Mexico. Passing out from the planted fields and making his way around an outcropping of trees, he drove over the cattle guard with a shudder, as the tires rumbled over the row of half a dozen pipes set just far enough apart to discourage cattle from trying to make their way into the wheat. The back forty, as the family called this part of the ranch, was where Bob had Russ working all week, repairing fencing. He came to a stop and pulled the binoculars out of their case affixed to the dash. He checked around the stock tanks first, only to find cattle. There was no sign of Russ's pickup. Engaging the parking break and putting the jeep in neutral, Matt got out of his seat and climbed into the back of the vehicle to scan to the south looking for the bright red of the pickup. He was about to drive north around another outcropping of trees when, finally, he spotted the flash of red color nestled under a tree near the river to the south. Hopping back into the driver's seat, Matt put the jeep in gear and headed south. As he drove towards the river, he decided that he really did not miss New York at all. He had always loved being in the field when he was in the army.

Approaching the pickup, he figured that his new life was really the best of both worlds. He had all the comforts of home, a family, and he got to spend his days outdoors, doing something useful. As he drew near to where Russ had parked, he realized that he was in a terrific mood. Smiling like an idiot, he decided he was grateful for whatever this new life would bring.

Drawing from his brief stint as a drill instructor, he abruptly altered his expression from one of pleasantness to appearing as if he were completely pissed off. The transformation took place in a heartbeat. Deliberately slamming on the brakes, Matt jerked the jeep to an abrupt stop, throwing up a cloud of dust.

Matt reached back for the assault rifle and exited the jeep, his mock fury directed at Russell.

"Dammit, Russ, We have been trying to reach you for almost half an hour! You better have a good reason for not answering, damn it." Following the tracks towards the sandy drop-off down near the river, Matt saw the fence was completely down and a post had washed away, probably during the last down pour.

As he approached the downed fence he finally spied Russell, or at least his booted leg entangled in the barbed wire. Drawing near, he realized that the post that Russ had been trying to re-string the wire on, had given way, taking Russ with it. Russell was apparently standing in the wrong spot and went over the cliff edge of the small sandy washout. His right leg, now entangled in wire held him suspended upside down, his body hanging off the edge.

"Russ?" Rushing to where he lay suspended, by his bleeding leg, Matt could see he was really hurt. He ran to Russell's side, and realized the post he had been working on was now suspended on top of him and was preventing him from moving.

"It's going to be all right, Russ. I got you now. How long has it been?"

The sound out of Russell's mouth amounted to nothing more than a moan, but Matt made out what he thought was half an hour. He examined the mess and realized it was too tightly bound to unwind.

"Wire cutters. Where are the cutters you were using?" Russ pointed towards the beach near the rushing water of the Brazos. Turning to follow with his eyes where Russell pointed, he laid down the AR14 against some scrub brush and scrambled down the sandy slope to recover the wire cutters from where they landed in the young man's fall. Climbing quickly back up the slope, Matt carefully cut away the bottom two strands of wire attached to the roughhewn tree branch that the post was made from, leaving the last strand to hold the post in place until Matt could position himself to take its weight. Moving around to Russell's other side, he shifted his shoulder under the post and, making sure of his footing, he cut the last strand. The wire popped loose, singing as the tension on it was released. Standing up straight again as if lifting free weights, Matt threw the post aside and Russell screamed. The post now out of the way, Matt could see that the young man's leg was hyper extended. He was really surprised that he was even conscious. Thinking he really wished he had some help to support Russ while he cut the wire binding his leg, he realized Russ would be in shock soon, if he wasn't already, so he needed to get this done.

Matt maneuvered along the sandy slope, under the younger man, and used his bent left knee, to support Russell, his left boot planted atop a small grassy plant, to keep it from sliding down the slope. Using his left arm, he cradled Russell's back and head. Stretching as far as he could reach, he used all the strength in his right arm to cut the wire above Russell's boot. After several failed attempts due to his awkward position relative to the task, Matt realized Russ was in trouble if he didn't achieve success quickly. Truly angry now, and more than a little frustrated, he screamed and squeezed the handles of the wire cutters. Finally, he could feel the wire cutters beginning to make headway. Squeezing with all he had, Matt finally severed the wire and freed him, but Russell was out cold, the pain taking him as the tension was released.

"Well, Russ, you being unconscious for what is next, is probably the best, because it is going to hurt like a son of a bitch." He dropped the wire cutters and moving his left arm under Russell's arms, he used his right to pull him back up the sandy little cliff. Once there, he laid him out on the flat ground. Next he repositioned the young man so he could pick him up again to carry him over his shoulder as he had done in combat more often than he cared to think about. He took Russell to the back of his pickup and laid him carefully on the tailgate and then climbed up after him to move him up further onto the bed of the truck. Placing a tool bag under his head, he grabbed an extra gas can strapped to the side of the bed to elevate Russell's legs, and then ran over to the jeep to grab a tarp that was folded up in the back. He returned to the pickup and after getting Russell's keys from his pocket, he covered him up and used his water bottle to try to wake him up again.

Squirting him with water and slapping him lightly, Russell returned to consciousness with his eyes fluttering weakly.

"Welcome back, Russ. I need you to stay awake for me, ok? Here, take a small sip or two and I will get you out of here."

He nodded.

"Hang on, Buddy. It won't be long now. I have to grab my rifle, and I will be right back. Matt started to run back toward the river, but realized he needed his cell to get the women to call for an ambulance, and changed course to the jeep to grab his phone from the caddy between the seats. Reaching the jeep, he quickly grabbed the cell phone and saw that he had seven messages. Tapping the icon for the first one he listened.

"We need you back here now! The Feds came, and they have Daddy! They had a federal warrant for nonpayment of the EPA fines. They are claiming we are terrorists because of what is going on in the news. Matt, where are you?"

Chapter 39
Once More Unto the Breach

Catherine paced back and forth in front of the two folding tables that were the heart of their makeshift headquarters in the church meeting room. She blinked and rubbed her eyes to relieve at least some of the fatigue. It was only three o'clock in the afternoon, but she was exhausted to the core, having only slept approximately eight hours since Monday. As today was Thursday, it just wasn't enough. Sadie was becoming more and more agitated with her, but what could she do? The size of the group had exploded. They had a lot of volunteers now that fewer and fewer people were working, but the need in the community was far outstripping their resources. If the local Kroger's manager hadn't diverted much of his last truck to the group they would not have been able to feed people past last weekend. She knew she just needed to focus, but the task was becoming difficult. She knew the soup kitchen they were running here at the church needed some fresh meat, but...

"Catherine. Catherine, Honey, you need to take this call. It's your mom." Sitting up in her chair, it dawned on Catherine that she had just fallen asleep.

"Sadie? What time is it? How long have I been out of it?"

"Not long enough. It is five-thirty, and I wouldn't have awakened you now, but it sounded important." Catherine took the offered cell phone.

"Momma, what's going on? Sadie said it was important?"

"They came for your father, Katie. federal agents just arrested him."

"Arrested him! Arrested him for what? They don't arrest people for EPA crap! You called Uncle Jerry, right?" She suddenly felt wide awake as if someone had just poured ice water down her back. Glancing down at her arms as she spoke, she saw chill bumps as her mother responded.

"They said that... They said that Bob, well, all of us, are terrorists now that Governor Miller has told the government in Washington they were acting illegally. They don't like that we won't comply anymore." Catherine felt the fear and heart-break penetrate her soul as her mother began to cry on the other end of the phone. Looking up, she saw Sadie, Dennis and Ginny stop what they were doing to stare at her in horror, as they listened to her half of the conversation.

"Oh my God, Mom, I am so very sorry! We all knew that the Feds passing NDAA a couple of years ago would end up this way, but I can't believe we have come to this." Searching inside, for that core of strength she relied on so often lately, she continued.

"Mom, listen to me. It is going to be ok. They aren't Nazis at least not yet, anyway. We have been hearing about federal agents of every kind harassing people all week. We believe that they are shipping in every agent they have to try and pressure Texans. It looks like they want us to make the Governor back down. You have Meg, Annie and their guys with you, right?"

"Yes, Honey. Matt is here and taking good care of us. Russ got hurt today, but Annie and Meg took him into town to see the doctor. He dislocated his leg and is in a lot of pain, but Annie called and said the doctor thought he would be ok."

"Good. OK, I want you to call me every day with what's happening there. I know Uncle Jerry is going to take care of this, and I will come home as soon as I can, ok?

"Of course, Katie, I know what you are doing is important. Your group has been on the news a couple of times now. Anyway, I love you, and I hate to bother you with this, but I knew you would want to know. Matt is here, and he is very capable. Mr. Robards, at the church, said that he would have a couple of the single young men come out to help with things a couple of times a week until we figure out what to do."

"Mamma, of course I want to know. Don't ever hesitate to call if you need me, or just need to talk, ok? I love you." Closing her eyes, she could feel the stress tearing at her. She swallowed, and put all the confidence she could muster into her voice. "Tell everyone hello, and if you can talk to Dad, you tell him, for me, that we aren't going to let the bastards win this."

"I will, Baby-Girl; I will. God bless you. Take care. I will call you."

"I love you Mamma. I will talk to you soon." She tapped the green phone icon to end the call, set the phone down, and shrugged at the blank faces staring at her.

Catherine, her face grim, wiped the beginning of a tear from her eyes. "This is a freaking train wreck! That's what it is. The Fed bastards need to figure out how to care for people, not just think about how to maintain their power."

Dennis looked pissed. Catherine saw the vein on his forehead turning bright red, which meant he was likely to explode at any minute. Catherine stood up, placing both hands flat on the table, staring at each of them with a sober expression.

"OK, nothing has changed. We have been getting this sort of news all week. We win by staying peaceful and continuing to resist the fascists. Governor Miller is depending on every Texan to be the kind of men and women who know the price and the value of freedom. We lose now, and we will be little more than slaves."

Sensing Sadie walk up behind her, she sighed as she felt the touch of her partner's reassuring hand on her shoulder. Chase began to speak, but paused at the sound of urgent footsteps running down the hall to the conference room. The footsteps turned out to be Drake's, as he emerged through the door.

Drake was in uniform, and he was out of breath. It took him a moment to catch his breath so he could speak.

"There is some sort of confrontation going on at Fort Hood. We are receiving ham radio reports of sporadic fighting around the base. C-130s began landing at the airstrip on the east end of the base this morning before dawn. The President apparently ordered the Frist Cav and the Fourth Armored Division to occupy Austin and to back up federal agents. They are planning on arresting our elected officials."

Catherine felt, as well as heard, the room take a collective gasp.

"Do we know if they are going to try and force us to abandon the Constitution?" Drake's fiancée, Ginny asked. She looked from Catherine to Richard Franks, the group's de-facto lawyer. "I thought we said we were technically on solid ground, since we are the ones upholding the Constitution."

Drake shrugged as Catherine motioned to Chase to find a television. "I'm afraid what's right and the facts on the ground don't always match up, Sweetheart," Drake said to Ginny.

Catherine snorted loudly, another indication of her exhaustion, and looked at her friends. "The last communication anyone's heard from the Tea Party group in Killeen was that Major General Harrington, Fort Hood's CG, told the President that his position on the conflict with Texas was political in nature, and the United States Army should not get involved. At least we know the orders he gave a couple of days ago, were that Fort Hood would not be getting involved on either side." Looking down for a moment she completed her thought. "If they are landing troops in C-130's, they are probably trying to relieve the base commander and - or take possession of his equipment, so they can carry out the orders that General Harrington refused to obey."

Sitting down again, she looked at her team. "Let's face it, Guys, this is a mess. At every level, and in every organization around the country, people are going to splinter. I have said for a few years now that we had really developed into two cultures. We all know there are Americans who like the idea of being cared for by a progressive style government. Soldiers take an oath to defend the Constitution against all enemies, foreign and domestic, but they also swear to follow the orders of the President who is the Commander in Chief. Two days ago, Dennis was telling us how more than a few soldiers just left to avoid being confined when the General said that he was sitting things out. Most of the guys in uniform agree with freedom and limited government but not everyone.

Dennis nodded. "The guy I talked to lived next door to a colonel in the First Calvary. He said General Harrington ordered mass formations and spoke to the troops. He said that what was going on was an unprecedented constitutional crisis. He said the CG told them that he was not going to put down American citizens who are defending the U.S. Constitution, he swore he would uphold. He basically stated that anyone who didn't believe they could follow his orders through the crisis would be relieved and conducted off the base. He issued orders requiring everyone to declare straight up front which way they would go in this. He apparently lost like twenty percent of his people."

Ginny responded, her eyes wide with fear. "So the guys that are there, are kind of on our side? Or at least, they are not against us?"

"I think so," Catherine said. "Ginny, that is why I think the Feds are trying to take the base. God help them. This thing is really getting ugly, quickly!"

Chase returned with Pastor Tom. Drake moved out of the way, and the guys moved the television on its rolling cart into the corner of the room. Catherine smiled at him. "Thanks Tom. Have you been watching the news?"

He shook his head no. "I was working the food line. We are out of bread again. Martha Jennings has some of the ladies making bread from scratch, but we are not keeping up really."

"You guys are doing an amazing job. Just do your best. Anyway, you may want to see this. Drake said there was fighting at Fort Hood, so we are trying to see what is going on there."

She watched the blood drain from Tom's face as Chase plugged the cable into the outlet.

"...that, according to sources near the President. Asked to reply, Governor Miller stated this afternoon that the state of Texas bears no ill will towards the government of the United States of America. He emphasized Texans are Americans too, but we are an honorable, law abiding people, and as such, we are bound by the Constitution of the United States of America, and not by any international group, or the UN. He stated while the financial crisis is severe, and Texas stands ready to do our part, to help our neighbors, we will not, under any circumstances, relinquish our rights and freedoms. He said, and I quote: "Our liberty is granted by God and not Congress, and as such, cannot be revoked by any fiat of the Executive Branch or the United States Congress..."

As Catherine watched Governor Miller, flanked by key legislators, she realized that whatever happened, nothing would ever be the same. As she glanced around the room, she saw commitment on every face.

"...once again reiterated that it was their solemn duty to defend the constitutional rights of the citizens of the great state of Texas."

"Rick, this is Tina in New York. That is an extraordinary statement. Do you get the impression that people there really believe they can just do as they please, regardless of the federal government mandates? Is this going to turn into some sort of civil war, on top of all of the catastrophes that the world is facing? Can they truly be that selfish?"

"I am with the Governor now, in Amarillo, Texas. He is moving about the state, making the case with all seriousness. He has mobilized the National Guard here to guard key facilities, and we have unconfirmed reports that, even now, local law enforcement is deputizing people to set up checkpoints at the borders."

Catherine smirked at the news anchor's dumbfounded expression, as the correspondent continued.

"Wendy Keller, the Governor's spokesperson, told me yesterday that Governor Miller is still hopeful Americans everywhere will realize that although the situation is dire, their constitutional freedoms are too important to give up even in the crisis facing us all. Back to you, Tina."

"Thank you, Rick, let us hope that Texans come to their senses soon." She looked back into the camera. "Back to our lead story. Sporadic fighting continues through out the country, as Americans from all walks of life continue to struggle with the current crisis. Today in the Pentagon, over thirty service members were killed in a conflict over the chain of command, as many military commanders continue to try and avoid becoming involved in putting a stop to the rebellious acts of those few Americans who flatly refuse to comply with Presidential requests. In Fort Hood today, additional fire fights were reported, as negotiations continue between Major General Ronald Harrington, the now relieved commander of Fort Hood, and Lieutenant General Rob Beckley, who the President sent there to replace him. Sources close to the negotiation told Fox News, that although he would deeply regret to order airstrikes on an American military base, he would do so if he were forced to...."

Catherine picked up the remote and turned off the coverage. "Come on, Guys. We have things to do. We can pick up on this later. I am relatively certain it is not going to go away any time soon."

Drake nodded his head in agreement. "Let me know if you need anything, Kate. My partner is covering for me, but I really need to get back."

"Thanks Drake." He waved at the group and headed back out the door.

"Alright, where were we?" Catherine looked at the pastor. "Tom, please let us know if we can do anything more to help with the food. I'm thinking we are not going to be able to count on MREs from the Feds after all, so see if we can get some guys over to the grain elevators, and produce growers, etcetera, to see if they can help us out. I know Nellie wasn't counting on having to mill flower this soon, but maybe she can show people what to do, so that we can get that going. Oh, and don't forget to find out what they need while you're there."

Turning back to her ad hoc staff, she took a deep breath. "OK, so back to the item we tabled earlier. I know we don't have the time, and we are struggling, but I now think more than ever, that we need to get our guys on busses, and go to Governor Miller's speech at Dallas City Hall, when he gets here Saturday. The speech is at noon. I believe we really have to show him and the world we are behind him. He is putting his life on the line for us. We owe him the same courage in return."

Catherine took a breath and looked each of her team in the eye. "If the progressive bastard politicos in DC think they can back us down by putting innocent people in camps then they have another thing coming. I admit it is personal now, but if you will pardon my anger, screw them!"

Dennis jumped to his feet. "She's right, Guys. I say we do this. We have a large group, so we need to do this."

Catherine watched the reactions play across her team's faces as each of them climbed to their feet. Acknowledging their decision, she smiled weakly.

Ginny gave her a look of encouragement and wrote a note to herself. "I will put together some tweets and email and get the call tree moving. If the event is scheduled for noon on Saturday, we only have a couple of days to get people organized and get the transportation together." She turned to Chase and gave him her most appealing look of a damsel in distress. "Chase, do you think you could reach out to the guys you know, to see if we can get some busses for transportation?" She turned to Catherine and continued. "You know they are going to need us to pay for the fuel for the busses. Can I take what we need out of the silver reserve to pay for it?"

Catherine cringed, knowing they really could not afford it, but she also knew that Janice had called last night to tell her the Dallas event was going to get national coverage.

"Of course, Ginny, I don't like spending that either, but we have to show our support now when it counts." Smiling at Lacy, the only teenager in the little group, she made another request. "Lacy, can you go through the signs we made up for the awareness drive, and get with our guy over at Lone Star signs by Highway Sixty-Seven, to see about a couple of vinyl banners."

"Sure, Kate, no problem. We've saved most of them. We just lost the ones the union guys got to before Drake and Johnnie got there to break it up."

"Great! Now we just need to see how many people we can get to show up. There is going to be a lot of coverage, so I'm thinking we need to get there early, say like eight o'clock to get a good visible spot that will get noticed." Turning to Dennis, she gave him a sheepish look. "Can you get a couple of guys to go hang out Friday night, so we have good intel on what folks are doing, should anything go awry. I will call my Uncle Jerry to see if he can get a hold of someone on the Governor's team, to let them know we are going to have his back."

Dennis smirked. "Oh boy, a night in a sleeping bag in February at Dallas City Hall! Just the way I like to hang out on Friday." His look of consternation turned into one of slyness, however.

"No problem, Kate, you got it. We will make sure we are good to go. Maybe Pastor Tom could save us some of that bread they are making for some sandwiches." He looked at Tom with a cheesy, but hopeful, smile on his face.

Tom rolled his eyes. "I will see what we can do, but you and Ginny will need to get me some idea about numbers of people who are going," Tom said.

Catherine smiled and nodded at the little team. "We are doing a good job, Guys, I know that we are all tired, but we are keeping people on their feet. I am proud of you all." Wiping her bloodshot eyes, and looking down at her hand written notes, she added one more point.

"I am not sure what to expect on Saturday but winning hearts and minds is critical. Remember we are there to be peaceful supporters of the US Constitution and The Bill of Rights, etcetera. We are going to have to go all MLK with this. You know damn well that the enemy will be looking for people to pull off sides. God knows there is more than enough violence going on around the country as it is. Getting people hurt and killed will not get anyone what they want. Make sure you hammer that idea home as we drive up in the morning." About ready to make another point, Sadie raised her hand and shot Catherine an exasperated look.

"Sorry Sadie, what do you have?"

Looking out around the table for some support, she made her own request. "I know a few of you guys are burning the candle at both ends. I think if we are going to be able to help people in the long run, this effort cannot be driven by only a few people. We need to decentralize. I want you all to send Catherine, Dennis and a few of the others home to get some sleep. I am sorry, but you cannot hope to win with no rest. You will make mistakes and that is a biological fact."

A few of the guilty leaders around the table started to respond, but Sadie stared them down with an imperious look that no one wanted to question. "Good. I see my years as a nurse were not wasted. Catherine, get your things; I am taking you home. I expect the rest of you who haven't been home in days to do the same. Pick someone from your teams and hand things off to them. It is important for your health and for the group to have resilient leadership."

Catherine rolled her eyes, but she realized her partner was right and grabbed her things to follow Sadie out of the door.

Setting out on foot, to walk the couple of blocks from the church to the house, Sadie smiled at Catherine. "I really appreciate you not giving me grief on the sleep thing. You know they are all trying to follow your example."

Catherine nodded, but her words caught in her throat. Taking a breath, she made her point. "I just hope this rally thing is a good idea. The world has gone completely nuts. I really worry about the future."

Chapter 40
Family in Crisis

Megan led her uncle Jerry over to where Matt, Russ, Annie, and her mom were talking by the fireplace. Taking a mental picture of her family, she reflected that her mom, as always, sat in her favorite rocker at the far end of the room. Russ was on the couch resting there after tearing the ligaments in his right leg the previous day. Matt had just returned from working on the tractor and was now sitting on the hearth next to the perch she had just left. Annie was in Daddy's brown leather club chair, with Bridgett in her lap. As her uncle and Megan approached the family, she noticed Jerry did his best to smile to hide the grim face he wore when she answered the door a few seconds earlier.

Megan sighed at the hopeful look on her mother's face as she took a breath to speak.

"Jerry, were you able to find out anything about Bob? Do you know what they've done with my husband?" Her mother asked. Megan shivered with fear. She knew that if the news were good, her uncle would not look so distressed.

"I'm sorry, Beth. Sheriff Percy doesn't have him here. They took Bob and a few other people charged with tax issues to Dallas. They told me they are being held in the Dallas Federal Building for questioning. Apparently anyone in the state of Texas that ever had anything to do with an anti-government rally or Tea Party event and has the misfortune to have federal attention for any reason is being looked at. The sheriff and I both agree this is a political measure to get Texans to bring heat on our elected officials. The Feds want us to get our leaders to back off our resistance stance and to be flexible about the Constitution. They are cutting money to everything they are supposed to fund in the state. That is, our course, all but meaningless at this point, anyway. More and more people every day are refusing to accept dollar denominated payment for goods and services, and if they do take dollars, prices are hyper-inflated like nobody's business."

Megan suddenly noticed how completely exhausted her uncle appeared. Obviously, Matt saw the same thing as he got up and walked into the other room and pulled in a chair from the dining room, motioning for him to have a seat. Megan resumed her seat on the hearth as Matt looked at her uncle with concern.

Nodding gravely, Matt headed towards the kitchen. "I will get you something to drink."

"Thanks, Matt," Uncle Jerry said. "Anyway, everyone in town is in an uproar, and I don't mind saying they are fighting mad. With all of the violence being reported around the country, and news about the standoff at Fort Hood, it is getting really hard to keep people calm."

Her man returned momentarily and handed Uncle Jerry a glass of iced tea as Russell struggled into more of an upright position, careful to keep his injured leg immobilized.

Strained from dealing with his pain, Russell's temper broke free. "We need to be angry! We need to fight back. The bastards are breaking every law on the books, and we're just supposed to take it because they think that they are all that?"

Taking in a deep breath, Matt spoke up. "Look, Russ, nobody is arguing that what the federal government is doing isn't wrong. Still, open fighting like this, or anything like the so called Civil War stuff that the idiots on TV are calling this, is not something anyone wants. If things proceed very far down this road, hundreds of thousands of innocent people, and possibly many more than that, will end up getting killed."

Megan's eyes were wide with disbelief. She knew her mind arrived at this angle coming to fruition over a month ago, but seeing it affect real people whom she loved felt like being in a car wreck. It was as if she were suddenly jolted, the glass that was her life, shattering with the impact. She felt tears come as Matt continued.

"I'm not saying we don't defend our freedom. That's why we are spending effort on the defenses here on the ranch. We must, in fact, but we must do absolutely everything possible, and then some, to keep this mess from getting worse. The President and the D.C. types will not want to admit they screwed the pooch. They all have enormous egos, and no politico would ever want to have this sort of stain on his record. You can bet the guy is sitting there in the White House, imagining himself as Abraham Lincoln, even now. Every soldier and every citizen at every level has to make the decision of which way to go in this kind of crisis. We are supporting the law as it was written, and they have the guy the country elected as president, and the last hundred years or so of culture, moving us away from our founding documents. This is not an easy thing, and we have to keep cool heads for everyone's sake."

Megan gave her fiancée a weak smile, and patted the hearth where they were sitting. Looking at her mother, she saw that tears were also rolling down her cheeks. Beth Danvers's voice quivered as she stood. She paused to make sure she had her family's full attention. "I want my husband back. I can't sleep, and I worry about his health. He has never been any good at holding his tongue when his temper is up, but things can't continue like this. What the President is trying to do is wrong, giving away our land, our labor and most of all, giving away our sovereignty is something we just simply cannot abide. Matt is right. We must be peaceful, but this family will support Governor Miller, and that is all there is to say. Am I clear?" Megan's heart broke, seeing the grief behind that soft, but resolute, little voice.

Uncle Jerry spoke first. "Don't worry, Beth. We will have the Governor's back, and it is going to be ok. I am not sure how, but with God's help, it will be ok. I can go to Dallas tomorrow to see what I can do about getting Bob back. If they won't let me see him, I'll talk to the press. The national media is in Dallas anyway for Governor Miller's speech taking place tomorrow." He was going to say something further when his cell-phone rang. He listened for a moment and looked up at everyone mouthing an apology. "Excuse me; it is Sheriff Percy."

He walked towards the kitchen to take the call, and Megan stood up to hug her mom. "I love you, Mamma."

Annie set Bridgett on the floor and went to her mother as well. "We all do." Annie's voice was sad but sincere. "We love you, and we have friends. I know somehow God will see us through this. We are just going to have to have faith."

"Thank you, Girls. I love you both dearly. I know we will do our best, and all will be fine. I am more than grateful to have my girls here with me, or at least, no further away than Dallas. So many families are separated right now. We really are very blessed."

As the family hug broke off, Meg followed Annie's gaze as concern suddenly overtook her features. Looking in the same direction, she saw her exasperated uncle gesticulating ferociously, almost throwing his phone at the wall. As he turned towards the rest of the family, he obviously realized they had noticed his outburst.

"Beth, I am not sure I know how to say this, but Sheriff Percy just told me federal agents are on their way out here right now to confiscate your property for non-payment of the EPA fines."

Megan wasn't sure she had heard him right when she heard the sound of her mom's coffee cup shattering on the floor at her feet. In shock, she looked over to her mom, to see that she suddenly appeared pale and fragile. Megan reached for her as she collapsed. Annie too, moved to catch her mother. Together, they moved her to the club chair and sat her down. Matt moved the ottoman over and added a throw pillow for good measure as Annie scurried to clean up the shattered coffee cup. Her family surrounding her, Megan sighed with relief as her mother's eyes opened.

Matt smiled down at his future mother-in-law. "It will be ok, Mom. I promise." He looked at Megan and shrugged helplessly. "Annie, I need you to get some water for your mom when you take that to the trash. After you get her the water; however, I want you to go into the bedroom. You are pregnant, and although I am hopeful this will not get out of hand, I know your dad would not want you to take any chances."

Annie looked stunned. She was obviously not expecting what she just heard. "Matt! What makes you think I will be any safer in there? You think they won't search the house?"

Matt wheeled on Annie so fast, Megan jumped right along with her sister. "There is no time for an argument. Move your ass and don't argue with me." His head whipped to Russell. "Tell her, Russ."

"Go on, Annie. He's right, and you know it. We'll be alright."

Matt's expression softened. "Besides, Annie, I need you to hook up that field telephone that I picked up a couple of days ago. Just screw the two speaker wires down, that I brought into the laundry room from my over-watch position, up the hill, and put batteries in the phone. We have the walkies, but it won't take them very long to jam our radios, once they get organized."

Shocked, Annie blinked and stormed off towards the laundry room. Matt then turned to his fiancée. "Megan, you need to keep your mom talking, and don't let her get up for a few minutes." He took two steps back to the fireplace and gave Jerry a knowing look as he grabbed his AR-14. "I am going to need you to keep the Feds distracted any way you can for like fifteen minutes so. I need to get some of my gear and get to my spider hole on the hill above the house." Her uncle clearly wanted to ask him what he planned, but Matt had already turned back to her and Russ. "You two need to have your pistols out of site but ready. I need you to keep control of things in the house. I want to be clear, here. Don't shoot anyone unless they are actively using force, or about to use force to hurt someone. Am I clear?"

Megan realized that her head was shaking in agreement before she could even process Matt's statement.

"Good! Megan, take the radio. Turn it on and set it back on the mantle, but put it behind that vase, so it's out of sight. Oh, and use electrical tape from my work belt to keep the talk button keyed, so it is transmitting. I want to be able to keep tabs on what is going on in here."

Megan suddenly felt as if she couldn't breathe. "What are you going to do, Matt?"

He gave her a helpless shrug, and turned to leave when her uncle grabbed his arm his eyes asking the obvious question of her fiancée.

Matt pulled free and took a breath looking at them with sadness in his eyes. "I'm going to do everything I can not to hurt anyone, but I promised Bob I would look after the family, and I mean to do just that."

Megan looked on, terrified, as he and Uncle Jerry took each other's measure. She did as Matt requested, and Matt sprinted over to the French doors. Turning the handle and pulling the door to him, he glanced back at the family for a second or two and gave her a bleak look only able to offer her a helpless expression of loss. He fought to turn his resignation into a smile of sorts and turned to walk through the door.

Megan watched as he gently closed the mostly glass door and darted off to the left towards the garage. Turning to her mom, she realized she had no idea what to say. She was all but paralyzed with foreboding, she realized. They waited, with big eyes, for they knew not what, for their lives might change irrevocably. Finally, Megan resumed her seat on the hearth, as Annie, clearly angry at being pushed aside, returned with the water. She handed the glass to her mother and turned to leave. Taking two steps, she paused and turned to her husband. "Where is your pistol, Russ?"

He reached for the drawer of the end table, and Annie smirked. "That's what I thought. You didn't even realize I put it by the door earlier." She sighed and walked over to the rustic cabinet next to the front door where her uncle kept his vigil looking out in the direction of the highway. Megan watched as she opened the drawer and took her husband's pistol, still in its clip-on holster, and headed back towards the fireplace. Megan could see that Annie was visibly struggling to maintain control of her emotions as she returned to hand Russell's weapon to him.

Megan wondered suddenly if Annie's expression mirrored how she looked prior to her trial by fire a few weeks ago in New York. Annie reached down and put Bridgett on the couch by her husband's feet and turned on her heels, moving off towards the bedroom.

Tense now and not at all comfortable with the angles she had available to her, Megan reached into her purse beside the fireplace for her own 9MM Glock. Careful to keep the barrel pointed away from the others, she pulled the slide and laid it on the mantle beside her covering it with a couple of her mother's magazines from the caddy next to the fireplace.

The wait only endured for a few minutes. Megan gave her mom a reassuring smile when Uncle Jerry announced from the dining room, next to the double set of French doors that Matt had just exited that he could see dust from a vehicle moving down the road up to their home.

"Here they come. I am guessing it is just one or two vehicles for now. I hope Matt knows what he's doing. This could get out of hand quickly."

Meagan took a breath. "He has served in Iraq and Afghanistan, and he saved my life two weeks ago. He knows what to do. We are just going to have to trust that things will be ok."

"No!" Her mother, shaken but still firm with conviction in her voice, made her own announcement. "What we are going to have to do is pray. There's no way we can hope to navigate something like this successfully on our own. If we are to overcome this assault on our home, it will happen through divine providence. If it is God's will that we get past what is coming down the road, we will have nothing to worry about." Her mother made eye contact with her. "Megan, Russ and you too, Jerry, let's bow our heads now, and give thanks for our family and for the country." Megan saw their heads drop a bit, as she too, lowered her eyes to the floor in submission.

"Dear Lord, please be with this family as we face the unknown. If it's your will, keep us safe and protect us from evil. Please keep Matt and the men coming down the road safe, as we all do as we must. Let us not be blinded to your will by our own desires or our pride, that all may benefit in the end. I would be grateful, Lord, if you watch over Bob and help him to keep his temper in check. Please also be with our leaders that tragedy not consume this nation and the world. Amen."

"Amen." Megan repeated and looked up. "I love you guys. It is going to be just fine. They will probably just serve us some sort of order, or something. It won't amount to anything, not today, at least."

Russell nodded his head in agreement. "Meg's right, Mom, it will just be a bunch of trash talk, and they'll leave."

Megan glanced from Russell to her mom to see a sad little smile play across her face as she gathered herself for what was coming. She folded her hands in her lap, and her face took on a peaceful expression.

"It looks like its two SUVs," her uncle announced, loudly enough to be sure the radio picked up. "They are getting out. Looks like four of them, but two of them are staying out by the front gate. The others are coming in. I'll go out and see what I can do. Wish me luck."

Megan watched, along with the rest of the family, as her uncle walked out onto the pleasant terracotta tiled patio festooned with flowers. Megan noticed he left the door open behind him. She thought she could almost smell her mom's herbs reaching out to her comforting her senses with their welcoming scent. Moving a little to her right, to better see out the window, she saw the lead agent approach her uncle. He put on his professional face and handed the younger of the two men a business card as she had seen him do many times. What she didn't expect was that the agent rolled his eyes, crumpled the card and discarded it. Her uncle scurried to stay up with the two men as they all but pushed him bodily out of their way.

She could see the older of the two agents was clearly agitated by whatever Jerry had just told him, but he stopped and turned to face her uncle. They both gesticulated heatedly with the older agent directing his younger colleague to proceed into the house.

"Ok, guys, here we go."

Her mom, now calm, replied. "Stay calm, everyone."

The younger agent appeared to Megan to be about her own age. She realized that she immediately disliked the man at a primal level as he didn't so much as hesitate at their front door, but rather, just walked right on in to the living room from the patio as if he owned their home. Snorting, she realized that he probably did hold that opinion.

"Beth Danvers?" The man's eyes scanned the room. No one responded, and the young agent appeared confused about what to say next. Megan decided the guy must be a complete idiot as even the dumbest guys she had ever known would realize that her mom, as the oldest woman present, was obviously who he sought.

Finally realizing her mom was the person to whom he needed to deliver the official looking document in his hands, he took a couple of steps towards the end of the great room where the family was seated. Megan could almost imagine the man in a black uniform and jackboots the Nazis always wore in the movies. She saw that Russell was trying to stand, but with a look from her mother, he thought better of the idea. As Russell struggled to get into a better position, Bridgett growled at the man, and jumped down off the couch onto the floor. Megan drew in a deep breath hoping the dog didn't make matters worse.

She glanced towards the patio to see that the senior agent who had pushed Uncle Jerry aside would be in the living room any second. It dawned on her, as the confrontation unfolded, that her hands were visibly shaking.

Russell sneered at the younger agent as his partner came up behind him. "You have no right to be here, Dude. This is a private home, and we have done nothing against the law, so you need to leave."

The older agent rolled his eyes, frustrated with his counterpart's inaction and grabbed the documents from his partner. Obviously impatient at having to be here, the older man snarled a reply. "This house is hereby confiscated under provisions of the National Defense Authorization Act, under sections 301, 302, or 303 of the Act, 50 U.S.C. App. 2091.

Megan's mouth dropped in horror as the man kicked the dog aside, took a step, and dropped the document onto the blanket now covering her mother's legs.

Beth Danvers made no effort to reach for the document as she serenely sat in her chair. "I am afraid, Agent, you will have to deal with my attorney. You can find him standing behind you. He is the man you people assaulted in my front yard."

"Lady, the government considers you to be out of compliance with federal regulations, so you don't own a front yard. This structure and all of the property titled to you and your husband are now the property of the United States Government. Because I'm a generous man, I will allow you and your family an hour or so to pack a few belongings," The older agent said.

Megan saw that her mom paled, but her expression remained unchanged. "Is that what you believe, Agent? The EPA's ill-conceived attempt to steal our property rights is still an open question. The Supreme Court decided clearly that federal agencies exceeded their authority in harassing citizens. We have not been charged with anything, and if I recall the Bill of Rights, and I do, United States citizens are innocent until proven guilty. Now, I would like you to leave my home. You are trespassing, and I would hate to have to call the sheriff on a federal agent."

The younger man laughed. "We already contacted them. Our back up resources will be here any time now, I think, to escort you off this property." As the younger agent looked out the front glass, Megan followed his gaze to see the dust from several more vehicles approaching.

Megan could feel irritation mounting by the second. It felt like a movie, she realized. Here she sat, in the house she grew up in, the house her grandfather built, listening to two arrogant bastards threaten her family. Looking at Russell, she noticed his hand disappear beneath the afghan that was covering him. They locked eyes as she very subtly shook her head, silently mouthing for him to chill.

She was doing all she could to keep her emotions in check. She glanced through the large windows on the front of the house to the court yard, to see the two other agents, who had accompanied the two standing before her. The agents in the courtyard strained to follow the action from their post at the gate. She almost missed seeing Matt darting from around her Daddy's pickup over to the SUV furthest from the house. Her attention was quickly brought back to the situation at hand, however, as her uncle spoke again, his voice dripping with scarcely controlled hatred.

"They are not using the issue with the EPA, Beth. They are creating a fiction that paints us as terrorists because folks here dare to stand up against their unconstitutional and possibly criminal acts. They are misusing statutes, and they know it, but they also know that we cannot really fight it very well."

The senior agent gave an exacerbated sigh. "Civil-asset forfeiture is based upon property, not people, being associated with criminal acts. Your property, Mrs. Danvers, has no rights. We are here to confiscate it, and once we do that, it is, in effect, presumed guilty. The burden will be on you to prove its innocence to get it back."

Megan shook uncontrollably, tears rolling down her face. Russell had to physically grab Bridgett to keep her from going for the man. It was clear the entire family was boiling with rage and indignation.

The younger agent chimed in, adding to his partner's comments.

"As your property is charged, not you, there is no right to a court-appointed attorney. You have no right to confront anyone, and we can use any evidence we like against you, hearsay or not. If you want to fight this, good luck. We will require that you pay a ten percent bond prior to any contest hearing. Times are tight these days; so of course, you will have to pay for our investigation against you."

As Megan listened, she realized that although what she was hearing was real, it felt more like a dream.

"I would add also there is no double jeopardy when property is involved, so if you do happen to prevail, we will just appeal, and or, re-file until we get the result we want."

Megan noticed the senior agent was growing tired of the conversation and glanced at his watch. "This property is public land now, and frankly, I'm tired. Your hour is ticking by. I suggest you begin packing a few things."

Angrier than she had ever seen her uncle, Jerry moved to stand behind the club chair, probably to avoid the temptation to strike the arrogant men before them. Livid, he responded to the agent's proclamation. "These charges and these actions are patently illegal. I demand that you leave, now!"

Megan's eyes darted from one family member to the other, taking her lead from her mom. Her mother remained motionless, with her hands in her lap.

The younger of the men grew suddenly agitated at the venom in her uncle's voice and rushed him. "Shut up old man! This is over, and you are wasting our time. You get these women out of here, or you will regret it!"

Beth began to reply again, but Megan couldn't take it any longer and moved her right hand towards the caddy to casually support her weight as she leaned to that side. She was terrified and still shaking with rage, but, at least she decided, it wasn't as bad as it was in New York.

Regarding the agents coldly, her retort was heartfelt, but her voice was shaky. "I always wondered what it was like for the people who faced the Nazis. I guess I know, now. Tell me, are you assholes building ovens, too? This is our home, and we aren't leaving. So now what? As I recall, it didn't go too well for the Nazis the last time." Megan raised an eyebrow chillingly, but was distracted as additional vehicles pulled up. Glancing outside, she saw two additional SUVs had pulled up next to the first two, and three Sheriff's vehicles blocked the road to the highway. Returning her eyes to the senior agent, she gathered her courage and gave him her most effective imperious look.

"Fine!" The senior agent growled. "If you want to play it stupid, it will be my pleasure to haul your asses in for impeding my duties. You and your mother are under arrest for interfering with a federal agent in the course of his duties. In fact, since your mother is listed as an owner of this land, we can hold her indefinitely, along with her blowhard husband." He looked to the younger man and spoke into a communications unit concealed in his sleeve. "Jeff, you two get in here; we are going to take them all." He looked at the younger man. "Cuff the one by the fireplace; I will take care of the mother myself."

Anxiety clamped around Megan's heart like a vice, and time seemed to almost slow to a crawl. Her right hand slipped the rest of the way into the caddy to grasp the cool grip of her Glock as the sneering young blond agent approached her. She glanced at Russell and then rolled her gaze quickly to indicate that he needed to deal with the senior agent. The younger man approaching her looked almost gleeful at the opportunity to manhandle such an attractive woman. The pistol grip now solidly in her right hand, she brought it up smoothly, her left hand automatically moving to support her right, as the barrel of the Glock came on line with the man's face, now only a couple of feet away. She met his eyes down the sights of her pistol, the new balance of power in the room suddenly beginning to dawn on him. His eyes went wide and his right arm automatically went for his own weapon.

Megan said nothing, only shaking her head slowly from side to side, her facing transforming into a disgusted grimace. Her target froze, judging her. She could see that he wondered if she would pull the trigger. "Go ahead, Asshole, try it, and it all ends for you right here, right now!"

His arm froze in mid motion as she heard Russell make his move on the senior of the two men. "Place your hands on your head, or you are one dead son-of-a-bitch." Russell's words dripped with venom.

Megan dared not look anywhere but down her own sights, but she could see her target's partner was just behind him, in the midst of his attempt to pull her mother up and cuff her. She had enough of a view of the older agent to see him turn, his body spinning to face Russell while drawing his side arm to shoot her brother-in-law.

The older agent's face was complete fury, as his weapon rapidly came out of its holster. Unfortunately for him, his arrogance did not account for Russell already having a solid sight picture, center mass. Three loud claps announced the three 45 caliber rounds fired from Russell's weapon. She thought that at least two of them hit him in the chest and neck. The impact of the rounds knocked him off his feet, and he landed in a heap between the couch and her mother. The sound of Russell's pistol reverberated in her ears as she watched the shocked realization replace the smugness on the younger agent's face.

"You heard him, put your hands behind you head and interlace your fingers. You even blink and I will kill you." Megan was pleased to realize that she actually had authority in her voice now. She also seemed to be shaking less. It pleased her that the man in front of her was the one who was pale and shaking. Slowly, he complied. "Uncle Jerry, take this jerk's weapon and cuffs. Looking over to the pony wall, separating the area in front of the bedrooms, from the great room, she knew that would be the best place she had to keep him under wraps. "I want his arms behind him, around the archway post." Megan stood slowly, keeping her weapon leveled at the agent. She saw Russell take the other man's weapon from where he dropped it, after being hit. Jerry moved to help her, as Annie's pale face poked out from the bedroom.

Glancing quickly at Annie, Megan realized that her sister had been screaming in terror from the moment of the first shot. The shock and terror on her face, when she emerged from the bedroom, morphed into relief as she realized that, for the moment, the family was ok. As Jerry grasped the younger agent's arms, the three of them moved towards the back of the house, and the post Megan intended to use.

She could see the two agents that were by the front gate were now almost to the house, running towards them, their weapons drawn. Behind them, four more agents were doing likewise.

Almost panicking, she forced herself to stay focused when she felt, as well as heard the deafening boom from where the SUVs were parked. The concussion was like nothing she had ever felt before. The windows all rattled and the still open French doors were blown inward, as if caught by a sudden gust of strong wind.

Smaller pieces of the vehicles began to rain down on the yard and swimming pool, with some of the debris landing noisily on the metal roof over the porch.

She heard Uncle Jerry close the cuffs with a series of clicks. She looked out in the yard to find four of the six agents knocked off their feet by the explosion. The one nearest the house started to reach for the weapon that he lost it in the blast. Megan gasped, hearing the AR14's sharp bark sending rounds just in front of the downed men.

Matt's voice rang out. "That's enough boys. I will let you crawl back out of here, but if you go for your side arms, that's going to be all for you. Fair enough?"

She smiled, seeing they clearly believed Matt's threat, and quickly began crawling backwards.

Her uncle looked at her blankly, and, as expected, her mother was bent over the agent who just threatened her, doing her best to help him. Russell was trying to get to his feet, as Annie charged into the room to keep him on the sofa.

Uncle Jerry breathed out loudly. "Now, what are we going to do?" Her uncle asked. "They're all over the place, out there. I would never have thought I would ever be the idiot criminal holding up in a standoff."

Looking out, she could see the remaining agents, and the sheriff deputies scrambling for cover behind whatever cover they could reach. She began to reply when Matt stuck his head in from the door to the garage. "Un-key the radio again, so we can communicate. I have to change positions." She turned in his direction, towards the door to the garage, but he was gone as quickly as he came. Oddly, Seeing Matt caused her both a sense of relief and made her want to cry again.

Chapter 41
Standing Together

Megan stared at the spot in front of the door, leading to the garage from the kitchen, where her fiancée had just been. Finally, it occurred to her that she had things to do. Turning back to her family and the problems right in front of her, she sighed. She looked down at the fallen agent. "Is he still with us, Mom?" She really hoped he wasn't dead, regardless of his intentions to do her family harm.

Her mother shrugged, working quickly to save the man before her.

Megan acknowledged the gesture, her expression grim. "Annie, Uncle Jerry, see if you can get Russ behind the pony wall. It is solid concrete, and we have nothing but glass and a frame wall in front of us out here."

Her mother looked over her shoulder at her daughter. "Megan, I need the first aid kit from the garage, and please grab some dish towels from the drawer in the kitchen. His vest took two of the shots, but this neck wound is bad."

Megan ran towards the garage, and following her example, everyone sprang into action. Opening the door, she leaned into the garage, and reached above the freezer, to grab her mom's first aid kit. She thought that the arrogant asshole was lucky her mom was an RN, and a very good one at that. On her way back through the kitchen, she opened the second drawer down on the end of the counter, and took out a hand full of dish towels. Her hands full, Megan rushed to her mom's side, as Annie and her uncle began lowering the blinds at the front of the house. Watching the feds in front of her home, she realized that the agents were quickly taking up covered positions, and she saw rifle barrels already coming to bear, pointing in their direction. Her anxiety spiked as the hopelessness of her family's situation began to truly sink in.

Hyped up on adrenalin, Megan snapped at her sister. "Dammit Annie, don't do that in full view. Do it from one side. Don't think the bastards won't shoot you." Stunned, Annie moved quickly behind the wall, separating the French doors and the large plate glass window as she lowered the blinds and twisted the slots, thus making the room suddenly much darker and less visible to the outside.

Turning back to the matter at hand, Megan looked down to her mom who was feverishly working to stop downed agent's wounds from bleeding. Sighing, she handed her the first aid kit. "Here you go, Momma, we need to get behind the pony wall. Can we move him?"

"Not yet dear, you go. I have to finish sewing some of this up to get this bleeding stopped, or he will die." Megan wanted to argue, but knew that it would be pointless.

"What can I do to help?"

"Just stay out of the way, Dear. You keep doing what you are doing. Matt may need something, and you are in charge now, so run on dear."

In charge? She thought. She was the middle daughter in a house full of women. She was never in charge of anything in this house. That was one of the reasons that she loved her life in New York. No one there knew that she always played second fiddle to her older sister, or worse, lived in the shadow of her father who was always in charge of any group of which he was a part. Watching her mom open up her kit to take out a scalpel, some gauze and packing, she felt disoriented, trying to think of what to do next. A moment passed, and her mother looked up at her.

"Go on, I will be just fine."

Frustrated, Megan got to her feet and walked back behind the low wall that separated the main room from what passed as a hall in front of her home's bedrooms. Making eye contact with Russell as he reloaded his weapon, she shook her head in dismay. He shrugged and looked at her pleadingly. Shaking badly, he looked almost sick. It occurred to her that he just shot a federal agent, and was probably in one hell of a lot of trouble. Not that all of them in the house, were not in more trouble than she wanted to contemplate. Chiding herself, she realized that it did not take a prodigy to run the angles on what was likely in store for them, but for the moment, she needed to give her brother-in-law some support.

"Are you ok Russ?"

"I'm fine, I guess. Did I kill that guy?"

"No Russ; not yet, anyway. He had on a vest. Mom is patching him up right now."

Russell exhaled loudly. "He didn't give us any choice, you know."

"I know, Russell. Their actions were beyond the scope any rational citizen could endure.

From behind her, cuffed to archway post, the younger agent found his voice, finally.

"You are all screwed, you know. Interfering with a federal agent is nothing compared to what you will get for this. The President declared martial law. We have the legal right to shoot every one of you people. If my boss dies, Kid, you will definitely get the death penalty, and I am not talking twenty years from now, either. You inbred hicks, out here, don't get to just abandon the country just because things are tough."

Her blood instantly boiling, Megan spun around, slapping the man hard across the face.

"You don't get it, do you, you arrogant prick? We are the victims here. We are the ones standing up for the Constitution and for what is legal. The political class in DC just doesn't have a clue. Any competent statesman that put the country over their own petty desires, or their stupid party concerns for power could see that they squandered any right to governance."

The young agent snorted. "You are the one who doesn't get it, Kitten. The world you knew is over. It isn't about individualism anymore. From now on it is about teamwork and managing resources to the benefit of everyone."

Shaking with rage, Megan realized that she wanted to hurt the man before her. She took a breath and responded. "You are right about the old paradigm being over, but your belief in some sort of collective solution, that strips Americans of our rights, is the very reason you will lose. We are free people, and we are right to defend ourselves." Megan gestured with a sweep of her arms. "You think that this little drama is the only thing going on. It will happen over and over and over again, and not just in Texas. Americans are born free and once the initial shock of the disaster subsides, your masters will have their hands full. Do you seriously think that you can just steal from us and hope to control one hundred to two hundred million freedom loving Americans, once they realize what you tyrants are really talking about?" She shot him an imperious look. "You think that you and your socialist UN buddies can even take Texas in a fight when we are defending our homes and our very freedom? You better hope we don't have to find out. You idiots don't know the first thing about a real fight."

The younger agent began to reply, but she cut him off.

"It took you months to take out Libya. You people had no idea what to do about Egypt, or about what's happening with Iran. You debated for years about whether to do anything in Syria. You think that we give a damn anymore about parties out here. We don't. Your political masters in both parties have sold us all out, and we have had all that we are going to take. Look at what is happening in Fort Hood right now. If anything, the military will be with us."

The agent blinked, shocked as much by her words as he was from the stinging red mark on his face. "You red-necks will never dare stand against the rest of us. Texans think that they are so tough, but you will be begging us for leniency when this plays out."

She was about to reply when her uncle interceded. "Matt is asking for you on the radio, and he told me to relive this guy of his walkie-talkie. They don't need to listen in unless we want them to."

She nodded and gave the egotistical bastard another dirty look and moved down to where Russell and Annie were sitting behind the wall.

"Matt, it's me."

"Hi there, Babe, Jerry says that you are doing a really good job. Are you guys holding up ok in there?"

"I guess. No one is hurt but one of the FBI agents. We have one guy cuffed and mom is working to try and save the other one. Russ nailed him, but his vest took two of the rounds. He took one in the neck though, so she is sewing him up."

"Good. Ok I am in a good concealed spot, where I can see pretty well. They know that I am out here obviously, but they have yet to really take the chance to come look. I will let you know if they make any big moves, so you need to have someone listening for me at all times. If we lose communications assume that they are coming. Also, I need you to shut all of the blinds and get everyone into the back of the house. Ok?"

"I already did. Mom is still working on their wounded guy, but she will come when she can."

"Perfect. Good girl. I will make you into an operator before you know it."

Megan snorted. "I sure hope not. This is a colossal mess. I'm scared, Matt. We are in such trouble." Turning her back to the others, she took a couple of steps into the kitchen. Staying close to the wall, by the door leading to the garage, she moved the blinds just enough to see out.

Beyond the still burning chassis of the destroyed SUV, she saw that agents and local law enforcement were setting up a command post while uniformed officers scrambled to control the quickly growing crowd. The perimeter appeared to be set up on the edge of the rise, on the road in from the highway.

Sighing, she returned her attention to her fiancée. "You do realize that we are likely screwed. The feds are not going to just let this go even if they do have more pressing issues."

"It isn't good, Babe. We didn't exactly have a choice, did we? On the other hand, what is happening in the country is unprecedented.

With your governor talking like he is, maybe it works out. At least it could work out, assuming his team doesn't cave on us. With any luck, they will give us a pass as a part of whatever deal gets made. If there's no deal, it's anybody's guess what happens."

"Well, nothing to do for it now, anyway. You know I love you. I am really sorry for getting you into all of this."

"Stop it Meg. I do what I think is right. Let's play this out, and hope for the best."

"You're right, I'm sorry."

"Forget it. Ok, so Jerry is going to get their radios. Take one and reach out to them. We need to get them talking."

"Sure, Matt."

"The first thing they will want is to gain intel about what is going on in there. They will want to talk to their guys, but only give them enough time to validate that they are ok. Tell them that one of their agents was wounded when he unlawfully attacked the family. Tell them your mom is an RN and is patching him up. They will want to evacuate him. We want that too, but we need to get something for it."

"Matt, I don't know if I can do this." Feeling jittery, she looked at her hands and realized they were shaking again. The situation was developing too fast to keep up with competently. She just couldn't believe how quickly her family's position was deteriorating. Sighing, she realized that her man really was amazing. When she and Richard would work out the angles in a situation, they typically had plenty of time, not to mention the staff support to figure out the response to take with a client or adversary.

"Look, Babe, I know it sucks, but you are perfect for this. It isn't any different than one of your negotiations at work. Anyway, some people are starting to show up out here. It looks like more cops and several more feds are out by the cattle guard, in front of the house. They have the sheriff and his people dealing with the folks from town, and there is a news helicopter, so we just need to keep things static for a while. We want to be sure that we have news footage to constrain what they can do."

"Matt, I love you. I just... Are you going to be ok out there?"

"I'm fine, Meg. They have a few flankers moving around. No doubt they want to find another way in, or locate who shot at them earlier. I will have to wait until dark to deal with that. You just keep your head in the game, OK."

"Sure Matt. Please don't do anything stupid. Are you sure that they won't stumble over you."

"I sure don't intend to. As for finding me, my spider-holes are really well hidden. There is no guarantee, but I am pretty well concealed, and my spider holes blend into the environment, so I should be ok. As you know, I have a couple of surprises for our friends, if they are kind enough to approach the house like I think they will. They are already poking around over by where one of my flash bangs is set out. Well, I have got to go, I have company. Being smart goes for you too Meg, alright? I will check back in say thirty minutes."

Realizing that Annie was behind her, she turned, her eyes closed to shut out the uncertainty. Annie nodded with understanding and she sighed, Megan handed the radio back to her. Annie smiled weakly and turned to make her way back behind the pony wall.

Taking another look outside, Megan realized that there were at least ten more law enforcement vehicles out front than were there before. Looking down towards the road, she shuddered when she realized that there were several dozen of her neighbors past the yellow tape at the cattle guard. It looked like Sheriff Percy had his hands full, arguing with them. Turning away, she walked towards the archway that led to the great room. She really wanted her mom behind there now, whether she liked it or not.

As she passed her prisoner, an explosion from behind the house rattled the windows. Her heart caught in her throat, and the younger agent sneered at her. "Who is that guy? You know he is just going to get himself, and probably the rest of you killed."

"It's none of your damn business, Fed. You had better hope that explosion was caused by 'That Guy' and not one of your people." She moved in on him aggressively, to whisper in his ear. "I am a good person, but I am not sure how long my even temperament will sustain, should something happen to my family. Have we an understanding, Agent?"

Backing away again, she considered him, awaiting his response. The man before her said nothing, but Megan realized that he had goose bumps. Nodding at the man, she smiled coldly at him, channeling her mentor's terrifying mildness. "You think that we didn't consider that you people would come and try to steal what is ours? You were wrong."

His eyes wild, he swallowed. Megan thought that she could almost read him like a book as he desperately tried to assert authority into his voice.

"The name is Kellers, Agent David Kellers. Just to make things really clear to you people, you are all under arrest."

Megan considered him for a moment and rolled her eyes, resting her right hand on her holstered Glock.

Agent Kellers trembled ever so slightly. "No respect. That is the problem with you God-and-Guns types. All you people ever think of are yourselves. You could care less about anyone else."

"Do save your breath, Agent Kellers. It is quite simple really, you can believe in your socialist, collective salvation, all you like, but I suggest that it is quite past the time that your masters got it through their arrogant heads, that millions of Americans aren't interested. Maybe it is time that we all just get a divorce so that people like you can go live in your fairy land. No wait, that doesn't work for you, does it, because your fairy kingdom just collapsed, and you need someone to enslave, so that you can find a way to get around the economics."

She smiled an almost cordial smile. "Well, that was such a nice chat. Won't you excuse me? I fear that I am quite busy." She turned her back on him again and walked over to check on her mom.

"How is it coming, Mom?"

"I think it will be touch and go for him. He lost more blood than I care for, but I did my best for him."

"I know, Mamma. Let's get him behind the wall. We don't want him to get hit again, if they get stupid."

Her mother nodded. "OK, but try not to let his head move. I don't want him tearing out my sutures. We can drag him by the shoulders but I need you to support his head."

"Sure, Mom." The two women grasped his arms and lifted him partially, as they struggled to drag him behind the pony wall. Megan was able to more or less position herself behind him, to support his head with her right forearm, while her mother, on his left side, pulled him behind the cover of the pony wall.

"Where do you want him?"

"Down towards my bedroom will be fine, Megan."

Struggling with his weight, Megan and her mom finally got him to safety. Giving her a quick smile, her mom went to get a blanket and pillow.

Taking a breath, she looked up to see Uncle Jerry setting ammunition boxes and a rifle next to Russell. Handing her the pistol grip Mossberg, he looked gravely into her eyes. "Here Meg, I will do what I can, but you know this is not looking good. This kind of thing never goes well. Even with them initiating things, it will be a nightmare legally."

Megan smiled at him. "All we can do is our best. They will probably figure out how to cut power, but it's not hot outside, and we have more than enough food and water. The Cistern tanks from Daddy's rainwater harvesting set up are in here with us, and we have months of food, so we will just see what happens."

Agent Kellers smirked. "You won't need two days of food, much less months. Give yourselves up now, and I can promise you will not be killed."

Megan rolled her eyes. "I am afraid, Agent Kellers that I just don't..."

"Sis, it is them," Annie interrupted. "They're finally answering."

Megan nodded and looked at her uncle. "Can you keep an eye out for me, so I can talk to them?" Stepping over to her sister, she took the earpiece and mike from her sister. "Annie, if he says even one word, duct tape his mouth shut. I have grown weary of listening to him, I'm afraid." Megan saw that Annie's eyes flared, but she picked up the roll of duct tape from their little pile of supplies, and moved over to do as she asked, if needed.

Uncle Jerry smiled supportively. "Don't under estimate them Meg. Just because they are arrogant does not make them stupid, and they are trained."

Megan nodded and smiled.

"This is Megan Danvers. With whom am I speaking?"

"Megan, it is nice to meet you. I am Agent Rodney Kelso. I believe you know my colleague, Agent Ricks. You are the young woman that we have been looking for the past few weeks. You and Mr. Regan are clearly very capable. I am guessing that he is why I am going to have to explain the destruction of a government vehicle."

"Look Agent Kelso, you are illegally trespassing on Danvers property. You have taken violent action against us, and you are violating our civil rights. We are only doing what we have to do, to defend our constitutional rights. You have a wounded man in here and his partner is being detained for his own safety until we can sort all of this out."

"I see. Can I speak to Agent Marchant, to get his update then? I am hoping that we can see what we can do to work things out from there."

"I am afraid that your Agent Marchant is the one who is wounded. My mom sedated him. She is an RN and will do her best for him. Besides, my family is innocent of any wrong doing, and you know it. I am more interested in talking about you getting federal agents off of my property. Until DC starts following the law again you have no authority here."

"Ms. Danvers, assault of a federal agent is a very serious matter, and I am afraid that your state representatives have deluded you. States do not have the legal right to separate. That is well settled law. Can I speak with Mr. Regan perhaps? I really want to come to some accommodation before anyone else gets hurt. The situation in Killeen is bad enough. I don't want to see this get any worse. "

"I am afraid not, Agent Kelso, but Matt is standing right here. We will talk it over, and I will call you back in a little while."

"Good, that will be fine then. There is one other thing, however. I really do need to speak with Agent Kellers, if Agent Marchant is unconscious."

"I am very sorry, but I don't think that I need him telling you everything he has heard us talk about in here. Send me an email, and I will get you some pictures, so you know your people are ok. In exchange, you will leave the power on, so that my mother can see to care for your wounded man. Have we an arrangement, Agent Kelso?"

"We do Miss Danvers. Incidentally, I should tell you, however, that I have listened to hours of your former employer's surveillance tapes. I am afraid that his considerable talents of manipulation will not be as useful on me. Please do get back in touch soon, won't you?"

Megan exhaled loudly, suddenly feeling the strain that had landed on her shoulders over the past hour or so. She really wanted to go into her bedroom and cry. She realized that this fed was not to be under estimated. Closing her eyes, she knew things would disintegrate when she and her boss talked things through a month ago, but the idea that her parents were being victimized was literally making her nauseous.

Russell looked up at her. "You are doing great, Meg. I think you have this handled, I really do, but I have an idea if you are interested."

Renewing her grip on her emotions, she looked down at her brother-in-law. "What Russ?"

"The internet! If it's true that we can still get email, that they haven't cut us off yet, let's send out what is happening here to everybody. Matt said we really need the media. We should get them interested. This has got to be better than a stupid car chase, right?"

Megan smiled broadly. "You know what? For a dumb Okie, you are pretty smart. Write out what happened, but let Uncle Jerry take a look, before you send it. While you are at it, take some pictures of our guests so that we can show we are taking good care of them."

Russell smiled broadly. "Sure Megan."

Suddenly with nothing to do, Megan sat down across from her sister. Annie's eyes were red and puffy. She looked pale and miserable. "This sort of sucks doesn't it?"

Annie nodded her assent. "I just threw up again. I am just so worried about the baby. They are probably going to kill us all, like the guy said, and if they don't, we will still end up in jail. Can you imagine being pregnant in jail?"

Megan moved from across the little hallway, moving beside her baby sister leaning against the pony wall. "I don't know what is going to happen, but you are the one that has always had faith in impossible situations. Look at your husband there. He has been amazing. Matt is watching over us, and we are going to get our story out. I know that doesn't seem like much, but like mom said, we just have to hope for the best, and leave it to God."

Megan put her arms around her baby sister and hugged her close. "I love you." She smiled at her sister's trembling face when Russell interrupted.

"Holy Crap! This is turning into a real war guys. The Blaze is reporting that a bunch of people at Fort Hood were killed! The feds are denying it, but the headline is unbelievable."

Killeen Massacre, Hundreds killed in Federal Attack!

Megan felt like someone had just slugged her. "Well don't keep it to yourself. Damn it Russ, what are they saying?"

"Give me a second." The group was on pins and needles, including Agent Kellers. Russell scanned down the page on his laptop as the others stared at him.

Megan noticed him grimace as he read.

"Agents from the Departments of Homeland Security (DHS) and Alcohol Tobacco and Fire Arms, (ATF), supported by an unidentified special military taskforce, reporting directly to the

Executive Branch, reported that federal military forces have begun operations to contain rogue military units stationed in Fort Hood, Texas. Special contributor Eric Daning on the ground in Killeen reports that approximately six to eight fighter aircraft flew in from the East at approximately 8:00 AM, CST this morning, dropping munitions on the base which is the home of both the 4th Armored Division and the famous First Cavalry Division."

Megan glared at the stunned look on Agent Keller's face as her own shocked reply escaped her lips. "Oh my God, you have got to be kidding me."

Agent Keller's expression turned immediately to one of indignation. "Well, I hope you are happy. Look at what you started."

Megan was on her feet before she even realized it. "Look what we started! The idiots in DC and New York are the ones that caused all of this. I know, because I am guilty of ignoring what was right too. Now, I suggest you shut your mouth, or you are going to see what my bad side feels like. It seems to me that it is your socialist tyrant buddies that are raising the stakes."

Keller stared sullenly at her but did not retort further.

Russell looked at her to see if she was done.

"Sorry Russell. Go on."

"Right." He cleared his throat and continued. "Sources speaking on the condition of anonymity have confirmed that initially the number of attacking aircraft was much higher, with up to two dozen aircraft initially being tracked on radar, but the federal air operation appeared to fall apart as many of the attacking aircraft diverted from their squad mates and began landing at various locations around the state of Texas just prior to the attack.

Annie smiled. "So it isn't one sided then. Some of our guys are going to join us or at least stay out of it."

Russell, now frustrated, exhaled loudly. "Do you guys want me to read this or not?"

"I'm sorry, Russ. Nobody will say anything else."

Russell sighed, but continued reading. "Additionally, sources confirmed that two aircraft were shot down by ground forces protecting Fort Hood. When asked about the apparent splintering of the military at all levels, and the use of special teams, bypassing the traditional chain of command, the White House declined to comment.

In a related ongoing story, federal spokesperson Wendy Scott noted an apparent massacre taking place in Killeen, Texas, a town located next to the post at Fort Hood. She said the terrible events were apparently an unrelated event, caused by activist associated with a group of Solidarity protestors along with members of The American Brothers of Islam. Early reports indicate that approximately three-hundred people, who were protesting the military, began rioting following a police shooting of one of their members.

"The altercation began after the group was confronted by a group of local residents. The friction quickly blossomed into a complete breakdown of civil authority after a resident shot and killed a protestor who was attacking one of the residents. Police officers present were quickly overwhelmed, as several hundred protesters rushed the main gate. The well-armed protesters began shooting indiscriminately killing dozens of civilians. Amongst the casualties was CNN Reporter, Janice Tate of Dallas, Texas. According to witnesses, both police and military security officials defending the post then opened fired on the protesters."

Russell continued reading, but shook his head in disbelief as he did so.

"Remaining attackers were quickly repelled by military reinforcements from the base. The tragedy occurred when the protestors turned their wrath on defenseless civilians in the nearby town of Killeen Texas."

Megan could see that her mother fought back tears as Russell read the post.

Russell just sat there, with a blank look on his face when Annie broke the silence. "Oh my God! They just said that Janice Tate from CNN was killed. Isn't that who Katie was partnered with?"

With tears in her eyes, her mother nodded in confirmation. "Yes, she was. Poor Kate."

Annie looked down, her face a mask of shock and disbelief. "I guess that we aren't the only ones with problems. I just can't believe that the federal government would do this to us."

Looking over at her uncle, she caught his eye. "Are they doing anything?"

"Not that I can see, Sweetheart. You should probably check in with Matt though. There has to be hundreds of people out there, including some media trucks."

Feeling exhausted by the tension, she reached to take the field phone's handset from Annie when her sister held up a finger to stop her. "Sis, it's Agent Kelso again."

"Tell him to wait, and give me the phone."

"Matt, are you there? They are calling again. What are you seeing? What do you want me to do?"

"Hey, Babe, just breathe. You are doing just fine. There is a real crowd starting to gather out here. Looks like the Sheriff has his hands full with crowd control, just down the hill, but don't let on that you know that, unless you can get it from a source other than me. We don't want to give them any clues about my vantage point. The Feds are staying close to their command post. They are really undermanned, so I doubt that they will try anything for a while. I am betting that the FBI has their hands full all over the place. They will likely try to bluff us into feeling helpless."

Megan's eyes darted over to Kellers. His eyes shifted down and to the right. Tilting her head, she considered him carefully.

"Just a moment, Matt, there is something I have to do." Deciding that Kellers was planning something, she acted. Grabbing the duct tape from atop the pony wall where her sister had laid it a few minutes earlier, Megan tore off a strip, and smiling sweetly, she motioned to Annie for some help. With her sister's help, she applied the tape across the Keller's mouth.

Returning to the field phone, she closed her eyes to focus on what Matt would say.

"OK, so I will keep stalling them then, right? Russell just put out our message on Facebook and sent it as a news tip to the Blaze. I would guess that the media types will jump all over it, so I am thinking that we are getting our side of the story out there."

"You got it, Babe. Just keep up the tweets or whatever you guys are doing."

She smiled at his easy going way, and signed off. "Love you. Talk to you in a while."

"I love you too, Meg."

Handing the phone back to her sister, she walked over to Kellers, tearing off another strip of tape. For good measure she taped over the man's cuffed hands, binding them even tighter together. She didn't want any surprises. There were going to be enough as it was; she was sure.

Chapter 42
With a Whimper, Dies Power

Confused and disoriented, Catherine's eyes fluttered open to see a spinning ceiling fan. Blinking, she rolled to her right to see that Sadie wasn't there. It was then she realized that she smelled spaghetti or something very similar to it. As she lay there gathering her wits, she began ticking off the things she should do. First on the list was to check in with the group to make sure everything was ready for tomorrow's rally supporting Governor Miller. That thought, colliding with the smell of spaghetti instead of the freeze dried ham and powdered eggs they had been eating, made her heart jump, awakening her fully. She reached over to grab her cell phone to see what time it was. Looking at it, it read: 1:30 which meant she had been asleep for like eleven hours. Swinging her legs out of bed, she grabbed her robe and headed for the kitchen.

Stepping into the little dining room, Catherine saw Sadie planted in front of the television in the adjoining parlor. "Hey, why didn't you wake me?"

"Because you needed the rest, and everything for tomorrow is under control. I was about to come get you, though. Things in the news are not looking very good. There is fighting at Fort Hood. The isolated incidents, posturing, and threats we saw on Thursday have turned into a full blown conflict.

Catherine plopped down heavily beside Sadie and stared at the images of Military Humvees moving past the cameras, with soldiers manning SAW Automatic weapons standing in the back. "My God, this is going to be a mess. What is the Governor saying?"

Sadie shook her head, indicating she didn't know. "I just got up a little less than an hour ago, and I was in the kitchen until just now. All I know, so far, is there was some sort of massacre of average citizens yesterday by a large group of protesters in Killeen. General Harrington sent MPs to assist the cops there. They are reporting that the President ordered airstrikes on Fort Hood, but apparently most of the pilots either refused, or simply landed their planes at various airports here in Texas. There is random fighting all over the place. Cops, soldiers and citizens everywhere are splitting into different camps based on world-view. They even said that some military guys on the ground shot down some of the planes that were doing the air strikes."

Catherine felt numb. She felt like she was watching a movie, but she knew that wasn't true. It was all too real, and Americans were killing each other. "Oh my God, this is the last thing we need. The country is broken, and all the bastards in Washington can think to do is to try to hang on to their power?"

As they watched, the image switched from a shot of military forces surrounding the Pentagon, back to Fox News reporter, Mitch Barnett, in Texas, who was putting a microphone in front of a very serious looking Governor Dorie Miller.

"Governor, the Supreme Court has issued an injunction, reaffirming that states do not have the authority to disregard federal mandates. Doesn't that invalidate your administration's position that Texas is acting legally?"

Governor Miller stopped abruptly on his way to his waiting aircraft, and turned on the reporter. Giving the camera a frank look, he responded. "Mitch, first off, you are well aware the Supreme Court also stated unequivocally that the actions taken by the President in disregarding the Constitution, are also illegal. There isn't one thing the federal government has done in this crisis that is constitutional. I'm sorry, but there comes a time when a leader must stand up for what's right. Texans are demanding to be represented. Secondly, I took an oath to defend the Constitution of the United States, and to do what is best for the people of Texas. Giving away our land to foreigners, and selling our citizens out, to what amounts to indentured servitude is not going to happen under my watch."

Catherine noticed the dismay on the reporter's face as he countered the Governor.

"But Governor, how can you claim to uphold the Constitution, while disregarding the fact that the federal government is sovereign over the states?"

"Mitch, this isn't an academic debate. People are dying, and Texans will never yield to an international body. Not one of the President's committees or emergency powers were derived constitutionally, so the best we can do is ignore them. If the President thinks he can pressure us into giving up our freedom by flooding the state with federal agents to harass our citizens, then he is sadly mistaken. Furthermore, his actions are blatantly in violation of the law."

"Does that mean that you intend to wage a civil war, Governor?"

"The state of Texas has not taken any such action. We are simply ignoring illegal mandates and federal overreach. The President can either retract his unconstitutional mandates and work honestly to solve the issues before us or we are at a standstill. I might add, that those issues were caused by Washington DC in the first place. Failing the President's recognition of our constitutional rights, Texans will do what we must to defend the rule of law and our freedom. Now, if you will excuse me, I have work to do. Good day, Mr. Barnett."

Catherine felt Sadie's hand cover hers. She turned to look at her partner.

Sadie sighed. "Living in interesting times is really way overrated."

"You can say that again, Sadie. I hope we have a good crowd tomorrow. The Governor needs us to back him. The world needs to see that Texans are in this for the duration."

"We will, Catherine. People know what's at stake. I just wish Washington would worry more about getting our guys home from other countries and caring for people, instead of selling us out and regulating everything." She smiled and patted her thigh. "Let me go finish up with lunch. You just sit there and wake up."

Catherine leaned in and kissed her, as she got up. "I love you, you know."

"I know." She headed for the kitchen and Catherine turned back to the television, switching to channel four, to see the local news. It was, of course, another government sponsored commercial about fuel rationing. She quickly muted it as Maggie walked over demanding attention. Catherine smiled at the dog, as she scratched her head. It occurred to her that regardless of how bad things got, Maggie was always there for her. The boxer always warmed her heart. Turning her attention back to the television, she decided she would watch later. As her index finger sought out the power button, she froze, as an image of a stand-off flashed on the screen. The stand-off was at her parent's home in Mineral Wells. The screen reached out and clenched her heart with fingers of steel as federal agents were moving back and forth in combat gear, as if preparing for an assault.

Wracked with fear and guilt, she sat in shock for almost thirty seconds before scrambling for her phone on the coffee table. Terrified, she fumbled with the phone, tapping the screen to reach out for them.

The number rang once and the ringing was replaced with a simple message.

"This number is currently out of order. Please check the number you are dialing or try back later."

"Shit!" Catherine immediately began dialing the numbers of her mother, her sisters and Russ, each of them giving her the same result, as she watched the large crowd being held back by the sheriff and his deputies. The federal agent being interviewed explained to the Channel Four reporter that the family was sought for numerous violations of federal law and for the attempted murder of an FBI agent.

Looking through the cutout between the kitchen and the dining room, Catherine saw her distress reflected on Sadie's face as she rushed into the front room. Catherine looked up at her, terror gripping her heart as her phone rang. Sadie sat next to her as she grasped the phone.

"Hello!"

"Kate, Ginny and I just saw what is going on in Mineral Wells. What can I do?"

"Oh, I don't know! How about getting my parents the hell out of there! My God, Drake, the bastards are going after my parents. Why them? If they want to harass me so badly, there has to be an easier way."

"Hang on a second, Kate. You're assuming it is about you. Your dad is pretty connected. Maybe they're trying to get to our representatives."

Dammit, Drake, there is no way they tried to kill anyone unless it was self-defense. This is really it! The bastards are not leaving anyone any room to work things out."

"I know, Kate, I know. Let me see what I can find out. If I hear anything I'll call you back."

"I appreciate it, Drake. Thank you.

Catherine watched, with Sadie at her side, for approximately fifteen minutes when the phone rang again.

"Hello."

"Catherine Danvers? This is Ted Knight, I am with CNN. Janice Tate was a friend of mine. I understand you are the daughter of Robert and Beth Danvers. Can you give me your reaction to what is taking place at your parent's ranch? We understand your parents are Tea Party activists, and are known for holding anti-government sentiments."

"Are you insane? My family is being harassed by the FBI and you want my opinion? My parents are the most upstanding people I know. I resent the implication that believing in the rule of law and the Constitution somehow makes a person suspect."

"Ms. Danvers, we are going to air a profile of your family. You can participate in this by giving us an interview, or we can go with what we learn on our own. Don't you want to have some input?"

"How about you go screw yourself, you rat-bastard, inbred, dim witted, little weasel! People like you, are so corrupt, you wouldn't know anything about getting a news story right! Don't call here again."

Her blood boiling, Catherine stabbed at the end call icon furiously. The phone rang again, before she could even lay it on the sofa table. Looking at Sadie, she realized this was not going to stop.

Sadie shrugged. "Just turn it off, Honey. I'll call Drake and let him know what's going on. He can call on my phone, to get ahold of us."

"Thanks, Sadie. I appreciate it. I just need to see what they're saying."

Turning her attention back to the television, the screen switched from her family's home to the reporter, standing on the road to the house, just below the rise where the FBI and Sheriff's department deputies were doing their best to deal with what had to be thousands of people. Cars were parked up and down the road from the highway, on both sides of the road. People were everywhere. Her friends and neighbors were witnessing this just as she was.

The young reporter, his face serious, continued his overview. "As reported earlier, the standoff began yesterday afternoon, and escalated into an armed conflict. The controversy stemmed from the Danvers family refusing to comply with EPA Regulations affecting their use of the property. Despite being given repeated opportunities to rectify the issue, the Danvers family simply refused to acknowledge their legal deficiencies." His countenance became one of disappointment and dismay as he continued. "Now, having recklessly wounded an FBI agent, the family has escalated the matter. Agents here have indicated they will absolutely bring these people to justice. I just spoke with Senior Agent-In-Charge, Rodney Kelso, who confirmed that the FBI was able to successfully negotiate the release of their wounded agent. Agent Bill Marchant will be released by the hostage takers, once their version of events has been broadcast. Inexplicably, in addition to Agent Marchant, four additional agents were apparently captured outside the Danvers compound last night. It is unclear how this could happen, but it seems the Danvers family still have multiple hostages."

"Sadie, can you get on the internet to find out what my family had to say? Try WBAP or Channel Four's web site."

"Of course, Honey. I will be right back."

Watching, with her heart already in her throat, she realized the agents gathered were no longer just milling about the area. It was clear that they were now forming up into a group. As an armored personnel carrier appeared at the edge of the screen, coming up the road from the highway, it became obvious that something was happening. Her heart felt as if it had suddenly stopped beating all together. The dark clad figures, in full combat gear, were assembling around the tracked vehicle.

"Sadie!"

Staring in horror at the images, she screamed at the television. "My God, I think they are going to murder my family! Dear God, help us!"

Sadie rushed back into the room. Catherine felt herself being drawn into her partner's arms, as the images continued to play across her screen. She saw the agent who had just addressed the reporters walk over to the darkly clad figures, giving them some sort of speech. He then returned to the table they had set up as a communications station, as the dark figures behind the APC checked their weapons.

Heart broken and unable to even breathe well, Catherine felt the tears begin to streak down her face as the conversation in the communications tent drug on for several minutes. "My God, Sadie, how can this be happening?"

"I know, Honey. Just pray. It's all that we can do."

The screen showed the agent throw something in exasperation. He then turned towards the waiting dark figures and gave a hand signal. A puff of smoke rose from the vehicle's exhaust and it began to creep forward, toward the front of her childhood home.

Crying desperately now, she could hardly see what was happening. She could hear the reporter saying something about the abuse of federal power, when she felt Sadie shaking her.

"Honey! Catherine, look. Look at the crowd! The bystanders are rushing in on the Feds!"

Catherine looked up, blinking and wiping at her eyes to clear her vision. It was true. What must have been over a thousand people were rushing past the Sheriff and his people. In minutes the dark figures in combat gear were overwhelmed. One agent raised his assault rifle to a firing position but was suddenly thrown violently back from the apparent impact of a bullet.

Catherine held her breath as her neighbors and people from town continued rushing past the FBI men. She noticed one of the deputies begin to level his pistol at one of the men running past him, when Sheriff Percy grabbed his arm, shaking his head. Speaking into his shoulder mike, he ran over to the communications tent. Civilians were streaming in all directions, but most now were moving towards the house.

Within minutes, the front of the house was completely enveloped. Average people from every walk of life surrounding it, and linking arms, as others wrestled with the darkly clad agents. Her heart jumping, almost painfully, she recognized one of Megan's friends, Wendy Everett, nervously standing with a little girl beside what must be her husband. The man stepped forward, pulling a Bible from his coat and began to read. Catherine realized she wished desperately to know what he was saying. Whatever it was, the effect on her neighbors was profound, and it was immediate. As a group, every man, woman, and child seemed to lift their heads as one, offering only defiance to the dark clad men. Suddenly, they no longer appeared to be nervous,

Stunned, Catherine and Sadie both gasped when the Sheriff drew his pistol and aimed it directly at the agent in charge. Townspeople had now opened the back hatch of the APC and were herding the FBI men into a small depression near the road to the Danvers home, prodding them along with their own weapons.

The Sheriff handed off the agent in charge to one of his men, and walked calmly over to the reporter. The stunned man just stood there, his mouth agape as the camera rolled.

"My name is Sheriff Percy. I am the chief law enforcement officer for Palo Pinto County, Texas. As you may have noticed, I have just arrested federal agents who, in my estimation were illegally attacking a family without cause. Until such time as I am instructed to do otherwise by Governor Miller, or his designate, I intend to hold these men in custody pending further instructions. I have known this family my entire life. They are in no way, criminals. As you can see, the people here are simply not going to submit to federal overreach any longer." The sheriff reached up to reposition his baseball cap and continued. "Well, that's it, Boys. I have nothing further to say on the matter at this time, and I am going to ask you to leave these folks be." Nodding courteously at the reporter, he picked up the radio that the lead agent had been using and depressed the talk button.

"Beth, Megan, Jerry, this is Sheriff Percy. I can't promise what will happen, but whatever comes, the community is behind you all the way. We just arrested the Federals bothering you. I would like to come in and take custody of your other prisoners if that is ok with you all."

Catherine leaned against Sadie and closed her eyes.

&

"Crap! No way it was already morning. The soothing harp music on her iPhone alarm was persistent. Catherine heard Sadie gasp, followed by an expected complaint.

"Damn it, I just want to sleep."

Catherine chuckled softly. "I don't know who's worse at getting out of bed in the morning, you or me." She reached out for her iPhone and looked at the time. The screen read 5:30 in the morning. Lying there, flat on her back, she blinked away the sleep. Her partner sat up in bed, but was doing much the same thing. A minute or two passed, when Sadie swung her feet out to find the floor, as Catherine too, got to her feet.

"You go first, Sadie. I'll see about coffee, and take care of Maggie." As Catherine headed towards her bedroom door, her eyes followed Sadie's shapely figure as she stumbled towards the bathroom. Smiling, she decided nobody could help but admire the way she looked in silky blue tap pants and a cotton tank top.

Clicking on the television, she did not stop to see what it had to offer. As always, Maggie was on her heels the moment she emerged from her bedroom.

"I know, Baby, I've got you covered." She patted the boxer's head and made her way to the back door. She loved to watch how Maggie was so happy and unaware of the issues of the day. A little consistency was good, she thought.

Moving back towards the little kitchen, Catherine began the process of making their usual powdered eggs and reconstituting a scoop of freeze dried ham for their breakfast. She thought again how grateful she was to have saved more coffee than she could use. Some people were out already, and she found it to be a great barter item.

As she robotically went through her morning routine, she checked off what she needed to do. As of her call with Dennis last night, it sounded like things were pretty quiet at Dallas City Hall. There was security everywhere and the media trucks were already set up, so Dennis took the opportunity to chat with some of the media support guys. Good for him. It was always good to build relationships. Realizing the eggs were about done, she sprinkled a hand full of cheese across the top, and dished them onto two plates as Sadie sat down at their little table.

Catherine brought in their meal, setting the plates down just as her phone rang. Sadie smiled at her partner. "Do you want me to answer it?"

"That would be great Sadie, thank you."

"Hello."

Sadie's expression turned pensive, and she nodded. "I understand. Just a moment."

Retrieving the rest of their breakfast from the kitchen, Catherine gave Sadie a questioning look.

"Who is it?"

Sadie covered the speaker with her hand. "It's Dennis. Our guys are early." Uncovering the mouthpiece, she continued. "Dennis, here is Kate now."

Catherine smiled her thanks and took the phone from her partner.

"Hello."

"Hi Kate, looks like some of our guys are early risers. One of our buses just showed up ahead of schedule. There is a good crowd down here already, so I think we should make quite an impression on the media types." Catherine smiled at Sadie as she picked up a piece of toast. "Cool, I really appreciate you guys hanging out overnight, and it was a great idea to chat up some of the media techs, by the way."

"Um, Kate, I don't quite know how to tell you this, but we were talking about the massacre at Fort Hood last night. The guys I was with said that a CNN reporter was killed by the protestors when they went nuts in Killeen. I am really sorry, Kate, but that reporter was Janice. I know she was your friend, and I don't know if you had heard, so I felt I had to check."

The moment of stunned silence turned into two before Catherine responded, her voice barely above a whisper. "Thank you for telling me, Dennis. I didn't know." Catherine closed her eyes against the pain. "I will get there as soon as I can."

Dennis started to reply, but Catherine's hand shaking, she put down the phone once again forced to deal with another loss and the emotional pain that accompanied it.

Sadie looked questioningly about what had just happened, concern and fear consuming her expression.

Catherine paused and picked up a piece of toast, thinking that life no longer seemed real. Of all people, Janice was the last person to end up like that. They had gone their separate ways weeks ago, but still, she could feel tears tracing a path down her face. Clamping down hard on her emotions, she replied to her partner's unasked question.

"Dennis said Janice was killed yesterday. She was in Killeen. She was always so courageous when it came to getting a story. She never did understand the real world. She just couldn't see things as they are."

"Catherine felt Sadie's hand encompass hers, as her partner exhaled. "I'm so very sorry, Honey. If there is anything I can do..."

Catherine stopped her with a hand gesture. “Not now love. I just can’t let myself dwell on it now. Is it ok if I just repress?”

“Whatever you want, Catherine. I just want to take care of you.”

Catherine nodded. “Thank you.” I love you for that. Let’s just get moving before I fall apart. We need to get up there I think.”

“Sure, Honey, just eat your breakfast and we are out of here.”

“You are really bossy, you know it?”

Sadie smiled gently, and nodded that she did, as Catherine quickly cleaned up her plate.

As she rose to take their dishes to the kitchen, she continued. “Please keep emphasizing that we must remain passive, regardless of any harassment from the feds. We have to be MLK today. Please help me emphasize that, ok? Now that the people of Mineral Wells have backed the feds down, I suspect they will be out in force today.”

“We will, Kate. Don’t worry. You, Dennis, and Drake are doing a great job.”

Catherine smiled weakly at her partner and shrugged. “I am sure things will hit me at some point, but for now, we need to get to the church. Some of our guys were early enough that one of our busses already left.”

“Alright, Catherine, but know you are going to have to grieve, whether you like it or not. It’s just the way human beings are wired.”

Catherine wiped at her eyes with her sleeve and took a deep breath. “If you can get our stuff together, I would appreciate it. I will go get my shower, so we can get out of here.”

“OK, Sweetie, I love you. When we get back this afternoon though I want you to take some time to think about Janice, and maybe try your folks again.”

“Sure Sadie, I will. Thanks for keeping after me about taking care of myself.” She smiled weakly and headed for the bathroom. “I just hope nobody gets killed today.”

Chapter 43
Phoenix Ascension

Sitting on one of the lawn chairs the team brought with them, Catherine was stunned at the turnout she was seeing for Governor Miller's speech. Again, she was grateful for her uncle's contacts with the Governor's team and for Dennis and Chase's contacts from last night. Governor Miller's press advisor came over almost as soon as she stepped off the bus from Cedar Hill, to make sure that her group had a great location. The Governor was to be positioned just south of the reflecting pool, facing north-east, towards the biggest part of the mall area, where most of the crowd was already standing.

Looking at her phone for the time, she realized they still had another twenty five minutes or so to wait before things got underway. Governor Miller would be standing right in front of her people with the Dallas City Hall building to their right, and the reflecting pool to their left. She wished Sadie was with her for this, but she knew her helping out in the medical tent was obviously the best use of her skills.

As she scanned the sea of faces, she noticed there were cameras everywhere on the Mall. Fox News and CNN, she noticed, had set up over by the flag poles across the reflecting pool from her people. The other outlets were also there, poised between the flag poles and the green space, north of the plaza. She thought this was definitely going to be a day to remember. Media trucks were parked up and down Young Street. She smiled at the thought that the feds were going to hate Texas getting this kind of coverage.

Catherine hated the reasons that brought everyone here, but she decided she felt useful, and for once in her life, people needed her, and they didn't really care if she didn't fit their preconceptions.

It occurred to her that she felt guilty because, regardless of all of the struggle and uncertainty, she was content for the first time in her adult life. Catherine spotted Drake kissing Ginny who was manning a table with Tea Party literature on the other side of the reflecting pool. She lifted a hand to wave at her friends. Ginny smiled and waved back. Catherine leaned down and reached into her little red six-pack cooler to grab her bottle of cold water and watched the crowd. Moments later Drake walked up.

"Hey, Kate, is this crowd off the hook or what? I was just talking to a good friend of mine with the Dallas PD. He said they still have people flowing into the downtown area. They already have people standing around in pretty much every open space near city hall. They are calling in extra officers now to deal with all of this."

Looking across the plaza, she could see reporters moving through the crowd. "It will be interesting to see how all of this gets portrayed. They cannot miss how many people are coming out in support of the governor."

"True enough, Kate, true enough." Hearing some movement on his right, she followed Drake's gaze as he looked back towards the City Hall building. An attractive young woman with blonde hair, up in a bun, and dressed in a navy blue business suit exited the City Hall building and made her way to the podium. Trailing her were a handful of military officers.

Catherine got up from her lawn chair to see better, as Drake leaned in to comment.

"Not sure about all of those guys, but the general officer with the grey hair, just behind the woman is John Barker, the Texas Adjutant General. He is a Major General, and commands all National Guard forces in the state of Texas."

"Really, thanks Drake. He looks like a serious guy. Did your folks ever find out if all of his people will support the governor?"

Drake's face became serious. "As of Wednesday, all the senior leaders but two are with us. Those who declined were relieved and replaced by their XO's. At the lower levels it's more chaotic, but commanders are pretty much letting anyone go who doesn't feel what we're doing is right. It is too early to tell for sure, but I think we are keeping like two thirds or more of those currently serving. On top of that, apparently National Guard recruiters are being inundated with people wanting to sign up. Also, for what it's worth, a lot of those leaving now were just wanting out regardless and are taking the opportunity to not get involved either way."

Kate nodded. "Well, I guess we will hear what he has to say soon enough."

As the woman reached the podium, she smiled confidently at the crowd before her.

"Ladies and gentlemen, my name is Dana Limon. I am Governor Miller's media coordinator. On behalf of Governor Miller and his staff, I would like to thank you all so very much for coming out today. The Governor will be out shortly." She scanned the crowd and smiled, shaking her head to acknowledge the applause that was already washing over the crowd.

"We are deeply appreciative, and we are humbled by the amazing turnout that Texans around the state have given us in these extraordinarily difficult times. As I am sure you all are aware, we have been visiting cities and towns around the state, explaining in person, to citizens what is happening and what your elected representatives are doing to uphold our sacred duty to the citizens of this great state. Times like these are challenging, but Texans are a resilient and hearty people and...." The applause from the crowd hit Catherine like a tidal wave.

After several minutes the blonde woman resumed. "Thank you all, really. Looking out at your banners, posters, and the United States flags, I can see already that you understand clearly the Governor's message today. I must say we are grateful for that understanding, so I will get right to what will happen next. We will soon play the National Anthem after which Governor Dorie Miller will come out. The Governor will present his speech and answer a few questions. Again, God bless you all. God bless Texas, and May God bless the United States of America. With his help this nation will, once again, find its way back to greatness."

As the woman stepped back, Catherine looked around at the crowd to see if she could gauge the mood of the people present. Glancing at Drake, she could see he too seemed to have the same idea, as his eyes darted from the spectators milling around the reflecting pool to the media types standing near their impromptu sets with their producers and technicians. Following his gaze, Catherine decided it was obvious the media were clearly nervous.

Pointing at the media trucks she shook her head with dismay. "Are you picking up on the anxious vibe from those guys?"

Drake tilted his head, considering what he was seeing. "Actually, I think you are right. They are definitely wigging about something, aren't they?"

"Yep, that's what it looks like to me. What do you think that's about?"

"I have no idea Kate, but keep your eyes open."

Catherine nodded. A little on edge now, she continued to scan the crowd, a feeling of dread creeping more and more into her thoughts, as the minutes passed.

Noticing people beginning to stir near the podium, she saw the governor's media consultant had returned to the microphone. The soldiers came to attention, and the woman looked out over the crowd.

"Ladies and gentlemen, please rise for the National Anthem."

Catherine heard the familiar notes floating majestically out over the loud speakers. Already standing, her hand went to her heart as the music washed over the crowd infusing everyone in sight with pride as it played.

Oh, say can you see, by the dawn's early light
What so proudly we hailed at the twilight's last gleaming?
Whose broad stripes and bright stars, through the perilous fight,
O'er the ramparts we watched, were so gallantly streaming,
And the rocket's red glare, the bombs bursting in air,
Gave proof through the night that our flag was still there.
Oh, say does that Star - Spangled Banner yet wave
O'er the land of the free and the home of the brave.

As the lilting strains of the song died away and the roar of the cheering crowd increased in volume and tempo, Governor Miller exited the building surrounded by Texas State Troopers. As he reached the podium, he smiled and waved, then waved again. The applause impacted Catherine's ears like thunder, as whistles and cheers continued for several minutes. The citizens gathered on the plaza seemed unwilling to stop.

Catherine watched as Governor Miller approached the podium. The brilliance of his signature smile contrasting starkly with his warm dark skin, along with his distinguished manners was captivating. Somehow the man made her feel better, and he had yet to say a word. She thought the man simply projected confidence to all by his presence. His record as a Marine Corps officer, leading men in combat in both Iraq and Afghanistan, was more than impressive, and his charisma was undeniable. Grasping the podium with gusto, his security detachment fanned out in a loose semicircle around him, with Dallas City hall to their backs and the reflecting pool on the front to their left.

"Thank you, Cindy. Again, thank you all for coming out today. I know we're all challenged these days, but I cannot help but marvel at the beautiful day the Lord has given us for this conversation." Again the crowd erupted in cheers. Governor Miller raised his hands, quieting them down after several seconds. "Ladies and gentlemen, although it seems like an eternity ago, it was only last week that the President of the United States addressed this nation about the grave financial crisis in which we find ourselves. It has only been a little over one week, or if you like, eleven days. I wish I could stand before you all with some easy and painless answer to the troubles we all face, but I am not here today with any such message.

As the President said in his speech, the entire world has experienced an unprecedented financial challenge. We all know this to be true. What seems to be lost in all of the reporting , however, is not only why, and who is to blame, but how is it that the answers to this profound crisis are, amazingly, already all thought out and ready to be implemented. The President said he thanked the leaders from around the world for their willingness to help resolve the issues confronting us all. Furthermore, he informed us world governments had been working for years to develop how nations would manage just such a crisis." As he paused to let his words sink in, Catherine looked over to see Drake, already shaking his head in dismay.

"The President said he regretted our constitutionally guaranteed rights and liberties would, by necessity, have to be temporarily set aside."

Governor Miller's hand slammed with a crack on the podium, the microphone broadcasting the gesture throughout the plaza, and Catherine's heart jumped. "I say, No! There isn't an American alive who should accept these statements. The rights enumerated in the Constitution and in the Bill of Rights are not issued by Congress, and they are not given to us by the President. They are ours, freely given to us, by almighty God. I will not be a party to any tyranny that seeks to do away with these rights! We have a process to amend our Constitution and to make deals with foreign powers, and forming committees to rubber stamp plans made years ago by an oligarchy of so-called 'elites' is not how Americans are to be governed!"

Again Catherine looked over at Drake, this time seeing him smiling for the first time today as the crowd cheered. She realized she too felt more hopeful and had goose bumps all along her arms as the governor once again quieted the crowd.

"I agree with him that Americans are more than their check-books. I agree we are the acts of kindness as we help our neighbors, and we are indeed, the resilient pioneers who settled this land, but those values are not what the federal government, or the UN, or Europe, as a whole, are talking about. They are talking about collectivism, the outright taking of American property and indenturing our citizens. This is something no American should tolerate. I was not elected to speak for the men, women and children of other states, but I will be damned if I will not uphold my oath to defend the constitutional right of Texans against all enemies, foreign and domestic."

Catherine was stunned by the power and conviction in the man's voice, as was the crowd who erupted into unprecedented adulation. She realized at that moment she wanted to follow him wherever he led.

Looking at Drake, he smiled at her. "He is the guy, Kate. It scares the crap out of me and all, but I'm in. I am going to follow him. God help us all; you can just feel that this is the right thing." Catherine smiled as her friend stood on his toes a moment looking around obviously wishing Ginny was at his side.

When the crowd finally died down to a low roar again, Governor Miller continued. "The road ahead will be hard, but we are working on the details of how to get through this. For now, know that Texas is rich with resources, and we will be concluding agreements in partnership with private industry in the coming weeks to begin selling refined petrochemical products, as well as other goods and services to keep things running through the crisis period. In the meantime, I have signed legislation sent to me on Thursday, to suspend, until further notice, the force of all federal law in Texas, until a statute by statue review can be done regarding the constitutionality of these mandates, in the context of the current crisis. This suspension includes income and capital gains taxes, as well as any other funds paid by Texans to the federal government until such time as constitutional governance is restored at the federal level. Instead, an alternative system of taxation will be rolled out in coming days, to fund basic governmental requirements as we work through this crisis."

The roar of the applause was deafening. Catherine blinked with surprise at the energy of the crowd. As she looked at the faces on the plaza, she realized that here, at least, people were wide awake and standing up for freedom.

Again, the governor motioned for quiet, smiling broadly at his reception. "I encourage you all to..."

Catherine watched as the group of state troopers suddenly surged forward, tightening their protective circle around their charge, with one of the agents stepping in close to update his boss.

The Governor's head turned sharply towards the security man.

Finally beginning to process that something big was coming, she heard multiple deafening explosions behind her. Turning her head, she heard several shots fired to the south, followed by people shouting and what was likely the screams of whoever had been hit.

Turning towards the explosions, her eyes went wide with disbelief. Staring south at the tumult, she realized that the bangs were tear gas grenades. Frozen, she witnessed multiple five ton military trucks as they simply rammed the police cars parked sideways on Akard Street to block traffic. The police cruisers were pushed aside as if they were made of tin. The trucks turned onto the plaza and immediately began disgorging black clad figures in full riot gear. The dark figures instantly began forming up for an assault.

"Ginny! Ginny!" Drake called out to his fiancé whom Catherine spotted, too far away from them to reach now. "Damn it!" Feeling Drake drag her next to him, Catherine looked back to see still more darkly clad figures emerging from the building. It was obvious that a firefight was taking place inside, from the sound of several of the large plate glass windows shattering, mixed with the sound of gun fire. Panic ensued instantly. The large crowd began to shriek with fear and panic, but there was simply nowhere to go. She realized even more vehicles had moved up on the other side of City Hall, along Evray Street.

Over a span of thirty seconds, Catherine's world disintegrated into a maelstrom of gun fire, tear gas smoke, and screaming citizens. Everyone around her was stunned. As her mind struggled to cope with what was happening, it dawned on her they were quickly being hemmed in by the rapidly advancing federal agents.

Shocked, but oddly clear headed, it felt as if she suddenly had an electric current running through her. Catherine turned. "We have to surround him," she yelled over the din to her best friend. She pointed at the Governor who, with his guard, was pinned in along with the crowd. "You said that the National Guard is with us. We need to buy them some time."

Not waiting for his reply, she instead grabbed Cole, who was to her left, and moved forward towards the podium, and the beleaguered state troopers who, like everyone else, looked overwhelmed with only their side arms to stand against what were basically armored assault troops. Charging ahead, waving her arm like she was wielding a sabre, she screamed, "Let's go! Grab our folks. We have to make a human shield, to protect Governor Miller!" Not even bothering to look back, she charged into the storm, the black clad feds just behind her. As her reality slowed to a crawl, and her nerves tingled with the adrenalin pumping through her veins, she dodged a woman with an infant, desperately trying to get away from the City Hall and the gun fire. Reaching a spot just a few feet in front of a deputy, she nodded and winked at the pale man, nervously standing his ground between her and the Governor.

Turning back to look towards the spot where she had been standing, she realized not only had her people followed, but so too, had a great number of the other citizens on the plaza. It appeared the vast majority of those on the plaza had caught on to her plan, and were scrambling, not to get away, as was likely the plan of the assaulting force, but rather to form ranks of human beings to surround the Governor. The crowd was suddenly like a living entity, pulsing with energy, as Texans rapidly locked arms around their elected leader.

Drake locked his arm around hers as everyone continued to yell to keep it going. "Come on, the more ranks, the better! The time to fight for our freedom is now!"

As the smoke increased, she realized that the Feds were deploying more tear gas. Nudging Drake, she pointed at a canister several feet away. The smoke increased quickly, and Drake broke off from her, running towards the smoking canister, kicking it towards the reflecting pool. She saw others doing the same thing, and once again, she heard the tempo of gunfire increase. A woman a few feet away spun and fell, as she was hit multiple times by rifle fire. Drake had just turned to head back to her, when she saw an agent approximately thirty feet away take aim at his back. She took a breath to yell for him to duck, but she never got the chance. The agent leveling his rifle to shoot him was suddenly knocked off his feet from a shot fired from behind her, his blood, bright red, pooling where he fell.

Drake reached her smiling, but the smile turned instantly to concern. “Now that was cool, right?”

She pointed at the fallen agent. “He had a bead on you.”

They both began to look around for who was defending them, as another young man followed Drake’s example, but unlike her friend, he was hit twice and collapsed after kicking a canister into the water. The sound of more and more gun fire erupted around them. Catherine could see agents now trying to shut down the media. More canisters landed, and again, citizens ran out to kick them away. Catherine could hear screams of hatred now, as the agents, finally adjusting their tactics, began to rush towards the circle to pull away the civilians protecting their governor.

Catherine could see the agents just north of her were beating two men with batons who were doing their best to shove them back. As an older man went down, blood pouring down his face, the crowd surged forward, overwhelming the half dozen agents nearest him. Suddenly several federal agents found themselves on the defensive as the crowd charged into federal ranks. Completely enveloped, the agents were now being drug to the ground as citizens punched and kicked them and pulled their masks from their faces. A woman, of at least sixty, used pepper-spray on one of the downed agents who was now on the ground being kicked. She sprayed him directly in the face and screamed her fury at the top of her lungs.

The agent, now blinded and having lost his assault rifle to the crowd, grasped for his side arm and pulled the trigger several times. One of the rounds hit the older woman just under her chin, blowing off the back of her head. She collapsed immediately, falling on top of him, knocking his pistol out of his hands. A teenager next to them picked it up and fired twice at the agent, killing him as well. The young boy was obviously shocked, but didn’t even hesitate as he turned the weapon towards other agents, and began firing. A moment later, he too fell, hit in the chest.

"Bastards!" Catherine yelled through her tears, as more and more people in the crowd began falling as they were shot by the now out of control agents. Citizens who had earlier not been able to get onto the plaza were now rushing in from outside, attacking the federal agents with whatever they could find. Another agent only fifteen feet away was taking aim at the crowd when he was hit in the face. This time, as Catherine turned, she could see there were blue uniformed snipers on the roof of the City Hall. As more and more of the agents fell, she realized the Dallas police were picking off anyone who was attempting to use deadly force.

The shooting went on for what seemed like an eternity, but in reality, it was only minutes before she noticed that the feds began to realize they were hopelessly outnumbered. The military trucks had now been taken over and many of the agents, who were healthy just minutes before, lay motionless on the plaza.

The smell of blood and ozone permeated the air, as did the rank smell of human waste. Still crying, she sagged into Drake's arms when she noticed more military vehicles, rolling onto the plaza.

Her heart jumped in horror, as despair began to overwhelm her senses. Crying so hard that she could barely see, it took over a minute for it to dawn on her that the new arrivals were flying Texas flags from their radio whips. Several Humvees rolled to a stop approximately thirty feet in front of the knot of Texans surrounding Governor Miller. The rifle fire suddenly stopped as Texas Guardsmen flooded out of the now steadily arriving trucks. Drake had her by her arms looking her in the face as he steadied Catherine. "Stand here a moment. Don't move." She watched Drake run off through the crowd. Her heart seized up knowing he was looking for Ginny.

From behind her, she felt more than heard someone pushing past her from within the cordon. As she began to turn, someone nudged by her. Wiping her tears away with the back of her hand, she could see that the uniformed man in front of her was smiling.

"Excuse me, Ma'am. I need to get out there."

Beginning to feel any strength drain from her body, she watched as General Barker gently moved her aside and strode forward, returning the salute of an officer in full combat gear stepping out of one of the Humvees.

"Status, Colonel?"

"I have our guys sweeping the area, Sir. I will have air defense in place in like ten minutes, and I have two cobras in the air now, until we can get a handle on things."

"I am sorry it took so long. We had trouble getting in past all of the civilians."

She sighed with relief when she saw through the crowd that Drake was clutching Ginny to him. They spoke a moment and smiled at each other. After several minutes passed of watching people doing what they could for the wounded, Catherine realized she was somewhat in shock as Drake nodded and walked back in her direction. Catherine realized that she felt really weak all of the sudden and looked questioningly at Drake. He smiled back at her in return.

"It's the adrenalin wearing off. You'll feel better in a few minutes."

"Oh, my God, Drake, I can't believe this. They're animals. Look at all of this."

"Yes, they are, Kate. Look at the media guys though, they filmed the whole thing. I bet you anything this whole thing went out live. The world probably just saw us beat these guys. That doesn't mean anything about tomorrow, but it cannot hurt."

Megan nodded and took in a deep breath as she once again noticed the older woman splayed indignantly across the dead agent. "My God, Drake, my God! I may be sick."

"I know, Kate. The price of freedom is never cheap. Come on. Go sit back in your lawn chair before you fall down. I am going to go get a head count of our guys."

Catherine felt Drake physically guide her by the arm towards their original spot on the plaza. He reached down, grabbed the tumbled chair and righted it. "Come on, Kate; just sit for a bit until you feel better." He then moved off towards where she saw Dennis standing with a few of the others, when a man behind her spoke.

"Excuse me, Miss." Catherine turned to see Governor Miller standing in front of her while the man's security detail looked unhappy with their charge. His body man was frowning and with a hand on the governor, the man tried to urge Miller away to safety. The Governor held up a hand to stop them. "What you did just now was amazing. What happened here today is really bad, but it would have been infinitesimally worse if you hadn't done what you did. Can I ask your name?"

Catherine blinked in stunned disbelief for almost two seconds before standing. "Sorry, Sir, I am just a little freaked out. I'm Kate Danvers. I lead the Cedar Hill Tea Party."

She saw a winning smile chase the grim expression from his face. "Now, that does not surprise me. Jerry Danvers...?"

Catherine nodded confirming that he was her uncle.

"I know your uncle pretty well, and I believe I met your father once too. Did you get that bruise on your face today?"

"No, Sir that happened last weekend."

"I see. You are going to start taking better care of yourself, but I am grateful for your actions today."

Kate nodded. "You're welcome, Sir."

"Speaking of your father, I want you to know I won't rest until he is home with his family, along with all the other decent folks the federal government is using as human pawns."

He grimaced and looked at her sincerely. "I probably owe you my life, young woman. I'm sorry," his eyes scanned the carnage, "that you had to see this kind of thing. If there is anything that I can ever do for you, please ask me." The governor watched, with a military eye, the scene before them, ensuring the care of the wounded was getting underway. His concern was evident, but he turned back to Catherine.

"I am sorry too," Catherine said, her face grim as she too watched history playing out before them. "I served in the army for four years, but this is something I hope I never go through again. Regarding doing something for me, you are doing what I would ask of you. You are supporting our constitutional rights." She looked into his eyes. "That's it, Sir. As long as you support freedom, Texans will follow you."

The Governor acknowledged her comments, as Drake returned to her. "I can't predict what will happen, Miss Danvers, but I will do my level best. It won't be an easy journey, but I think that we'll get through these times."

She nodded, and turning her head slightly, she smiled at her friend. "Yes, Sir. I think you're right about that." Turning her gaze to Drake, she continued. "This is my friend, Drake Sabol. He is a police officer in Cedar Hill. We brought a few hundred people here to show our support."

Drake shook hands with the governor. "It is nice to meet you, Sir. I want you to know the guys in my department are all behind you."

With difficulty, he tore his attention away from the woman before him, to greet Drake. "Of course, officer, thank you for your service."

"It was an honor, Governor, any time." Looking to Kate, he continued. "We're still checking on everyone. I'll let you know when we have everyone accounted for."

"Thank you, Drake. I just hope ..."

Drake cut her off. "It isn't your fault if we have losses, Kate."

She looked down, as the Governor indicated to his security team he was ready to move on. Pulling her chin up to look at him, the Governor smiled knowingly. "Your friend is right, you know. It is never an easy task to lead, but I thank God you did." He released her and turned to leave, but paused as he did, considering her closely. "I'd like to talk with you some more at some point, if that's ok."

Catherine smiled. "I would be honored, Sir."

He smiled his thanks, and motioned to his team that it was time to catch up with General Barker, when Ginny ran up to the little group, breathing heavily.

"Kate! Kate, the Feds captured the medical station. The bastards arrested Sadie. The medical tent was located on the northeast corner. They were all taken before we even knew what was happening!"

Kate felt as if her heart had stopped. Blinking, she felt lightheaded as her knees buckled. Drake and Governor Miller both lunged to catch her. Guiding her gently to the pavement, Governor Miller barked orders over his shoulder. "Colonel, they took our people from an aid station located on the north end. I want those people back, and I mean right now!"

Drake stared intently into Catherine's eyes, as he too, spoke over his shoulder. "Ginny, get me our water bottles."

Somewhat detached from reality, Catherine watched those around her moving and talking. She wanted to participate, but just could not seem to quite clear her head. She wanted to cry. She just could not take another loss. She just kept replaying the same thought, Please, God, keep Sadie safe.

Chapter 44
Cat's Paw

Her head pounding, Sadie tried to sit up, only to find that her arms were pinned behind her with handcuffs. She felt as if her head would explode. Exhaling, she struggled to roll onto her elbow, in an effort to gain some insight into what had happened to her.

The last thing she remembered was the black clad agents rushing the medical aid station, located on the east end of the building. Four of them rushed around the south edge of the building, just a few feet from the aid station where Sadie was treating a young girl who had cut herself on a broken bottle. The agents stormed into their tent, yelling at everyone to get down on their knees. Brenda, the nurse coordinating the aid station, demanded that they leave them alone, as they were only there to provide care to anyone needing it. Horrified, Sadie recalled the shock on the fifty-something year old woman's face, as the lead agent forcefully slammed her onto the pavement. Sadie shuttered, recalling the sound of Brenda's head smacking against the pavement.

As soon as Sadie dropped to her knees, the mother was pulled roughly to her feet, knocking over the folding chair she had been sitting on next to her child and was hand-cuffed. Her daughter was handed off to another agent who rushed the child away from the building towards South Ervay Street and a waiting bus. The mother began struggling and screaming, as her daughter was taken, but like Brenda, she was slammed to the ground. Sadie remembered seeing Brenda's eyes dilated and non-responsive, and a clear fluid draining from her nose. Sadie had reached over, to check on her and...

Now awake and thinking on it for a moment, it dawned on her that Brenda, the mother and her daughter were all she could recall. It occurred to her also that she too, must have been knocked out. Sadie wondered what happened to the little girl and her mom, and said a quick prayer that they would be ok. Angry, but terrified, she finally managed to at least sit up. Blinking, she focused on her surroundings. Looking around, she realized that she was in the back of a military vehicle, probably a Humvee, she guessed. She was alone, but the acrid smell of vomit on the bed of the truck, near where she was dumped, made it obvious that she hadn't been alone very long. She tried to make out what she was seeing through the little plastic window in the flap that covered the rear of the vehicle.

She knew she was in trouble. She hadn't felt this frightened, since the two Iranian men tried to kill her and... "Catherine! Oh my God, Catherine. Let me out of here!" Sadie now realized that she could hear gun fire, nearby. Struggling, she began scooting towards the back of the Humvee. As she reached the tailgate, she worked to get onto her feet. She couldn't stand up all of the way, but she knew that she had to get to her feet to have any chance of escaping.

She didn't know where here was, but her heart screamed one thought at her conscious mind. That thought was that she had to find Catherine. Looking out of the faded clear plastic of the back cover, she decided that she was likely still in the downtown area, probably close by, if the weapons fire was any indication. She noticed that two of the black clad agents were desperately working to unload something out of another Humvee. As one of the men moved aside, she could see that what was being unloaded was actually not a what but a who. They were moving a wounded man to a military tent set up a few feet away.

Taking a deep breath, she leaned forward, using her body to straddle the tailgate. She used her left foot to balance herself, while she swung her right over the back, searching desperately for anything to use as a foothold. Not finding one, she whimpered, as the tailgate dug into her breastbone from the weight of her body pressing down on the narrow tailgate. Taking another breath, she squirmed, moving her left foot over the tail gate and pushed as hard as she could, with her hands cuffed behind her. The sensation of falling, lasted a fraction of a second, before the jarring impact of hitting her chin on the tailgate, shot pain through her already pain wracked head. She fell in a heap, behind the vehicle.

Shaking her head to clear her senses, she realized that one of the agents offloading wounded from the three other vehicles saw her. Her heart seized, and she rolled onto her knees. Gritting her teeth to endure the pain, she climbed awkwardly to her feet, and did her best to sprint in the opposite direction of the pursuing agent. Running blind, she only took two or three steps before she heard boots slapping the pavement behind her, and then she felt the man grab her hair, pulling her back. Once again, she lost her balance, falling backwards as her feet outran the rest of her body.

Landing on her backside, this time, she looked up to see a man with expressionless eyes in his thirties aiming his rifle at her.

She snarled at the agent. "Go ahead; why not shoot an unarmed prisoner? That is what you Feds do, right? Shoot women and kids, and anyone else that doesn't do what you say."

"On your feet, Bitch, you and your traitorous friends are the ones to blame here. Now that you are awake, you are going to make yourself useful. You're a nurse, right? Thanks to your asshole friends, there are wounded that need attention, and you are going to help out or you won't like what happens to you."

Sadie glared at the man, but again, rolled onto her knees and climbed to her feet. The man grabbed her arm and guided her back towards the military tent. "How many people have you monsters killed today, anyway?"

"Who knows? We aren't the ones that started this mess, but you will see that we are going to end it."

As they approached the tent, Sadie could smell blood, vomit, and urine in that all too familiar cocktail of smells that she associated with the trauma of gunshot wounds. Closing her eyes, she said a prayer for her partner. Please God, please watch over her. We are trying so hard to protect people. Please don't let her be dead.

Arriving at the front of the Fed's aid station, she saw at least ten people working feverishly over converted folding tables filled with wounded. As she scanned the aid station, she was surprised to see that there were a few federal agents, but the vast majority of the anguished, blood soaked people before her were the same people that, like her, had come to support Governor Miller.

She felt the agent's grasp tighten, as he roughly spun her to face away from him. She then felt him lifting her arms slightly, as he inserted a key to unlock her handcuffs.

Spinning her back to face him, he grabbed her chin in his gloved hand. "I don't have time for babysitting. You have a medical skill that we need. Use it. If you run again, I will personally shoot you in the back. Do you understand?"

Sadie, glowered at the man, but looked at the wounded and nodded. "They're my people; I will do what I can."

The agent pushed her, and she stumbled, losing her balance, but she recovered. Moving past two more FBI agents in full combat gear, she entered the tent. She was assaulted with the painful screams of more than a few wounded people. The tan canvas tent was large, but not nearly large enough to contain the human wreckage that lay ahead of her. Clamping down hard on her hatred and the tears that were threatening, she put the desperate wails of her patients aside, her professional mask thankfully descending to protect her humanity from the human carnage before her.

A slight man, with dark hair, going grey at the temples, looked up at her. His blood covered hands pressed packing into the grave stomach wound of what was likely a ten year old boy. He regarded her closely. "Are you the nurse?"

"Yes. What can I do?"

"What is your name and skill set?"

"Cline, I am an RN. I was a trauma nurse at Presby before all of this."

The man sighed, relief obvious on his features. "Good." He nodded at the table next to him. "Relieve the nurse next to me.

Do what you can for them. I have almost nothing for pain. Only the most severe get anything until we get some help down here, got it?" Not waiting for an answer, he raised his voice, speaking over his shoulder through the wails of the child, on the table in front of him. "Wendy, Nurse Cline will take it from here. Get out front, to triage the wounded coming in."

The woman looked up at her, relief washing over her face. She smiled weakly and handed Sadie, her stethoscope. "This one is a sucking chest wound. I have a Ziploc bag from a break room taped over the wound." She nodded and headed out of the tent.

Making eye contact with the man on the table, Sadie smiled reassuringly. "I've got you now. You are going to be fine. I am sure ambulances will be here any minute. It looks like the nurse did a good job patching you, so I am going to roll you onto your side, ok? That will help you breathe a little easier. Let me know if the pressure increases, I don't want a bunch of air between your chest wall and your lung, ok?"

She could see the man was scared, but he jerkily nodded his understanding.

"Good, let's get you outside then, so that you can rest until we get you to the hospital. Tell someone if the pain gets significantly worse." The two agents moved up to help the man out of the way. The agent on the left gave her a sympathetic look, as he helped lift the man from the table. Two more agents brought in what appeared to be a teenager covered in a massive amount of blood. As the boy was pale and unconscious, Sadie began by checking his pulse. She couldn't feel anything at the wrist, so she tried for his carotid artery. Still not finding a pulse there either, she took a deep breath and prepared to begin chest compressions, when the agent that chased her down, pushed his way into the tent carrying a fallen comrade.

The doctor, who seemed to be running the aid station, looked up exasperated. "Jacobs, just what the hell do you think you are doing? Take that man out front. You need to set him down, now. Wendy will evaluate him."

The agent snarled, his teeth bared, his shoulder soaked in blood; he stood over the much smaller doctor. "To hell with that, Doc. We take care of our own first!"

Furious, the doctor looked up from his task. "Agent Jacobs, get out! We deal with people in order of their wound's severity, period!"

Agent Jacobs glared at the doctor and then down at the now unconscious child. He snarled before noticing Sadie's patient on the next table. "Fuck that!" He took two steps towards her.

Alarmed at the intrusion, Sadie glanced quickly at him but tried to tune him out, focusing on not losing count.

"That is the little bastard that shot my partner. I will be dammed if he gets treated before him."

Sadie was terrified but focused. She dared not look back at the monster. "Doctor, get him out of here, or this guy will die."

The doctor stopped what he was doing and looked at the furious agent. "Jacobs, you are experiencing combat stress. You are too senior of an agent, and not the kind of guy to be a problem. Please go."

Again, the agent on the left, standing watch at the tent opening, took a step forward. "Come on Jacobs; let's see what Wendy can do. I'm sure they will get to your partner really quick, ok? We are all Americans here. Come on Jacobs; let these people work."

His teeth grinding, Agent Jacobs clearly clamped down hard on his emotions, the muscles in his jaw straining, so hard that Sadie wasn't sure which way he would go. A moment passed, and the agent turned and stormed out of the tent.

Sadie knew that she had to get her patient breathing, or he was doomed. Tiring quickly, she switched from doing compressions to administering mouth to mouth resuscitation. Thankfully, the young man finally started breathing on his own, relieving the building fear in Sadie's heart that she was going to lose him. Sighing, she reached over for bandages and the suture kit to begin patching up what she could when she heard automatic weapons fire just outside the tent, and the agent remaining at the tent's entrance pulled the slide on his rifle chambering a round and darted out the opening.

Fear seized her yet again, but she continued to work, praying that bullets didn't tear though the tent, killing her or those around her. She glanced momentarily at the doctor, her eyes meeting his. She could see the stress residing there matched her own. Focusing back on sewing up a profusely bleeding vein in the young man's shoulder, she tried to tune out the screaming just outside. She could hear Wendy yelling as the gunfire continued for several seconds. Hearing death ricocheting off of the pavement she realized that she could smell the cordite from the weapons fire. Again glancing up, she saw that the doctor, stood motionless over his patient, his eyes tightly closed as if blocking out the sounds of battle. Men were cursing just outside the tent now. It was too chaotic to make out what was being said, other than disgust in Agent Jacob's voice. "Fuck it. This isn't over not by a long shot."

"It is for you, asshole. On your knees, you know the drill. Interlace your fingers behind your head!"

Sadie's head whipped toward the tent opening as did all of the others working in the aid station. A moment turned into two, when a tall man in fatigues and full combat gear, stepped through, into the tent with his rifle ready, but lowered so as not to directly threaten anyone inside. His bright blue eyes were alert but kind as he inspected the medical staff in the tent.

"My Name is Lieutenant Anders. I'm with the Texas National Guard. I apologize for any inconvenience, but I'm afraid my team, and I will have to detain you all until we can guarantee your safety. It is my hope that we can get you all on your way before too long." The man smiled sheepishly.

The doctor's expression was grim, but she decided that his head nod indicated his acceptance of the situation. A nurse at the back of the tent began crying nervously, her relief obvious in her demeanor. "Please don't leave. We need protection and supplies for these people."

Sadie felt some of her tension ebb from her body as she continued to work. Tying off the suture she was working on, she glanced over her shoulder at the soldier. "Lieutenant, several of us were taken from the aid station on the plaza. Can you tell me... Um, how bad is it?"

Fearing the worst, tears welled up in her eyes, as desperately, she looked hopefully at the young army officer. He looked down at his boots. "I'm sorry, Miss. It isn't good. A lot of people were killed, as you probably guessed, but the Governor is ok, and our people are now securing the area. I am very sorry for all of this, Ma'am."

Sadie's breath came in gasps, as bloody hands dabbed at her eyes. She was terrified for Catherine, but realized she would just have to focus on the need in front of her and hope that God would take care of her partner. The worry was oppressive. She realized just how real it all was. She knew now that regardless of whether Catherine was alive or not, she was now firmly committed to freedom.

Chapter 45

The Liberty Equation

Annie ran her fingers through her hair as she left the bathroom, having just thrown up for the third time since lunch. Regardless that it had been almost a week since her family had faced off with the FBI, she was still really nervous about things. Obviously, being pregnant, Annie knew she was supposed to throw up a lot, but she still could not help but blame some of it on what had happened. She reflected that, regardless of how quiet it had been for the family the past few days, almost no one thought it was really over.

Sighing, she gathered her thoughts and plopped down in her favorite spot, the leather club chair near the pony wall, across from where Russell and Matt obsessively watched the ongoing national drama.

"...That's it for your Mid-Day Update, but, as always, leave it right here on FOX News for the latest in our continuing back to back coverage of the latest events in the world financial disaster, and of the numerous violent conflicts at home and around the world. Coming up next, Senior Political Anchor, Tina White. Tina?"

"Thanks Brad. In a special alert aired first on Fox an hour ago, the number of western states throwing their weight behind the so-called Constitutionalist Movement has grown yet again, since the tragic events in Dallas last weekend. As first reported late Monday, the state of Oklahoma announced that it concurred with Texas that the federal government's actions could no longer be construed as legal. Two days later, Kansas and Arizona both vowed to rapidly push through legislation ratifying the Constitutionalist viewpoint. Darla Phillips, Governor of Arizona, stated yesterday that her state saw no other legal or moral option but to stand with the U.S. Constitution as written even in times as dire as those before us. As events unfold and the situation nationally continues to deteriorate, additional state legislatures are apparently finding themselves more and more on their own as it becomes challenging to even keep food, water and power available to Americans. Wyoming, Idaho and Utah are all widely expected to join Texas in disavowing D.C. in coming days."

Annie looked at Matt and sighed. "Does that mean the fighting will stop, and the Feds will stop trying to force us to do stuff and steal our land?"

Matt shrugged. "Anyone who answered that question like they knew what was going to happen would be a liar. Nothing like this has ever happened. It is anybody's guess what will happen next."

Annie thought she just wanted it all to end, but every day the news was filled with one tragedy after another. Her mind continually replayed the headlines. Gang members had all but taken over large portions of Atlanta. The fighting in Maryland and California between citizens and law enforcement was horrific. Of all the tragedies being reported, the massacres in Fort Hood, her family's own standoff, and now the massacre in Dallas, were keeping her up at night. Feeling her emotions about to overwhelm her yet again, she closed her eyes and willed herself to calm down. She knew Katie was ok, and she said she would come home to visit soon. Still, she just wanted things to be normal again.

"Annie? Are you ok, Honey? Are you still nauseous?"

She opened her eyes. "I'm sorry, Russ, what?"

"It's ok Annie," Matt interjected. "I was just saying that there is no telling what will happen next, but it is really good news that other states are seeing our side of things. It will be really hard for Washington to make the states do anything since they no longer have infinite amounts of cash to spend. They have an unbelievable number of problems to deal with, without looking for even more trouble."

"I hope so. I don't know how people cope with all this. I hate wars and fighting. I hate it; I don't know what I would have done if Katie had been one of the people killed last weekend."

Matt and Russell both smiled sympathetically. "It will be pretty rough for a while," Matt remarked, "but the US really is a very wealthy nation. We will pull through this. People are just going to have to remember how to be more self-reliant, and neighbors will have to help each other like the folks here did for us. When you were in the restroom, they said that Congress had degenerated into chaos. They are not getting any consensus on anything at this point."

Russell got up and hobbled over to sit on the arm of her chair. "That's right Annie Girl; it really is going to be a whole new world. I think it might be a much better one. After all, we aren't telling people in New York or LA how to live. If they want to be socialists, they can; we are just going to stick with the U.S. Constitution here. No reason for them to fight over anything. Like Matt said, our congress people left Washington on military planes this morning. I guess it will be pretty weird for a while, and the leader types will have to figure things out, but at least, we won't be some kind of UN slaves."

With sudden tears in her eyes, Annie cursed yet again due to the abundance of hormones in her body. Grasping her husband's arm for comfort, she looked earnestly at Matt. "Is all this going to be worth it? So many people have died. How can it be worth what is happening?"

Annie wiped at her eyes with her sleeve. "I can't help but wonder if it would really be so bad to just give them what they want? I don't want to live that way and everything, but they are saying that they don't even know for sure how many have died in all of this, but that it is going to easily be over thirty thousand people." Annie paused, thinking about her words. "Surely, we could change it all back to the way it's supposed to be later."

Matt rose off the couch. Saying nothing, he paused by her chair. Squatting down to look intently at her, he smiled sympathetically. "I'm sorry, Annie. Nothing about conflict is pleasant or glorious or anything but a stupid waste. The only thing worse would be the loss of freedom. Communist regimes have murdered millions. Ask your folks about East Germany. Did you know that over two hundred thousand men, women, and children have risked their lives trying to get away from that kind of collectivist ideology? If we don't continue to stand up for freedom, that could happen to us. Thousands were killed in East Germany alone. If you add guys like Pol Pot or Stalin, the number literally climbs into the millions, and that is just off the top of my head."

She felt Matt squeeze her arm reassuringly as he stood once more. "Freedom is never free, Annie. It is expensive in fact, but well worth the price." She noticed that Russell looked up at Matt and nodded. "Anyway, I need to wake Megan from her nap." Chuckling, he moved towards the archway between the great room and the walkway in front of the bedroom. "She gets cranky if she sleeps too long."

Annie sighed. "I guess I am not much of a patriot, am I? I'm sorry Russ. I embarrassed you, didn't I?"

"You would never embarrass me, Sweetheart."

Annie smiled at her husband and nodded. "I'm ok now. You need to go back and lie down. Come on, Russ." Annie got up and helped Russell hobble back to the couch. Once he was down, she picked up two throw pillows and propped up his leg. Looking up, she noticed that he watched her closely. "What?"

"Just noticing how beautiful you are, Annie girl. I love you."

"I love you too."

Moving closer to him, she leaned down and kissed him on his forehead as her mom called from the kitchen.

"Honey, can you go out to the freezer in the barn and bring in half a dozen steaks. I want to make this dinner nice for your sister and her friend." Beth Danvers sighed. "I mean, her partner. Anyway, pick out some of the really nice cuts, will you dear?"

Annie kissed her husband on the forehead and started for the door. "Sure, Mom."

Her mother smiled at her as she passed. "And Annie, keep your chin up, Honey. I know all of this is frightening. It is for all of us. I miss your father too, but the Lord is still watching over us. I don't think that it is an accident that the family is for the most part healthy and whole." Annie nodded and grabbed the door knob when she felt her mother's hand on her shoulder. She turned. "I love you, Honey, and so does your dad. I know that being pregnant, you feel really vulnerable. Anyone would worry about the world they were about to bring a child into, but, regardless of this mess that we are living with, you just hold on to your faith, it will all be fine."

Annie smiled. "Thanks, Mom, I'm ok. I just hate hearing about all of the terrible news every day. I can't help but think about how many families out there, just like ours, are just being destroyed."

"I know, Honey, I know. That's what faith is all about, isn't it? Believing in salvation is about believing in that, which you cannot prove. Anyway, go get the steaks. I want them to defrost slowly."

Annie smiled. "Thanks, Mom, I'll be right back." She turned and headed for the front door.

As her hand touched the doorknob, Russell yelled after her. "Annie! Your pistol! You know we don't leave the house unarmed."

"All right, Russ, fine." Reaching into the drawer on the cabinet by the door, she grabbed her holstered nine millimeter pistol, clipped it to her jeans and headed out the door, only to be pounced upon by Bridget, who was demanding that she throw a tennis ball for her to chase. Annie obliged, and the little Pomeranian raced after it, bringing a smile to Annie's face.

She sauntered across the covered patio and out into the sunshine and the thick Saint Augustine grass. The sun warming her, she realized life would go on, and as bad as things had been, the family was blessed. It could have been much, much worse.

She was about halfway to the front gate when Bridgett raced back to her and dropped the tennis ball proudly at her feet with her tail beating madly. She bent down to ruffle the dogs fluffy lion-like mane with one hand, as her other darted in quickly to grab the ball. She stood and threw it again. The ball ricocheted off a lounge chair and almost landed in the pool. Instead, it bounced back onto the grass, after being deflected by the raised lip of the coping surrounding the edge of the swimming pool. Again, Bridgett raced off after the ball, and Annie took the opportunity to slip out of the courtyard and out into the open parking area out in front of the house. Closing the gate behind her, she angled to her left, passing in front of the family's vehicles, on her way towards the long metal building the Danvers used as their barn. Walking past the paved drive in front of the garage, she sighed, this time happy to be home where she grew up. She knew she was blessed to have her family with her. She had always loved the ranch, but now it occurred to her how incredibly lucky she was to have this refuge in the storm that was breaking across the country, and, in fact, across the whole world.

Reaching the door to the barn, she breathed in deeply to smell the sage bushes planted to either side of the doorway. She turned the knob and walked into the building, flipping the light on as she went. The florescent bulbs flickered and slowly came to life, as she made her way past her Daddy's work bench to the old freezer. As happy as she had just been, she realized that without him home it all seemed wrong. He should be here. Her uncle called every day, and even went to Dallas to check on him, but in light of events, the Feds would not even let her uncle into the building to see her father, regardless of the fact that he was his lawyer.

He said that the experience was surreal. Texas officials made no attempt to interfere with any of the federal employees still willing to go to work there, but the federal building was surrounded day and night by Texas National Guard soldiers. Her uncle said that from what he could find out, the soldiers were making sure that Texas citizens arrested by federal law enforcement were not going to be allowed to leave the state.

Now, back to being depressed again, she sighed, as a moment of nausea reminded her that regardless of anything else, being pregnant and awash with hormones was likely part of the constant barrage of emotions. She leaned in to pick out the steaks that her mother asked for, and set them on the shelf next to the freezer. Standing on her tip-toes, she stretched to reach up to the top shelf for a plastic shopping bag. Finally grasping one, she began placing the steaks into the bag. A moment later she closed the freezer and turned to leave. Seeing her father's empty bench in front of her, abandoned and sad, she wondered if she would ever see him again. She decided she would put on a brave face for her mom, but her depression was overwhelming.

Annie walked past the bench on the way to the door, and paused by her dad's coffee cup, left in the very place he had set it down several days ago. Reaching out to touch the cup, a weak smile turned into a grimace. "Please, Lord, take care of us, and please take care of Daddy." Sniffing away a tear, she headed for the barn door and the sunshine.

As the metal door clanged shut behind her, she stumbled as she had done a thousand times over the cracked and uneven concrete pad, just in front of the door. Regaining her balance, she was grateful no one saw her clumsiness. Rolling her eyes, she headed toward the front gate when she saw a black SUV had just made its way up the rise in the road that led to the parking area out front of her home. Freezing, she realized that it was quickly approaching the house. She knew there was no way she could get inside before it arrived.

Annie just stared blankly at the approaching vehicle for almost three seconds before it occurred to her that she was completely out in the open. As her mind finally began to function, she looked around and decided her best bet for any cover was Matt's pickup. Now awake to the reality approaching her, Annie sprinted towards the truck. Crouching down, she dropped the shopping bag with the frozen steaks on the gravel just to the left of the front passenger side tire. She crouched low, breathing hard. If only she had some way to warn everyone that Feds were here without giving away her hiding place. Almost hyperventilating, she realized she had very few options. If only she had her cell phone! Finally, her mind racing, she reluctantly pulled the 9mm Glock awkwardly from its holster. Nervously, she pulled back the slide to chamber a round. Peeking over the hood, she could see that the SUV was almost to the parking area. With the windows tinted, she could not even tell how many were coming. Her mind scrambled with what she should do. Her hands trembling with fear, she leaned against the front tire of the truck. One thing was for sure, she desperately needed help.

That is when she realized she could communicate. Turning to peak back over the hood, she leveled the pistol, aiming at the grill of the approaching truck and pulled the trigger several times. Four shots rang out, sounding like staccato thunderclaps, as the hollow point bullets struck the radiator and driver's side light. The vehicle rolled to a stop immediately, approximately twenty feet in front the courtyard gate. Ducking back down Annie fought to keep from crying, hoping that Matt was paying attention inside. Listening for what she was sure would be swarms of agents flowing out of the truck she could hear the SUV doors opening and a man yelling at someone to do something.

Carefully, she peeked out towards the house to see if Matt and her sister were coming. She thought she saw movement inside, but could not be sure. Turning to look towards the Feds, she heard her Daddy's voice.

"It's OK, Annie, it's your dad! This man is just getting me home. Put that thing away!"

Annie's heart stopped. Her mind was processing her dad's voice, but her heart just could not believe it. Slowly, her pistol still readied, she glanced cautiously over the hood of the pickup to see her dad, walking towards her. A man in a suit stood passively behind the driver's side door.

As she stood, she blinked, and even shook herself to clear her head to make sure that what she was seeing was real. A long moment passed as her father approached. Finally, completely overwhelmed with emotion, she dropped her pistol on the hood and sprinted around the front of the truck, running headlong towards his open arms, crying so hard she could barely see.

Reaching him, she felt his strong arms envelop her, lifting her off her feet as he swung her around in a circle, the same way he had done when she was little.

"Daddy, are you home to stay? How? Why did the bastards let you go? You aren't going back, right?"

"No, Honey, I won't be going back. It seems your sister made a friend from New York City, who was able to help me out." Bob Danvers set his daughter down, but Annie could not exactly bring herself to let go of him completely. Wiping her eyes, she could see that, other than her husband, the house had emptied out and everyone was running towards them, including Matt, who was carrying his assault rifle.

Once past the gate to the Spanish garden, her mom actually sprinted to where she and her father stood amongst the vehicles. Annie stepped back to give her mom full access as Beth Danvers slammed into her husband with enthusiasm grasping him in her arms. Annie watched, a smile plastered on her face, as the relief washed over her in waves. Megan drew up beside her sister. Annie noticed Megan was almost as emotional as she was. Giving the family some space, Matt walked warily up to the FBI agent. As they spoke, Annie got the impression that he seemed to know the guy. Turning back to her parents, she felt her heart lift watching the joyful expressions on her parents' faces as they began to move toward the house. Her mom, smiling back at her, nodded her head back towards the barn. "Honey, please go get a couple of more steaks. Tonight is going to be the biggest celebration this family has ever had."

"Meg, dear, please go ask your fiancée and Agent Ricks to come in and relax," her father said.

Annie turned to do as she was told. This time, she felt almost as if she were floating as she moved towards that barn. She noted that Megan was already moving towards the SUV where Matt was talking to the Fed.

"Don't forget your pistol, Sis. I can see that you left it on the hood of the truck. You will be wondering what you did with it," Megan called out.

Annie was so happy she almost skipped the whole way; and this time, she knew she would be delighted to see her Daddy's work bench.

Chapter 46
Epilogue

As she passed Indian Creek Road just west of town, Catherine exhaled some of the stress she was feeling. Having just driven through Mineral Wells, Catherine knew, as did Sadie that her pointing out the local highlights in her hometown was really just her way of covering her nerves at taking the woman with whom she had now committed to share her life home. At least she wasn't ill this time. Reflecting on this same trip with Dan, she recalled she was actually nauseated, and Janice wouldn't come at all. Now, she was nervous, but this time she was older and had confidence in who she was and in what she believed. With Indian Creek Road now in her mirror, she turned and smiled at her partner, grateful that Texas Army National Guard rescued her and the other medical staff. At a glance, Sadie appeared to be completely normal; yet as Catherine gazed into her eyes, she could still see that haunted look that everyone in her group who witnessed last weekend's assault now had.

Shaking off her reverie, she smiled weakly. "Well, it won't be long now. It's just a little further up the highway to our turn off."

"Catherine, you know your family loves you a lot. I am sure everything will be fine. I really liked your folks when we met last time, and there are much larger things to worry about these days than you and me."

"Thanks, Sadie. You always see right through me, don't you?"

"I do try, Sweetie. I am really looking forward to this, if you want to know the truth. After the last couple of weekends, I just want to feel as normal as possible. After they rounded us up, and all the shooting started, I was terrified I would never see you again." Sadie's voice cracked as she finished her sentence.

Catherine nodded her head in solemn agreement. "I keep seeing it every time I close my eyes too. I will never forget the teenaged boy who died begging for his mother. I still just cannot believe American law enforcement could be capable of what happened. God, I hope the last few days of the country taking a breath gives people some time to think about where this can go if they don't start acting like adults for once."

Glancing over, Catherine could see in her eyes that Sadie, too, was fighting the images. She turned off the highway and drove over the cattle guard onto the Danvers Ranch past the sign that she, her sisters and her father had placed at the entrance to their property.

Sadie smiled as she read the sign. *Welcome to the Danvers Ranch.* "I feel at home already. I love the little flower bed around the base. Flowers are always so cheerful."

Catherine smiled in spite of herself. "I remember when my Dad made all of us come out here to put the sign up. I was mad because I wanted to go into town with my friends. Annie was always little miss cheerful, and loved doing stuff like that. Of course, my other sister, Megan, acted like she wanted to help just to make me look like bad. She always did know just how to play our folks."

Sadie chuckled, as she turned from watching the passing ranch land filled with scrub trees to trade a significant look with Catherine. "You know, however it goes with your family, I love you. Even if it is a little awkward, we will get through it just fine."

Catherine took a sip from her travel mug, and replaced it in the center console's cup holder. "I know you're right, and I'm glad to get away from the grind we have been through since everything went into the toilet. Honestly, after last weekend, I could happily hide out here on the ranch for months, eating good food and only having to worry about the occasional disappointed glance."

"Catherine, your parents were just fine when they came to check on you after we were attacked. I am sure they would prefer some stunningly handsome doctor on your arm, but do you really blame them? If we can find a way to have children someday, wouldn't you want them to have as normal a life as possible?"

Catherine considered what Sadie said, as the Jeep climbed up the little hill where the house stood presiding over the Danvers' property. She knew Sadie was right, but she just wasn't ready to admit it yet. Still, as she approached her childhood home, she smiled at seeing it. The mission house and long metal barn were always the same. It warmed her heart that as crazy as the world had grown in recent weeks, other than a few different vehicles, what she was seeing before her hadn't changed at all, since she last looked at it in her rear-view mirror, following the divorce. The timelessness of the ranch was calming. Being here made her feel safe for the first time in months.

As she crested the hill, Catherine's eyes locked immediately on the unfamiliar vehicle with a shot out head light, awkwardly parked twenty feet from the house.

Turning to Sadie, she grimaced. "Does that SUV look to you, like what I think it looks like?"

Sadie's eyes went wide, as she shook her head that it did. "Maybe you should call to see if they sound ok."

"Right, good idea." She glanced over to her partner. "Would you get the number ready for the Mineral Wells sheriff, just in case?"

"Sure, Catherine, just give me a sec."

Catherine stopped the Jeep at the top of the rise, and pulled her nine millimeter and her cell phone out of her purse. Sliding the pistol in between the seat and the center console, she tapped the number for the house phone. The phone rang and then rang again. Each ring stretching her nerves tighter and tighter, until Catherine wanted to scream. After the third ring, she looked over at Sadie with a look of alarm on her face. She was about ready to have Sadie dial the Sheriff when Annie's voice answered.

"Danvers residence."

"Annie, is everything ok in there?

"Of course, Katie, Daddy is home. He just got here like thirty minutes ago. Are you and Sadie on your way? We are going to have a huge celebration."

"Damn it, Annie, you guys almost gave me a heart attack. You could have called to let me know. Why is an SUV shot up out front?" She exhaled loudly, and looked at Sadie, rolling her eyes in frustration. "How did you guys think I would react to a Fed vehicle out front, with holes in it?"

Taking in another deep breath, she started to chastise her sister further, when she could hear the phone being taken away on the other end.

"Kate, is that you, Honey? Are you here?"

Sighing, Catherine swallowed her vitriol and responded. "Yes, Momma. We just got here. We were about to call the cops!"

"You are right, Dear. I'm sorry. Your Daddy just got home. I guess we were all just so happy that we didn't think to call you. You and Sadie come on in here, Sweetheart. I want the whole family where I can see everyone."

"Ok, Momma, we will be there in just a moment."

Catherine put the Jeep back in gear and moved it forward parking it to the right of the vehicle's older cousin. As she put the vehicle in park, her emotions overwhelmed her. Unable to stop them, she felt tears running down her face.

She felt Sadie's hand take hers. Looking at her, she was suddenly helpless, her emotional armor completely destroyed. Sadie was smiling again, the momentary tension forgotten already.

"Catherine, it's ok to cry, Sweetheart, your dad's home. What wonderful news! I can't believe it. I wonder why they released him. Maybe letting political prisoners go is a good will gesture, after what they did last weekend. Maybe it is the beginning of the end."

Struggling to regain control, Catherine returned her pistol to her purse. "I wouldn't count on it, Love, but whatever the reason, I'll take it."

Sadie already had her door open and was reaching back in for her purse. She smiled at Catherine. "Come on, let's get inside. I haven't seen unbridled joy in ages, and I desperately want to."

She reached for her own door handle, as both sets of French doors opened at the house. Emerging from the Jeep, her tears threatened to restart again as her dad walked off the porch and into the courtyard, followed by her mom and her sisters, Annie and Megan.

Suddenly, overwhelmed with emotion, Catherine didn't even get a chance to reply before Sadie sprinted towards the gate.

"Oh boy," Catherine exhaled and steeled herself for the coming encounter as she walked after her partner and struggled with her emotions.

She was almost to the gate when Sadie reached her family in the middle of the yard. She was stunned to see her dad pick Sadie off her feet embracing her in a massive hug, spinning her around in a circle. Stunned, she looked on with unbelieving eyes, as her family warmly embraced her partner.

Her mom smiled and waved at her. "Get over here, Slow Poke!"

As she came through the gate, she realized her mouth was hanging open. Megan, who had her arms around a guy she sort of recognized, released her man to suddenly trot forward towards her. Surprised, Catherine's eyes went wide when her sister broke into a run as she approached.

Megan pulled her tightly into an embrace as the two women met at the gate. "God, Sis, it's great to see you," she whispered. "We were all watching the coverage. I cried the whole time." She felt her sister release her, and pull back to look into her eyes. "You were amazing, Kate! You really were."

Catherine smiled, and her tears once again won their battle against her determination not to cry, as her family enveloped her.

Listening to her family as they discussed the disaster befalling the armed forces in Europe and the Middle East, Catherine considered taking a final bite. She shivered at the thought of what it would be like to be so far away from home right now. Deciding she was full, she laid her fork down on her plate with a soft clink as Matt discussed what he thought of the news.

"It won't be easy, but our guys are smart, well equipped and they are tough. We have good commanders, and they will make the best of things."

Catherine wondered what she would do. Her thoughts were interrupted by the sensation of Sadie gently caressing under the table with her fingernails her bare arm. She turned slightly, to see that her partner's attention was totally engrossed in the conversation. She smirked, as her dad responded.

"I am not saying they aren't smart or tough Matt, I just hate to think of what they are getting into, trying to drive all of our equipment north to give to the Israelis. I cannot believe that the Arabs are going to let that happen"

"I don't imagine the Islamists are very happy about the matter. They are demanding that Washington turn over all of our equipment to them, just like we are doing in Europe, as our guys get ready to come home."

Matt reached out for his glass of tea. He took a drink and returned the glass to the table, and smirked. "Admiral Foxglove has three aircraft carrier task groups and one hell of a lot of firepower on the ground. Apparently, once they had the civilians and most of the support folks out of the country, he realized he had an opening. It looks like he is giving everything we have on the ground there to the Israelis."

Matt smiled, taking on the countenance of a wolf. "Our commanders decided they could just drive north and kill anyone that gets in our way. He has more than enough air power to cover the movement, and by the way, Iran is not the only one with nukes. Think about it, Bob, he has an armor heavy, mobile force with no rear area to protect. He has the complete loyalty of his people and the ability to resupply our guys from the sea. Now that he told the President where to go, he has no political masters at home to tie his hands."

"My God, Son, I cannot even begin to imagine where all of that will end. He has guts, but he will have to come home eventually. You can bet the President will not be kind when that happens."

Matt chuckled. "Who said that home will be the East Coast? He could sail his fleet into Houston. For that matter he could just stay in Israel after the conflict is over. With a three carrier task force, the Israelis would not be a nation to trifle with for some time."

Pushing her plate away, Catherine said a silent prayer as a momentary quiet fell across the table. She prayed for everyone in harm's way, and prayed Israel would survive. She realized she couldn't recall the last time she had been this full, much less had steak, potatoes, and a salad as the cause of that sensation. The smell alone of her father's perfectly seasoned steaks, grilled out on the patio was unsurpassed. Having just eaten more than she should have, Catherine still savored the cut she had just devoured. Her dad had a way with meat. She liked her steak medium, so each bite all but melted in her mouth.

She and Sadie had been the center of attention since their arrival an hour ago, supplanting for a brief time, her father and his FBI benefactor, Agent Ricks.

She looked over at him now, as he sat across from Sadie, next to Matt. He seemed to be a nice enough guy, but she could not help but be suspicious when her father relayed how Ricks had signed him out of his temporary prison in the heavily guarded Federal Building in Dallas.

Even with Texas soldiers surrounding the building, it just seemed odd that they would be able to get away.

She noticed Matt regarded the man in much the same way she did, but it was also obvious that her father had clearly asked him to back off. Deciding that she simply had to explore the matter, she opened her mouth to speak when Sadie unexpectedly took up the gauntlet.

Sadie smiled brightly at Ricks, giving him one of her looks of complete absorption in what he might have to say. "Agent Ricks, I cannot tell you what an incredible blessing your actions today were for the family. It is nothing short of amazing that you were able to get Mr. Danvers away from your people. I am not sure, however, that I understand exactly how in the world you were able to do it."

Catherine smirked inwardly, knowing full well that, regardless of the fawning expression on her face, Sadie was on the same scent she was. She then tilted her head, her eyebrows rising, as an expression of anticipation and curiosity crept onto her face.

Somewhat embarrassed, Agent Ricks collected his thoughts, as he sat down the sparkling glass of red wine, from which he had just taken a sip. "Well, I suppose it was a risk, but I didn't really think so. The holding space was not as secure as a normal FBI holding facility. Due to the number of detainees in custody, We-um... the FBI, that is, temporarily converted part of our fifth floor office space into a holding area."

Catherine glanced at her father to see that the topic of discussion was not his favorite. She quickly looked back towards Ricks.

He took another sip of wine. "Due to my legitimate concern with Miss Danvers," he nodded in Megan's direction, "I had been in Dallas for the last week and a half in an effort to locate her and Mr. Regan. I had an official transfer request on my laptop for a prisoner from two weeks ago. I just changed some of the relevant pieces of information, and the date, and printed it off. It was as simple as folding the document and walking up to the fifth floor." He smiled slyly. "No one questioned that I might want to talk to my subject's father, as he was conveniently in FBI custody. With Texas soldiers surrounding the Federal building, I simply walked him to a side door. I asked our agents standing watch on the door if your people had arrived to make the exchange. They were confused, of course. I handed them my paperwork, and they opened the door for us. We simply walked up to a sergeant standing next to the nearest tracked vehicle."

Catherine glanced at her father again, noticing that he didn't approve of the grilling of his rescuer, but she decided that she simply had to know why he did what he did. "You are a clever man, Agent Ricks. Like my family, I am very grateful for your taking the chance that you did. What I don't understand, is why you did it. Are you trying to make some sort of arrangement with my sister?"

She looked at Megan for a moment, as she continued. "Or are you perhaps uncomfortable with the actions of the people in D.C.?"

Ricks acknowledged the question with a nod. "Like most Americans, we watched your stand last weekend. I realized, at that point, that people down here are just different. You were actually going to stand on principle, regardless of the odds. I have been thinking about what my duty was since the President gave his speech. The balance of public outrage at what happened last weekend is getting worse, not better. I don't think the country can afford to start shooting at each other, so yesterday when Israel officially recognized Texas's right to follow the Constitution independently, until such time as political differences could be worked out, I decided my oath was to the US Constitution, even if that meant disobeying my superiors." He looked down the table at her dad, his face serious. "I knew your father had a connection to some of your political leaders, so I decided to try to make arrangements. To be brief, I am throwing in with Texas. For good or ill, I would rather support the Constitution than what DC is trying to do."

Catherine realized that what she was hearing made sense, but it was a lot to take in. Realizing her mouth was open again, as she stared at the man incredulously, she snapped it closed and swallowed. "Fair enough, Agent Ricks. Thank you for answering the question. Again, I am grateful to you for what you did, and I hope that you are right about Americans not wanting to see more of last weekend. I don't know that I will ever be able to not see that day every time I close my eyes. There is enough tragedy happening without us doing it to ourselves."

Her father placed both hands flat on the table and coughed. "We have been blessed in this country for over two hundred years. It has been over a hundred and fifty years since we have had this level of division. We can get past this if we can find a way to have honest conversations about issues. That's why patriots like Agent Ricks here can make such a large difference. We need to find ways to reach out. It will become almost impossible to stop, if the kind of violence that we have seen in recent weeks really gets going."

Catherine looked at her father for what felt like the first time. She saw the man she had always known, but looking at him now, seeing his vulnerability and the concern etched in his face for all he held dear, she realized that just maybe she wasn't any different than anyone else. Everyone was just as scared of what lay ahead as she was. She knew now she could endure whatever was to come. She let out a low sigh, realizing for the first time in years that she felt accepted and whatever happened she would be OK. Watching her father, she gave him an understated smile and realized she felt a peaceful contentedness settle into her soul. She decided that never again would she wait so long to come visit her family.

Her dad's head tilted slightly to the left as he noticed the change in her, causing him to pause momentarily. After a moment, he returned her smile with a nod of approval.

Standing at the head of the table, Bob looked at each person sitting there. "We must stand on principle, and defend the freedoms God gave us, but when we can, we must focus on reaching out to help others and share our principles. The world is suffering, and it is up to us to make folks realize God is there for them too and that they can have a better life, if they just will reach out and grab it."

Author's message to Americans from all walks of life.

I hope you enjoyed "Phoenix Republic" as much as I enjoyed writing it. I wrote "Phoenix Republic" because I love my country and desperately want to help find a way for all Americans to find a way to live together.

It is my belief that there is far more that binds us together than separates us. The problem, as I see it, is American culture tends to encourage people to get on a team and support that team, right or wrong. Most of us view our environments through the prism of what our "team" promotes as its core values. My question for you is this:

Do you believe in one-hundred percent of what your team says you should believe?

I'd love to hear from you. Here's how...

If you liked the novel, it would be amazing if you would take a moment to "*Like*" us on Facebook. Also, if you want to take a look behind the scenes or interact with me and other readers, check out the following links.

Website

Phoenix Republic – The Lone Star Gambit: http://www.daniellewedgeworth.com/

Blog

Phoenix Republic Lone Star Press: http://phoenixlonestarpress.wordpress.com/

Facebook

Danielle's Facebook page: https://www.facebook.com/DanielleEWedgeworth

Twitter

Danielle's Twitter handle: @Danielle_Wedge

www.ingramcontent.com/pod-product-compliance
Lightning Source LLC
Chambersburg PA
CBHW051932020726
47501CB00001B/96

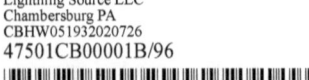